"Why was fighting for your country

more _____ *us?"*

Grace caugh _____ k's face and drew in a shaky breath. "I'm sorry. I shouldn't have said that."

"Dammit, Grace, don't apologize. And don't you dare shut down on me, not now. I'd rather you be honest than that."

She turned. The room felt like it was closing in around her, and she opened the window. Folding her arms across her stomach, she breathed in the rain-scented air as the damp breeze cooled her heated cheeks. She heard Jack's chair scrape across the ceramic tile, felt the heat from his hard, muscular body as he moved in behind her. He wrapped his arms around her and lowered his face to the side of hers. "I love you. I never stopped loving you."

But for seventeen months he had...

Acclaim for

The Trouble *with* Christmas

"4 Stars! This is a wonderful story to read this holiday season, and the romance is timeless. This is one of those novels readers will enjoy each and every page of and tell friends about."
—*RT Book Reviews*

"A fun and festive tale, flush with small-town warmth and tongue-in-cheek charm. The main characters are well worth rooting for, their conflicts solid and riveting... The tone is sweet, yet sexually charged—that kiss in the closet could power Rudolph's nose for an entire year."
—*USA Today*'s Happy Ever After blog

"Mason will please fans of zippy small-town stories."
—*Publishers Weekly*

"The first in a new series called Christmas, Colorado, and already I want to pack my bags and move there... Humor, snowflakes, a little drama, and romance made this a sweet afternoon read by the fire."
—CaffeinatedBookReviewer.com

"A humorous, heartwarming tale that tugged at my heart-strings while tickling my funny bone."
—TheRomanceDish.com

Christmas in July

ALSO BY DEBBIE MASON

The Trouble with Christmas

Christmas in July

Debbie Mason

FOREVER

NEW YORK   BOSTON

Copyright © 2014 by Debbie Mazzuca
Excerpt from *It Happened at Christmas* copyright © 2014 by Debbie Mazzuca
All rights reserved. In accordance with the U.S. Copyright Act of 1976, the scanning, uploading, and electronic sharing of any part of this book without the permission of the publisher constitutes unlawful piracy and theft of the author's intellectual property. If you would like to use material from the book (other than for review purposes), prior written permission must be obtained by contacting the publisher at permissions@hbgusa.com. Thank you for your support of the author's rights.

Forever
Hachette Book Group
237 Park Avenue
New York, NY 10017

www.HachetteBookGroup.com

Printed in the United States of America

First Edition: June 2014
10 9 8 7 6 5 4 3 2 1

OPM

Forever is an imprint of Grand Central Publishing.
The Forever name and logo are trademarks of Hachette Book Group, Inc.

The Hachette Speakers Bureau provides a wide range of authors for speaking events. To find out more, go to www.hachettespeakersbureau.com or call (866) 376-6591.

The publisher is not responsible for websites (or their content) that are not owned by the publisher.

This book is dedicated to my mother, Jean LeClair, who taught me to believe in myself, to believe in my dreams, to stay strong through the bad times and fully embrace the good times. She is my best friend, my biggest cheerleader, and a woman whom I greatly admire and love.
Thank you, Mom.

Acknowledgments

This book kicked my butt and so did my editor, Alex Logan. It would have been easy, and much less work for her, to simply accept it as is. She didn't. She made me look at the story with fresh eyes, then gave me the time, support, and encouragement to take the book where it needed to be. And for that she has my heartfelt gratitude. Every writer should be so lucky as to have a butt-kicking editor, and I'm very thankful for mine.

To the entire team at Grand Central / Forever, you're truly the nicest, most talented, creative group of people I have ever had the pleasure to work with. Much thanks to the sales, marketing, production, and art departments for all their support and work on behalf of my books. Especially my publicist, Marissa Sangiacomo; Jamie Snider in managing editorial and copy editor Janet Robbins; art director Diane Luger and her team; and Madeleine Colavita and Amy Pierpont.

Many thanks to my wonderful agent, Pamela Harty, for all her efforts on my behalf.

I'd also like to extend my sincere thanks to Major Brant Enta for his willingness to share his expertise and his experiences in Afghanistan with me. His insights were a tremendous help.

And thanks to April Speake and Ruth Wilson from The Home Front Cares for allowing me to reference their wonderful organization. The Home Front Cares program provides support for Colorado's military families. For more information, go to http://www.thehomefrontcares .org/index.htm.

A huge thank-you to my daughter Jess and my friend Lucy Farago for taking the time to read this book in its early stages. As always, your comments and suggestions are much appreciated. And thanks to my writer friends Allison Van Diepen and Vanessa Kelly for always being there to offer encouragement and support. Thanks also to my niece Kelsey Mazzuca for shamelessly pimping her auntie's books.

To my family and friends, I wish I had enough room to mention you all by name. Please know how grateful I am to have you in my life.

Most of all I'd like to thank my husband, Perry, and my children, April, Jess, Nicholas, and Shariffe, for all their love, support, and encouragement, and for putting up with me when I'm on deadline. And thanks to my adorable grandbaby, Lily, for the hugs and kisses and making me laugh. Love you all so very much.

Christmas in July

Chapter One

Till death do us part.

Grace Flaherty, owner of the Sugar Plum Bakery, tried to drown out the wedding vows she couldn't get out of her head by humming a song. Her breath hitched when she recognized the melody—"Amazed," her and Jack's song. It was as if he knew what she was going to do and tried to stop her. A warm spring breeze wafted through the screen door, and she closed her eyes, letting its soft caress soothe her aching heart.

Today was her husband's thirty-fifth birthday, and the day Grace said good-bye to him.

"I'm sorry, Jack. I can't do it anymore. I can't keep pretending you're coming home," she whispered as she put the finishing touches on the cake, tying a yellow ribbon to the tiny white picket fence that circled the pink fondant house.

Since the day Jack's Black Hawk went down in

Afghanistan and he'd been listed as MIA, she'd clung to the hope he'd come home to her and their two-year-old son. But where hope had once sustained her, now, seventeen months later, the gossamer threads held her in limbo. The not knowing was making her crazy. She had to move on with her life and somehow heal her broken heart. And the only way she knew how to do that was to let Jack go.

Kneeling on the stool beside her, her son Jack Junior dumped a bottle of blue sprinkles onto the stainless steel prep top instead of the cupcake she'd given him to decorate.

She sighed, prying the bottle from his small fist.

"Me do." Under a tumble of curly dark hair, a frown puckered the brow of his sweet face. "Mommy sad."

So sad that it hurt. "No, Mommy's happy." She gave him a hug, touching the tips of her fingers to her cheek to ensure there were no tears. Grace had been schooled at an early age to hide her feelings, and it amazed her how easily her son picked up on her emotions. Then again, she could never hide her feelings from his father, either.

Forcing a smile, she handed him a miniature American flag. "Put it on your cupcake," she said as she attached one to the Victorian's front porch. His hand darted in front of her. "No…" She swallowed a frustrated groan when he smashed the flag in the wildflower garden, taking out two poppies and a sunflower.

If she didn't hurry up, he'd destroy the cake. She quickly retrieved the chocolate sugar plum from the refrigerator. Typically, the sugar plum contained an engagement ring or a wish. This one held Jack's wedding band, a good-bye note, and a wish for her future. A man's man, her husband didn't wear jewelry and had only worn the ring on their wedding day. Their life had been filled with such promise then, promises and dreams, like the house on her cake. But while her dreams with Jack might be over, she was determined to create new ones for her and her son. Different dreams, but just as bright.

Instead of hiding the sugar plum in the cake like she always did, she placed it beneath the house. She couldn't risk someone finding it, but she needed the sugar plum to be there. It wouldn't be her signature cake without it. And lately she'd been receiving letters from people whose sugar plum wishes had come true. Something her silent business partner and friend—not that Madison McBride knew what the word *silent* meant—had been happily exploiting. Grace didn't believe there was anything magical about her cakes, but if there was a chance...

The stool wobbled as Jack Junior tried to get down. "Me go party," he said, referring to the gathering Jack's friends had organized to celebrate his birthday at the Penalty Box tonight.

After putting in twelve hours before picking up her son at the sitter—two of her employees had called in sick that morning—the last thing Grace wanted to do was spend an emotional evening with the citizens of the small town of Christmas, Colorado, who believed with all their hearts their hometown hero would one day come home. It wasn't as if she could plead a headache or heartache and drop her cake off and leave. They expected her there, as upbeat and as naïvely positive as they were.

At the thought, Grace wearily scooped her son into her arms. "As soon as mommy's cleaned up the kitchen, we'll go."

"No!" Wriggling in her arms, he tried to break free.

She couldn't handle his Flaherty temper right now, but nor could she leave the bakery in a mess. She put him down and reached for the broom. "Here." She handed him the dustbin. "Let's play catch the sprinkles."

After an exasperating five minutes, even though the black-and-white tiles were clear of sprinkles, Grace reached for the mop, then stopped herself. She was being ridiculous. Instead, she searched for something to occupy her precocious son while she cleaned the prep top. She latched on to the cupcake liners he'd dumped onto the counter and sat him on the floor at her feet. "Can you put these back in the tube for Mommy?"

He nodded. She ruffled his baby-soft hair before turning to clean up the icing and sprinkles. The crushed flowers called to her. She needed the last cake she made for Jack to be perfect. When an over-the-shoulder glance revealed her son to be engrossed in his task, she reached for the gum paste and cutter.

Less than ten minutes later, she'd replaced the last of the three flowers in the garden and turned to her son. "Jack..." He was gone. Panic overwhelmed her as the memory of another child who'd gone missing on her watch came back to haunt her. She pushed the thought aside as her gaze darted to the narrow space between the industrial ovens and refrigerator.

"Jack, it's time to go to the party," she cajoled, kneeling to look under the prep table. At the sound of a shuddering crash from the front of the bakery, she uttered a panicked "Jack" and shot to her feet, racing through the swinging doors.

Chunks of wet plaster had knocked over a round bistro table, water gushing from a hole in the ceiling above. In one breath she was thanking God her baby hadn't been hiding under the table, while in the next she was crying out his name, her voice ragged with fear.

"I've got him, Grace," a deep male voice called from the kitchen. Sawyer Anderson, Jack's childhood best friend and owner of the Penalty Box, came through the swinging doors with her son in his arms. The former captain of the Colorado Flurries, a professional hockey team, Sawyer had been there for Grace since the day Jack went missing. Incredibly good-looking and laid-back, he was the one person she'd been able to share her fears with. The one person who understood why she couldn't keep pretending Jack was coming home. His support made it easy to be with him. Only lately, it'd been too easy.

She reached for Jack Junior, who wrapped his small arms around Sawyer's neck. She laid a palm on her son's back, the steady rise and fall of his breath and the warm body beneath his navy T-shirt calming the panicked gallop of her heart. "Where did you find him?"

"Back alley. I was coming to check on you..."

She closed her eyes. She'd been so focused on making sure the flowers were exactly right that she hadn't heard the screen door open.

"He's fine, Grace."

"Only because you were there. If you..." She shook her head, trying not to think of what could've happened. Of what had happened that long-ago summer. "Thank you."

From beneath the ball cap pulled low on his dark-blond hair, he scanned her face, then lifted his gaze to the ceiling. "Shit," he muttered.

"Shit," said her son.

Grace shot Sawyer a don't-you-dare-look as he fought

back a laugh. "Jackson Flaherty, what did I tell you about using the S-word?" Grace's sweetly innocent child had been spouting expletives with an alarming frequency, and now it seemed she'd discovered the reason why.

"Me no say shit, Mama, me say shh." He grinned at Sawyer, who'd lost his battle with laughter.

She narrowed her eyes at the two of them. Sawyer winced. "Okay, buddy, I'll make you a deal. No more S-words this week, and Mommy'll bring you to the bar for a root beer float on the weekend." He raised a brow at her.

"Bribery?"

He shrugged. "Worked for me."

Obviously it worked for her son, too. He nodded. "Me like beer."

"I'm sure that's just what your mother wanted to hear," Sawyer said, handing her Jack Junior. "We need to do something about the leak."

Distracted by her son's safe return, she'd forgotten about the gaping hole in the ceiling. She wished she could ignore it completely and the dent it was going to put in her meager bank account.

Leaning over the table, she called to their tenant, "Stu, are you up there?"

"Stu, up there?" her son echoed.

"He's not there, Grace. Get me the keys."

"How can you be . . ." She caught the sympathetic look in Sawyer's eyes. "You think he skipped out on us, don't you?" She groaned. "Jill's going to kill me. She wanted to put him out when he didn't pay last month's rent, but I thought . . . Jill's right. I am a sucker."

Hefting Jack Junior higher on her hip, Grace rounded the display case and opened the cash register drawer.

"You're not a sucker," Sawyer said as he followed her. He took the key she retrieved from under the tray and held on to her hand until she looked at him. "You were just trying to give the guy a break. Nothing wrong with that."

There wouldn't be if she could afford to, but she couldn't, at least not yet. Stu, a recent divorcé whose wife had had an affair and gotten both their home and their children in the settlement, had easily garnered Grace's sympathy. She hated the thought she'd been played.

"I could be wrong. Maybe he didn't skip out on you. Give me a couple of minutes upstairs and—"

She shut the register drawer and locked it. "I'll go with you."

"You sure? He might have left the place a mess."

"Oh, I didn't think of that." Going into the apartment was hard at the best of times, and this was not the best of times. There were too many memories of Jack there. It was one of the reasons Grace had moved in with her sister-in-law a year ago, the other being the extra income from the rental.

Jack Junior held out his arms to Sawyer. "Me go, Da. Me go you."

A soft distressed cry escaped from Grace, her arms tightening around her son.

Sawyer bowed his head, then raised his eyes. "I wish, buddy," he murmured as he rubbed her son's head and held her gaze.

She averted her eyes, nervously clutching the neckline of her white blouse. "Sawyer, I can't—"

He lifted his hand to caress her cheek. "Yeah, I know. It's too soon. But—"

"What the hell's going on here?" Jill, Grace's

sister-in-law, snapped, keys jangling in her clenched fist as she strode through the front door. Eyes the same vibrant blue as her brother's were dangerously narrowed beneath her dark hair, her blade-sharp cheekbones flushed with Flaherty temper.

Grace went to take a guilty step back. But Sawyer, with a gentle yet firm grip on her shoulder, held her in place. He gestured to the mess on the floor. "There was an accident. I'm going up to see what I can do."

Her sister-in-law looked up at the ceiling. "Son of a—"

"Jill," Grace interrupted her in an exasperated tone.

"Sorry." Hands on the hips of her tan uniform pants, Jill's lips flattened. "So Stu decided to leave us a good-bye present when he skipped out, did he? Wait till I get a hold of the little pri—"

Sawyer cut her off. "I'll take care of it. Help Grace get the cake and Jack Junior to the party." The look in his eyes dared her to argue.

Which she probably would, because when Jill and Sawyer were in the same room together, fireworks were guaranteed. Jack had always thought his sister had a crush on his best friend. She'd been their shadow growing up. If their interactions of late were anything to go by, Jill no longer loved Sawyer; she hated him. Grace released a grateful breath when her son broke their silent standoff. "Me go party."

"Right." As quick as Jill's anger flared, it dissolved with one word from her nephew. "Are you going to show me the cake you and Mommy made for your daddy?"

Jack Junior nodded as Jill took him from Grace's arms and headed for the kitchen. He looked back at Sawyer and opened his mouth.

Don't say it, Grace prayed. *Don't call him Da*. Jill

would never understand that it was normal for a little boy without a father to be looking for one. She'd blame Grace for spending too much time with Sawyer. Given what he'd just said to her, maybe she'd be right.

"See you at the party, buddy. Save me a piece of cake." Jack Junior grinned. "Me have beer."

"Nice, Sawyer. Now you're corrupting my nephew."

"Don't listen to her," Grace said as she went to drag the garbage pail over to clean up the mess.

"I'll take care of it." Sawyer stopped her with a hand on her arm. "Don't let her get to you, Grace. You're not doing anything wrong."

"I know. It's just..." She shrugged, then looked up at him with a smile. "Thanks for everything."

"It's not your thanks I want," he said before heading for the door.

*   *   *

With the cake in her arms, Grace walked the half block along Main Street with her son and Jill. Jack Junior giggled as his aunt swung him up the street by his hands.

"No wonder he'd rather walk with you than me," Grace said.

Jill laughed. "Mommies aren't supposed to be fun."

"Thanks." Grace *wasn't* fun; she was boring and overprotective. She used to wonder what it was about her that her adventure-loving husband had fallen in love with.

Jill cast her a sidelong glance. "I was teasing. You're a great mom." She stopped, lifting a protesting Jack Junior into her arms. "Are you okay?"

No, I've just said good-bye to the man I loved with all

my heart, and if you ever found out, you'd never forgive me. "Tired. It's been a long day. Not to mention the ceiling caving in and Stu skipping out on the rent." Grace sighed. "I'm sorry. I should've listened to you."

"I'm sorry, too, about earlier, with Sawyer. It's just seeing the two of you…" Jill held the door to the bar open with her shoulder. "Jack's coming home, Grace. You still believe that, don't you?"

I wish I did. "Of course I do," she said, smiling in response to the greetings their friends called out. It seemed like half the town had crowded into the rustic-looking bar with its exposed log walls and wood-planked floors. Jack Junior reached for one of the hundred yellow balloons that were tied to the chairs and bar stools.

Gage McBride, Christmas's sheriff, came over. "Hey, Grace, Jill." He kissed both their cheeks and took the cake from Grace, setting it on a nearby table. His wife, Madison, who was not only Grace's partner and friend but also the town's mayor, took Jack Junior from Jill and untied a balloon from the back of a chair. "Here you go, sugar."

Madison smiled at Grace then rolled her eyes when Nell McBride, Gage's great-aunt, sauntered over with her best friends, Ted and Fred, in tow. "Here we go." Madison sighed.

Gage, standing behind his wife, grinned. "You'd better give me Jack Junior."

Madison handed him off to her husband and took a seat, rubbing the barely noticeable baby bump beneath her floral sundress. "I'm sitting, okay?"

Ted pulled out a chair, and Fred plunked Madison's pink-sandaled feet on it. "Now, you stay put, girlie," Nell ordered.

The three of them shared a couple of their memories of Jack before moving off to join their friends at a large table near the jukebox.

"Gage, you have to talk to them. I can't take five more months of this," Madison complained.

Her husband leaned over and kissed her. "I'll give it my best shot, honey. But the three of them are almost as stubborn as you are when you set your mind on something."

"Hey, I'm not stubborn."

Gage snorted. "Come on, buddy," he said to Jack Junior, "let's go play some air hockey."

Grace felt a sharp twinge of longing. In the beginning, she and Jack had been as head over heels in love as Gage and Madison. She wondered if she'd ever have that again. The thought made her feel horribly disloyal. But who was she trying to kid? The citizens of Christmas, especially Jill, would never forgive her if she moved on with someone else. And it wasn't as if she'd leave town. Her father's military career had taken them all over the world, and Christmas was the only place that had ever felt like home.

"I'll be right back," Jill said.

Madison pulled out a chair. "Come sit with me."

"How are you feeling?" Grace asked as she took a seat.

"Not you, too. I'm fine." Madison looked at her closely. "But you're not. Do you wanna talk about it?"

"We had a minicatastrophe at the bakery. There was a leak in the apartment and part of the ceiling came down. Sawyer's . . . What's wrong?"

"Nothing."

Grace arched a brow.

Madison grimaced. "It's Gage. He's worried Sawyer—"

She was right. They'd never allow her to move on. "We're friends, that's all."

"Forget I said anything. And don't worry about the leak. Your insurance will cover the damage. Plus, I have an idea that's going to make us rich." Grace's skepticism must've shown, because Madison said, "I'm serious. I've been thinking about all those letters. We're going to create a story about a Sugar Plum Fairy being the one who granted their wishes. We'll sell T-shirts, and books, and wands... Anything we can think of, we can sell."

Grace could almost see the dollar signs flashing in her business partner's blue eyes. She didn't want to be a downer, but she had to ask, "Umm, won't there be an issue with copyright? There's a Sugar Plum Fairy in *The Nutcracker*."

"The Sugar Plum Cake Fairy, then. My friend Vivi can write the stories. Can you do the illustrations?"

Grace nodded. As a little girl, she'd loved to draw, but had stopped the day her sister died. It wasn't until Grace started working on the designs for her cakes that she rediscovered the joy, the deep sense of satisfaction she got from drawing.

"Fantastic. I'm so excited about this, aren't you?"

"Yes, it's a great idea." Anything that had the potential to increase the bottom line was welcome news to Grace. She just didn't know where she'd find the time to do everything, but it was exactly what she needed right now. The perfect way for her to move on with her life.

Madison glanced at the door and reached for her hand. "Okay, just breathe."

"What..." She followed Madison's gaze and swallowed, hard.

Jill followed behind their friends—the twins Holly and

Hailey and Sophia and her sister-in-law Autumn—with a life-size cutout of Jack tucked beneath her arm.

A warm hand gently squeezed Grace's shoulder. Brandi, one of Sawyer's waitresses and another of Grace's friends, set a drink in front of her. "This'll help. It's a Hero. Sawyer named it after Jack."

"Thanks, Brandi," Grace murmured, wrapping her fingers around the cold, frosted glass.

"What do you think?" Jill asked, setting up the cardboard likeness beside Grace as the other women took their seats around the table. They placed their orders with Brandi while commenting on the lifelike Jack in his desert camouflage fatigues and Kevlar vest, a helmet tucked under his arm, his sexy grin flashing perfect white teeth in his deeply tanned face.

"There's nothing hotter than a man in uniform. And Jack Flaherty was—" Autumn, the owner of Sugar and Spice, the woman who made Grace's chocolate sugar plums, quickly corrected herself. "—*is* hands down the hottest man I've ever seen."

He was. And looking at him now, Grace felt the same heart-stopping punch of attraction she did on the night he strode into the Washington ballroom to receive his Medal of Honor.

Sophia, owner of the high-end clothing store Naughty and Nice, pointed at Jack and in her heavily accented voice said, "Yes, and he is coming home with me tonight."

"Grace?" Jill said, looking hurt.

She took her sister-in-law's hand "It was a great idea, Jill. It's like he's here with us."

Jill smiled, her eyes bright. Brandi came back with their drinks, and they lifted their glasses. "To Jack."

Everyone in the bar followed suit, and then, one after another, they stood to share their stories about Jack and their prayers for his safe return. By the time they were finished, Grace had downed two Heroes.

Jill clapped her hands. "Okay, time for cake."

They cleared the table and placed the cake in front of Grace. She stood, relieved that her emotional torture would soon be over. Gage, with Jack Junior in his arms, took his place beside Madison.

Sawyer came up behind Grace and whispered, "Hang in there. Not much longer."

Before she could turn to ask how it went at the apartment, Jack Junior yelled, "Da, Da." And put his arms out.

Grace's breath seized in her chest.

Several people said, "Aw," while her friends quietly sniffed. "He'll be home soon, buddy," Jill said, swiping at her eyes.

Grace wheezed out a relieved breath. Thank God, no one seemed to realize he'd meant Sawyer.

But Sawyer did. "How about that root beer float I promised you, buddy?" He went to take Jack Junior from Gage, who gave him a hard look before passing him over. Of course Gage would notice, Grace thought miserably.

"Me want beer."

Everyone laughed as Sawyer carried her son to the bar. After they sang "Happy Birthday" to Jack, Grace cut the cake while Jill handed out the pieces.

She reached across Grace, bumping into her. "Sorry," she said when Grace stumbled.

The knife jerked and hit the house, toppling it over, revealing the chocolate sugar plum underneath.

"Hey, no fair, it's supposed to be hidden in the cake," someone grumbled.

Grace sucked in a panicked breath and dove for the sugar plum. Jill beat her to it.

Her sister-in-law laughed. "Finally, I got a sugar plum."

As Jill opened it, Grace wished the floor would open up and swallow her whole. Jill's laughter ended on a choked sob. "How could you? How could you give up on him?" she said, her voice a strangled whisper.

"Jill, let me explain," Grace called after her sister-in-law, who strode for the door.

From behind the bar came a shrill whistle. "Everyone quiet," Sawyer yelled, directing their attention to the flat screen behind the bar where a newscaster announced breaking news. Sawyer turned up the volume. "We have just received unconfirmed reports that the four crew members of the Black Hawk that went down in the mountains of Afghanistan seventeen months ago have been recovered...alive."

Chapter Two

From where he sat behind his desk, the doctor made a nervous sound in his throat when Chief Warrant Officer Jackson Flaherty unfolded his large frame from the chair opposite him. "Chief Flaherty, if you'd be patient a bit longer, I'll—"

"With all due respect, Doc, I ran out of patience two days ago." Jack winked, rapping his knuckles on the dark polished wood. "There's a steak calling my name and a gorgeous woman waiting for me, so I'll be on my way. If I have any problems, I'll be in touch."

The doctor looked like he'd swallowed his tongue. His bald head bobbed a couple of times before he recovered his voice. "I realize after your experience you're anxious to get on with your life, Chief Flaherty, but there are some things you need to know."

Experience? Interesting choice of word to describe over a year in captivity, Jack thought, but let it go. He was due some serious R and R and had already lost several days being debriefed, poked, prodded, and analyzed. It was standard procedure, but there were other things he wanted to be doing—like Maria DeMarco, the reporter they had been sent in to rescue when the RPG— rocket-propelled grenade—brought down his Black Hawk seventeen months ago.

The beautiful, voluptuous brunette was exactly the type of woman Jack was attracted to. Smart and aggressive, she was an adrenaline junkie like he was, and more importantly, she wasn't looking for a ring on her finger. During their captivity, with an attentive audience, they'd had little opportunity to do more than talk and steal a kiss or two. And even though they'd had the freedom and privacy to do a whole lot more while they were on the run, all they'd managed was one very hot, very steamy makeout session.

He planned to rectify that now.

Jack headed for the door. "Thanks, Doc, I'm sure I'll figure it out." Learning the blow he'd taken to his head in the crash had stolen the last four years of his life had taken some getting used to. But what no one seemed to understand was that Jack felt lucky just to be alive and back in the good old U.S. of A. There were a lot of guys who'd lost far more than he had.

"Wait, you can't go. Your sister's on her way. She should be here shortly."

Jack stopped in his tracks and swung his gaze to the doctor. "What do you mean, my sister's on her way?" Jill hadn't mentioned coming to Virginia. He'd told her that, once things were squared away on his end, he'd head to Colorado. But now that he thought about it, she had sounded like she was holding something back during their conversation. At the time, he'd put it down to shock at his return.

Avoiding Jack's gaze, the man shuffled the papers on his desk and cleared his throat. "Under the circumstances, I thought it best for a family member to be present when—"

The cell phone Jack had been given pinged. He held up a finger, cutting off the doctor's explanation, and read Maria's text. Once he finished, Jack narrowed his eyes at the man who was putting a serious crimp in his plans. "Thanks to you, Doc, I'm going to have one unhappy woman on my hands." Hot-tempered and dramatic, Maria's reaction to this latest delay in their one-on-one time would no doubt be over-the-top. Her intensity was a little unnerving at times, but his hope that she'd bring some of that passion into the bedroom outweighed the discomfort.

"You don't know the half of it," the doctor murmured.

Before Jack could question the man's odd remark, another text popped on the screen. He swallowed a frustrated oath. Maria was on the base. He shouldn't be surprised. The woman was also tenacious and enterprising. Two traits he admired, but not necessarily when they were applied to him.

"I'll be back in a minute," he said, opening the door to step into the corridor.

"Jack," Maria called, her white do-me shoes clicking on the shiny tile floor as she strutted toward him wearing a body-hugging white dress that showed off her cleavage and a whole lot of bronzed skin. He doubted it was only her impressive journalistic creds that got her past security.

"Hey, I thought we agreed I'd give you a call when I was finished up here, and we'd meet back at the hotel," he said, unable to keep the frustration from his voice.

Pulling her lush red lips into a playful pout, she stepped into his space, bringing with her the appetizing scent of vanilla musk. "I got tired of waiting. I thought you'd be happy to see me." She walked her fingers down his chest. "I love a man in uniform, but I'm really looking forward to seeing you out of yours."

He grimaced and wrapped his hand around her fingers before they walked any lower. "About that, I'm going to have to take a rain check. My sister's due to arrive any minute now. I want to spend some time with her."

She stared at him. "You can't be serious." Then, with a calculating look in her dark eyes, she wound her arms around his neck, rubbing against him like a cat in heat. "Come on, Jack, we've been waiting so long to be alone. You can spend time with your sister tomorrow."

With the loss of his memory, Jack didn't know exactly how long it'd been since he had a woman in his bed. At that moment, his body was reacting like a teenager who was about to get laid for the first time. But no matter how much he wanted to indulge in a few rounds of hot, sweaty monkey sex, he wouldn't blow off his sister. It'd been the two of them against the world for as long as he could remember.

A silver-haired officer making his way down the hall aimed a censorious look in their direction. Jack went to remove Maria's arms from his neck. "This isn't the place for this. Why don't I call you—" Before he could finish, she stretched up and fitted her lips over his. He lost all train of thought with the feel of her hot, sensual mouth on his, her voluptuous curves pressed against him. Her tongue was halfway down his throat when the short hairs at the back of his neck stood at attention. The electrical buzz was his internal warning system and had saved his ass in the past. Oddly enough, the damn thing went off that night in the desert when he and Maria were about to make love and stopped him from going any further. The last thing he'd wanted to do was put his men at risk because he couldn't keep his zipper zipped.

Just as he was about to pull back, he heard a soft gasp from behind him. A sharply uttered "Soldier" brought him swiftly to attention. He extricated himself from Maria and turned to face their audience.

His sister, a shocked expression on her face, gaped at him. Jack saluted the grim-faced older man standing beside her. After what he'd survived, Jack figured the general needed to cut him some slack. Jill recovered and ran into his open arms. "Jack," she cried, burying her face in his chest.

He held her tight. His little sister had been the only person he'd been worried about when he was stuck half a world away. She was the reason he never gave in or gave up.

She eased back, but didn't let him go. "I can't believe you're here. I almost didn't recognize you." She half laughed, half cried, touching his beard.

He'd wondered at her initial reaction. But he supposed with the beard and long hair, he did look different. "You've changed, too. Older than I remember." He teased, making a joke of his memory loss. He wanted Jill to know he was okay with it, didn't want her worrying about him.

Maria nudged him, arching a dark brow.

Right. "Jill, this is Maria DeMarco. Maria, my sister, Jill."

His sister's gaze narrowed when Maria placed a possessive hand on Jack's arm. With a curt nod, Jill stepped back.

Jack frowned, confused by her reaction. Before he had a chance to fill the uncomfortable silence, the general intervened. "Ms. DeMarco, I think it's time for you to leave."

What the hell was going on? First his sister and now the general. Granted, given where they were, the kiss was inappropriate, but their rudeness was uncalled for. "Sir, that's not your call to make."

"You don't know how wrong you are, son. Jill, take your brother into Dr. Peters's office. Ms. DeMarco." He reached for Maria.

Dark eyes flashing from the general to Jack, Maria jerked her arm away. "What's going on?"

His sister tugged on Jack's sleeve. "Let General Garrison deal with Ms. DeMarco."

"What's gotten into you, Jill? No one's going to *deal* with Maria. She's with me and—"

Garrison got in his face. Thick-necked and barrel-chested, the older man wasn't as tall as Jack, but he had about forty years' worth of practice intimidating soldiers. Jack wasn't intimidated. He was pissed. And he wasn't about to stand around and let them treat Maria like crap. "Come on, let's go." Taking her hand, he sidestepped the general.

"No, Jack," his sister called after him, "you can't do this. You can't do this to Grace."

Jack froze on the spot, slowly turning to face his sister. "What did you just say?"

Garrison put an arm around Jill's shoulders and held

Jack's gaze. "You're married. You have a wife and son. Peters was worried how you'd take the news and wanted to wait until we were here to support you."

"Bullshit." But even as he spat out the word, he knew they had no reason to lie.

"You're married to my daughter, Grace. Your son's name is Jack Junior." There was both pity and anger in the general's voice.

Nervously biting her bottom lip, Jill pulled two pictures from her purse. She held them out to him.

With his heart beating in his chest at the speed of machine gun fire, Jack left Maria's side and took the photos from Jill. The willowy blonde in the wedding dress looked like her name, a classic, delicate beauty. He stood beside her in his uniform, gazing down at her with a soft, loving expression on his face. And all he could think was why the hell had he done it? Years ago he'd made a promise to himself never to marry. What was it about this woman that had made him break that vow? He'd seen firsthand what being married to a military man did to a woman. And the military was his life, always would be.

He felt his sister's gaze upon him and looked at her in stunned disbelief. She gave him a watery smile. "You loved her."

He shifted his attention to the other photo and speared his fingers through his hair. There was no doubt the little boy with the mischievous grin was his.

Maria moved in beside him and studied the pictures. "He looks like you," she said with a soft smile, reaching for the photos.

Jack held them away from her. For some reason, he

didn't want her to touch them. She looked at him, seemingly surprised by his reaction. "I'm sure there's an explanation for this, Jack."

Yeah, he'd lost his fucking mind.

"Maybe you and your wife were estranged and—"

Garrison cut her off with a terse "Ms. DeMarco, I'll see you out."

This time, Jack didn't intervene.

*   *   *

"Are you okay?" his sister asked as she drove the SUV down I-70. She'd been asking him a variation of the same question since their flight landed at the Denver airport two hours ago.

Maybe if he told her the truth, she'd quit asking. "How do you think I am, Jill? I have a wife and son I don't remember, and I was messing around with another woman." And there'd been no one to stop him. He'd gone up with a new crew that morning. But still, it seemed odd that he hadn't mentioned his family before the crash. He'd called Quinn, Holden, and Josh on the way to the airport. They'd been as shocked by the news as he was. Maybe Maria was right, and Jack's marriage wasn't as happy as his sister and father-in-law believed.

"You didn't know you were married." Chewing on her bottom lip—it was a nervous tic Jill had developed at six—she cast him a sidelong glance. "Grace doesn't have to know. I won't say anything and neither will her dad."

Lying went against his moral code, but Jack wasn't stupid. He didn't plan on telling the woman who'd been waiting for him to come home about the other woman in his life. At least not right away. And when he finally got around to calling Maria back—she'd filled his voice mail—he'd make it clear that she had no place in his life now.

"What's Grace like?" he asked. He'd been relieved when Jill called her from the Dulles airport to tell her not to make the trip to Denver. Jack had been reeling from the news of what he'd lost, the knowledge he had a wife and son. Still was. He needed a few more hours to get his head around everything. It was why, when he'd sensed his sister was going to hand him the phone, he'd ducked into a barbershop for a shave and haircut to avoid talking to his wife.

"She's amazing. She's sweet and kind, a bit reserved and quiet, but not in a stuck-up sort of way." She gave him a wry smile. "When you first brought her to meet Nana and me, I thought she was one of those rich society girls. She was too perfect and polite. But she's not like that at all. I know she doesn't sound anything like the girls you dated in the past, Jack, but you were crazy about her. I'd never seen you as happy as when you were with Grace."

His sister was right about one thing: Jack dated bad girls. And from everything Jill said, his wife fell in the good-girl category. The same girls he'd avoided once he was old enough to know the difference. They were the ones who wanted a ring on their finger. "But?" he asked when Jill averted her gaze.

"Nothing."

"Shortstop, I know when you're holding out on me. Spill."

She released a shuddering breath and reached for his hand. "I missed you so much. I can't believe you're actually here."

"I missed you, too." He squeezed her hand, and she blinked back tears. "Do you want me to drive?"

"No way," she said on a choked laugh. "You drive like a maniac. I'd have to arrest you."

True. There was nothing Jack liked better than taking the mountain roads at breakneck speed on his Harley. His grandmother used to accuse him of having a death wish. He didn't. He'd needed the rush and the excitement, needed to test his boundaries. The small town of Christmas had been as much a prison as the one he'd just escaped.

Because there'd been nothing or no one to jog his memory in Afghanistan, Doctor Peters was confident Jack's memory would return fairly quickly once he was in familiar surroundings. Jack was counting on it. He didn't plan on trading one prison for another.

"You going to tell me what you're holding back?"

Her fingers tightened on the steering wheel. "You were different when you came back. You'd only been home for a few months when you re-upped. I know it was because of Charlie, but it was hard on all of us, especially Grace. You'd only been married eight months when you deployed, and you had been gone a year. So for you to voluntarily leave again, yeah, it was tough. And then not a week later, we got word you were MIA."

His wife and son weren't the only ones he'd forgotten. He hadn't remembered that his grandmother had died three months before he'd returned from his initial deployment. But it wasn't the news of her death that had knocked him on his ass. He never got along with his grandmother. No, it was learning of the death of his best friend and copilot Charlie in Dr. Peters's office that had him struggling to keep it together.

"Grace's father is a general. She knew what she was signing up for." And that's the only reason he could come up with for breaking his vow to remain single. She knew the score and wouldn't fall apart like his mother.

"Really, Jack? How exactly does someone prepare for that?"

He might not remember his wife, but that didn't stop an anxious knot from tightening in his gut. "She's okay, isn't she?"

"She's strong. She's not like Mom, if that's what you're worried about."

It was, but he wouldn't admit that to his sister. "I wasn't. And you were there for her, you and the general."

"A lot of people supported her, but she blamed her father for pulling the strings that allowed you to go back to Afghanistan, Jack. She hasn't spoken to him much since you went missing."

That explained the comment the general had made to Jack when he'd pulled him aside at the airport. He'd said his daughter didn't forgive easily and advised Jack not to tell her about Maria.

"I'm sorry to hear that," he said as they turned off the highway and the scenery became all too familiar. Feeling hemmed in by the mountains and the memories, he opened the window, breathing in the pine-scented air.

"Welcome home, Jack," his sister said softly.

"Thanks, shortstop." He didn't bother reminding her that Christmas had never felt like home. He frowned when they turned on to Main Street. "I thought we were going to your place? Jill?" he said when she didn't respond.

Instead she said, "Oh, look, Jack," and pointed to the old-fashioned lampposts decked out with yellow ribbons, the pastel painted shops with the "Welcome Home" signs in their windows. She glanced at him, her eyes bright. "I know how you felt about Christmas, but please give it a chance. You're not the town bad boy who almost burned down the church hall and flooded the school anymore. You're our hero."

He didn't feel much like a hero. And there were a few other incidents his sister didn't know about, but now wasn't the time to enlighten her. "It's real nice that they went to all this trouble. I do appreciate it." Oddly enough, he did. Crowds lined the sidewalks, spilling out of what used to be his grandmother's bakery. He took in the purple-and-white-striped awning and the sign above. "I'm surprised with what Libby's sales were that someone opened another bakery. Looks like they put in some serious coin."

His sister followed his gaze and chewed her lip.

He was already nervous enough about meeting his wife and son, and Jill wasn't helping matters. "Would you stop? You're going to gnaw your lip off. What's going on?"

"Nothing," she said, pulling alongside the curb. "Gage got married. His wife, Madison, is the mayor, and she, ah, owns the bakery. She's supersmart and a financial whiz. The bakery's doing really well. Wait until you see the changes. It looks great. And, um, Madison offered to hold your welcome-home celebration there. We thought it was a nice idea. You're not mad, are you? I know how you felt about the bakery when Nana owned it, but..."

"Jesus, dial it back a notch. I barely made out what you said."

"Sorry. I guess I'm a little nervous." She looked over the crowd and opened the driver-side door. "I can't believe how many people have come out to welcome you home."

She was nervous? At that moment, Jack contemplated sliding into the driver's seat and heading for Fort Carson. His sister frowned. "Aren't you coming?"

"Yeah." He forced a smile. "Lead the way."

Chapter Three

Grace glanced out the window to where the citizens of Christmas stood three deep along Main Street. Inside, the bakery was just as crowded with well-wishers. She struggled to keep her frustration and, if she was honest, her resentment, from showing. She'd wanted her first meeting with Jack to be in private. But it wasn't as if she could send everyone on their way once they'd started arriving an hour ago. Jack had known them a lot longer than he'd known her. And at least he remembered them.

"If you're not careful," Madison said, prying Grace's fingers from the strand of pearls at her neck, "you're going to choke yourself."

Grace unclenched her hand, letting it fall to her side. "I didn't realize...Thanks." She managed a smile. She was as nervous to see Jack as she had been on their first date. Scratch that. She was beyond nervous. She should've ignored Doctor Peters and her father's wishes and gone to Virginia. The worst of it would be over now. But no, Grace Garrison Flaherty always did what she was told. You'd think at thirty years old she would've broken the habit by now.

Maybe she would have if the few times in her life when she'd done and said exactly what she'd wanted to hadn't ended in disaster. It was probably for the best she'd obeyed the men's wishes after all. Especially since Jack Junior had come down with the flu the night they'd learned his father was alive.

She kept a watchful eye on her son as he played with Madison's stepdaughters, Annie and Lily, at one of the tables. Raising her gaze, she met Sawyer's. Since that night at the Penalty Box, she'd barely seen him.

Of course, because he was a good man, a good friend, he'd repaired the damage Stu had left behind and lent a hand when they moved back into their apartment. But so had plenty of people, making it easy for Sawyer to avoid her. She was grateful he'd only avoided *her* and not Jack Junior.

Grace hoped in time they'd get back to the way they once were. She didn't want what happened between them to put a strain on Sawyer and Jack's friendship. Not that anything had actually happened, but she knew it had only been a matter of time before it did.

Cheers erupted out on the street. *He's here*, Grace thought, pressing a hand to her stomach in an effort to calm the nervous flutter. A look of concern in his eyes, Sawyer took a step toward her. Then, with a slight shake of his head, he shoved his hands in his jeans pockets and leaned against the wall.

Her throat tightened, and she barely managed to get the words out. "Come here, baby. Daddy's home."

Jack Junior glanced at Sawyer. *Please, no, not now*, Grace thought, and hurried to the table, scooping her son into her arms.

"Damn reporters," Madison muttered when Grace returned to her side, her narrowed gaze moving from the window to Grace. "You didn't happen to make a sugar plum cake for Jack's homecoming, did you?"

Between Jack Junior being sick and getting the apartment ready for Jack's arrival, she hadn't had time. Grace cast an anxious glance at the glass display case that held the cupcakes and cookies she had on hand. Madison patted her shoulder. "Don't worry about it. I just thought we could take advantage of the publicity. But since we can't…" She smiled up at her husband. "Sugar, can you do something about the reporters?" Madison gestured to the men and women who shoved microphones and cameras into the faces of the crowd on the sidewalk. The corner of Gage's mouth twitched, and he playfully tweaked his wife's ponytail. "I'll see what I can do."

Grace self-consciously touched her own hair. With the number of people who'd come out for the event, she hadn't noticed the reporters until Madison brought them to her attention. She should have. When her mother had called earlier, she'd warned Grace there would be a media frenzy.

Helena Garrison wanted to make sure her daughter behaved like a proper military wife, that she was suitably attired, suitably prepared. She'd wanted to ask her mother how exactly she was supposed to prepare to see the man who'd forgotten her, her and their son.

Grace ignored the thought along with the dull ache that accompanied it. After what Jack had survived, she had no right to be hurt. And maybe it was for the best. They'd have a chance to reconnect without the memory of that last night coming between them.

Madison wrapped an arm around her shoulders and frowned. "Grace, you're trembling. Maybe you should sit down."

Madison's comment drew the attention of Dr. McBride. Despite being in his sixties, the dark-haired man was as good-looking as his son. "I'm fine," Grace assured him, tightening her hold on Jack Junior, who wriggled in her arms. "Baby, don't..." She trailed off when everyone started to clap and whistle, to shout, "Welcome home!" Her husband's commanding presence filled the entrance to the bakery.

He stood there in his uniform, as breath-stealingly handsome as she remembered. "Jack," she whispered, her voice breaking under the strain of the emotion welling up inside her. He'd looked different in the photos they'd released from Afghanistan. His wavy dark hair had been long, his strong, masculine jaw hidden behind a full beard. Now his hair was shorter, the shadow on his jaw accentuating, rather than hiding, his movie-star good looks. But his eyes were the same startling blue in his deeply tanned face as they'd always been. And now they lasered in on her.

She felt the weight of the crowd's attention as they parted to make room for her to go to her husband. Desperate to think of something to say, uncertain what to do, Grace felt a hot flush work its way up her face. Madison took Jack Junior from her and gave Grace a nudge in her husband's direction. She wanted to run to him, to throw herself in his arms, but there was a guarded look in his eyes that held her back. *He doesn't remember you*, she reminded herself. *He doesn't love you.* As if Jack sensed how close she was to losing her composure, sympathy darkened his eyes, and he reached her in three confident strides. He hesitated for a heartbreaking moment before drawing her into his arms.

When he did, she buried her face in the crook of his neck and breathed him in. For months she'd wrapped herself in his sweatshirts, worn them to bed, drawing comfort from the warm, spicy scent that was his and his alone, until one day that faded away, too, just like his memory of her.

A sob escaped from her parted lips, and then another. The tears she struggled to contain rolled helplessly down her cheeks. His strong arms banded around her, his large hand moving in comforting circles on her back. "Don't cry," he murmured, his breath warming her ear. "It's going to be okay."

She wanted to believe him, wanted to believe his memory would return along with the man she'd fallen in love with. Not the one who'd left for Afghanistan seventeen months ago. Cocooned in his embrace, she pushed her doubts away. All she needed to do was show him how happy they'd once been. She nestled deeper in his arms and immediately sensed his discomfort, the stiffening of the corded muscles in his back. Embarrassed, she pulled away and swiped at her tear-streaked face. "I'm sorry. I didn't mean—"

Jack Junior broke free from Madison. "No hurt my mama," he yelled.

"No, baby, it's okay. They're happy tears." Grace knelt down, opening her arms to him. "He wasn't…" Jack Junior zigzagged past her to hurl himself at his father.

*   *   *

Jack couldn't take his eyes off the woman who'd fallen apart in his arms. He hadn't been prepared for the hard punch of attraction he'd felt from just holding her, from breathing in her soft, feminine scent. She smelled like wildflowers and cinnamon, and for a split second, he caught a wisp of memory. They were laughing in a meadow as he twirled her in his arms. Princess. He'd called her princess.

He didn't know if the memory was real or not, but the name suited her. There was something regal about the way she held herself in the prim and proper yellow dress she wore, a strand of pearls at her neck. Jill was right. With her honey-blonde hair pulled back from her perfect oval face, his wife looked exactly like the snotty rich girls he'd once avoided. Until he looked into her liquid gold eyes and saw the warmth there, the warmth and the love.

But there was no love in the electric-blue eyes of the little boy who sank his teeth into Jack's leg. Jack winced and reached for him. The kid let loose an ear-splitting shriek. Jack reared back, holding up his hands. "I didn't touch him."

"I know you didn't," his wife assured him and went down on her knees beside the little boy, trying to pry his jaw open. "Jackson Flaherty, you stop that right...Ouch."

At his mother's pained cry, the toddler loosened his grip on Jack's leg. Reaching for her reddened finger, he kissed it and gave her a dimpled smile. "Owie better." He scowled at Jack.

"I'm so sorry," she said, coming to her feet with the little boy in her arms. "He's never done that before. Jack Junior, you apologize to your daddy this instant."

The little boy buried his face in his mother's neck and shook his head. "It's okay," Jack said, and tentatively reached out to touch him. "He was just protecting you." His voice was gruff as he stroked the toddler's dark, curly hair. *Son.* He had a son.

"No, it's not okay, but we'll talk about it later." Her lips curved in a soft smile. "He's a lot like you, you know."

"I think his teeth are sharper."

She laughed. "No, I mean he looks just like you."

Her laugh was rich and warm, and it caused his chest to tighten the same way looking at his son did. He managed a smile. "I haven't gotten a good look at him yet."

"Hey, baby." She nudged his son's chin up. "Say hi to your daddy."

"He no Da." The little boy pointed to someone in the crowd. "He Da."

His mother blanched. "I-I..." She cleared her throat. "It's just—"

"Hey, Jack. It's good to have you home," Sawyer Anderson interrupted her, coming to stand by her side.

The little boy flung himself into Sawyer's arms. "Me want beer."

"Maybe later, buddy," Sawyer said, extending a hand to Jack.

And if Jack wasn't mistaken, there was a challenge in his best friend's eyes when he did. Jack's narrowed gaze took in the three of them. For some reason, the sight of them together irritated the hell out of him. He shook Sawyer's hand, hard. Sawyer firmed his grip. So did Jack.

"It's good to have you back, buddy." Gage McBride intervened, pulling him into a bear hug. "Let it go. It's not what you think," he said for Jack's ears alone.

"You sure about that? Because it doesn't look that way to me," Jack muttered, even as he realized he had no right to judge. He'd been fooling around with another woman. But *he* hadn't known he was married, he reminded himself. *She* did. And so did Sawyer.

As though Gage and Sawyer's greetings signaled the end to Jack and his wife's one-on-one time, everyone crowded around him. Jack kept an eye on Grace and Sawyer while accepting hugs and pats on the back. Jill said something to the two of them, holding out her arms to his son. Grace looked like she was trying to explain something to Jill, but closed her mouth when Sawyer put a familiar hand on her shoulder. The little boy went happily into Jill's arms.

His sister shot Sawyer a dirty look before making her way to Jack's side, apologizing to two of his grandmother's friends for the interruption. "I'm going to put Jack Junior down for a nap. I won't be long. You okay?"

He didn't know if he was or not. Half the people in here had wanted to run him out of town at one time or another, and now they were treating him like a hero. It felt like he was in a movie, and they'd forgotten to give him the script.

And the possessive feelings for a wife he didn't know or want confused the hell out of him. He was about to tell his sister he was good when he felt a gentle hand on his arm. "Yes, I'm very happy he's home," his wife responded to Mrs. Tate's question, then smiled up at him. "You must be tired. Why don't you sit at one of the tables, and I'll bring you a cup of coffee?"

Her comment brought about a flurry of concerned questions. Nell McBride, wearing a stars-and-striped

T-shirt with a matching red streak in the front of her curly white hair, took his arm. An old friend of his grandmother, Nell had never failed to remind him what a disappointment he'd been to Libby. The older woman ushered him to a table and pulled out a chair. Her friends Ted and Fred stood behind her. They looked like the two guys from the movie *Grumpy Old Men*.

Jack looked for his sister in hopes she would rescue him, but she headed out the door with two young girls following behind her.

Sawyer came over to the table. "I'll catch up with you later."

"Yeah, seems we have a lot to catch up on," Jack said with a meaningful look at his wife, who walked toward them carrying a cup of coffee and a platter of cupcakes and cookies. Her gaze shot from him to Sawyer, and she stumbled. Jack reached out to steady her at the same time Sawyer did.

Nell sighed. "Let go of her before she spills the coffee." She took the platter from Grace. "Thanks, Nell," his wife murmured in her cultured voice, then handed Jack the cup. He kept one hand on her slender arm until Sawyer lowered his.

"Call if you need anything, Grace," Sawyer said.

She gave a jerky nod and cleared her throat. "Would anyone else like something to drink?"

Fred and Ted each asked for a cup of coffee. The band of tension across Jack's shoulders loosened when the door closed behind Sawyer.

"She's a good girl that wife of yours," Nell said, pulling out the chair beside him. "Your grandmother would be proud of what she's done."

Before Jack could ask what she meant, several people he'd gone to school with came to say hello. He relaxed in the chair, when about an hour later, the crowd started to thin out. He caught sight of Grace cleaning tables and frowned. Every so often she'd checked in with him, making sure his cup was filled, that he had enough to eat. The same as she did for everyone else. He didn't understand why she was playing hostess and not the attractive owner, who spent most of her time working behind the counter. Maybe they were short staffed and his wife had decided to pitch in. She seemed to be good friends with the woman. Now that he thought about it, his wife seemed to be friends with most of the people who'd crowded into the bakery. Obviously, she'd spent a lot of time in Christmas while he'd been gone.

Gage, who'd been manning the door, ambled over. "Reporters promised to give you some space for a few days, but that's about all I can guarantee. They'd probably lose interest if you gave one of them an interview." He handed Jack a card. "This guy wasn't as aggressive as the rest."

"Maybe you can put in a plug for the bakery."

With a laugh, Gage shook his head at the woman who'd come to stand beside him. "You're shameless, you know. Jack, this is my wife, Madison."

She nudged her husband then smiled at Jack, extending her hand. "It's great to finally meet you. You've had a lot of people praying for you."

Jack stood and shook her hand. "Thanks. It's nice to meet you, too." He looked around, taking in the changes to the bakery that he'd hated as a kid. "The place doesn't look anything like I remember. You did a great job fixing it up. And your cupcakes are amazing."

The woman gave him a confused look. "I didn't—"

Nell snorted. "She couldn't bake a cupcake to save her life. You should've seen what she did to my gingerbread. This is all your wife's doing. I told you your grandmother would be proud of what Grace has done. She's turned the place around."

No, there must be a mistake. Jill said . . . So this is what she'd been keeping from him. He was going to kill her, but before he did, his wife had some explaining to do. "Will you excuse me a minute? I need to speak to Grace."

Chapter Four

As her father's social secretary, Grace had single-handedly organized dinners and events for hundreds of people from diplomats to heads of state. Unlike Jack's homecoming, each and every one of them had gone off without a hitch.

They'd been perfect.

Grace mentally reviewed what had gone wrong today and came to the conclusion it was her fault. She'd bowed to the pressure of the citizens of Christmas and allowed her son to meet his father with everyone looking on—with Sawyer in the room. And then Jack and Sawyer had gone all Alpha male with their I'll-bring-you-to-your-knees handshake and I'm-keeping-an-eye-on-you looks.

Surprisingly, they appeared to be fighting over her. Surprising because Jack didn't seem to want much to do with her, and she didn't understand his acting all possessive. Then again, he *was* an Alpha male. Even though he didn't remember her, she was his wife and that'd be all the excuse he needed to stake his claim. Besides that, Sawyer had egged him on. From what she knew of their friendship, Jack wouldn't have needed much egging. The two men were fiercely competitive.

She clunked her head against the screen door and contemplated escaping into the late-afternoon sunshine if only for a few minutes. Instead, she took a deep calming breath of warm, lilac-scented air before closing and locking the door. Since their friends and neighbors had begun clearing out when she'd taken refuge in the kitchen, it wouldn't be long before she and Jack were on their own. Grace didn't know whether she was happy about that or not. She wasn't sure how she was supposed to act around him or what she was supposed to say.

Dr. Peters had told her to follow Jack's lead. To talk about their past, but if she sensed he was overwhelmed to back off. After the living conditions he'd endured for the last seventeen months, she was sure the meal she'd prepared—his favorite, roast beef—and their comfortable apartment would make him feel welcomed and relaxed. That thought alone eased some of her anxiety.

Now if Jill had managed to settle Jack Junior down for a nap, he'd be easier to deal with, too—and less prone to violence. And if she was really lucky, her sister-in-law would also be in a better mood. Grace didn't think she could put up with any more of Jill's censorious looks or remarks. It didn't seem to matter that Jack was home now. Jill obviously hadn't forgiven Grace for giving up on him.

Today hadn't helped.

No matter how much she wanted to, Grace couldn't stall any longer. She took one last look around the gleaming kitchen before going to rejoin the others. She pushed through the swinging doors at the same time as Jack and slammed into him. It felt like she'd run into a brick wall. His large, calloused hands closed around her upper arms. "Sorry. Are you okay?"

Oh, how she'd missed his deep, raspy voice. Missed the way he called her princess, missed how often he told her he loved her, missed the way he teased her and the way he shouted her name in the throes of passion. His brow furrowed. "Did I hurt you?"

She blinked away the memories and smiled. "No, I'm..." Her smile faltered when she noted the tic in his clenched jaw, the furious light in his incredible blue eyes. "What's wrong?"

He gently moved her back a couple of steps then released her. His firm lips flattened as he took in the kitchen.

"Jack, what is it?"

She knew him well enough to see that he was struggling to keep his temper in check. He drew his gaze back to hers. "Who owns the bakery now?"

"We do, of course." He cursed under his breath, and she briefly closed her eyes. He didn't remember. And Jill hadn't told him. What had she been thinking?

But Grace knew exactly what her sister-in-law had been thinking. When Jack had come back from his year-long deployment, it'd been hard to know what had angered him more: Charlie's death, his grandmother dying and leaving them the bakery, or the colicky baby Grace couldn't get to stop crying. Everything and everyone set him off back then. "I'm sorry. I thought Jill had told you."

"No, she didn't," he muttered, looking around the kitchen once again before returning his hard, unyielding gaze to her. "How long have you been running the bakery?"

She walked away from him and nervously picked up the cloth she'd folded over the sink. "Pretty much since Libby died," she said as she went to wipe the prep top. She scrubbed at a faint scratch on the corner. "Business is improving. The expansion loan is almost paid back, if that's what you're worried about."

He came to her side. His tall, leanly muscled body brushing against hers sent a familiar rush of desire through her as he took the cloth from her hand. If the irritated look on his gorgeous face was any indication, he didn't have the same reaction. "Stop it. I'm not worried about the money."

He'd always hated the bakery, and she loved it. She'd found herself here. Made a place for herself in a town she loved. "Then I don't understand why you're angry." But of course she did, she just wished she didn't.

"It's a good two-hour drive from my place. What do you do when the weather gets bad? Who looks after your son?" His gaze was probing yet wary, as if he knew the answer but hoped he was wrong.

Grace stiffened at his reference to Jack Junior as *her* son and struggled to keep the emotion from her voice. "He's *our* son," she said quietly. "We live in your grandmother's apartment. I sublet your place in Fort Carson. It didn't make sense—"

He threw the cloth on the table. "Is Jill upstairs?"

"Yes." She nodded. "But, Jack, we need to talk about this…" His long, angry strides took him through the swinging doors before she finished. A few choice words popped in Grace's head, but she didn't let them out of her mouth. She didn't swear, no matter the provocation.

And she had lots of provocation. Jack had shut her down before, and she wasn't going to let him do so again. The bakery was too important to her. Somehow she had to get him on board. Because if he decided to sell it out from under her, she wasn't sure she'd be able to forgive him.

Grace was about to go after him when Madison, looking over her shoulder, entered the kitchen. She turned her attention to Grace and pulled a face. "Sorry, I had no idea he didn't know about the bakery."

"It's okay. I didn't, either. I thought Jill told him."

"It's gotta be hard for him to come home and find everything's changed. But I'm sure once he gets used to it, he'll be happy with what you've done to the place."

Grace absently picked up the cloth. "It's not about the changes. When he found out Libby left us the bakery, he wanted to sell."

Madison stilled Grace's hand with hers. "We're here, so he must've changed his mind, right?"

"No." She didn't like to talk about her personal life, but as her business partner, Madison deserved to know. "Jack wasn't himself when he came back. He had a lot to deal with. I thought"—she shrugged—"it was a great opportunity for us, but he didn't see it that way. He left before we'd settled anything, and then a few days later, we got word he was MIA. I needed the bakery more than ever then. I couldn't make myself sell it."

"You said Jack used to do the bakery's books, right?"

"Yes." Jack and his grandmother weren't close, but he took care of everything for her. He was a man who took his responsibilities seriously. He'd never let hard feelings get in the way of doing what he felt was his duty.

"Well, there's the problem. I would've had the same

reaction he did. But once he realizes how well the business is doing, he'll be fine. If you want, I'll go over the books with him."

"He more or less told me it's not about the money. Jack didn't get along with his grandmother. I think the bakery reminds him of that."

"After what he's been through, I'm sure whatever happened between them will seem inconsequential in comparison. And even if he says the money doesn't matter to him, it will once he sees how well you're doing. You just have to sit him down and talk about it."

She wished it were that easy. "I'll try."

"You do that. I don't want anything to stand in the way of the bakery's success." Madison tapped her chin. "Let me write down a few talking points for you."

Twenty minutes into Madison's talking-points presentation, Gage came looking for his wife. He glanced at the papers. "What are you up to?"

"You saw how Jack reacted to Grace owning the bakery. I thought it would be helpful if she could hit him with some hard facts. Once he sees—"

Gage rubbed the back of his neck. Madison stopped midstream. "I don't like when you do that. You always say something I don't want to hear."

"Give him a break, honey. He's just come home. He has a lot to take in."

Gage was right. Grace should've followed Jack instead of letting Madison distract her. Granted, she had kind of welcomed the distraction. Part of her didn't want to deal with Jack and the fallout over her decision to keep the bakery. "How angry is he, Gage? He and Jill aren't going at it in front of Jack Junior, are they?"

Gage gave her shoulder a comforting squeeze. "No. Jack Junior's napping, and they were talking, civilly, when I left with the girls about fifteen minutes ago."

That didn't mean they would be once they were alone. The siblings had both inherited the infamous Flaherty temper. "I'd better get up there."

"Just one more thing." Madison went to jot something down. Gage snagged the pen from her. "Oh no, you don't. Grace has to get upstairs, and we have to get home. Nell took the girls to her place. I figure we have the house to ourselves for an hour or two."

"Oh yeah?" Madison grinned, then gave Grace a quick hug. "We'll talk tomorrow," she said before asking her husband, "Did you mention the barbeque to Jack?"

"Yeah. We thought we'd have a few people over Saturday for a Memorial Day barbeque," Gage explained to Grace. "He said he was good with that. Okay with you?"

"Yes, that'd be great. Thank you."

"Perfect. I'll talk to Jack about the bakery's very bright future then," Madison said with a satisfied smile.

Gage put his hands on his wife's shoulders and steered her through the doors. "You're going to be too busy cooking to do much talking, honey."

"You're not serious, are you? I was joking about me cooking," Madison protested as they walked to the front door.

Following them onto the sidewalk, Grace smiled. She couldn't help but wonder if she and Jack would ever get back that same easy familiarity.

"Don't worry, Aunt Nell says she'll give you a hand." Gage winked at Grace, checking the door she'd just locked before leading his grumbling wife away.

Grace waved and opened the purple exterior door. As she climbed the narrow staircase, she listened for sounds of a knock-down drag-out fight. Surprisingly, it was quiet.

She opened the door to their apartment and walked down the hall to glance in the living room on her right. Jill sat in the middle of the blue area rug with Jack Junior, surrounded by a pile of colorful wooden blocks. "Wow, nice…castle," Grace guessed, dropping a kiss on her son's head. "Where's Jack?" she asked her sister-in-law.

Jill canted her head toward the kitchen. "See how tall you can make it, buddy." She came to her feet, following Grace into the other room. "He went for a run."

The last time they'd had a fight, Jack had left and disappeared from her life for seventeen months. Grace's knees went weak, and she sank onto the straight-backed chair. "I wish you'd told me you didn't say anything about the bakery to him. He was furious."

Arms crossed over her chest, Jill leaned against the counter. "I'm sure he wasn't too happy about his son calling Sawyer 'Da' or the way the man was drooling over you, either."

"Don't do this, not now." Grace dropped her face in her hands. "I don't know how to make this right. We have enough to deal with without him feeling like I went against his wishes."

"You don't have to say anything." Jill's voice lost its sarcastic edge. "I told him he agreed to you keeping the bakery before he re-upped."

Grace jolted upright. "You did what?"

Her sister-in-law shrugged. "You said so yourself, you have enough to deal with without this coming between you." Jill glanced out the window over the sink. "I don't want to give him a reason to . . ." Her voice trailed off.

"You don't want to give him a reason to what?"

"Nothing. It's nothing."

"It's not nothing, Jill. You lied to him. What am I supposed to say when he gets his memory back?"

"We'll deal with it then. Right now, you have to focus on making him remember what you had together. You still love him, don't you?"

"Of course I do. How can you even ask me that?" Jack had been her one and only love, and it was hard to have Jill question Grace's feelings for him. Nothing had happened between her and Sawyer. Grace didn't have anything to feel guilty about. Not about Sawyer at least. But she did feel guilty she'd been ready to move on, to let Jack go, and now she felt guilty about the lie Jill had told him. Only Grace wasn't sure she could tell him the truth. At least not until he saw for himself how well the bakery was doing.

"I'm sorry. I know you love him." Jill glanced at her watch. "I'm going to head out. You guys need some time alone together."

"I thought you'd stay for dinner at least." It was ridiculous how nervous Grace was to be alone with her husband.

"I'm tired, and I have an early shift in the morning." Jill sniffed. "Smells good, though. Save me some leftovers."

Grace checked the temperature on the roast before heading into the living room after her sister-in-law. Jill kissed her nephew good-bye, and Grace followed her to the door. With her hand on the knob, Jill turned and drew Grace into a one-armed hug. "I'm sorry I've been such a bitch. You're my best friend, and I love you. It just hurt to think…Never mind, he's home now." She pulled back, swiping at her eyes. "I can't believe it. He's really home."

"I know. And his son bit him." Grace half laughed, half sobbed. "What am I going to do, Jill? He doesn't remember us." Grace hadn't been able to tell anyone how much that hurt. It made her feel forgettable, as if he hadn't really loved her, at least not enough to remember her.

For years after her sister Faith's death, her parents had forgotten about Grace, too. They'd been grieving, she understood that, but underneath their grief had been blame. She'd wondered if subconsciously Jack blamed her for Charlie's death. Thanks once again to her father, Jack came home two weeks early when Grace, exhausted from dealing with a colicky baby while trying to run the bakery, had ended up in the hospital. It was then that his best friend and crew chief was killed.

"One day at a time, remember?"

That's what they used to say to each other. It was how they'd gotten through those first horrible months and the equally horrible ones that followed.

The door opened as they gave each other one last hug. Jack, wearing a gray T-shirt and sweatpants, looked from Jill to Grace. "What's wrong?"

"Just happy you're home." Jill hugged him, then lifted her head from his chest. "Ewh, you're all sweaty."

"Yeah, I need a shower." He drew away from her and lifted the bottom of his T-shirt to wipe the beads of perspiration from his forehead. Grace's gaze dropped to the deeply tanned washboard stomach he revealed. She hooked a finger in her strand of pearls. *Oh my.* Before he caught her ogling his body, she dragged her eyes back to his face. Blue eyes locked on to hers as he lowered the

T-shirt. Jill snorted a laugh and patted his arm. "I'll leave you two alone. Three," she corrected at the sound of toppling blocks.

"I thought you'd stick around for a while." There was a hint of desperation in Jack's voice as he glanced from Grace to the living room.

Oh, great. Her reaction to that brief flash of naked abs probably had him worried she was going to jump him as soon as Jill left. Or maybe he was worried about which limb their son would gnaw on next. Then Grace reminded herself that he didn't think of Jack Junior as his son, and that was more hurtful than what he might think of her. "I'll talk to you tomorrow, Jill," she said as she walked toward the living room.

Attempting to ignore their quiet conversation in the hall, Grace knelt beside her son. "Do you want to help mommy get dinner ready?" She forced a bright smile and piled the blocks in the bin.

Jack Junior nodded, and Grace nattered on about peeling carrots and potatoes while organizing the blocks into neat rows. "How does that—" she went to ask her son when she noticed Jack leaning against the white plaster pillar, watching her with an unreadable emotion in his eyes. "I didn't see you there."

"Sounds like you guys are going to be busy for a while. Mind if I take a shower?"

Unconsciously her gaze flitted over his incredibly masculine, broad-shouldered frame. She'd memorized every glorious inch of him, knew where every freckle was, knew how to touch him to drive him wild with passion, knew how to make him laugh. "Grace?"

Heat suffused her cheeks at the memories, and she

cleared her throat. "Not at all. There's clean towels on the bed for you. Everything else is where you left..." She grimaced and pushed the bin aside. "You probably don't remember where anything is. I'll show—"

"Don't worry about me," he said, cutting her off. "I'll find what I need." He came to crouch beside them. His gaze roamed her face, a gentle smile curving his lips. "I know this is as tough on you as it is me. I'm sorry if my reaction earlier made it harder. It'll take me some time to get used to the changes, that's all." He handed her a block as if it was a peace offering.

Her son, who'd been quietly sizing up the big stranger beside him, grabbed the block and held it to his chest. "Mine."

"Jack Junior," Grace said with an exasperated sigh, then apologized. "He's a little possessive of his things right now."

Jack shrugged and held her gaze. "So am I. I never did like to share. Still don't."

Chapter Five

Jack flattened his palms on the beige tiled wall, letting the hot water sluice over his body while the day played through his mind. He kept circling back to images of his wife. In the space of a few of hours, he'd already hurt her. He felt bad about it. He'd have to try harder to guard his reactions, to watch what he said around her. He shouldn't have referred to their son as hers. And he probably shouldn't have made the comment about his not liking to share, either. But it was true.

It wouldn't be the first time he'd fought over a girl with Sawyer. They'd been doing so since grade school. Neither of them had a type back then. Female about covered it. But as they got older, Sawyer had gravitated toward the sweet, reserved, intelligent ones while Jack went for the uninhibited rule breakers. The possessive knot in Jack's gut twisted tighter. He was good at reading people. It'd been how he knew to trust Aasif, the man who'd helped them escape their captors three weeks ago.

Now Jack's gut told him his best friend was in love with his wife.

Grabbing a bottle of shampoo, he squeezed a glob into his palm. The scent of wildflowers permeated the steamy enclosure. *Grace.* He closed his eyes, and the image from the meadow flashed behind his lids again. Only this time it was clearer, he could feel her in his arms, hear her warm, rich laughter, see the love in her golden eyes. She kissed him. It was a no-holds-barred kiss—passionate and uninhibited. He realized then the images were more dream than memory.

He wasn't surprised he was fantasizing about her. It'd been a long time since he'd had a woman in his bed, and his wife was beautiful. A cool and contained beauty, who he imagined would be as reserved in the bedroom as she was outside of it. There was no way she'd kiss with the wild abandon of the woman in his fantasy.

He swore as the water turned cold. The image in his head disappeared along with his body's reaction to it. Good thing, he decided, as he quickly washed before turning off the shower. He stepped from the glass enclosure and wrapped a towel around his waist. Tugging a smaller one from the towel rack, he rubbed his hair dry while walking into the bedroom.

There was a light tap on the door. "Jack?" Grace peeked her head into the room. She blinked, and her cheeks pinked. "Umm, sorry." She held up the cordless phone, covering the receiver with her hand. "It's my father. He insists on speaking to you," she said with an apologetic smile.

He'd left a message for the general to call him. He'd wanted to check on Aasif. To make sure Garrison followed through with his promise to protect the man and his family from retaliation.

"No problem," Jack said. If his wife's reaction to catching him in a towel was anything to go by, she was a prude. He'd been right. She had nothing in common with the woman he'd been fantasizing about. Once again he found himself wondering what it was about Grace that he'd fallen in love with.

"Don't let him keep you on for long. Dinner is almost ready, and I made your favorite." She smiled at him. "Roast beef."

He hated roast beef. His grandmother had served it every Sunday. It'd been as tough to swallow as her two-hour sermons. He forced a smile. "Great. I'll be out in a minute."

At the disheartened look on her face, his chest tightened. Obviously the last seventeen months had exhausted his talent for hiding his true feelings.

"You don't like roast beef anymore, do you?" she said, handing him the phone. She made it sound as though not only did he not like roast beef, he didn't like her. If he was going to hurt her every time he opened his mouth, maybe he should leave.

He took the phone and nudged her chin up with his knuckle. "If you knew what I've been eating for the last seventeen months, you wouldn't ask that. Two minutes. I promise."

She smiled, revealing an adorable dimple in her cheek. Jack was surprised he hadn't noticed it before. The dimple made her seem more approachable, sweet. "General, thanks for getting back to me," he said, his gaze following her from the room.

* * *

Jack leaned back in his chair at the kitchen table. "That was amazing. I think I've finally figured out why I married you." He couldn't believe he'd just said that. He'd been thinking it, but to say it . . .

Her smile faltered. He reached for her hand. "Grace, that's not what I meant to say."

He didn't remember enjoying a meal or the company as much. Grace kept the conversation light and amusing. She had him laughing out loud with her stories about Gage's wife and Nell McBride, and it'd been a long time since he'd laughed that hard.

"It's all right," she said in a painfully polite tone of voice. Pushing back from the table, she came to her feet. Her movements were controlled and graceful as she started to clear the table.

He stood up and touched her arm. "I'm sorry. It didn't come out the way I meant it."

Jack Junior looked up from his high chair and frowned. "Mommy, sad?"

Smart kid. Jack tried to think of something to say that would take away the defeated look that stole the light from her eyes.

"No. Mommy's happy, baby." She smiled.

His son eyeballed him. Picking up a Yorkshire pudding covered in gravy, he fired it at Jack's head. Jack caught it, gravy splattering down the arm of his white shirt.

Grace's eyes widened on a horrified gasp. "Jackson Flaherty."

"Relax. I had it coming." Jack smiled. "He's got a pretty good arm for a two-year-old."

"I do not find this the least bit amusing, Jackson Flaherty."

"Are you talking to me or him?"

"Y-you," she sputtered.

He could see, like when he entered the bakery earlier, no matter how hard she tried to keep it together, she was close to losing it. He carefully took the plate from her hands. "You've had a tough day. Why don't you go and put your feet up? Jack Junior and I will take care of the cleanup."

She laughed. Not the warm, rich laughter of earlier. She sounded half hysterical. "*I've* had a tough day? You've come home to a woman and son you don't know from Adam. A woman you don't like and a son who doesn't like you, and you think *I've* had a tough day. And...and you hate the bakery and this apartment, and roast beef isn't your favorite anymore." She finished on a hiccupped sob.

He put the plate on the counter and drew her into his arms. "I love your roast beef. And I like you and my son just fine. It's a lot for all of us to take in, Grace. It's not going to be easy, not right away." He framed her face with his hands and eased back to look down at her. The tip of her nose was pink, her beautiful eyes tear-filled. "I'm sorry I hurt your feelings. I was trying to make light of the situation. It was stupid."

"It's all right," she said, her voice husky. "I'm being overly sensitive. I—"

Jack Junior tossed his red plastic plate and cup onto the floor. "Me down."

She pulled away from Jack and went to their son. "Why don't you go and sit in the living room and watch TV? The apple pie won't be ready for another forty minutes. I'll get him ready for bed," she said, lifting the toddler out of his high chair.

Jack agreed, but as soon as she left the kitchen, he got started on the cleanup. The sounds of laughter and splashing coming from the bathroom down the hall made him smile. He was tempted to join them, but didn't think his son or wife would appreciate his company. He'd screwed up. He thought about staying with his sister. But he didn't want to leave. He wanted to get to know his son. And there was something about Grace that drew him to her.

The dishwasher was loaded, and he was drying the last of the pots when Grace returned with their son in her arms. The little boy's hair was damp and curly, and he had on a pair of powder-blue pajamas with trains on them. "You didn't have to do the dishes."

A couple of honey-blonde strands fell over her flushed cheek, and splotches of water marked the front of her yellow sundress. Her feet were bare. "I didn't mind." Jack smiled. "I think my job was easier than yours."

She looked down at herself and gave a rueful laugh. "Next time you get bath duty."

"I'd like that, but I'm not sure how he'd feel about it."

"You'd like daddy to give you a bath, wouldn't you, baby?" Jack Junior buried his face in her neck. "I read to him before bed. I thought maybe you'd like to join us."

"Sure," Jack said, his voice inexplicably rough. The timer dinged as he dried his hands on the tea towel.

"I have to take the pie out," Grace said, handing him the little boy.

He was relieved when his son didn't put up a fuss. It felt like a minivictory of sorts. The little boy was a warm, comforting weight in his arms. His damp curls brushed against Jack's chin as he played with the buttons on Jack's shirt. He smelled like baby powder.

Jack struggled to contain the emotion welling up in his eyes. Grace stood watching them, a tender expression on her face. She turned away and set the pie on the counter. Giving him, he imagined, a moment to get himself together.

He cleared his throat. "He's pretty cute when he's not biting me or throwing something at me."

She gave him a dimpled smile. He really liked that smile. "You can bring him into our...your room, and I'll get the books."

As he walked to the bedroom, he realized he hadn't given much thought to their sleeping arrangements. He'd assumed that they'd be sleeping together. But given the situation, it made sense that they wouldn't be. At least earlier today it would've made sense. Now he wasn't so sure.

With his free hand, he pulled back the white duvet and crisp white sheets. The little boy released a delighted squeal and dove from Jack's arms onto the mattress. He grinned. "Okay, you stay right there."

His son bounced on the bed while Jack changed into a clean T-shirt. He was debating whether to climb in when Grace entered the room. "Can you turn on the bedside lamp? Thanks," she said when he did as she asked. She shut off the main switch, and the taupe-colored walls were cast in a soft, diffused light.

She seemed shy when she crawled into the bed beside their son, and Jack climbed in the other side. "Read *Love You*," his son said.

Grace sighed. "Okay." She pulled a book from the bottom of the pile on the bedside table.

"You don't like that one?" Jack asked, glancing at the title: *Love You Forever*, by Robert Munsch.

"Yes, but you have to promise you won't laugh if I cry."

"Be serious. A kids' book makes you cry?"

"All right, tough guy. You read it." She handed him the book.

Halfway through, he handed it back to her. "I promise. I won't laugh."

Her eyes sparkled with amusement as she propped the pillows behind her.

Sliding an arm around her narrow shoulders, he drew her closer and tucked his son more comfortably between them. "Better?" he asked.

She nodded, hesitating for a moment before she rested her head against his chest. Her voice caught as she started to read, but this time he knew the story wasn't responsible for the emotion. He kissed the top of her head, inhaling the soft scent of wildflowers as he did. "We're going to be okay."

"I hope so."

* * *

"I guess I didn't do such a good job loading the dishwasher."

Grace gave a startled yelp and nearly dropped the plate she held. She looked up to see Jack coming into the kitchen with an amused expression on his face. "You just about gave me a heart attack," she said.

"Sorry about that." He walked to her side and took the plate from her hand, sliding it behind the others. "How's that?" His lips twitched.

"Fine," she said, unconsciously straightening the plate.

She grimaced when she realized what she'd done. "Sorry, I guess I'm a bit anal."

"Maybe just a little." He smiled, then looked out the open window, a gentle breeze ruffling the curtains. "Beautiful night."

"Yes, beautiful," she murmured, taking in his strong, masculine profile, his thick, sleep-tousled hair. She'd spent so many months praying for him to come home that it felt surreal having him standing beside her now. She wanted to touch him, wanted him to hold her in his arms like he had earlier.

He glanced at her. Embarrassed, afraid he could read the desire on her face, she turned and closed the dishwasher. "I can reheat the pie if you'd like a piece." Her fingers trembled as she gestured to where it sat on top of the stove.

"Sure, if you'll have one with me."

"I really shouldn't." She pressed a hand to her stomach.

His eyes slid over her pink checkered sleepshirt, and a fluttery sensation came over her at the warmth in his gaze. She found herself leaning toward him. "Don't tell me you're watching your weight," he said.

She blinked, quickly straightening, wondering how she was going to keep from touching him, from begging him to kiss her like he used to. "No. I don't sleep well, and eating this late doesn't help," she said, her voice husky. Self-consciously, she cleared her throat.

He leaned against the counter, crossing his arms as he studied her. The movement pulled the white stretchy fabric tight across his broad chest, and she found herself paying more attention to the corded muscles in his arms than the flicker of concern in his laser-blue eyes. "You always have a problem sleeping or is it more recent?"

This was ridiculous. She couldn't think straight. *He doesn't feel anything for you. He doesn't want you*, she reminded herself sternly. The thought had the same effect as standing under an ice-cold shower. At least she could think clearly again. "Jack Junior took a while before he learned nighttime was for sleeping. I think it messed with my internal clock," she answered, adjusting the temperature on the oven. In truth, she hadn't slept through the night since Jack went missing. She'd been able to deal with the fear during the day, but it haunted her at night. But like her lusting after him, it wasn't something he needed to know.

"What do you do to help you sleep?"

Pray. Imagine what it would be like when you came home. Figure out how I'll go on if you don't. "Warm milk with a banana."

"I'll have to remember that."

She wondered if he meant for her or for him. If he was having trouble sleeping, it was something she needed to know. Despite how peaceful and sweet they'd look lying together in the big bed, Grace knew enough about PTSD to be cautious and had returned Jack Junior to his crib. The military trained their warriors to cope with being captured. And Jack was one of their best. But that didn't mean warriors didn't break. He hadn't been fine when he left.

"Are you having trouble sleeping?" she asked, placing the pie in the oven. He didn't answer right away, and she glanced over her shoulder.

His gaze slid up her legs to her face. As if embarrassed to be caught checking her out, he uncrossed his arms and shoved his hands in his jeans pockets. It was somewhat heartening to discover he wasn't totally immune to her.

"No, not at all. Why?"

"So you're not having nightmares or flashbacks?"

"Is that why you didn't leave Jack Junior in bed with me?"

"No, of course not. I didn't want him to fall out or for you to roll over on him." He raised a brow and held her gaze. She sighed. "Okay, so the thought crossed my mind."

"If you were worried about it, you should've asked me. For the record, I don't have PTSD."

"It's a little early to say that for sure. There can be a delay in symptoms."

"We'll have our pie, and then we'll talk about—"

Stunned, she interrupted him. "You want to talk about it?" She'd begged him to open up to her last time, to help her understand what was going on with him. But every time she did, he'd shut her down.

"Honestly? No. I'm one of the lucky ones. I survived. I came home. But you have legitimate concerns, and we should discuss them."

This was the man she'd fallen in love with, the one she'd prayed would come back to her. At that moment, the desire for him to remember her, to remember them, was painful. She had to remind herself she was lucky to have him home at all. She forced a smile. "I appreciate that. Thank you."

Opening the cupboard, she took out a plate. He reached around her and took out another one.

"I said *we'll* have our pie and talk. That's the deal. Take it or leave it," he said when she went to object.

"I told you—"

"Yeah, I know what you told me, but I don't believe

you. I'm home now. You don't have to worry about me anymore."

"How did you know?"

"Let's just say you wouldn't make a very good poker player."

"Is that right? Well, how do you explain the fact I beat you every time we played?" She grinned at his shocked expression.

"Huh. I wouldn't have taken you for a poker player. What did we play, Five-card stud, Texas Hold'em?" he asked as though he didn't believe her.

She took the pie out of the oven. "Strip poker."

"Sorry, I missed that." He leaned into her, his warm breath ruffling her hair. "What did you say?"

"I think you heard me just fine," she said in a breathy voice, trying not to melt into his lean, muscled body.

"Maybe I'm in shock. You don't strike me as the strip-poker type."

"What type do I strike you as?" she asked, placing first his slice of pie, then hers, on the plates. She handed him his. "I have ice cream if you'd like. Häagen-Dazs dulce de leche." She wondered if he remembered the brand was his favorite.

"Do you even have to ask?"

"You remembered."

"Yeah, I remembered," he said quietly.

As she took the container from the freezer, he said, "Bridge. I would've figured you for the type of woman who played bridge. When I first saw you, that's who you reminded me of—wealthy women who do lunch and are involved in good causes. Elegant and refined, polite and cultured." Grace kept her back to him so he wouldn't see the face she made. He could be describing her mother. "You're also sweet and have a great sense of humor. And you're a wonderful mother. Our son is lucky to have you."

She blinked back tears, pretending to fight with the ice cream lid. She didn't want him to see how his words had affected her. "Thank you."

They were lovely words, but that's all they were. She didn't think the qualities he ascribed to her would be enough for him to fall in love with her again if his memory didn't return.

*   *   *

Her narrow shoulders slumped, his wife leaned over the sink to close the window. Her sleepshirt rode up her toned thighs as she did. What had he said to upset her now? Jack wondered. Maybe she'd feel better if he told her she also had the most incredible, long legs he'd ever seen and a dimple that made him smile every time it winked at him. Both were true, but she might take it the wrong way and that'd get him into trouble.

He didn't want to mislead her. If he didn't get his memory back, he didn't know if he was willing to stay married to a woman he wasn't in love with. A woman who had her heart set on keeping the bakery and living in Christmas.

There was no question he'd honor his responsibilities. But Grace deserved someone who loved her. Not someone going through the motions. As much as he knew that in his head, his gut protested, tightening once again in a possessive knot. He knew of one man who would happily step into his shoes—Sawyer.

Jack shoved the thought aside. He'd worry about the what-ifs later. Right now his mission was to take care of his son's mother, to make sure she was healthy and strong. It didn't matter that Jack didn't love her now. He must have loved her once. He'd married her. And she loved him and had suffered because of it. His mother had suffered, too. Only Jack and Jill had been too young to do anything about it. His father had died on a military mission in Honduras, and his mother had never been the same. She'd tell them she was fine, same as she'd tell the neighbors and his grandmother when she called. She'd said it so often they believed her. Until the morning Jack found her in her bed, cold and unresponsive, staring unseeingly at the ceiling after chasing back a bunch of sleeping pills with a bottle of wine.

He hadn't thought about that morning in a long time. He sure as hell didn't want to think about it now. Jack took the plates from Grace. "Why don't we sit in the living room?" he said when she looked like she might suggest eating in the kitchen. The chairs looked good but were damned uncomfortable.

"Oh, okay," she agreed.

"You sure you don't mind?" he asked at her disconcerted expression. He'd lay odds no one ate anywhere but in the kitchen. The woman was a neat freak. Since he wasn't, he imagined that'd been a bone of contention between them. So what exactly was it that they had in common? he wondered.

"Of course not. This is your home. You can eat wherever you want."

He didn't have the heart to tell her the apartment had never felt like home. His memories of growing up here weren't happy ones. And the changes Grace had made didn't help. The place looked like it belonged in a magazine.

Jack set Grace's plate on the coffee table, then sat on the couch with his. Settling in, he put his feet up.

She came into the room with a glass of milk and napkins. Wrinkling her nose, she set a coaster on the table before putting the drink down. Unfolding a napkin, she placed it under her plate.

Jack fought back a laugh. He must've driven her nuts. "You okay with me putting my feet up?"

"Yes. Absolutely."

He didn't think she realized she was frowning at his feet. He offered her a spoonful of pie and ice cream. "Come on, just one bite. You don't know what you're missing." He waggled the spoon in front of her.

Her gaze flicked from the spoon to the couch. "I'm good." She smiled, then placed a napkin on the cream-colored fabric between them.

Damn, she was cute. He grinned and tucked into the pie. As they ate in companionable silence, Jack found himself relaxing. It was nice to be with a woman who didn't feel the need to fill the silence.

"That was the best pie I've ever eaten," he said once he'd finished. Resting the empty plate on his stomach, he folded his arms behind his head and reclined against the back of the couch, closing his eyes.

It wasn't long before he caught a hint of wildflowers, then felt the gentle pressure of Grace's hand as she removed the plate. He opened his eyes.

"I'm glad you liked it." She smiled, then searched his face. "You're tired. Would you rather wait until tomorrow to talk?"

He slid his feet off the table and sat up. "No, might as well get it over with." Elbows on his knees, he dragged his hand down his face before he looked at her. "How much do you know?"

"Most of it, I think." She repeated the conversation she'd had with her father after Jack's initial debriefing in Afghanistan.

"I'm surprised the general told you as much as he did." For reasons of national security, some of what her father had told her wasn't meant for public knowledge.

"I used to work for him. I have TS security clearance. Well, I did have."

Jack couldn't believe it. His wife had top secret security clearance. "What exactly did you do for him?"

"Basically I was his girl Friday. I did everything. But mostly I acted as his hostess and arranged all his social functions, many of which included heads of state and foreign dignitaries. You'd be surprised how much you learn in a social setting." She gave him a dimpled smile.

His jaw dropped. "You were a spy?"

She laughed and shook her head. "No. I watched and listened and relayed what I saw and heard to my father. It seems I have a talent for fading into the background." She smiled again, but this time it seemed a little forced.

He studied her, intrigued by the revelation. "Did I know about this?"

She nodded. "We met at one such function. It was when you received your Medal of Honor."

"Were you watching someone then?"

"Yes, and you kept distracting me. Sort of like you're doing now."

So much for hoping she wouldn't notice. "Your father pretty much covered everything. There's not much left to tell."

"You were held captive for seventeen months, Jack. You were subjected to torture." She held up a hand when he went to object. "In the beginning, you were beaten, whether you remember or not."

She was right. They were lucky they'd survived. If Josh—a medic—hadn't been on board, they might not have. "If I'd been alone, it would've been worse. We kept each other's spirits up. We were focused. We did everything we could to stay in shape and healthy so that, when the opportunity arose, we'd get out of there. We never gave up. That's what kept us going."

They talked for another hour, and he did his best to answer her questions honestly and set her mind at ease. It wasn't as difficult to talk about as he'd thought it would be. But that was mostly because of Grace's military background. She knew more than the average citizen. It made it easier to open up to her about his experiences. And she had a way of getting around his discomfort. If she sensed him shutting down, she steered the conversation in another direction, then circled back without him realizing what she was up to. She would've made a great spy.

"I imagine it was more difficult for Ms. DeMarco. You were trained to deal with situations like this, but she wasn't. Have you heard how she's doing?"

His internal warning system kicked in, the back of his neck tingling. He concentrated on not reacting. "She'd been in the theatre before, so she was as prepared as she could be. It wasn't easy for her, but for the most part, she held it together." He had to shut this down. He didn't want to think about Maria, let alone talk about her. She'd texted him several times today, but he hadn't responded. Sooner or later, he'd have to.

"Were you able to talk to her or did they keep you separated?"

"About nine months ago, they moved us, and the new guards were more lax. We were allowed more freedom," he said with a goal to steering the conversation toward the escape instead of Maria, then realized the minefield he'd be tiptoeing through. "We were able to communicate with her then."

"She was lucky you were there for her." His wife's sweet, trusting smile felt like a punch in the gut. If she knew . . . No, he would do everything in his power to make sure she never found out.

Grace opened her mouth, and Jack braced himself.

From the back bedroom, his son called for his mother. Jack had never been more grateful for an interruption in his life.

"I'd better go to him," she said. "It means a lot to me that you talked about this, Jack." She placed a soft kiss at the corner of his mouth. "Thank you."

"You're welcome." He stroked her silky hair, the tension leaving his body. That'd been too close for comfort.

She drew back and smiled, coming to her feet. As she picked up the plates and glass, she said, "I'd love to meet your crew and Maria. We're planning a big Fourth of July celebration, maybe they'd like to join us. It would be nice for all of you to be together that day, don't you think?"

Chapter Six

Grace opened her eyes, taking a moment to get her bearings. After finally getting Jack Junior settled last night, she'd fallen into a dreamless sleep on the narrow cot in his room. It was the best sleep she'd had in months. Jack was right: having him home made all the difference. Remembering their conversation last night, she smiled. He'd opened up to her, and more importantly, when she'd kissed him, he hadn't pulled away.

It wasn't often Grace was up before her son, and she decided to take advantage of the opportunity to have a leisurely shower. As she slowly eased off the bed, the frame squeaked. She waited for her son's curly, sleep-tousled head to pop up. Surprised when he didn't awaken, she tiptoed to his crib.

"Jack Junior," she cried, flying from the bedroom.

"Hey. It's all right. I've got him, Grace," Jack said, coming from the kitchen.

She sagged against the wall, placing a hand on her chest. "I thought he got out of his crib on his own. I have dead bolts on the front door, but there's no telling what he'd get into."

"Relax, he's fine," Jack said, standing before her wearing a white T-shirt and gray sweatpants, a spatula in his hand. "I caught him coming out of the room."

"I never heard a thing. How did you keep him quiet?" she asked.

Jack grinned, looking outrageously handsome and pleased with himself. "Food."

Grace came to an abrupt stop at the entrance to the kitchen. Her son, strapped in his high chair, naked except for his Pull-Ups, shoveled pancakes in his chocolate-covered mouth. His hair, stuck together with what she assumed was syrup, stood on end in clumps. She opened her mouth, then caught sight of the counter and closed it. It looked like Jack had lifted the beaters from the mixing bowl while they were still on. Batter was splattered from one end of the white Corian countertop to the other, with splotches dotting her pristine white curtains.

"Did I do something wrong?" he asked, looking from her to their son. "I checked with Jill before I gave him the pancakes."

Grace managed a smile. She didn't have the heart to tell him, no matter what his sister said, their son wasn't allowed chocolate and syrup. He was hyper enough without adding a sugar high into the mix. "No, it's fine." She gave Jack Junior a good-morning kiss on the only clean place she could find, his ear.

"I made coffee. Want some?"

"Yes, please," she said as she straightened. Jack handed

her a cup. "Thanks. Did you sleep okay last night?" she asked, taking a sip of coffee.

He nodded, pouring batter into the electric frying pan. "How about you? That bed didn't look very comfortable."

"I didn't have a problem falling asleep. I must've been out of it not to hear him get up. I'm glad you were here," she said, keeping an eye on her son, who was digging chocolate chips out of the last of his pancake. Setting her mug on the counter, she took a dishcloth from the bottom drawer and turned on the tap.

Jack shook his head with a low laugh. "I wondered how long it'd take before you had to clean him up." He turned off the tap and took the cloth from her. "Leave him be. He's having fun. A little mess never hurt anyone."

"A little? It'll take me at least an hour just to get the syrup out of his hair. I'll probably have to cut it." She hoped not. She loved his long, curly hair.

"Might not be a bad idea. Cutting it, I mean. Hair like that'll get him teased. He looks like a girl."

"He looks adorable. And he's two. No one's going to tease a two-year-old."

"Two and a bit, but I still say he looks like a girl." He shrugged and turned back to the frying pan. "Your pancakes are ready."

"No, I'm fine, thank you. I don't eat breakfast."

"Everything's always fine with you. Anyone else ever notice that?" He flipped three pancakes onto a plate and handed it to her. "Sit and eat."

"Anyone ever tell you that you're bossy?" she asked, surprised when the words popped out of her mouth. Obviously, she was miffed at his comment about Jack Junior's hair.

"Plenty of people." He pulled out the chair for her. "Sit."

"And you don't care, do you?"

"Nope." He set the plate in front of her. Well, that hadn't changed. He'd never cared what people thought of him. She'd always admired his self-assurance.

"What about you? Aren't you going to have any?"

"Already did." He got himself a coffee and joined her at the table, motioning for her to eat.

She sighed and cut a small piece. "I'm never going to be able to finish all of this."

"Try." His expression turned serious. "You need to put on some weight, Grace."

Her cheeks heated. She'd wondered if he still found her attractive. Now she had her answer. The piece of pancake got stuck in her throat. She took a sip of coffee. "I've always been on the thin side." He never seemed to mind before. But maybe because he'd loved her then, he'd been more careful of her feelings.

"Grace, I didn't mean—" Jack Junior banged his sippy cup, cutting off his father. Then the phone rang, drowning out her son's me-want-more chant.

"I'll get him. You get the phone," Jack said.

She felt him watching her as she took the call. It was one of her employees. The new girl she'd hired hadn't shown up for work. Given Jack's reaction yesterday, the last thing Grace needed was for there to be problems with the bakery.

"Everything okay?" he asked when she hung up.

About to say *fine*, she caught herself. "I have to go to work for a few hours. But don't worry, I'll call the sitter."

Lifting his son from the high chair, Jack frowned. "Why? I'm here."

Grace's stomach did a nervous jitter at the idea of leaving him alone with their son. Jack had no idea what a handful he could be. "He likes going to the sitter. She looks after two other boys his age. They have a good time together. It'll only be—"

"I want to spend time with him, Grace."

Of course he did. She was being totally insensitive and ridiculously overprotective. "I'm sorry. I just thought you might have things you needed to do."

"I don't." He made a face, holding his son straight-armed away from him. "Whoa, buddy. You're deadly." He handed him to Grace.

"Since it's going to be just the two of you this morning, you should probably learn to change his diaper. Come on."

"I'm pretty sure I can handle changing a diaper. And it's not like he's going to do *that* more than once a day."

"After what he ate for breakfast, I wouldn't be so sure." He winked. "Good thing you're downstairs, then."

*   *   *

By the time Grace got Jack Junior cleaned up and herself ready for work, an hour had passed. Jack surprised her by once again cleaning the kitchen. She did her best to ignore the streaks on the counter and the crumbs on the table. She'd take care of it later when he wasn't around.

Sitting Jack Junior on the area rug in the living room, she pulled out the bin with his train set and the bin with his blocks. His father joined him on the floor. Grace had written Jack a list of dos and don'ts, including a schedule of activities, nap times, and snack times. "I should be finished by lunch, but if I'm not, I made up a plate of leftovers in the fridge," she said, handing him the list. "Everything else you need is in his bedroom. I left instructions on the change table."

Jack looked from the piece of paper to her. "You're kidding, right?"

"What do you mean?"

"I'm not some fifteen-year-old babysitter, Grace. I'm his father. I think I know how to look after my son without consulting a list."

"I'm sure you do, but children like routine. And—"

"What he needs, Grace, is to play outside and get some fresh air, burn off some energy. He's a boy. They're physical."

"Believe me, I'm well aware of that. But until you've spent more time with him, I think it's best for you to stay indoors. We can go out when I get back, Jack."

Her son looked up from dumping his blocks out of the blue plastic container and pointed to himself. "Me Jack."

"You're Jack Junior, and he's Daddy." A daddy who was starting to tick her off. Who did he think he was acting like he knew more about their son than she did?

"They're calling for rain this afternoon. We'll take a walk this morning. What do you think, buddy? Wanna go for a walk with Daddy?"

Grace gaped at him. She couldn't believe he'd over-ridden her like that. Who did he think...his father, she reminded herself, and it looked like she better get used to sharing the decision making. It wouldn't be easy. But there were some benefits to sharing responsibilities, she decided. Her husband had some poopy diapers in his immediate future.

"No. You Jack."

His father sighed. "Okay, buddy. You're little Jack, and I'm big Jack. How's that?"

"'Kay." He nodded.

"Good, let's go." He scooped their son off the floor and came to his feet. Jack looked at her and raised a brow.

"Fine," she said, ignoring the twitch of her husband's very fine lips. She walked to the front hall closet and opened the folding door. Taking the harness from the top shelf, she handed it to him.

"We have a dog that I don't know about?"

"Very funny. The harness is for little Jack. And I'd appreciate you not fighting me on this. He's really fast, and this keeps him safe."

"I'm not putting my son on a leash, Grace. No," he said when she opened her mouth to protest.

"But, Jack—"

He placed a finger on her lips. "I think I can handle a toddler."

*   *   *

Standing outside the barbershop on Main Street, little Jack eyed the revolving red, white, and blue striped barbershop pole. "You sure you won't change your mind?" Dan the barber asked Jack for the second time. The gray-haired man with the matching Fu Manchu mustache had come out of his shop when he'd spotted Jack and his son passing by. "The weather's getting warm. His head's going to get itchy under all that hair. And if you don't mind my saying, he looks like a girl. I'll give him a nice buzz cut same as I used to give you."

"I'll keep it in mind, Dan, but I don't think his mother...Shit," Jack said when his son took off down the sidewalk.

"There, between the red Jeep and the black one." Dan

pointed out the two vehicles parked alongside the curb. Right before he shot onto the street, Jack snagged the back of his son's green T-shirt. He took a couple of deep breaths to calm his rocketing pulse, then crouched in front of little Jack. "Don't ever do that again. You could've gotten yourself killed." Jesus, he sounded like his grandmother. "You have to hold my hand, buddy, or we're going home."

He'd planned to stop by the station to visit Gage and his sister, but now he had second thoughts. "You wanna go to the park?"

"Yeah, park." His son nodded, taking Jack's hand.

Since they had to pass the bakery to get to the park, Jack lifted him into his arms. Better safe than sorry, and no sense getting his mother all worked up.

Sure enough, as they passed the bakery, he spotted a familiar honey-blonde head in the window. Grace ducked before little Jack got a look at her. Jack appreciated that because his son hadn't been overjoyed when he'd discovered his mother wasn't joining them. His cell rang. He had a good idea who it was since he'd given Grace his number when they'd gone their separate ways. Balancing little Jack on his hip, he dug in his jeans pocket for his cell.

"He's good, Grace." After what had just happened, he had a better understanding of her earlier concerns, but he couldn't help being irritated at her need to check up on him.

"I know. Are you going to the park?"

"Yeah. Is that okay with you?" Some of that irritation leaked into his voice.

"Of course. I just wanted to warn you about the yellow house with the slide. He's sneaky, and there's another way out."

"Did anyone ever tell you that you have control issues?"

"No, because I don't."

Jack caught sight of old man Murray sitting on his front porch. The white stucco two-story was four doors down from the bakery. "That you, Jackson Flaherty?" Murray called out from his rocking chair.

"Yes, sir, it is," Jack responded, even though the last thing he wanted to do was talk to the old man. He'd been the bane of Jack's teenage existence. "Grace, I'll see you when I get back."

"Is that Patrick?"

"Yes. I'm hanging up now."

"Be nice, Jack. He's old, and he hasn't been feeling well."

"Good-bye, Grace."

He thought he heard her mutter a not-so-nice word, but he must've been mistaken. His wife wasn't the type of woman who swore. Then again, he hadn't thought she was the type of woman who played strip poker or spied for her father. She was full of surprises, this wife of his.

He found himself smiling at the thought as he approached Murray's front porch. The old man had been one of his grandmother's friends. That alone put him on Jack's list of people to avoid in Christmas. But he'd been raised to be polite to his elders.

"Sorry I couldn't make it to your homecoming yesterday. I was feeling poorly."

Jack was surprised he'd want to come. "I hope you're feeling better. Say hello to Mr. Murray, buddy."

His son framed Jack's face with his small hands and looked him in the eye. "No. Go park now."

Jack grinned. The kid was something else.

Under a head of thick white hair, Murray narrowed his rheumy eyes. "He's just like you, that one is. Gonna give his poor mother a run for her money. Gracie's a sweet girl, works real hard, too. You better be plannin' on sticking around this time, boy-o."

"I am." He forced a smile. Cantankerous old coot. It wasn't like it was Jack's fault he hadn't been around. Leave it to Murray to conveniently forget that.

"Men who are there for their wives and sons, who stick around when the going gets tough, they're the real heroes. You remember that, Jackson Flaherty. Tell Gracie when she brings me my supper tonight I have some lilacs for her. She likes my lilacs."

"I'll let her know. I better be on my way. Little Jack wants to go to the park."

"Where's his leash? Gracie always has him on one. He's a little devil, you know."

Now Jack was pissed off. "He's not a devil. He's an active two-year-old."

The old man snorted. "Two and a bit, and you'll find out soon enough."

"See you around, Mr. Murray." Not if he could help it.

As Jack walked away, he told his son, "Don't you pay any attention to him, buddy. You're a good boy." He didn't want little Jack growing up listening to crap like that. They'd never let Jack forget that he'd been a hell-raiser, and now they were painting his son with the same brush.

"Me good boy."

"Yeah." Jack smiled. "You're a good boy."

"Jackson. Hello, Jack." Two older women strolled down the sidewalk toward him.

"Aw, shit," Jack muttered at the sight of Mrs. Tate and

Mrs. Wright. Just what he needed—more of his grand-mother's friends. They were like ants, the warm weather bringing them out of the woodwork.

"Aw, shit," his son said with a grin.

Jack grimaced. "Shit."

"Shit," his son echoed.

Grace was going to kill him. "No, that's a bad word, buddy. We can't say the S-word."

"'Kay. Me have beer?"

Where the hell had that come from? Maybe Grace was right and they should've stayed home after all. He managed a smile for the two older women. "Hi, Mrs. Tate, Mrs. Wright. You ladies enjoying the nice weather we're having?"

"Yes, we are. And we're so glad you're home to enjoy it, too, Jack. We've prayed for you every day since you went missing, you know." The diminutive Mrs. Tate beamed. She reminded him of one of those apple dolls his grandmother used to collect.

"Thanks, I appreciate that."

"Seems like we've been praying for you since the day you came to live with Libby, Jack. The good Lord must've gotten tired of hearing your name and decided to answer us this time around." Mrs. Wright, a white streak in her dyed black hair, wheezed a laugh and patted his arm.

"And a good thing he did," Mrs. Tate added. "Your poor wife is fading away. You better take care of her, you hear? She's a good girl."

"I plan to, Mrs. Tate," Jack said with a strained smile, relieved when his son started squirming in his arms. "Little Jack's getting restless. I'd better get going. You ladies have a good day now."

Mrs. Wright frowned. "Where's his harness?"

"Grace couldn't find it," Jack lied, heading down the sidewalk with a wave. He released a gratified breath when they reached the path to the park. Despite it being a perfect late-spring day, the playground was empty. He spotted a couple of bikers and joggers on the tree-lined trails that bordered the green space. Thankfully, no one Jack recognized.

Twenty minutes later, he wished he would've listened to his wife.

"One more time and we've gotta go," Jack called from where he waited at the bottom of the yellow slide for his son. "Hey, buddy," he said, walking to the ladder leading into the plastic yellow house. He stuck his head inside. *Shit*.

"Lose something?"

Jack jerked, banging the back of his head. He pulled himself out and turned to find Sawyer with little Jack tucked under his arm.

"Swing. Me swing," his son demanded when Sawyer handed him off.

"Who is he, Houdini?" Jack asked once he was able to breathe again. "The only way down is to jump." And it was a good six feet.

Sawyer, wearing jogging shorts and a wifebeater, followed him to the swing set. "That ever stop you? The kid has no fear. It's kind of scary. Where's his harness?"

"Not you, too." Jack groaned, sliding his son into the swing.

"I'm not exactly a fan of the leash, but I can see why Grace uses one. He's a handful." Sawyer took a seat at the picnic table beside the swing set.

"Yeah, unfortunately I've had firsthand experience. You're not going to tell her about this, are you?"

"No." Sawyer stretched out his legs and folded his arms behind his head. "So, other than almost losing your son, how's it going?"

If Jack hadn't seen and heard what he had yesterday, he might've felt more comfortable opening up to Sawyer. He wanted to. They'd once been as close as brothers. But he wasn't sure what they were now. "Good to be home."

"Glad you feel that way. I wasn't sure you would."

"Higher. Higher," little Jack yelled, pumping his legs.

Jack complied, then asked Sawyer, "Why's that?"

"You weren't exactly thrilled to find out Grace had taken over the bakery and moved into your grandmother's apartment when you came back."

"Why would I agree to her keeping the bakery, then?"

"Grace tell you that?"

"No, Jill."

"Maybe you should talk to Grace about it. You, ah, weren't yourself when you came back, Jack. You know that, right?"

"So I've been told." Before yesterday, the loss of his memory hadn't seemed like a big deal. Now it did, and it was starting to get to him. After Grace had gone to bed, he lay awake, trying to force the memories to the surface. It felt like he was digging through concrete with a spoon. All he ended up with for his efforts was a headache. He rubbed his temple to ease the beginnings of another one.

Sawyer came to stand beside him. "You okay?"

Dr. Peters had told him to take it easy for a while. But Jack had never been one to follow the rules. "Yeah. Still adjusting to the time change, I guess."

"Tell that to someone who doesn't know you as well as I do. You don't have to play the tough guy, you know. You've been through a lot."

Jack appreciated his concern. He began to wonder if he'd misjudged the situation between his best friend and his wife.

"Uppy, Da." Little Jack held up his arms to Sawyer.

Chapter Seven

As Grace sat at the table in the bakery, she felt the weight of a dozen pairs of eyes upon her and looked up from the heart she'd drawn on her copy of the agenda.

"Anything you want to contribute, Grace?" Madison grinned, obviously aware her mind had been elsewhere.

Grace gave herself a mental pinch, returning her attention to the topic at hand. Just because she'd rather be upstairs with her husband and son than here debating the merits of holding a hamburger-eating contest on the Fourth of July didn't excuse her lack of participation. She was vice chair of Christmas's Economic Development Committee, after all. "If Holly and Hailey are willing to organize the event, I don't see the problem. But for food-safety reasons, we should have someone oversee the person cooking the burgers. We…What?" she asked when Hailey snorted and Jill rolled her eyes.

"We agreed to the contest." Madison pressed her lips

together in an effort, Grace imagined, to hold back a laugh. "We've moved on to the dignitaries who will be attending."

"Oh, sorry," Grace murmured.

Sophia, a Latino beauty who sat beside Grace, patted her hand. "If I had a husband who looked like yours waiting for me, my mind would not be here, either."

"Forget her mind not being here. Grace, you shouldn't be. You have a lot of lost time to make up for. If Jack was my husband, you wouldn't see me for at least a week. We'd be locked in my bedroom, and we'd only come out to eat. Maybe," Brandi said with a suggestive waggle of her eyebrows beneath her teased, bottle-blonde hair.

"Yeah, who needs to eat when you have Jackson Flaherty taking care of all your other appetites. Although, strawberries, whipped cream, and chocolate sauce wouldn't go amiss. You could slather all that sweet goodness over that hot body of his," Hailey said with a wink.

"Come on, you guys. He's my brother," Jill complained when Hailey and Brandi continued to describe what they'd do to Jack...in detail.

Grace released a heartfelt sigh. Their suggestions sounded good to her. But until Jack got his memory back or miraculously fell in love with her in the next few days, she'd have to be satisfied with a very active fantasy life.

A pink-cheeked Mr. Hardy of Hardy's Mountain Co-op cleared his throat. "If you don't mind, can we get back to the topic at hand?"

"Mr. Hardy's right, get a grip on your hormones, ladies," Madison said, shuffling through the pile of papers in front of her. "As of now, our only dignitary attending the Fourth of July celebration is Ethan. What about your father, Grace? Has he agreed to come?"

"I haven't asked him yet, but I will."

Jack was rumored to be up for another medal after leading his crew and Maria DeMarco to safety. The committee members thought Christmas's Independence Day celebration was the perfect place for him to receive the honor. What they didn't understand was approval for a Purple Heart took much longer than a few weeks. But Grace's father was good at pulling strings—like the string he'd pulled to have her husband attached to the mission that led to his going MIA.

Grace squashed the memory and added, "What do you all think of inviting Jack's crew and Maria to come? We could—"

"Why?" her sister-in-law interrupted her, looking at Grace like she'd sprouted another head. "Did you talk to Jack about this?"

"Well, yes, and he thinks..." Grace began, then realized she wasn't sure how he felt about the idea. He'd been rather noncommittal, which initially had struck her as odd. Until she'd reminded herself that he'd just finished reliving his experience as a POW and it probably hadn't been the best time to broach the subject. Then little Jack had interrupted them before they could explore the idea further.

"He thinks what?" Jill prompted.

Grace didn't want to admit that she wasn't sure of his opinion. She didn't want them thinking she didn't have a clue as to what was going on in his head. It was hard enough having everyone know he'd forgotten her. "That it's a nice idea. And I don't understand why you apparently think it's not, Jill. But I'll discuss it with him again tonight."

"Don't bother. If we invite them, we'll have to pay for

their flights and accommodations, and our budget can't handle the added expense."

Since when did her sister-in-law worry about budgets? That was Madison's department. Jill was there as a representative of the sheriff's department to deal with security issues. "I'm sure they wouldn't expect us to cover their expenses, Jill."

"You're a better person than me, Grace. No way would I invite that woman to come to town. She has man-eater written all over her," Brandi said, arms crossed over her black-and-white-striped uniform T-shirt.

Grace frowned. "You're not talking about Maria DeMarco, are you?"

"Who else would I be talking about? Did you see the pictures of them coming off the plane? The woman was on your husband like white on rice. What? It's true," Brandi said when Hailey elbowed her.

Of course Grace had seen the pictures. She'd devoured them. And Brandi's interpretation of the images didn't match hers. "Don't be ridiculous. Jack's a gentleman and was simply helping her down the steps. After what she's been through, it's no wonder she'd need someone to hold on to." Brandi didn't understand the camaraderie that developed between soldiers like Grace did. They became family, and Maria was now a member of theirs.

Brandi went to say something, but Madison gave her a pointed look before directing her attention to Grace. "I think it's a great idea. Talk to Jack about it tonight, and I'll have a look at the budget."

Jill made a show of checking her watch then pushed her chair back. "I, ah, I have to meet someone. E-mail me the minutes, Maddie."

Without saying good-bye, Jill strode out the door into the teeming rain, pulling her jacket over her dark, shoulder-length hair. Something was obviously up with her sister-in-law, but Grace didn't have time to think about it. Madison was already moving on to the next item on the agenda.

"Okay, guys, to date, forty people have signed up for the Fourth of July Triathlon. If we can get our numbers up, we can make money off the event, and it's great exposure. Plus, we're giving half of what we raise to The Home Front Cares. So, any ideas on how we can generate more publicity?"

Mr. Hardy volunteered to put flyers up around town, and Hailey had a list of Colorado running clubs she was going to get in touch with.

"Okay, that's a good jumping-off point, and I'll send out another press release. Nell's taking care of social media." Madison eyed the registrants' sheet with a frown. "How come none of you have signed up?"

Grace sunk down in her chair. The Home Front Cares provided support for veterans and was a cause near and dear to Grace's heart, but she couldn't sign up. Not only were the 5K running and 10K biking events beyond her current endurance level, she couldn't swim. Well, she could, but she hadn't been in the water since the day her sister drowned.

Obviously Grace wasn't the only one who didn't want to be steamrolled—and Madison was very good at steamrolling—because Hailey quickly intervened with a question about the plans for Christmas in July. Since the event was near and dear to Madison's heart, the tactic worked. And Madison, much to everyone's relief, began going over the plans for the week of July 24.

"Now, next year"—Madison passed around copies of an artist's rendering of Santa's village—"I'd like to have the first phase completed in time for Christmas in July. What do you guys think?"

They all agreed that it was a great idea and would be a good way to increase summer tourism, but Mr. Hardy worried about financing the venture.

"As to the costs," Madison began, addressing Mr. Hardy's concerns, "I'm putting together a deal with a couple of suppliers who will give us a substantial break on the cost of material in exchange for advertising on-site. And, as you know, the council has agreed to reinvest the profits from the sale of the house on Sugar Plum Lane into the development fund."

Grace loved the idea of a Christmas village and was already thinking of ways to incorporate the Sugar Plum Cake Fairy into the plan, but she had to work to put a smile on her face. Now that the house on Sugar Plum Lane was being put up for sale, she could forget her dream of one day living there. She'd fallen in love with the old, abandoned pink Victorian the moment she saw it. The once-grand house reminded her of the one down the road from her grandmother's. Grace had spent many an afternoon enviously watching the happy family who lived there.

But she'd always known it was a pipe dream. Even if they could afford the Victorian, Jack would never agree to it. He didn't like the idea of being tied down to a house. His aversion to putting down roots had never been an issue for Grace, not until they had little Jack. An anxious knot tightened in her chest at the thought of all they had yet to resolve. One thing at a time, she reminded herself. For now, she'd concentrate on helping Jack get his memory back. They'd deal with everything else later. The thought loosened the knot in her chest.

Twenty minutes later, Madison adjourned the meeting and everyone pitched in to help move the tables and chairs back in place. Madison cast a speculative eye at the window as she and Grace pushed a table beneath it. "You should build a ledge here and use it as a showcase, Grace. You could do a Christmas theme in July. Actually, we should discuss window displays at the next meeting."

"That's a great idea. I'll—" She frowned at the sight of Jill walking by with little Jack in her arms. She was followed closely behind by Jack, who held an umbrella over their heads.

"I'll be right back," Grace told Madison, then went outside. Standing under the awning, she called down the street, "What's going on?"

Jill opened the door of her SUV, glancing from her brother to Grace. "Little Jack's coming for a sleepover."

Grace ran down the sidewalk. Jack angled the umbrella so she could duck beneath it. "I wish you would've asked me," she said as a gust of wind tugged on the edges of her son's yellow raincoat. Grace began doing up the snaps. "Didn't you have to meet someone?"

"They canceled at the last minute. And little Jack wants to come for a sleepover, don't you, buddy?"

"Me go auntie."

Of course he'd want to spend time with Jill. Now that they weren't living under the same roof, her son undoubtedly missed his aunt. "I guess it's okay," Grace reluctantly agreed and cupped little Jack's face with her hands. She kissed him. "Be good for auntie and call me before bed."

"'Kay." He nodded.

As Jill belted him in the car seat, he blew Grace a kiss. She smiled, fighting back a wave of emotion, and blew him one back.

Jack ducked his head to look into her eyes. "We'll go get him if he's lonely." A smile tugged on the corner of his mouth. "Or if you are."

"I'm fine."

"Sure you are." He gave her ponytail a gentle tug before handing her the umbrella, then leaned into the SUV to stuff the bag on the floor. "See you tomorrow, buddy," he said as he backed out, ruffling his son's hair.

Jill closed the door behind him. "You know he's safe with me, don't you?"

Unlike her brother, Jill knew exactly what her nephew was like. Although, after finding Jack and little Jack passed out when she'd checked on them earlier, Grace had a sneaking suspicion her husband had discovered what a handful he could be. "Of course I do. It's just that I've never been away from him all night before."

Jill hugged Grace and whispered in her ear, "You guys need some time alone. Maybe you could, you know, try out some of Hailey and Brandi's suggestions. Just don't tell me about it if you do." She pulled back with a grin and opened the driver-side door.

Thankfully Jack was too busy to hear what his sister said. He was responding to the greetings from several committee members as they ran for their vehicles.

"Bye, guys. Have fun. Don't do anything I wouldn't." Jill laughed as she got in the SUV and closed the door.

Jack raised a brow. Before Grace could make light of his sister's remark, Jack held up a container. "Murray called to see where his supper was, and he's got a leak he wants me to check out while I'm there. I shouldn't be long."

She went to return the umbrella.

He closed his hand over hers. "No, you take it. I'm good." His voice was gruff, his eyes no longer holding hers.

She followed his gaze. Her rain-splattered beige blouse clung to her, her lacy white bra clearly visible. Self-consciously she placed her arm across her chest, pretending to rub her shoulder. "Thanks," she murmured.

"You're welcome," he said, his lips curved in that dangerously sexy smile she remembered. He'd smiled that way before he kissed her the first time. She wondered if he wanted to kiss her now. She didn't realize she'd tipped her head, her lips parted expectantly, until he turned and walked away.

A disappointed sigh drifted past her lips as the rain tapped on the umbrella. She watched Jack head up Mr. Murray's flower-lined walkway, remembering how her husband used to kiss her. How he used to make love to her as passionately and as tirelessly as he did everything else. As though he sensed her watching him, he turned on the porch's top step. "Don't worry, I'll be nice. Now get going before you catch a cold."

He hadn't changed. Some women might find his protective, take-charge attitude a little off-putting, but Grace had always been a sucker for an Alpha male. Probably because she'd grown up surrounded by them. Besides that, he was an incredibly gorgeous Alpha male.

Jill was right. All they needed was some time alone together. No doubt Hailey and Brandi would make good use of the opportunity if they were in Grace's shoes. Too bad Grace wasn't as confident in her ability to seduce her husband as her friends were. As he raised his hand to knock on the door, she took in the wide expanse of his shoulders beneath the black Windbreaker, the well-worn jeans molded to his amazing butt and powerful thighs. Maybe it was time she got her sexy back.

*   *   *

Jack walked into the apartment and set down the purple lilacs the old man had given to him for Grace. Shrugging out of his jacket, he gave an appreciative sniff. His wife was one hell of a cook. He'd been inhaling one of her meatballs when his sister walked in earlier. A meatball he promptly choked on when Jill repeated the conversation going on in the bakery.

He knew he should've shot down Grace's suggestion last night, but he hadn't been able to figure out what to say without raising her suspicions. And now, from what Jill said, he'd better come up with something fast, because Grace was determined to pursue the issue. His wife may appear fragile and sweet, but when she wanted something, she was as single-minded as a heat-seeking missile. He froze with the coat hanger in his hand.

Where had that come from?

No matter how hard he tried to push on the door to his memories, it remained firmly closed to him. At least when it came to his wife and son. He had no trouble remembering why he'd been hell-bent on leaving Christmas as soon as he was legal. Which was something he had to talk to his wife about. He'd been too busy calming his sister's fears about Maria to question her about what Sawyer had inferred. No matter what Jill said, no matter how much he'd supposedly loved his wife, he wouldn't have agreed to live in Christmas permanently.

"Jack, is that you?"

"Yeah," he said and hung up his jacket. Toeing off his sneakers, he picked up the flowers and made his way to the kitchen. His wife stood by the stove wearing a frilly white apron over black slacks and a white blouse. She looked put together in a don't-mess-me-up kind of way. He doubted she owned a pair of jeans. Something else they didn't have in common. He lived in his.

She rested the wooden spoon across the top of the pot and turned to him with a smile. "They're beautiful."

He handed her the lilacs. "I think old man Murray has a crush on you. He was singing your praises the entire time I was there." When he wasn't reminding Jack what a tool he'd been as a kid.

She opened a cupboard and went to reach for a crystal vase on the top shelf. "Do you mind?" she asked.

His body brushed against hers as he retrieved the vase, and a slow burn of awareness heated his skin. He'd had the same reaction when he stood under the umbrella with her, inhaling her floral scent while his gaze took in the intriguing hint of curves that her wet blouse revealed.

Turning on the tap, she said, "You used to bring me wildflowers."

Huh. That surprised him. He wasn't a hearts-and-flowers kind of guy. He wondered if the man she thought he was ever existed. "Probably because you smell like them."

"Oh."

"That's not a bad thing, Grace," he said in response to the face she made. "You smell nice."

"Nice. Nice is good," she said as if it was anything but. *Flaherty, do yourself a favor and keep your mouth shut.*

She placed the vase in the center of the white tablecloth, then began rearranging the candles and salt and pepper shakers. It took her several tries before they met with her satisfaction. Jack had to hold himself back from taking the candles from her and plunking them on the table, and saying, *That's it.* Underneath her calm and cool demeanor, his wife was a control freak. She looked at the table, smoothed the linen tablecloth one last time, and walked over to the stove.

"I hope you're hungry," she said, dumping a fistful of pasta into the boiling pot of water.

He wasn't. "Starved."

"Good. I wasn't sure you would be. I seem to be missing half the meatballs." She gave him a dimpled smile.

He laughed, the leftover tension from his visit with Murray melting away. Odd how, since Grace was so tightly wound, she had that effect on him. "Busted. But it wasn't only me. Jill took some, and I gave a couple to Murray."

"I'm surprised you shared."

"Me, too. I don't think I've ever tasted meatballs that good. What's your secret?" Her smile faded. "Did I say something wrong?" Did he even have to ask?

"No, it's just…I'm sorry. It's not your fault. I keep forgetting you have absolutely no memory of us." While she stirred the sauce, she glanced at him. "We spent our honeymoon at this amazing bed-and-breakfast in Casperia, Italy. Roberto, one of the owners, taught us how to make these incredible dishes. Everything was fresh. They produced their own olive oil and cheese. We'd pick tomatoes from the garden, and they were warm from the sun and smelled real, you know." She scooped up a meatball with the spoon and cupped her hand beneath it. "Close your eyes and see if you can guess the secret ingredient."

There was something incredibly sexy about Grace at that moment. It was the way she talked about the food. Her eyes lit up with passion. Her face captivated him. He could look at her all day and never get tired of it.

"You have the most amazing eyes. Anyone ever tell you that?"

"You." She smiled and lifted the spoon to his mouth.

He rested a hand on the curve of her hip and opened his mouth, then did as she asked and closed his eyes while savoring the moist, spicy meatball. "Hot Italian sausage," he guessed, although he wasn't sure it was a guess. Somehow he'd known, even before he said it, that hot sausage was the secret ingredient.

Her eyes widened. "You rem…" she started, then corrected herself. "You're right. I was going to bet you that you couldn't guess. Good thing I didn't."

"What would I have gotten if we had?" Answers, that's what he wanted. An answer as to why his sister had lied. But he liked this playful, lighthearted side to Grace and didn't want to ruin the moment. No sense in upsetting her when he could just as easily ask Jill.

She cast him a sidelong glance, her delicate jaw setting in a determined line before she said, "A kiss."

"Sounds good to me." It did. He hadn't been able to get the kiss he'd shared with the woman in the meadow out of his head. A woman who looked like his wife.

"It does?" she asked in a surprised tone of voice.

He took the wooden spoon from her and rested it across the top of the pot before placing his hands on her shoulders, turning her to face him. "Yeah, it does," he said and lowered his mouth to hers. Her eyelids fluttered closed as she leaned in to him. Her body a warm, supple weight. He smoothed his hands down her back, brushing his lips, slowly, gently, over hers, drawing her closer. He wanted her closer.

A needy whimper escaped her parted lips as she wound her arms around his neck. Bringing her body snug against his, she tangled her fingers in his hair. Jack had thought to take it slow, to get one small taste of her, but from the way she drew the tip of her tongue across the seam of his lips, she wanted more. She coaxed him to open, short-circuiting his brain with the feel of her tongue caressing the inside of his mouth with hot, greedy strokes. It was an unbelievable kiss—passionate and uninhibited.

Grace *was* the woman in the meadow.

She rose up on her toes, and he looped one arm around her waist, threading the fingers of his other hand in her soft, sweet-smelling hair. *Mine.* The thought echoed in his head at the same time the phone rang.

Her frustrated groan reverberated against his mouth. He wanted to voice his own frustration when she drew away from him. Cheeks flushed, her eyes heavy-lidded with passion, she gave him an apologetic smile and went to answer the phone. "It's probably little Jack."

By the time she finished talking to Jill, he'd laid their dinner on the table.

Jack pulled out a chair for her. "He okay, or do you want me to go get him?" He'd made some progress with his son today, but selfishly, he wanted Grace to himself tonight. Especially after that kiss.

"Thank you," she said, taking her seat. She placed a napkin neatly across her lap. "Jill doesn't think he's going to last through the night. But he'd probably pitch a fit if you went to get him now. She said she'll bring him home in a while."

"Inherited the infamous Flaherty temper, did he?"

She smiled and nodded. "I'm surprised you didn't see any signs of it today."

"Nope." The kid might be Houdini and a little stubborn, but he hadn't thrown a tantrum.

They talked while they ate, mostly about their son. As he'd noticed yesterday, his wife was an entertaining conversationalist. But unlike last night, it was harder for him to stay focused on the conversation. He'd catch himself staring at Grace's soft lips, reliving that kiss.

"Would you like some coffee and dessert?" she asked as she got up to clear the table. "I made tiramisu. It's one of Roberto's recipes."

"That would be a definite yes, then. Do you have any pictures of the place?"

"Tons. I'll get them." She set the dishes on the counter and went into the living room, coming back with three albums in her arms. "I should've done this yesterday. Dr. Peters thought it might help you remember."

Once she served coffee and dessert, she pulled her chair closer and opened the first album. It was of their honeymoon. She worked her way backward to the wedding. "If this is hard for you, we can stop," she said as she closed the second album.

It wasn't easy. Charlie, as Jack's best man, was in most of the photos. But Jack instinctively knew he had to do this. He wanted his memory back, and somewhere in these albums might be the key to unlocking it.

He knew the instant she opened the third album that he'd found the key.

She turned the page to a picture of her wearing a feminine white sundress, her arms held out from her body as she twirled in a lush meadow of vibrant red Indian paintbrush and white columbine. Her honey-blonde hair swung across her shoulders, her face lifted to the sun. "This is when you proposed. You planned a picnic for us. I had no idea what you were up to."

One by one, the memories flooded his senses: the night he met her, the first time he kissed her, the first time they made love, and the day he realized she was the only woman for him. He had fallen so completely in love with her that his reasons never to marry no longer mattered or made sense. Her military upbringing made her his perfect match. He knew whatever happened she wouldn't break. She'd stick by him, never give up on him.

Emotion swamped him as he looked at Grace, a soft smile playing on her lips, a strand of hair falling across her cheek, her delicate, fine-boned fingers tracing the photo. He loved her now as much as he did then. Theirs was a forever kind of love, an unforgettable love.

But he *had* forgotten her. If the situation had been reversed, he knew how that would've made him feel. He opened his mouth to tell her, and that's when the final memory clicked into place.

He remembered their last night together and what she'd said to him.

Chapter Eight

Grace was so caught up in the bittersweet memory that it took a moment before she realized Jack hadn't said anything. She glanced at him and caught the wary look in his eyes, the muscle pulsating in his clenched jaw.

"Is something wrong?" *Of course there is, you've pushed him too hard.* Dr. Peters had warned her it could take time, but selfishly she wanted Jack to remember her now. The kiss they'd shared had left her greedy for so much more.

He held her gaze, an emotion in his intent blue eyes she couldn't read. And for some reason, it set off a flutter of nerves in her stomach. "Jack, what is it?"

"I remember."

His low, flat tone of voice should have been her first warning that something wasn't right, but she was too happy to pay attention. She reached for his hand. "That's wonderful," she said, barely able to contain her tears.

"If you remember that day, it'll only be a matter of time before the rest of your memory returns."

"It's back. All of it. I remember everything, Grace."

She briefly closed her eyes and released his hand. It wasn't supposed to be like this. But deep down she'd known this would happen, hadn't she? Known they'd eventually have to deal with that night. Emotion tightened her throat, both joy and sorrow, and it took a moment for her to be able to say, "I'm sorry. As soon as I said the words I wanted to take them back, but I couldn't. You left." As she should've done that night, she swallowed the anger that welled up inside her. It wasn't easy. No matter the guilt she'd lived with for the last seventeen months, there was a part of her that hadn't forgiven him for leaving.

"Why?" he asked.

"Why what, Jack? Why did you leave when you promised you wouldn't? Why didn't you answer your phone when I called? Why was fighting for your country more important than fighting for us?"

Stop it, Grace. For goodness' sake, stop it before you say something you can't take back.

She caught the stunned expression on his face and drew in a shuddered breath. Pushing the chair from the table, she said, "I shouldn't have said that. Would you like more coffee?" She cringed as the inane words came out of her mouth. She sounded like her mother.

Jack reached for her as she picked up their half-empty cups. "Dammit, Grace, don't apologize. And don't you dare shut down on me, not now. I'd rather you be honest than that."

She turned and walked to the counter, setting the cups

beside the coffeemaker. The room felt like it was closing in around her, and she opened the window. Folding her arms across her stomach, she breathed in the rain-scented air as the damp breeze cooled her heated cheeks. She heard Jack's chair scrape across the ceramic tile, felt the heat from his hard, muscular body as he moved in behind her. He wrapped his arms around her and lowered his face to the side of hers. "I love you. I never stopped loving you."

For seventeen months he had. She bowed her head, a tear escaping beneath her closed lids. "I love you, too." She did; with every fiber of her being, she loved him. But it hadn't been enough to keep him with her. "If I could take back what I said, I would, but I can't. I missed you from the moment you walked out the door. I missed the man I married."

Against her back, she felt his chest expand. "I know. I was angry. Angry that Charlie was gone, angry that my grandmother had left us the damn bakery and that you were determined to keep it. I never wanted to live here, Grace. You knew that."

"You're right, I did. But the thing is, Jack, while you had a lot to deal with, so did I. I needed support, and I got lots of it in Christmas. And be honest, you weren't just angry about Charlie's death, you blamed me." It was the first time she'd voiced her suspicion. She hadn't wanted to believe it then, but she'd had a lot of time to think about his reactions since he'd been gone.

"No." He blew out a ragged breath, and his arms tightened around her. "Okay, yeah. Maybe. I thought if I had been the one in the pilot's seat instead of home with you, I could've kept the chopper in the air, and he wouldn't have died. It was survivor's guilt, Grace, and the only way I knew how to work through it was to get back there."

"Even though I asked you not to go."

"Yeah. I was no good to you the way I was. You or little Jack."

"I don't believe you gave our son a second thought. I could hardly get you to hold him or spend any time with him." She hadn't meant to say that, but it was true. The way he'd avoided their son had been painful to watch.

"I think I was afraid of him. He was so small and..." He hesitated.

"He never stopped crying," she finished for him. Grace had tried every remedy in the book to soothe their colicky baby, but nothing had worked. She'd been a permanent fixture in Dr. McBride's office. The man was a saint for putting up with her. She'd been a nervous wreck, and Jack hadn't helped. Dr. McBride had assured her that little Jack's colic would clear up. It did. Coincidentally, right around the time his father left.

Jack stepped back and turned her to face him. "I'm sorry I wasn't there for either of you, but I'm here now. Do you want me to stay?"

"How can you even ask me that? Of course I want you to stay." She blinked back tears. She couldn't lose him so soon after getting him back. Not again.

He cupped her face, wiping away her tears with his thumbs. "That night you told me if I left, you wanted a divorce. That you wouldn't be here when I came back."

"I was hurt and—"

A shocked gasp cut Grace off. Jill stood in the living room with little Jack in her arms.

*   *   *

Jack looked from his sister to his wife. From the furious expression on Jill's face and the distraught one on Grace's, it was obvious his wife hadn't shared their problems with his sister. This wasn't going to be pretty, Jack thought. Jill had been defending him since they'd moved in with their grandmother, and she had no qualms about fighting dirty. Jack knew how much she loved him, but he wasn't about to let her protect him at his wife's expense. Grace had been through enough. And no matter what his sister thought, he'd deserved everything she'd said to him that night. He was just glad she hadn't given up on him and moved on with her life.

"You asked him for a divorce? How could you? I thought you loved him. All this time—"

"Jill, that's enough," he interrupted her with a pointed look in his son's direction. "I'll take care of this, Grace. You get little Jack settled." He took his son from Jill's arms.

"No. Mama," little Jack cried and held out his hands to Grace, shooting a worried look at the adults in the room.

"How can you—" his sister began, temper flushing her cheeks.

"Knock it off. You're upsetting him," Jack said, giving his son to Grace.

"I do love him, Jill. Very much." Grace said quietly, patting their son's back. She held Jack's gaze, as if to make sure he knew it was true.

He smoothed her hair from her face and kissed her forehead. "I know you do."

"My mama. No kiss." Little Jack pushed him away.

Jack sighed. It looked like winning his son over would take some time. Lucky for him, he now had all the time in the world.

"You want a coffee?" he asked his sister, once Grace had closed the door to little Jack's room.

His sister scowled at the closed door then returned her attention to him. "Coffee? No, I don't want coffee. I want answers. This is bullshit, Jack. How could she do that to you?"

"Settle down, shortstop. I got my memory back. And Grace didn't do anything to me that I didn't deserve," he said, leading her to the couch.

She pulled her hand from his. "You got your memory back?"

"Yeah." He raised a brow. "You've got some explaining to do. Since when do you lie to me?"

She threw up her hands and flopped down on the couch. "What does it matter anymore? Grace was going to leave you." Jill gave her head a disbelieving shake. "She really pulled one over on me. Acting like the grieving wife when all along it was her fault you left. It was her fault those bastards held you prisoner for seventeen months."

"What's gotten into you? She's your best friend. She had nothing to do with my decision to re-up. That's on me, not her. And she had every right to be upset about it."

"Upset? She asked you for a divorce. You're a frigging hero going to fight for his country, and she asks you for a *divorce*."

Murray's comment earlier today about men who stood by their wives being the real heroes made some sense now.

Not that Jack wanted to give the old man credit for having any, but he did have a point. "It was in the heat of the moment. She tried to call me a couple of hours after I left, and I was too angry to answer." Scared that he'd screwed up the best thing in his life because he was afraid to be honest with her. The Flaherty temper that he'd learned to control through his years in the military had come back to haunt him and had nearly cost him his wife. "When I'd cooled down enough to think straight, I was going to call her. Only I didn't get the chance." He'd been going to get in touch with her after they'd returned to base from their mission. "She's here, Jill. She loved me enough to wait for me. She didn't give up on me. Seventeen months is a long time."

"She didn't . . ." His sister chewed on her bottom lip and glanced toward the kitchen. When she returned her gaze to his, her eyes filled. "I never gave up on you, not for a single second."

He put his arm around her and tugged her close. "I know you didn't."

"I don't care what you say," she murmured into his chest. "It's not right that Grace gave you an ultimatum. You don't do that to someone you love. Are you sure you want to stay, Jack? Are you sure you still love her?"

He frowned, pulling back. "Yeah, I am. What's gotten into you? Weren't you the one who reminded me just the other day how much I loved her? That hasn't changed."

"But you deserve someone who loves you, someone who knows how lucky they are to have you."

His sister had a serious case of hero worship. She always put him on a pedestal, and he was getting tired of it. He didn't deserve to be put on one. He was about to tell her that when she said, "Maria seemed to feel that way about you. And you—"

He shot an alarmed look toward the kitchen. All he needed was for Grace to overhear his sister's comment. "I'm only going to say this once, so listen up. No matter how it looked, Maria doesn't love me, and I don't love her. Nothing happened. I didn't want it to," he said. He only wished that was true.

"That's not how it looked to me," his sister muttered.

"Jill, I swear to God, if you say anything about this to Grace, I'll never forgive you. I love my wife. I don't want to lose her." And he was afraid if she found out about Maria, he would. That's why he didn't plan on saying anything. He hadn't responded to any of Maria's texts or phone calls, and he wasn't going to. Eventually, she'd give up.

"Then you better make sure your wife doesn't invite them all to the Fourth of July celebration. Because no matter what you think, big brother, Maria DeMarco wants you. Even Brandi commented on it during the meeting. What did she..." Jill tapped her chin. "Oh yeah, she said in the photos Maria was on you like white on rice. Called her a man-eater."

Jack dragged a hand down his face. "What did Grace say?"

Jill rolled her eyes. "Who, miss goody two-shoes? She said something corny about you being a gentleman, and how of course Maria would need your support after what she'd been through."

His wife was kind and sweet, but she was no pushover. She was bright and a good judge of character. And Jack was afraid once she had some time to think, she'd start asking questions, and he had no idea how to answer them. The last thing he wanted to do was lie to her. He had to come up with a reason not to invite them all to town. But first he was going to deal with his sister.

"You know what, Grace doesn't deserve this." He stood up. "Thanks for looking after little Jack and bringing him home, but I think it's time for you to leave." He held out his hand.

Her eyes widened. "You want me to leave?"

"Jack, what's going on?" Grace asked, coming through the kitchen. She looked from him to Jill.

His sister jumped to her feet and pushed past him. "Whatever. I'm outta here."

"Jill, wait. Don't go. Let me explain," Grace called out.

The door slammed, and Grace headed after her. Jack grabbed her hand. "Let her go. Give her some time to cool off." He didn't want Grace to talk to Jill right now. He didn't trust his sister not to throw Maria in her face.

"What did she say?"

"Don't worry about it. You know what she's like. She's overprotective. She'll get over it."

"No, she won't, Jack. She adores you. She'll never forgive me for asking you for a divorce."

"I love my sister, but I don't want to talk about her now." He drew Grace into his arms. "I've been gone a long time, princess. We've got some serious catching up to do."

She gave him that dimpled smile he adored. "What would you like to talk about first?"

There were a couple of things they had to talk about, but now wasn't the time. "You and me naked in a bed. Floor's fine, too." He walked her backward to the couch. "Or right here."

"We can't, not here. Little Jack could get out of his crib, and he'd, you know, see us."

Right, he'd forgotten about their son. Best to keep that to himself, he thought. He turned Grace around and steered her toward their bedroom.

She laughed. "Jack, wait. I have to clean up the kitchen."

He turned her to face him. "Are you frigging kidding me?"

She ducked her head and blushed.

"You're nervous." The thought never would've crossed his mind.

"It's been a long time. I've changed. I've had a baby, and—"

His comments about her weight had probably left her feeling insecure. *Way to go, Flaherty.* "Grace, I love you. I want you as much as I always did. Nothing will change that." He angled his head. "Unless you've decided you don't like sex anymore. Because, princess, you used to really like sex."

"Jack!" She lightly slapped his chest.

"What? It's true. You're one of the most passionate women I've ever met. It's one of the reasons I married you."

She snorted. "I thought it was my cooking."

He wrapped her silky hair around his hand and gently tugged her head back, drinking in every inch of her beautiful face. "God, I've missed you," he said.

"Oh, Jack." She blinked back tears, then moaned when he began stringing kisses along her delicate jaw and down her elegant neck. "Take me to bed."

Thank Christ. "Ow," he yelped at the sharp sting in his

calf. It felt like something had bit him. He looked over his shoulder.

"No kiss my mama," his red-faced son yelled.

Jack had the sinking feeling he was about to bear witness to *another* Flaherty temper tantrum.

Chapter Nine

Grace caught a glimpse of herself in the steam-fogged bathroom mirror and her earlier anxieties returned. She needed Jack to kiss her senseless again. He was good at vanquishing her insecurities—always had been.

She wrapped a towel around her and picked up the half-full glass of white wine from the ceramic tile beside the claw-foot tub. If their son hadn't interrupted them an hour ago, they'd be lying in bed now basking in the afterglow, the awkwardness of their first time making love behind them.

And for Grace, that's what it felt like, the first time. Jack would probably think she was ridiculous for feeling that way, but she couldn't help it. Seventeen months was a long time. More like thirty-five months if you included the year he'd been deployed. Grace didn't count the few times they'd made love before he re-upped. They'd had sex. They hadn't made love.

Setting the wineglass on the bathroom's granite counter-top, she released the clip from her hair. Face flushed from her bath, all she needed was a touch of mascara...and her husband, who'd gone for a run. Since he'd been ticked at her, it was possible she was going to all this effort for nothing.

Jack hadn't agreed with how she dealt with their son's temper tantrum. He thought she should ignore little Jack until he regained control. Their ensuing argument had left her frustrated. She'd done her best to hide her irritation, but she was pretty sure he knew how she felt.

The apartment was so quiet that the clock ticking down the minutes on the bedside table seemed overly loud and drew her attention. Her stomach knotted. Jack had been gone for over an hour. She realigned the tall pillar candle between the two smaller ones, trying to rein in her anxiety.

She wondered how long it would take before she stopped worrying about him every time he left the apartment, worrying that he wouldn't come back. Forever, if her past history was any indication. Eighteen years had passed since her sister died. Eighteen years and it felt like yesterday. The nightmarish loop of images had played more frequently in her mind since she'd had a child of her own, since Jack had gone missing. She couldn't shut them off no matter how hard she tried.

Someone probably stopped him to talk, she reassured herself as she retrieved a modest cream satin negligee from the dresser drawer.

She pulled the nightie over head and thought about calling Jill. Then nixed the idea. She was the last person her sister-in-law wanted to hear from. And Grace didn't want to worry her needlessly. Jill adored her brother. As far as she was concerned, he could do no wrong. Grace understood why.

With his mother barely functional after his father's death, Jack, at the age of ten, had taken on the role of head of the household. He'd made sure his little sister ate and got to school and to bed on time. And when they'd moved to Christmas, he'd been her protector, standing up to his grandmother on her behalf, accepting the blame for all real or imagined wrongdoings and the punishments that accompanied them.

He was the kind of brother every girl dreamed of having. But at times, like tonight, Jill's hero worship put a strain on their friendship and was the reason Grace never told her she'd given Jack an ultimatum before he'd left.

Jill wouldn't understand that Grace had been desperate that night. Desperate and scared that if she didn't somehow get through to Jack, she'd lose him forever. And that was why, while Grace was tucking her son into bed earlier, she'd unsuccessfully strained to hear Jill's conversation with Jack.

Grace was afraid she'd tell her brother about the sugar plum wish. How Grace had given up on him. Obviously Jill hadn't, but given her mood, Grace wasn't sure how long that would last. But maybe she was wrong, and their friendship meant as much to Jill as it did to Grace. She hoped so.

Placing the glass of wine on the bedside table, Grace crawled beneath the covers. As she propped the pillows behind her back, Jack's cell phone pinged on the bedside table. Grace reached for the glass of wine, and it pinged again. She eyed the phone. What if Jill had decided to text her brother? Casting a nervous glance toward the hall, Grace leaned over to read the screen. The texts weren't from Jill. They were from Maria DeMarco.

Grace debated whether or not to read the messages. Brandi's earlier comments popped into her head and, unable to overcome her curiosity, she scanned the texts. From what Maria said, she'd been trying to get in touch with Jack since he'd left Virginia, and he hadn't responded. The woman sounded ticked.

The proprietary tone of her texts set Grace's teeth on edge. Who did Maria DeMarco think she was? Taking a sip of wine, Grace reminded herself it was easy to misconstrue tone in a text. She put down the phone and glanced at her iPad. Ignoring the warning bells going off in her head, she Googled Maria.

As Grace clicked through the pictures, she took a large gulp of wine. That was the last time she ignored those bells. Maria DeMarco was beyond gorgeous. So far beyond that Grace decided the photos had to be air-brushed or the woman had a very talented plastic surgeon. Because really, how could breasts that large be so perky? Or lips that pouty and lush be natural? Grace's stomach did a nosedive when her gaze dropped from the pictures to the woman's bio.

Just like Jack, Maria was an adrenaline junkie. And if that wasn't bad enough, she was also brilliant and well traveled. She'd been an imbedded journalist for three years before she'd been held hostage. Grace clicked on the more recent photos. The one of Maria coming off the plane with Jack. Her cheek resting on his shoulder, the gorgeous brunette looked up at him as she clutched his arm. Jack still had a beard in the picture, and it was hard to read his expression, but she saw his smile—dangerous and sexy. Her stomach sank. No, she had to be mistaken. She scrutinized the photo, trying to get a better read on his body language.

"So, does this mean I'm forgiven for being an ass?"

She gave a startled yelp, her gaze jerking to where her husband leaned against the doorjamb, muscled arms crossed over his chest as he took in the candlelit room with a smile playing on his lips. He looked like he stepped off the big screen. Of course he did, she thought a little petulantly, tossing the iPad onto the bed. He and Maria DeMarco with their movie-star good looks were the perfect match. Stupid thought. Ridiculous thought. *Stop it, Grace*, she chided herself. She had no reason to be jealous. He was here, and he was hers.

The heated look in his eyes told her all she needed to know. She wasn't going to waste her energy worrying about a woman who lived over a thousand miles from Christmas.

* * *

His wife gave him an impossibly sweet smile. "Of course you're forgiven. I'm used to doing things my way, that's all. You have every right to voice an opinion on how we discipline our son."

Sure he did. Whether she'd listen to him was the question. Jack didn't think a two-year-old should be disciplined, and Grace had made it clear that she did. The exasperated expression on her face when she'd firmly put his son in the time-out chair, lecturing him on his behavior in a tone of voice Jack had heard Libby use often, had pissed him off. If his grandmother had lightened up with him, Jack doubted he would've pushed the boundaries as hard as he had. He didn't want the same thing to happen to his son.

He'd headed out for a run before he lost his temper. But all Grace had to do is smile at him like she was now and his earlier frustration would've evaporated. "If I'd known what was waiting for me, I would've cut my run short," he said, walking to the bed.

"I was worried about you. Maybe next time you should bring your phone." Her eyes darted to his cell, and a tiny frown pleated her brow.

He kissed her forehead and smoothed a hand over her silky hair. "Sorry. I ran into a couple of reporters. I'm not going to be able to stall them much longer. Might as well give them what they want so they'll leave us alone. You up for an interview in a couple of days?"

"Sure. Whatever you want."

"Whatever I want? I like the sound of that." He smiled, trailing his finger down her elegant neck to slide the delicate strap of her nightie down her arm. "Just let me grab a shower." Dropping a kiss on her shoulder, his eyes lit on the screen of the iPad lying open on the covers beside her.

He breathed deeply, holding back a curse. What the hell was wrong with her friends? If Brandi hadn't brought up the damn picture at the meeting, Grace wouldn't have felt the need to check it out.

That was the problem with small towns. No one could resist sticking their nose in everyone else's business. He and Grace didn't need to deal with this on top of everything else. As tonight had proven, they had a few things to work out before their marriage was back on track.

He wasn't going to let what happened—or didn't happen—with Maria hurt his wife. He loved Grace, and that was all that mattered. And as soon as he had his shower, he'd show her just how much.

The thought made him smile, and he didn't have to worry about covering his earlier reaction. "I won't be long." He pulled his sweaty T-shirt over his head on his way to the bathroom.

"Um, Jack. Maria texted you," Grace said, a nervous hitch in her voice.

He silently counted to ten before he turned to face her. "Oh yeah?" he said, instead of asking what she was doing reading his messages.

"I, ah, didn't mean to look, but..." She wrinkled her nose, then shrugged. "You might want to get in touch with her. She seems upset that you haven't responded to her previous texts."

"Huh, is that right. I don't know why." Her golden eyes narrowed slightly as she studied him with sharp intelligence. He'd seen her zero in on another man with that same intent gaze the night he'd first met her. She'd been doing the spy thing for her father. She'd fascinated him. She still did. But his pulse kicked up at the thought she now had *him* under her radar.

Play it cool, Flaherty. "I'll get back to her. You want me to extend the invitation to the Fourth of July thing?"

"Um, no, it's okay. It doesn't look like the budget will cover their expenses. Besides, I'm sure they'll want to spend the day with their family and friends, don't you think?"

"Yeah, I'm sure they will." He didn't like the idea that seeing him with Maria and Brandi's dumb-ass comments had caused her to retract the invitation. Not that he wanted them to come, not Maria at least. But it meant Grace was feeling insecure, and that was the last thing he wanted. Before the night was over, he vowed to wipe away her doubts.

"Don't fall asleep on me," he said as he closed the bathroom door. He thought about taking his cell phone with him, but that'd tip his hand. Same as if he told her to toss her iPad in the garbage.

He stripped off the rest of his clothes and turned on the shower. The bathroom smelled like Grace: delectably sweet and feminine. His conscience rebelled at the idea of holding out on her. Raising the shower head, he stepped under the stream of hot water. He didn't want to lie to her, and indirectly, that's what he'd done. It went against his code of honor. Honesty was important to him. If he expected it of those close to him, he had to hold himself to the same standard. He had to be honest with Grace and tell her about Maria.

She'd understand.

So maybe it'd be a little tough to understand that her husband had been attracted to another woman, had kissed another woman, had wanted to have sex with another woman...Fuck. She'd never understand. But she had to. He'd just gotten her back, and he wasn't going to lose her. And it wasn't like he'd known he was a married man at the time.. He hadn't betrayed her, not intentionally.

The water turned cold, effectively ending the conversation Jack was having with Grace in his head. So far, none of those imagined conversations had ended well. He turned off the shower and grabbed a towel. Maybe she was asleep. Towel-drying his hair, he opened the bathroom door. She was awake. The knot in his gut tightened.

She watched as he walked naked toward the bed. Her cheeks flushed, her eyes gratifyingly wide. "I forgot how beautiful you are," she whispered.

"Nah, too many scars for that. But you, you're beautiful, princess," he said as he crawled up the length of the bed.

Her eyes flitted to the iPad on the bedside table, her fingers curling in the modest neckline of her nightie. She gave him a small smile. "You always knew the right thing to say to a girl."

"To you, and only to you. I love you, Grace Flaherty." He couldn't do it. Not now. Seeing the pictures of Maria had done a number on Grace's confidence. And just because he wanted to clear his conscience didn't mean it was the best thing for his wife. In a few weeks... maybe.

He got under the covers and pulled her warm, lithe body to his. She tipped her face up, and he kissed her, tasting wine on her lips. His stomach turned. Ever since the morning he'd tried unsuccessfully to revive his mother, he'd had the same reaction.

Pulling away, he said, "You mind brushing your teeth, princess?"

Her hand shot to her mouth, an embarrassed flush spreading over her face. "Do I have bad breath?"

If he hadn't been entranced by the sight of her waiting for him in the candlelit room, he would've noticed the glass earlier. He gestured to the bedside table. "No, it's the wine."

"Oh, Jack, I'm so sorry. I forgot," she apologized as she scrambled from the bed.

"Don't worry about it." He felt like an ass for embarrassing her. His weakness embarrassed him. He'd surprised himself by telling Grace about it on their second date. He'd never talked about his mother's problem or his own with any of the other women he went out with. There'd been no need to tell them. He hadn't wasted time on kissing, never saw the point until he met Grace.

But on the night of their second date, he'd learned they had something in common. Her mother had invited him in when he'd picked up Grace at home. Helena Garrison might be good at fooling some people, but she couldn't fool Jack. He'd recognized the signs right away. Grace spent the first ten minutes of their date making excuses for her mother. In an attempt to put her at ease, Jack had confided about his own mother's drinking problem. He'd never forgotten the look on Grace's face. She'd been apologizing for Helena's condescending, superior attitude, not her drinking.

Grace had been right about one thing: her mother was a bitch. Jack couldn't stand the way Helena treated her daughter. He thought he'd blown his chance with Grace right then and there. But that was the thing about his wife, she always took him by surprise. He was pretty sure that was the night he'd fallen in love with her.

Thoughts of the past vanished at the sight of Grace backlit by the bathroom light before she flipped the

switch. She looked like an angel, fine-boned and fragile. His decision not to tell her about Maria had been the
right one.

"Better?" She smiled, leaning over to kiss him as she
slid under the covers.

"Yeah. Thanks." As much as he wanted to return that
kiss, there was a small worry niggling at the back of his
mind. "You never used to drink when you were alone.
Has that changed?"

"No, Jack. You don't have to worry I've become a closet
drinker while you were gone. I was a little nervous." She
frowned. "I guess a lot nervous, since I forgot how you
felt about wine. I thought a glass would relax me."

"What were you nervous about?" He hoped it didn't
have anything to do with Maria or his plan to put that conversation on the back burner would be shot. If she asked
him outright, he wouldn't lie.

"Us. This." She motioned to him and the bed.

He smiled, both relieved and amused.

"Don't you dare laugh at me, Jackson Flaherty."

"Ah, my wife, the little prude."

"I am not," she said in an offended tone of voice.

"No one knows that better than me." Passion darkened
her eyes as he slid his palm up her smooth thigh. "You
look like an ice princess, but in bed you act like her slutty
stepsister."

"Jack!" She tried to keep an annoyed look on her face
then started to laugh.

His chest tightened, and he lowered his mouth to hers.
"God, I love you."

"Oh, Jack, I've missed you so much." Her lips parted
on a needy moan as he slid his hand under her nightie,

touching and caressing her. He loved how responsive she was, the sexy sounds she made.

"You still seem a little nervous, Grace. I can take it slower if that'd help," he teased, nuzzling the soft spot just below her ear.

She tugged his head to her breast. "Who's Grace? I'm her slutty stepsister Ginger."

Chapter Ten

"You won't be disappointed," Grace assured the general manager of the Pines the next morning, barely able to contain her excitement. The Pines was a ritzy resort in Aspen. "Yes, we'll see you then. And thank you, thank you very much." Grace stood in the bakery's kitchen staring at the phone after she'd said good-bye. She couldn't believe it. If her sugar plum cake got the thumbs-up at the tasting, the Pines was placing a standing weekly order. A *huge* standing weekly order. She dialed Madison, but her call went to voice mail. It wasn't the type of news Grace wanted to leave in a message, and she decided to tell her that night at the barbeque.

When Jack wasn't around.

Because the thing was, no matter how amazing last night had been, and it had been off-the-charts amazing, Grace didn't fool herself that they had an easy road ahead of them. Jack would need time to adjust to being home, to civilian life, whether he'd admit it or not. And they hadn't even talked about the bakery yet. It was the IED—improvised explosive device—buried under the rug. Sooner or later, they'd have to.

Grace was hoping for later. She needed time to convince Jack that the bakery would provide a good living for them. If—when, she corrected herself—they got the contract with the Pines, she'd have the proof she needed to make her case. Because while Grace had enjoyed working for her father, it wasn't a job she would've chosen for herself. Her parents had done the choosing, and Grace didn't have the heart, or the spine, to say no. She'd always loved to bake, but until Jack's grandmother had left them the bakery, Grace had thought of it as a hobby. And now that she had a job she was passionate about, she couldn't see herself doing anything else.

The next hurdle would be to prove to Jack that Christmas was the perfect place to raise their son. Since Jack's experience in the small town had been less than idyllic, living here might prove to be the toughest sell of all. His memories of growing up in the apartment above the bakery weren't happy ones.

It was the reason Grace had renovated while he was MIA. She'd put half of what she'd saved from her years of working for her father into making the apartment a home, the other half on updating the bakery.

What she needed, she decided, were reinforcements to get him on board. At the moment, for obvious reasons, approaching Jill and Sawyer was out. The timer on the oven went off, and Grace transferred the cooled carrot-and-pineapple cupcakes onto the stainless steel prep top. As she spooned the cream cheese icing into the pastry bag, she came up with the perfect person to help her with Jack.

Nell McBride.

Madison had hated small towns as much as Jack, and thanks to Nell, look how that had turned out. Admittedly Gage had more to do with changing Madison's mind, but Nell was the one who'd set everything in motion. Enlisting Madison and Gage wouldn't be a bad idea. Given how set against Christmas her husband was, Grace needed all the help she could get.

Between the four of them, they were sure to come up with a plan to get him on board. Grace's good mood from earlier returned, then she looked up from piping the icing onto the cupcakes to see her sister-in-law push through the swinging doors.

"Good morning, Jill," Grace said with a hesitant smile, unsure what to expect from her sister-in-law.

"Yeah, morning." Jill focused on the cupcake in Grace's hand. "Thought you should know, Stu turned himself in this morning."

"Is he all right?"

Her sister-in-law gave her head a disgusted shake. "I don't get you. The guy wrecked the apartment, and you're worried about him. You're such a doormat."

Grace wrestled with her temper. Once she had it under control, she said, "He's had a lot to deal with, Jill. While he was fighting in Iraq for his country, his wife was living in their home with another man. He lost custody of his children." Grace stiffened as soon as the words came out of her mouth. She'd just handed Jill the ammunition she needed.

Jill slowly nodded. "Yeah, I guess you're right. My

bad. Amazing isn't it, how our soldiers are treated? What kind of woman asks their husband for a divorce while they're deployed, or for that matter, before sending them off to war? Gotta be hard for a soldier to concentrate on his job when he's dealing with something like that, don't you think?"

She didn't need Jill to point that out to her. The guilt had nearly driven Grace crazy. Her fingers clenched reflexively, the cupcake crumbling in her hand. "I tried to call him. You don't know—" She stopped herself from saying anything more. She hadn't told Jill how bad it was then. She didn't need to tell her now.

Jill flattened her palms on the counter. "What I know is that if you ever hurt him again, I'll tell him, Grace. I'll tell him everything." Her lip curled. "No wonder he didn't remember you."

Grace jerked as if Jill had slapped her. Closing her eyes in an effort to fight back tears, she turned to put the cupcake in the garbage. "He remembers me now," she said quietly.

"Whatever. I'm warning you, if you—"

"How's my two favorite girls?" Jack said as he entered the kitchen through the screen door with little Jack in his arms. He looked from Jill to Grace. "What's going on?"

"Nothing." Grace forced a smile. "Just busy. So many customers, so little time." She held up a cupcake and mentally rolled her eyes. *Brilliant, Grace, now you've handed Jack the ammunition he needs.*

His gaze roamed her face as he came to stand beside her. He leaned in, smelling like fresh air and sunshine, and kissed her temple before returning his narrow-eyed attention on his sister. "Everything good?"

"Peachy," Jill said, chucking little Jack under the chin. "How's my buddy today?"

"Cake. Me want cake."

Before Grace could tell him it was too close to lunch, his father handed him a cupcake.

Jill smirked.

Don't you have somewhere you need to be? Grace wanted to ask Jill, but didn't, because that would be rude. And Grace had been brought up to be polite, even when she wanted to shove the cupcake she was holding in her sister-in-law's face.

"Got something for you, big brother." Jill beamed at Jack, tossing him a set of keys.

He looked from the keys to his sister. "What's this?"

"Your new wheels. Happy birthday times two. Same goes for Christmas." Jill gave him a watery smile.

Jack looked shocked. So was Grace. And even though Jill was being horrible to her, Grace was moved by her love for her brother. Jill would do anything for Jack. Including, it seemed, working overtime to pay for the vehicle.

"Shortstop, you didn't have to do this. I can't—"

"No, don't argue. It's a gift, you can't refuse. Besides, Earl gave me a great deal. You being a hero and all." She grinned then added, "And you need wheels. Grace sold *your* truck to buy a delivery van."

Wow, nice, thanks so much for throwing me under the bus on that one, Jill.

Because she shared Jill's SUV, Grace hadn't needed a vehicle, but she should've realized Jack would. He'd loved that old truck, or so Jill had told her when Grace decided to sell it. But even her sister-in-law had agreed, that as business expanded, Grace needed a delivery van.

"Is that right?" Jack said, giving Grace an inscrutable look.

"Jack, I—" she began to explain.

Jill cut her off. "Come and check it out." She tugged on his arm. "It's black and badass. You're going to love it."

"Okay if I leave little Jack with you?" he asked as he handed Grace their son.

"Of course." Not really—she had a couple dozen more cupcakes to ice. But how could she say no after she'd sold off his precious truck? Her husband laughed at something Jill said as the two of them left the kitchen.

Grace forced a smile and pulled out the stool. "Did you have fun with Daddy?"

"No da. Jack."

"Jack's your daddy, baby. You call him Da."

His mouth set in a mulish line. "No. No like Jack."

Grace sighed. She'd already dealt with one angry Flaherty and wasn't up to going a round with another one. She placed little Jack on the stool and handed him an iced cupcake and a bottle of sprinkles. The way her day was going, he'd probably dump...He threw the bottle on the floor, and it shattered. "Me eat cake," he said right before he smushed the cupcake in his mouth.

She picked up one for herself.

*   *   *

Gage's wife handed Jack two cold beers and distractedly waved him off to join her husband on the deck. As soon as they'd arrived, Madison had dragged them into the kitchen, and her stepdaughters Annie and Lily absconded with their son. Jack had waited for him to morph from giggling toddler to screaming terror. He hadn't.

Scooping up a spoonful of red jiggly stuff from a crystal bowl, Madison shoved the spoon at Grace. "It tastes like crap. What did I do wrong?"

Ah, so this was the reason for the frantic phone call asking them to come early for the barbeque. His wife took a tentative taste, and her eyes widened. She looked around the room as if searching for somewhere to spit, then grimaced and swallowed.

Madison leaned on the island. "Can you fix it?"

"Umm, what is it?" Grace asked, casting a wary glance at the bowl.

"Don't worry, Madison, she can fix anything." Jack kissed his wife, who said for his ears alone, "Not this."

As he walked through the dining room on his way to the deck, he heard Grace say, "Of course I can. It's not that bad." He grinned. Grace never could hurt anyone's feelings.

Opening the patio door, he walked onto the deck.

Gage looked up from brushing down the grill on the mother of all barbeques. "Either you guys are early or my watch stopped."

Madison must've kept her emergency call on the downlow. "Early. Grace thought Madison could use a hand."

Gage snorted. "Or ten. Thanks," he said, accepting the beer. He clinked the bottle against Jack's and slanted him a look. "How you doing?"

Jack leaned against the cedar rail. "Great. Memory's back." And after last night, he finally felt like he had his wife back, too. Nothing like a few hours of mind-blowing sex to resolve the worries and doubts. He smiled, remembering how good it felt just to hold her in his arms again, to wake up with her this morning.

"So I heard. Grace looks happy." Gage nodded to where Grace was laughing with Madison as they set the table in the dining room.

"Yeah, she does," he agreed.

She hadn't looked quite so happy when she'd come in from work an hour ago. At first he thought it was because she felt bad about selling his truck and had reassured her as long as she hadn't sold his Harley, he was good. When that hadn't helped, he figured whatever he'd walked in on at the bakery earlier had been responsible for her mood. No doubt his sister had been giving her a hard time.

Jill had surprised him with the truck before he could call her on it. He still couldn't get over what she'd done for him. She was the best... best sister, that is. Her sister-in-law and friend skills needed some work. Since she was coming tonight, he planned on getting her alone for a few minutes to put an end to her blaming Grace for everything.

He drew his gaze from his wife. "Congratulations, by the way. Madison's great. Lily and Annie seem happy with their new stepmother." Seeing Madison's success in winning over Gage's daughters, Jack thought about asking her for some pointers.

"Thanks." Gage smiled. "Even the ex loves her. But between you and me, I'm kinda hoping we have a boy next. I could use some backup and a little less estrogen in the house."

"Feel free to borrow little Jack anytime." Jack winced. Good thing Grace wasn't around. "Forget I said that." He took a long pull on his beer.

"You've only been back a couple of days. Give him time. Remember, he's had all of his mother's attention for over a year, and now you're horning in on his territory. He's a cute kid. He'll get used to having you around."

"Yeah, a cute terror. I don't know how Grace does it. I turned my back for two minutes today, and he colored on the walls in the kitchen." It was embarrassing. He was a soldier, for chrissakes. He'd shot down planes, taken out the enemy, led his crew safely through the mountains and deserts of Afghanistan, and he couldn't handle a two-year-old.

Gage must have seen the frustration on his face and clapped him on the shoulder. "Being a parent isn't easy. Don't be so hard on yourself. You've been through a lot." Gage held up a hand when Jack opened his mouth to deny it. "Don't bother. Two brothers who were in the military, remember? They say hey, by the way. They're glad you made it back. Said to give them a call if you need to talk."

"Tell them thanks. How are they doing?"

"Don't see much of them. Chance hasn't been home since Kate died. Easton made it back in April for my wedding, though."

"I didn't get to talk to Chance at Kate's funeral. Must've about killed him to lose her." Jack couldn't imagine what he'd do if anything happened to Grace. Kate had been Chance's childhood sweetheart. They'd been married for two years when her car went off the road in a blizzard. She'd been six months pregnant at the time.

"For a while there, it was like he had a death wish. Can't say I blame him. I don't know how you go on after that." Gage's gaze went to his wife, who ushered Sawyer, Dr. McBride, and an attractive redhead into the living room, and he took a deep pull on his beer.

Jack figured a change of subject was in order. "Who's

the girl with your dad?" he asked, while he kept an eye on Sawyer and Grace.

"Karen. She's a nurse at the hospital."

"Huh, I always thought your dad would end up with Mrs. O'Connor."

"So did we. It looked promising at Christmas, but then...nothing. She's been on the campaign trail with Ethan. Both of them say hi. Eth's going to give you a call. He should be back in town in the next couple of weeks."

"Senator O'Connor." Jack smiled. "Has a nice ring to it."

"Yeah." Gage rolled his eyes. "He won't be able to get his fat head through the door if he wins."

Jack laughed. Gage and Ethan were best friends, as close as Jack had once been with Sawyer, who walked onto the deck with Gage's dad. Dr. McBride handed Gage a platter of steaks. "Your wife says to get cooking."

"How quickly she forgets she was in charge of the dinner tonight."

"Sorry, son, she's not allowed to lift a finger in the kitchen. Doctor's orders."

"Doctor's orders my ass. She put you up to that. My wife's got you wrapped around her little finger." Gage waggled his beer bottle at Jack. "You don't know how lucky you are. Your wife's an amazing cook. Mine can't boil water without burning it."

No one had to tell Jack how lucky he was. But before he had a chance to agree, Madison popped her head out the door. "I heard that, McBride. You have some serious kissing up to do if you want to get lucky tonight."

Jack wasn't sure, but Gage appeared to be blushing. He rubbed the back of his neck. "Honey, we have company."

"They're not company, they're family." She let out a gusty sigh. "Oh Lord, here comes Nell." The door closed.

Gage shook his head, and the rest of them laughed. Dr. McBride turned to Jack and gave him a once-over. "You look good, son. But if you have any problems, you don't hesitate to give me a call."

"That includes hangnails, Jack. He gets real concerned about hangnails. They might get infected, you know," Gage said with a straight face as he put the steaks on the grill.

"My son, the comedian." Dr. McBride patted Jack's shoulder. "I'm glad you're home. That wife of yours had me worried. She's lost too much weight. You make her eat, you hear?"

"I'll do my best, sir."

Flames shot up from the barbeque, and Dr. McBride moved to his son's side to offer his advice. While they good-naturedly argued, Sawyer said to Jack, "I hear you got your memory back."

"Yeah, I did."

"Glad to hear it. It was hard on Grace when she found out you didn't remember her and little Jack."

"Wasn't exactly easy on me, either. But it wasn't like I lost it on purpose."

"Yeah, guess so." Sawyer leaned against the rail and took a swig of his beer. Jack followed the direction of his gaze. Sawyer watched Grace through the window. "Gage's dad is right, you know. She's had a tough time."

"I'm aware of that, Sawyer. And I'm going to take care of her."

"Make sure you do."

Jack's fingers tightened around the neck of the bottle. Sawyer seemed to be confused as to whose wife she was.

Just as Jack was about to set him straight, Sawyer said, "I had an interesting conversation with Brandi last night."

Don't react, Flaherty. "Is that right?"

"Yeah, she's got this idea in her head that the woman you rescued has a thing for you. I checked her out. Gorgeous, stacked, and brunette. Exactly the type you used to go for, flyboy."

"*Used to* being the operative phrase." *Dickhead.* "I'm married."

"Yeah, but you didn't remember you were. At least that's what you said."

"You got something you want to say, say it."

Sawyer straightened and got into Jack's space. "You hurt Grace, and I'll tear you apart."

Jack pushed him. "Back off, Anderson."

"Okay, you two, knock it off," Gage said, flattening a palm on each of their chests. "You're not in high school anymore. Jack, you were always good in the kitchen, go help my wife. And Sawyer, I think it's time you and I had ourselves a chat."

*   *   *

"Umm, Jack, don't you want to sit with everyone else?" Grace asked, gesturing to where Gage and his dad were setting up a bunch of lawn chairs. Ten minutes ago, they'd piled into their vehicles to make it in time for the fireworks display at the park. Jack had laid their blanket behind a cluster of evergreens.

From the expectant look on his wife's face, *no* wasn't going to cut it. Didn't stop him from trying, though. "No one can see us here. We can make out." And he wouldn't have to listen to Nell and Madison talk about the bakery ad nauseam.

Grace looked torn. He stretched out on the blanket and gave a suggestive waggle of his eyebrows. She laughed. Jack was about to give himself a self-congratulatory pat on the back, when Nell McBride called out, "You two aren't going to be able to see the fireworks from there. We saved you a spot over here." She pointed to a patch of grass in front of her chair.

Grace wrinkled her nose. "She's right, and little Jack will put up a fuss if he can't see them."

"I doubt he'd notice. He's too busy being a dog." Jack got up and reached for the blanket. He really hated that leash. But at least his son was no longer clamoring for Sawyer's attention like he had throughout dinner.

Grace looked over to where little Jack crawled on the ground with Lily holding on to the leash. She went to laugh, caught Jack's expression, and grimaced. Picking up the other end of the blanket, she met him halfway and joined her hands with his. She kissed the underside of his jaw. "Rain check?"

Jack folded the blanket around her, bringing her tight against him. Then he dipped his head and captured her mouth, kissing her like he'd wanted to all night. The best thing about the dinner at Gage's had been having her at his side.

"Woof. No kiss my mama. Woof." Jesus, the kid was a bloodhound. Every time Jack went to touch or kiss his mother, he sniffed them out. Jack groaned against his wife's smiling lips.

As he moved his leg out of biting proximity, Grace crouched beside little Jack, who panted at her feet. She patted his head. "Are you having fun with Lily?"

"Woof." He nodded and licked Grace's hand.

Jack opened his mouth to give his opinion about their son pretending to be a dog, when Lily intervened, "Can little Jack have a sleepover tonight?"

"Oh, I don't know, honey," Grace began at the same time Jack said, "That's a great idea."

Maybe he should've curbed his enthusiasm, he thought as he met his wife's narrow-eyed stare.

His son's "Me stay Lily" thankfully drew her attention off Jack.

"We'll see. Let's go talk to your mom," Grace said to Lily, setting little Jack on his feet. She headed off in Madison's direction with the kids. When Jack didn't follow right away, she glanced over her shoulder. "Aren't you coming?"

"Yeah," he said on a defeated sigh, bracing for more not-so-subtle arm twisting from the Sugar Plum Bakery's defense team. As they maneuvered through the crowd to reach their dinner companions, several people stopped to talk to Jack. He was saying so long to his sixth-grade teacher, who told Jack she'd always thought he'd end up in jail—gotta love small towns—when a lanky guy with overlong reddish-brown hair and wire-framed glasses shuffled closer.

"Hi." The twentysomething kid cleared his throat and stuck out his hand. "I'm Stu Thomas. You, uh, probably heard of me."

"Can't say that I have. Nice to meet you, Stu." He noticed the boot and rifle tattoo on the kid's left bicep beneath the pack of Marlboros tucked under the sleeve of his grungy white T-shirt. "You serve in Afghanistan?"

"No, sir, Iraq." The kid shot a nervous glance over his shoulder. "I, um, just wanted to tell you how much I admire you. And to, uh, apologize. I ... I'm the guy who trashed your apartment." He finished on a rush.

News to him, and unwelcome news at that. Jack crossed his arms, eyes narrowed at the kid. "You wanna explain to me why you did that?" He shifted his gaze to Grace when she came up behind Stu. She touched the guy's shoulder. The kid practically jumped out of his skin, whipping around to face her.

"Grace." Stu's Adam's apple bobbed as he struggled to regain his composure.

Jack pulled Grace to his side. The kid was wired.

Grace gave him a confused look, then returned her attention to Stu. "Sorry, I didn't mean to startle you. How are you doing? I've been worried about you."

What the hell? Angling his head to look at her, Jack raised a brow. "Stu here tells me he trashed our apartment."

Grace gently squeezed Jack's forearm. "He hasn't had an easy time since he got back."

The kid's face flushed, and he shoved his hands in his jeans pockets. "I'm going to pay you back, Grace. Honest. As soon as I get a job, I'll pay you back."

She searched his face. "What happened?"

"It's not an excuse, but everything came down on me at once. I kind of lost it."

"What did Lisa do now?" she asked, explaining to Jack that Lisa was Stu's ex.

Stu's mouth flattened. "I got behind on my child support. She won't let me see the kids until I'm caught up. I had a job lined up, but it fell through."

The guy looked too young to have kids of his own.

Grace studied Stu for a couple of unwavering seconds,

then said, "I need help with deliveries. The job's yours if you want it. I can't pay you much, but—"

Stu looked like he didn't believe her. Jack had a hard time believing her himself. "Really?" the kid asked. "After what I did, you'd do that for me?"

"Yes, you can start tomorrow."

"You won't regret it, Grace. And I'll pay you back, just like I said."

She smiled and patted his arm. "We'll talk tomorrow. I'll see you at nine."

"I won't let you down. Thanks, Grace." He shook her hand, then Jack's. "It was an honor to meet you, sir."

"Keep your nose clean, got it?"

"Yes, sir."

"I know what you're thinking," Grace said as they walked away. "But he's going through a tough time and doesn't have anyone to turn to."

"He got a raw deal," Jack agreed after Grace had filled him in on Stu's story. "And I get why you feel sorry for him and want to help, princess, but there's something off about the guy. I want you to be careful around him."

"You sound like Jill. But you out of anyone should understand what he's going through, Jack. He needs to catch a break, that's all."

"We'll see."

Grace released a heavy sigh as Jill strode toward them. "What did he want?" his sister asked, eyes focused on Stu's retreating back.

"To apologize." Grace cut in before Jack could respond.

Jill snorted. "I don't trust the guy. I'm going to keep an eye on him," she said and started after him.

Jack hooked an arm around his wife's neck. "She's

going to find out, you know," he said into her ear, gently nipping the lobe.

"Not tonight she won't, and I'll be ready for her tomorrow." She made a face. "Maybe you could keep her busy for the next few days?"

"I'll see what I can do. It'll cost you, though." As he settled them on the blanket, he whispered in her ear what he'd expect in return.

She grinned and opened her mouth to respond, but little Jack plunked himself down on her lap before she could.

"Grace, you should've set up a booth and sold your chocolate cupcakes with the caramel centers. You would've cleaned up. Have you tasted her chocolate caramel cupcakes, Jack?" Nell asked.

Oh Jesus, here she goes again. He'd hoped she'd given up the ghost. No such luck. Madison leaned forward in her lawn chair. "Nell's right, they're incredible. Even better, they don't just taste delicious, there's a hundred-percent markup on those babies."

He shot Grace an are-they-for-real look. She gave him an apologetic shrug before turning to the two women. A silent exchange ensued, complete with eye and hand signals.

Jack didn't care that the bakery appeared to be running in the black. A solid balance sheet wasn't going to change his mind about keeping the place. All he'd heard growing up was how much his grandmother hated her life. How Libby and his grandfather hadn't had one because of the bakery. It'd been a legacy passed on from his grandfather's mother. More like a noose around her neck, his grandmother used to say.

Grace had always been a neat freak and a bit of a

perfectionist, but nowhere near what she was now. He blamed the bakery for that. Stress exacerbated the problem, and there was nothing, as his grandmother proved, more stressful than running a bakery. Sure, his being missing hadn't helped. But in his gut he knew where the true fault lay, and nothing could convince him otherwise. Now he just had to convince his wife. She'd already ended up in the hospital once because of the bakery, he wasn't about to let it happen again.

The whir of a rocket stopped his thoughts cold. A steel band tightened around his chest as a flash exploded in the night sky, lighting up the mountains in the distance. The acrid smell of burning rubber filled his nostrils. Grace cast him a sharp glance, then moved, with their son in her arms, between Jack's legs. He wrapped his arms around the two of them, burying his face in Grace's hair to breathe in her sweet scent. *It's just fireworks, you idiot. You're home now.*

Maybe not home exactly, not yet. But he was here with his wife and son and that's all that mattered.

Chapter Eleven

When Grace woke up to bacon and eggs and her favorite blend of coffee laid out on a breakfast tray complete with wildflowers in a bud vase, she thought she had the sweetest, most amazingly considerate husband in the world. At the moment, she was revisiting that opinion.

Jack raised himself up from where he'd been lying beside her on the bed and moved the cup of coffee from the tray to the bedside table. "Get used to it, princess. I'm going to fatten you up. You've got at least twenty pounds to go. And if I have to force-feed you to get you there, I will." He brushed his lips over hers. "Don't pout."

"I'm not pouting. This is my I'm-an-adult-and-can-look-after-myself face."

His firm lips curved as he lifted the tray from where it straddled her legs and stood up. "It's a pout."

If she was pouting, it was because he thought she

needed to gain *twenty pounds*. "I've put on five since you've come home."

"Good, only fifteen more to go. Ah, ah, no, you don't," he said when she went to get out of bed. "You need your rest. Grab a couple more hours."

Now he was being ridiculous and annoying. "I have to go to work. I promise, I won't be long." And she wouldn't be. Jack had planned a picnic for the three of them in the meadow this afternoon. Which admittedly put him back in the sweet and thoughtful category.

He set the tray on the dresser and turned, giving her a narrow-eyed look. She wondered if he knew how mouth-wateringly sexy he was standing there in only a pair of low-riding navy sweatpants, all that sleek bronzed muscle on display. "I shouldn't be more than an hour."

"We had a deal, remember? No more working twenty-four-seven."

Her brilliant plan of enlisting Nell and Madison to help change Jack's mind about the bakery had totally backfired. Jack had realized what they were up to—they weren't very subtle—and found them more irritating than persuasive, or so he'd told her last night on the walk back from the fireworks. At least Grace now knew exactly what she was up against. If they kept the bakery, Jack was worried she'd end up an overworked, stressed-out, miserable person. *Thanks a lot, Libby*, she thought a little testily.

So there she had it. She was the only person who could change his mind. Grace drew her gaze back to his laser-blue eyes and smiled brightly. "I just have to get Stu settled and check on Desiree. She's been with me a couple of months and still can't get the fondant to the right consistency...What?"

He sat beside her on the bed, giving her a look that seemed to say, *I love you, but sometimes you drive me nuts.* "Princess, you've got some serious control issues, and you're going to have to get a handle on them if we're going to make this work. Nothing's perfect, not even your fondant."

"My fondant is so perfect. And if I work with... You think I'm controlling?"

Rubbing his thumb over her knuckles, he nodded. "And a perfectionist."

"Oh, I see. So not only am I scrawny and exhausted-looking, I'm also a controlling perfectionist. It's a wonder you married me."

"Hey, don't be like that. I'm trying to be honest here. Part of why you're underweight and exhausted, Grace, is because you're a perfectionist. You don't let—"

"You forgot controlling."

"Look," he took her hand, "I didn't mean to hurt your feelings."

"You didn't."

"Yeah, I did. But, princess, I'm worried about you. And so is Dr. McBride."

"Jack, I love Dr. McBride, but—"

"Should I be jealous?"

"Ha-ha. You know as well as I do that Gage's dad is a worrywart."

"He's not the only one who's worried about you. And I'm not going to have people saying I don't know how to look after my own wife."

That was the thing about Jack: for the most part he didn't care what people thought or said about him. But when it came to the citizens of Christmas, well, they were his Achilles' heel. She squeezed his hand. "I'm fine. Honest. And if it'll make you happy, I'll eat more and hire more help. Okay?"

"All right." He kissed her forehead and stood up. "Why don't you sleep awhile longer? I'll go pick up little Jack."

"I still can't believe we didn't get a call from Madison in the middle of the night," she said, ignoring his question and leaning over the edge of the bed to pick her nightie off the floor. Meeting his heated gaze, she smiled and said, "Stop looking at me like that and go get our son."

"I like looking at you."

"I thought I was too skinny for your tastes."

He made a frustrated noise in his throat. "Did it sound like I didn't love every inch of your body when I was kissing my way up it earlier?"

"I guess not," she said as she pulled the white nightie over her head, her face flushing at the memory.

"You don't seem too sure about that. Maybe I should remind you."

"Go." She pointed to the door with a smile. "I'll make the sandwiches for our picnic."

"You're supposed to take it easy today, remember? I'll give Holly and Hailey a call, get them to make up some sandwiches for us, and stop by the diner on my way home with little Jack. Chicken club still your favorite?"

She nodded. "Don't get anything for little Jack, though. I'll make his lunch."

"Stubborn woman." He headed for the door.

"I should only need half an hour to get Stu and Desiree organized. But if I'm not here when…" He turned and raised a brow. She sighed. "Less than an hour, Jack. I promise."

"I won't have the bakery sucking the life out of you like it did Libby."

"Your grandmother hated the bakery. It's not the same thing."

"We'll see."

"Yes, you will." She swung her legs over the side of the bed and stood up, determined to get the focus off her and the bakery. "You know, all we've done is talk about me. We haven't talked about you and what you're going to do once you retire. It's something we need to discuss."

*   *   *

"We don't need to talk about it now," Jack said. It was a discussion he'd put off for as long as he could. They had enough to deal with, and he had no doubt his wife had her heart set on staying in town. If he decided to remain in the military, it wouldn't be fair to move Grace and little Jack. But if he didn't, could he really picture himself living in Christmas full-time? *Hell no* was his immediate reaction. "I don't have to make a decision for a while yet."

Her gaze jerked to his. "I didn't think your retirement was in question. You promised..." She trailed off then cleared her throat, focusing on the contents of the drawer she'd pulled out. "You've done six tours, Jack. You were a POW for seventeen months. You've put in your time."

He knew what she'd stopped herself from saying. He'd promised when they got married that tour would be his last. At the time, it was a promise he thought he could keep. Things had changed. In some ways, they'd changed, too.

"I don't know if I can give you the answer you want."

"I see," she said with a forced smile and headed for the bathroom.

"Come on, Grace, don't—" She shut the door.

What the hell? All he wanted was a month or two to figure things out. You'd think she could give him at least that. *Yeah right.* Grace wouldn't be able to let it go until she had every detail locked down. The apartment walls closed in around him, and he strode to the front door. Locking it behind him, he headed down the stairs and onto the sidewalk.

The sun's rays danced off the vehicles parked against the curb on Main Street, a warm breeze ruffling the blue and yellow flowers trailing over the hanging baskets. At least the weather, unlike his wife, was cooperating, he thought as he walked to his truck. Some of his frustration with Grace faded as he remembered making love to her in the meadow, proposing to her there.

The day might be perfect after all. All he had to do was distract her. Kissing seemed to work well. They didn't have any problems when they were making love. It was talking that got them in trouble. Then he remembered who he was picking up, and his plans for seducing his wife went out the window. Talking would be about all they'd be doing since his son wouldn't let him near his mother.

A candy-apple-red Mustang pulled beside Jack's truck, distracting him. *Hot set of wheels*, he thought with a low whistle. The whistle sputtered between his lips when his gaze went to the gorgeous brunette behind the wheel. He stopped dead in his tracks.

Maria.

Jack was screwed. Unless…His gaze shot to the narrow alley between the barbershop and hardware store only twenty feet away. Just as he was about to sprint for cover, Maria slid her oversize shades on top of her head, zeroing in on his position.

If the enemy had you in their sights, Flaherty, you'd be a dead man.

From the way Maria's full lips flattened, he still might be. And if the pissed-off brunette easing her bombshell body—shrink-wrapped in a white halter top and red jeans—from the Mustang didn't kill him, his wife would. All he could think, as he forced a smile on his face and started toward Maria, was he should've told Grace about her when he had the chance.

A bead of sweat trickled down his back. He couldn't risk Grace being blindsided by this. He had to get Maria out of here and ask Madison to keep his son a while longer. He glanced back at the apartment. Grace wasn't the type to spend an hour getting ready. If he was lucky, he had ten minutes to send Maria on her way. *What are you smoking?* he thought when the woman in question sashayed toward him with a determined glint in her eyes. His gaze darted to the storefront windows and sidewalk. At least the streets were quiet. For now.

Maria looked him up and down, then raised dark eyes flashing with temper. She stabbed his chest with a long, red fingernail. "I thought something had happened to you. But here you are, alive and well, looking as disgustingly gorgeous as ever, no sign of a broken hand or finger. What the hell, you couldn't pick up a phone? I was worried about you." Along with the anger, he saw the hurt in her eyes and felt like an unfeeling jerk.

He should've called her, and not just to avoid her hunting him down. It wasn't her fault. Neither of them had known he was married. They'd spent a lot of time together, come through hell and back together. They'd become good friends, and chances were, if he wasn't married, they would've become a whole lot more. He closed his hand over hers. "I'm sorry. I meant to get back to you, but I've been busy."

"Really, Jack, too busy to call me?" She gave an angry shake of her head, the sun glinting off her long, dark hair. "I thought we had something. I thought I meant something to you."

"You do. You're a good friend, and I'm sorry you were worried about me."

"Friend? Come on, I was more to you than a *friend*, and you know it. What—" Her voice was getting increasingly louder. Half a block down, Nell McBride got out of a red pickup with her cronies.

"I'm married, Maria," Jack quickly cut her off. "Things got a little out of hand over there, and I apologize for that. It was never my intention to hurt you, but I love my wife. I got my memory back a couple days ago."

"How nice for your wife. Kind of convenient, though, don't you think, that you forgot about her when we were over there? If it were me, I'd have a hard time buying that. Must have been tough on her when you told her about us. How did she take it, Jack?" she asked, her tone taunting and aggressive.

Somehow she knew he hadn't told Grace. He wouldn't confirm or deny. "My wife knows I love her. She knows she's the only woman for me and has nothing to worry about." The muscle in his clenched jaw pulsed. Problem was, he wasn't sure how Grace would feel once she knew about Maria.

Maria's dark gaze flitted past him, and a slow smile curved her full lips. "Are you sure about that?" She moved closer. Close enough that he could feel the heat radiating from her body, smell the sweet, cloying scent of her vanilla musk.

He took a step back as Nell and her friends glanced their way. "Look, Maria, I've got to get going. From now on I'll return your calls." In the back of his mind, he realized that was a dumb-ass thing to say. The woman had flown halfway across the country to see him. He wasn't going to get rid of her that easily.

"Oh, Jack." She gave a husky laugh and wound her arms around his neck. "You're not going to have to return my calls, you silly man."

"What do you—" The rest of his words got swallowed up in her hot and hungry kiss.

As he worked to extricate himself from the tight hold she had on his neck, she broke the kiss and murmured against his lips, "You can deny it all you want, but we had something. And I'm staying here until you figure that out. Because I guarantee if you'd been married to me, I'd be the last thing you forgot."

Jack ignored the dark scowl Nell McBride shot at him and Mrs. Tate's anguished, "Poor Grace." He wiped his hand across his mouth, so angry he could spit.

Maria eyes widened, and she took a step back.

"I'm warning you, Maria—" Jack began when a hand clamped on his shoulder and spun him around. He caught a glimpse of Sawyer's flared nostrils and bared teeth just before his fist slammed into Jack's jaw.

The force of the blow rocked Jack on his heels. It took a second to regain his balance. Once he did, he put a hand to his mouth, moving his jaw at the same time he stared down Sawyer. "Cheap shot, dickhead."

"Jack, baby, are you all right?"

He shrugged Maria's hand from his shoulder and focused on Sawyer. Sawyer glared at her then turned on Jack. "That's all you've got to say for yourself, you son of a bitch? You kissed another woman in the middle of Main Street while your wife watched. I warned you if—"

Jack's gaze shot past Sawyer. A picnic basket lay on the ground in front of the door to the apartment. He felt like the earth moved under his feet. He needed to get to her. Sawyer got in his face.

Fisting his hands in Sawyer's sweaty T-shirt, Jack gritted out, "Get the fuck out of my way. Now."

"You're not going anywhere near her, asshole." Sawyer planted his palms on Jack's chest and shoved.

"She's *my* wife, dickhead." Jack let go of Sawyer's T-shirt, drew back his fist, and got in a solid blow to Sawyer's gut. Jesus, the guy worked out. Jack shook off the pain in his hand while Sawyer recovered from the blow. He recovered faster than Jack expected, grabbing the back of his shirt as Jack went to jog past him.

Jack spun around and put him in a headlock. Sawyer grabbed him around the waist.

"What the Sam Hill has gotten into you two? Stop that right now before someone gets hurt!" Nell McBride yelled at them.

Jack looked up to see a crowd had gathered. *Just like the good old days*, he thought as he and Sawyer staggered down the sidewalk, each trying to gain the upper hand, neither one of them willing to let go. They lost their balance and slammed into the front window of the barbershop. Jack heard an ominous crack, and they landed inside the shop on the floor. Instinctively, he rolled on top of Sawyer to protect him when the rest of the pane of glass came down on them.

"Always have to be the hero, don't you?" Sawyer muttered, but some of the anger had left his eyes.

"Shut up, dickhead," Jack said and gingerly rolled off him.

Dan looked down at them. "Should've known there'd be trouble now that you're back in town, Jack. You owe me another window."

Sure he did, because if anything went wrong in Christmas, it was Jackson Flaherty's fault. He wasn't going to need a month to decide if he was staying or leaving. But after today, he wasn't sure his wife would be leaving with him.

*   *   *

Jack sent Grace another text: *Pick up the goddamned phone now.* After twenty unanswered phone calls and twice as many texts, he'd gone from desperate to a combination of panicked and pissed off.

"Leave her alone. She doesn't want to talk to you, flyboy," Sawyer said from where he sat beside him on the cot, craning his neck to look over Jack's shoulder.

"Mind your own business, dickhead. If it hadn't been for you, we wouldn't be sitting in jail."

"That's on your sister. I thought she was going to shoot me. The woman needs help. Gage should sign her up for an anger management course or something."

Or something. Not that Jack would admit it to Sawyer, but even he'd been worried Jill might pull the trigger. Her finger had looked a little twitchy when Sawyer started going on about how amazing Grace was and how Jack didn't deserve her. The crowd loudly agreed with his ex–best friend. Both his sister and Maria—who he wanted to strangle—had gone into pit-bull defense mode. Yeah, it had been a real shitshow.

Jack stood up and started to pace. The cell was a palace compared to the hole they'd been kept in, but being locked up was starting to get to him. It was one of the reasons he'd been texting and calling Grace nonstop. After the first couple of tries, he'd figured she wasn't going to answer. Didn't matter; he'd needed the distraction.

He wiped his damp forehead. "Jesus, it's hot in here. Town council must've cut Gage's budget," he said as a way to explain the sweat dripping off him.

A concerned frown furrowed Sawyer's brow. "Give me your phone."

"Use your own."

"I don't have it on me. I was jogging when I ran into you and Hot Stuff making out in the middle of Main Street."

It was getting harder for Jack to stay focused. He didn't bother responding. Instead, he muttered, "Where the hell is Gage?"

Sawyer took the phone from him, forcing him onto the cot. "I'll get you out of here, buddy. Take a couple of deep breaths."

Sawyer put the phone to his ear and walked to the front of the cell. Jack couldn't make out what he said, but it was obvious whomever he spoke to got an earful. Less than two minutes later, Gage strode through the main doors, exchanging a look with Sawyer before fitting the key in the cell door. "Sorry I took so long, but I had half the town jammed in the station and Nell, Mrs. Tate, and Mrs.

Wright in my office. It's not been a fun day so far, boys," he said.

Jack made himself take his time when all he wanted to do was bolt. Then again, his legs might give out on him and he'd embarrass himself further. As soon as he got on the other side of the door, the rock-hard muscles in his neck relaxed.

He gave Sawyer a curt nod and muttered, "Thanks." Taking his phone from him, he said, "But you're still a dickhead."

"Look it up in the dictionary and it'd have your picture there, flyboy, not mine."

"For chrissakes, you two are acting like you're back in high school. Grow up."

Jack started for the door. "I gotta go. Let me know what I owe—"

"Park your ass in the chair, Flaherty. You're not going anywhere just yet," Gage said in a don't-mess-with-me tone of voice.

Jack turned to see Gage taking a seat behind the desk one of his deputies had vacated earlier. "It's not like I'm leaving town. I have to talk to Grace and pick up little Jack."

"Don't worry about little Jack. He's staying at my place for the day. And I'd suggest you give your wife some time. She doesn't want to talk to you." Gage gestured for him to take the empty chair beside Sawyer, who had a smug smile on his face.

"Too bad. She's going to talk to me. So let's get this over with, shall we?" Jack said.

Gage's brows hit his hairline, then he read off a list of charges.

"You've got to be kidding me," Jack and Sawyer said at the same time as they pointed at each other. "It was his fault."

"Yeah, I thought that's what you'd say. And, Jack, just so you know, several women asked that you be charged with adultery."

"Bullshit. I didn't commit adultery. And even if I did...I did not," he snapped at Sawyer when he muttered that it looked like it to him, "you can't arrest someone for adultery."

"Relax, I know that. Giving you a heads-up is all. Women in town might give you a hard time."

"What else is new?" Jack muttered. He should've enjoyed the hero deal while it lasted.

"All right, so here's how it's going to go. All charges will be dropped, and I'm not fining either one of you. You'll split the replacement cost of Dan's window and do one month of community service."

At this point, Jack would agree to anything to get out of there. "Okay," he said and stood up.

"Fine," Sawyer grumbled, coming to his feet.

They both started for the door. "Ah, boys, don't you want to know what you'll be doing for the next month?" The underlying amusement in Gage's voice didn't bode well.

Sawyer and Jack shared a look then turned to Gage, who tried to keep a straight face. "There's a house on Sugar Plum Lane. An abandoned Victorian that should be condemned, but the historical society won't give the okay. Kids are playing around in there, and someone's going to get hurt. You two have one month to get it ready for market. I'll expect you there from nine to five Monday through Friday. And I'll be checking up on you."

"Hell no, I'm not working with him. Give me something else to do," Jack said.

"You think I want to work with you, flyboy? Come on, McBride, I have a business to run. I'll coach the kids' baseball team."

"You used to be afraid of the ball," Jack said. "I'll coach the baseball team."

"You've got a manager at the bar, Sawyer. And this is the only deal on the table, take it or leave it. But I'd advise you to take it. Wouldn't look good for either of you to have a record, and since my wife became mayor, the fines are pretty steep."

They muttered their agreement, and Jack pushed open the door. Sawyer followed after him. "See you tomorrow at nine sharp, boys." Gage chuckled.

"Dickhead," both he and Sawyer said under their breath. Jack lengthened his stride, ignoring the disgusted look the woman at the front desk shot him. "Bye, Sawyer," she tittered.

Jack rolled his eyes and headed for the door. Through the glass, he could see Nell and a bunch of older women standing on the sidewalk. Several feet away, his sister and Maria talked to Fred and Ted. He'd been hoping to avoid them all. He didn't want to waste time getting into it with Maria or the town's morality squad.

As Jack went to open the door, he heard the shots. He scanned the street, his muscles tensing, ready to go into defensive mode. A rusted-out brown truck trundled down the road. He dragged in a breath of fresh air as he pushed open the door, then spotted Maria on the ground. Fred, Ted, and Jill gathered around her. The three of them spoke to her in low, comforting voices. They knew what had happened. Everyone else gawked at her like she was some kind of freak.

"Show's over, folks," he gritted out, waving them off. He crouched in front of Maria and moved her hair from her face. She was pale, her eyes vacant. "Maria, look at me. It's Jack. You're okay. A truck backfired." His chest tightened when a low whimper escaped her parted lips. "Come on, sweetheart, look at me." He stroked her cheek.

She finally lifted glassy eyes to his, then glanced around, an embarrassed flush reddening her cheeks.

"Don't worry about them," he said, helping her to her feet. Jack looked at his sister, lifting his chin at the crowd. Jill nodded and headed for Nell and her friends.

Fred rubbed Maria's arm, and Ted handed her her sunglasses with a commiserating smile. "Don't you pay them no mind, missy. Me and Fred know what it's like. You're going to be fine. Jack here will take good care of you."

She murmured her thanks. The two men patted Jack's shoulder. "We'll handle the girls," Fred assured him before they headed off.

Jack wished "the girls" included his wife, because they were right: Maria was his responsibility.

"I feel like such an idiot," she whispered. Her hand shook as she swiped at her tearstained face.

Jack put his arms around her, angling his head to meet her eyes. "You and me both. If you'd seen me in the cell ten minutes ago, you wouldn't feel so bad."

"We're a pair," she said as he released her. She went to put on her sunglasses and gave a pained grimace.

Jack frowned and took her hand in his, doing a quick scan of the rest of her as he did. She'd ripped the knee of her red jeans, and there was blood on her abraded skin. "Better get you to the hospital and have you checked out."

She looked like she was going to object, then glanced at him from under her long lashes. "You might be right," she said, cradling the hand he'd released. "Will you take me? I don't think I can drive."

"Everything okay here, Jack?" Gage asked, coming to stand beside them. He glanced from Maria to the dwindling crowd.

Jack introduced them. "Maria fell. I think she might've broken her wrist. I'm taking her to the hospital."

Gage gave him an are-you-fricking-kidding-me look before he said, "I was heading over to see my dad. I can take Ms. DeMarco if you'd like."

Jack appreciated the offer. No one needed to tell him he was digging his grave a little deeper with his wife by spending more time with Maria. But he couldn't leave her with people she didn't know, not after what he'd just witnessed. His gut told him Maria was suffering from PTSD. If that was the case, she needed to get some help. He'd make sure she did. He owed her that much at least.

"Thanks, Gage, but I'll take her." He put his hand at her back and nudged her toward the Mustang, passing Sawyer, who leaned against the brick building.

Sawyer held his gaze. "Don't worry about Grace, Jack. I'll make sure she knows where you are."

Chapter Twelve

I'm not going to pick up, you...you no-good, lying rat bastard." Grace threw her cell phone on the bed. For all of ten seconds it felt good to release her hurt and anger. Until she thought of Jack kissing that woman again, right there on Main Street. It was devastating enough to see the man she loved with another woman, she didn't need the whole town to witness her humiliation.

From where she sat on the bed, Grace reached behind the bedside table to unplug the landline. She couldn't take any more sympathetic phone calls. Before she got the jack out, the phone rang.

She checked caller ID and closed her eyes for a second before answering. Forcing an upbeat, cheerful tone into her voice, she said, "Hi, Daddy, thanks for getting back to me."

She'd left a message for him earlier. Last night, Jack had convinced her to call him. He didn't want to be the reason for their distance. Grace loved her father, and their strained relationship had bothered her, too. It shouldn't have surprised her when he helped Jack deploy early. It was the same way her father dealt with his and her mother's problems. Probably the only reason her parents were still together was because of how little time they actually spent in each other's company.

"Honey, what's wrong?"

"Nothing, just a cold."

"You tell that son-in-law of mine he better take good care of my baby girl or he'll be answering to me," he said, using his general's voice.

Her throat clogged with emotion. Even after Faith had come along, Grace had been his baby. Parents weren't supposed to have favorites, but hers did. Faith had been their mother's. It was why, Grace believed, Helena had never been able to forgive her for what happened that long ago July afternoon at the river. The wrong daughter died.

She pushed the thought aside and gave her father the answer he expected. "I will."

"I was thinking your mother and I should come for a visit. We haven't seen our grandson in a while. How's he doing? Glad to have his father home?"

Dear Lord, she hoped he was referring to the Fourth of July celebrations and not now. It would be like a weird sort of déjà vu. They'd come to visit just before Jack re-upped. Given the state of Grace and Jack's relationship, the timing had been awful. Her eagle-eyed father hadn't missed a thing, other than her mother taking every opportunity to criticize and undermine Grace. By the time they left, Grace had zero confidence in her parenting abilities, and Jack was heading back to Afghanistan.

Grace decided to ignore her father's comment about the visit. "He's getting so big. I'll send you pictures as soon as I get off the phone. And Jack, well, I think it'll take some time to get used to having him around. For little Jack, I mean."

"It's not easy for any of you. But cut Jack some slack. He's been through a lot. He's a good man. I wouldn't have let you marry him if he weren't."

Her father loved Jack. He had from the very start. But Grace didn't think he'd be too happy with him right now. And she didn't know how much slack she was willing to cut him. "I'm sure it will be easier now that he has his memory back." Wow, even she couldn't tell that was a big, fat lie. And then she realized she hadn't told her father the news. "Oh, Daddy, I'm sorry. I should've called to let you know."

"Don't worry about it. Jack told me. We talk nearly every day."

Grace's stomach did a nervous dip at the news. Was her father the reason Jack had decided not to retire? Well, that was the least of her worries now, wasn't it?

Her father cleared his throat. "I hope this phone call means we'll talk more often. I've missed you."

"I've missed you, too. I shouldn't have blamed you. I was—"

"No, I shouldn't have interfered, baby girl. But it's in the past, so let's put it behind us. Now, I'm getting the impression this might not be the best time to visit. How about we come for that shindig you're putting on instead?"

"That would be perfect," she said, unable to hide her relief. "I'd love to see you . . . and Mother, of course. How is she?"

"Fine." His tone said otherwise. Helena had trained them well. At Faith's funeral, Grace had answered honestly when her swim coach had asked her how she was doing. Her mother's reaction had ensured she never made that mistake again.

Her father spoke to someone in the background. "You sound busy. I'll let you go."

"Never too busy for my baby girl."

They talked for a couple more minutes, then said their good-byes. Grace hung up and disconnected the landline. Her cell pinged. If it wasn't about little Jack, she'd ignore it. She'd talked to Madison twenty minutes ago. Madison had tried to make Grace feel better, saying how there was no way Grace could tell what kind of kiss it was from where she'd been standing. Grace knew a casual kiss when she saw one, and what her husband and that woman had shared was not casual.

Sadly, Jack's reaction to inviting the woman to the Fourth of July celebrations now made more sense. Her face grew hot as she realized how naïve she'd been. He must've thought she was such a fool.

Her cell pinged several more times, and she forced herself to look at the messages. *I'm not going to say I told you so, but I did. If you need me to kick your husband's very fine ass, I will. I'll kick hers, too. Not that it's fine. Call me.* She'd get back to Brandi later. She wasn't up to it right now.

The next text was from Sophia. Grace couldn't read it. Sophia texted in Spanish when she was angry. Grace imagined it contained several swear words and an offer to take Ms. DeMarco out. Because Sophia was a good friend and that's what she did. There were messages from

Hailey, Holly, and Autumn, too. A weak smile curved Grace's lips. At least her friends had her back.

If Jack and that woman thought the citizens of Christmas would give them an easy time of it, they better think again. Jack out of anyone should know what the people in town were like. The thought stuck a pin in Grace's self-righteous anger, and she felt a sudden pang of sympathy for him. Honestly, Jill was right. She was a doormat. How on earth could she feel sorry for him after what he'd done?

Because she loved him and didn't want him hurt, no matter how much he'd hurt her. And her father was right: Jack had suffered enough. At one time, he'd been the best thing that had happened to her. She'd felt like she could do anything with Jack by her side. And when she'd thought she'd lost him forever, she'd lost a piece of herself. So now that he was back, was she really going to give up on him that easily? From his texts, it didn't sound like he'd given up on them. He'd told her he loved her and asked for a chance to explain. She owed him that at least. And she owed it to herself and her son.

Her cell pinged again. She'd reply this time. Tell him to come home and they'd talk things out. If Jill thought that was added proof Grace was a doormat, well, too bad. What did she care what her supposed best friend thought when Jill had been the only one who hadn't contacted her?

Grace frowned. The sender information was blocked. She opened the attachment. It was a picture of Jack holding Maria DeMarco in his arms, smoothing her long hair from her face, a tender expression on his. It had been taken outside the sheriff's office. The back of Grace's throat ached, and her fingers curled in the front of her blouse.

There were several scenarios that might've explained that first kiss. Perhaps Maria had thrown herself at Jack. But Grace could see her husband's face in this one. There was no mistaking how deeply he cared for the woman.

And Grace had a boatload of experience when it came to actions speaking louder than words. *It was an accident, Grace. It wasn't your fault. We don't blame you.* Only to be shipped off to boarding school a couple days later and to her grandmother's for the holidays.

The intensity of her emotion scared her, and she took several deep breaths to regain control. How could he do this to someone he professed to love? Unless...unless he wanted to end their marriage but couldn't bring himself to tell her, couldn't bring himself to do it. He didn't turn his back on his grandmother, a woman who'd made his life miserable, did he? Of course he didn't; he was too honorable and responsible a man to simply walk away. What he wanted, Grace decided, was for her to do his dirty work for him, forcing her to make the decision.

"If that's what you want, Jack, I'll make it easy for you."

Her vision blurred as she flung open the closet door and grabbed his black duffel bag from the floor. She tossed it on the bed then walked to the dresser, fighting to open the drawer. Once she got it open, she scooped up a pile of boxers and socks, dumping them in the bag. She went back and gathered up his T-shirts, holding them at arm's length so as not to give in to the urge to bury her face in them and inhale him one last time. She stuffed them in the bag then went to the closet and pulled his jeans from the hangers. Jamming his clothes in the duffel, she forced the zipper as far as it would go and hefted the bag over her shoulder.

She marched down the hall and opened the front door. Tossing the overstuffed bag on the landing, she closed her eyes as she went to shut the door. She couldn't do it. Going back out on the landing, she knelt and neatly repacked the bag. When she was finished, she placed the duffel outside the door and went inside, sliding the dead bolt home.

Her legs trembled as she walked to the bedroom and picked up her cell from the bed. She went into the bathroom and started a bath, sending a couple of recent pictures of little Jack to her father while the water ran. She deleted the photo of Jack and Maria, then responded to Madison's latest text. *I'm fine. Don't worry about me.*

* * *

Jack sat between Jill and Maria on the hard plastic chairs. The place hadn't changed much. He'd spent a lot of time in the emergency waiting room as a kid, having one broken limb after another tended to. He glanced at his sister, who leaned across him to listen to Maria. He'd been glad when she'd accompanied the two of them to the hospital. Now, not so much.

He'd thought she'd come to chaperone on Grace's behalf. But it became clearer as they waited for Dr. Trainer to see Maria that that wasn't the case. The two chatted as though they were long-lost friends. They were talking about Jack as if he weren't there. And if either of them told one more story that made him out to be a goddamn superhero, he'd lose it. Leg bouncing, he tapped an impatient tattoo on the arm of the chair.

"No, it's true, Jill. You should've seen him. He took out two guards with his bare hands."

That's it. "Jill, since you're here, I'll get going. Let

me know how you make out with your hand, Maria. And talk to the doctor about your nightmares. Gage said he's a good guy." Jack had gotten Maria to open up on the way to the hospital. He'd been right about the PTSD. The fact Maria didn't seem to have anyone to support her only made it worse. But he was leaving her in good hands. Dr. Trainer had served time in the military as a medic and, if she was honest with him, he'd be able to help her.

"Oh, Jack, do you really have to go? I was hoping you'd stay. We haven't had time to catch up. I want to talk to you about my book." She rubbed his arm and pushed her lips into a cross between a pucker and a pout.

Huh, did she think that was sexy? He gave his head a slight shake and stood up. "Yeah, I do. I've got to go home and suck up to my wife. I have a feeling she's not going to be too happy about you kissing me in the middle of Main Street." There, he'd said it. He'd held back because of her episode. But listening to her talk about him to Jill made Jack uncomfortable. He wanted to remind her that he was a happily married man.

"Maybe Grace should've thought about that before she asked you for a divorce," Jill muttered.

Maria's eyes lit up with interest. He was going to strangle his sister. "Jill, can I talk to you for a minute? In private?" He reached for her arm.

"Jack, I'm so sorry. Why didn't you tell me? What kind of woman does that to a man—"

"She didn't ask me for a divorce," he grated out. But if he didn't get to her soon, she might. He unceremoniously tugged his sister from the chair. "Excuse us."

Jack dragged Jill to the emergency room doors. "What the hell is wrong with you?"

"Nothing," Jill said, pulling a sulky face.

"Don't give me that. You were practically offering me up to Maria on a silver platter. You're supposed to be Grace's best friend."

"So what. A little competition never hurt anybody. Maybe she'll realize what she has if she thinks she'll lose you."

"I'm warning you, do not encourage Maria. Grace and I don't need this right now." He raked his hand through his hair. "Don't you even care that she kissed me and Grace saw her doing it?"

"An old friend gives you a hug and a peck on the cheek and she can't handle that?"

"It was no peck, Jill. It was a no-holds-barred kiss, and I'm pretty sure Maria knew what she was doing. I think she saw Grace and decided to put on a show."

"Oh." She chewed on her bottom lip.

"Yeah, *oh*. My family's off-limits. Don't talk to her about us." He glanced at Maria when a nurse called her name. Maria mimed that she'd call him. He forced a smile and nodded. "Now I have to go and try to explain this to my wife."

"I'll stay and drive Maria to the lodge."

"Thanks. And while you're at it, see if you can convince her to leave. Tomorrow would be good."

"Uh, yeah, sure, but I don't think—"

He held up a hand. He knew what she was going to say, and right now, he didn't need to hear it. "Later," he said and headed out.

As he walked out of the hospital parking lot, Gage pulled alongside him in his white Suburban. The window rolled down. "You want a ride?"

"As long as it doesn't come with a lecture," Jack said as he opened the door.

Gage grinned then sobered. "How's Maria's hand?"

Jack put on his seat belt. "Swollen, but it should be fine. And it's not the hand that's her problem. She needs to talk to someone. Hopefully she'll open up to the doc." It bothered him that she didn't have anyone to turn to. If he could trust her not to pull shit like she had today, he'd encourage her to stick around until she got it together. He'd be there for her the same as he would for any of the guys.

"Do you?"

"No. I'm good. I get antsy in confined spaces, that's all," Jack said.

"Have you talked to Grace yet?"

"No, has Madison?"

"Yeah. I think you've got some major sucking up to do, buddy."

"Figured as much. Got any suggestions?"

"The truth." Gage slanted him a look. "There's nothing going on between you and Maria, is there? You can tell me, Jack. It won't leave here."

He trusted Gage, and he could use a sounding board. So he told Gage what had gone on between him and Maria in Afghanistan.

Gage released a low whistle. "Take my advice and get her out of town. I know you feel responsible for her. I understand and admire that. But I've got a bad feeling, if she sticks around, there's going to be trouble."

"You and me both. But right now I'm more worried about what to say to Grace. Should I tell her everything?"

"Yeah. Better coming from you than Maria. The

woman already told you what she wants. She doesn't seem the type to be easily put off."

"Understatement," Jack said as they drove over the wooden bridge. The fast-flowing creek tumbled over the boulders on its way down from the mountain lake where Jack and Grace would be picnicking now if not for Maria.

Gage's Bluetooth went off. "Hi, honey. You're on speaker. Jack's with me."

"Why are you with my husband, Jack Flaherty, and not with your wife?"

"Be nice, Madison. Jack's not the bad guy here. I'm bringing him home now."

"Hmph, I'll withhold judgment, for now. But if you hurt Grace, Flaherty, I'll hurt you. And I'll hurt you bad."

"For chrissakes, Madison, I'm the sheriff, and you're the mayor. You can't go around threatening people like that."

"It's all right, Gage. She's protecting Grace." And even if it was at his expense, Jack appreciated that. "If it makes you feel better, Madison, the last thing I want to do is hurt my wife."

A couple of seconds ticked by before she said, "See that you don't."

"Honey, I'll be home in a few minutes. Is there anything else you wanted besides threatening Jack?"

"Umm, we have company. So when you come home, don't...well, you know," she said with a thick Southern drawl.

Gage rubbed the back of his neck. "Who's at the house and what am I not supposed to do?"

"Jump me in the kitchen like you always do when you think we're alone, because we won't be," she whispered.

Jack laughed. Gage's grin faded when his wife continued, "Skye's come for a visit. Isn't that a nice surprise, sugar?" Her drawl was so thick that Jack wasn't sure that's what she'd said, but her husband seemed to understand her.

And he looked like he wanted to thump his head on the steering wheel. "How long is she staying?"

"Umm, looks like it might be for a while."

"A while as in a couple of days?"

"More like weeks." She sighed when Gage groaned.

"Oh, Skye, I didn't see you there. What are you talking about? I'm thrilled to bits to have you here. See you when you get home, sugar. No, I'm not nervous. I don't know why you'd—" They heard her say before she disconnected.

"So, who's the houseguest?"

"Madison's best friend, Skylar Davis. Sweet girl, but kinda crazy. Bleeding-heart liberal with more money than God. You don't want to get her in the same room with Ethan." Gage grimaced as he turned onto Main Street. "I hope she's gone before he comes home."

"They don't like each other?"

He snorted. "The night before we got married they liked each other just fine. It was once they sobered up and started talking instead of making out that we had a problem. They nearly ruined our wedding."

"Sounds like you're going to have your hands full, Sheriff."

"You're telling me." Gage pulled in front of the bakery. "Go work things out with your wife."

"I'll do my best. Thanks for the ride and for looking after little Jack. To think yesterday I thought my biggest problem was getting my kid to like me." He gave his head a weary shake as he got out of the Suburban. "Tell Madison I'll be over—"

"Don't worry about it. I'll bring him home. Gives me an excuse to get out of the house. I have a feeling I'll need one."

At the sight of the basket lying on the ground outside the purple door, it took some effort for Jack to smile. "Thanks."

"Good luck."

"I think I'll need it," he said as he closed the door of the Suburban and walked over to pick up the basket. Halfway up the stairs, trying to figure out what to say to his wife, he spotted his black duffel bag outside the apartment door.

He'd need a lot more than luck. He'd need divine intervention.

Chapter Thirteen

If these two were his divine intervention, someone upstairs had fallen asleep on the job. "I'm good, boys," Jack called back to Fred and Ted, who stood on the sidewalk loudly voicing their doubts about his tree-climbing abilities.

The older men sauntered down the lane between the two buildings, coming to stand beneath the oak tree Jack's great-grandfather had planted eons ago. Situated at the back corner of the bakery, its leafy branches brushed up against his old bedroom window—his son's now. Grace should know better than to think a locked door and unanswered calls would keep him away. And damned if he was going to let her kick him out because of a stupid misunderstanding. He loved her and only her. He wondered if she'd believe that after he told her what he had to.

Shoving his doubts aside, he jumped and grabbed hold of the low-hanging branch.

Fred scratched his whiskered chin. "Little old to be climbing trees, don't you think?"

Jack pulled himself up and swung his leg over the nearest branch. "Thirty-three isn't old." He grunted, then realized he wasn't thirty-three. He was thirty-five.

He pushed down the anger at the time the bastards had stolen from him with the reminder that he was one of the lucky ones. Look what the kid, Stu Thomas, had come home to. At least Grace hadn't given up on him, hadn't moved on with her life. She sure as hell had more reason to do so than Stu's wife. Yeah, Jack was one of the lucky ones.

"Seem to remember you falling out of this here tree a time or two when you were a young whippersnapper. You're old now, might not bounce back as quick as you did then," Ted observed.

"I'm not old," Jack repeated as he climbed higher. He pulled himself onto a branch. It creaked under his weight. *Shit.* He wasn't old, but he was considerably heavier than he'd been back then.

"What's that you said?" Ted asked.

"Turn your hearing aid up," Fred told his friend then returned his attention to Jack. "So, you and Grace doing that role-playing thing we hear all the young gals talking about these days? Who are you supposed to be, Romeo?"

Role-playing. Nope, he wasn't going to touch that one and latched on to the branch over his head instead.

"The girls weren't talking about Romeo, Fred. They were talking about that Christian Grey character in those dirty books they're all reading. You know, the one Nell had her nose buried in the other day."

If he had his hands free, he'd stuff his fingers in his

ears. The last thing he wanted to think about was Nell McBride reading a "dirty book." Now, Grace...He smiled at the thought.

"Yeah, yeah, you're right. Jack," Fred yelled up, "if you want to spice up your love life, forget Romeo, pretend you're that Grey fella from...What's the book called?" he asked Ted.

"Hang on a sec. I'll text Nell. You want me to ask her to loan you the book, Jack?"

"No. My love life's fine." It had been until today. He swore under his breath when he spotted Murray limping up the alley toward them. Could he not do anything in this damn town without drawing a crowd? If Fred and Ted were his divine intervention, Murray was hell's response.

"Not from what I hear, it isn't, boy-o." The old man scowled up at Jack. "You get down from there right now. I know what you're up to. You leave that girl be. I told her she should've let the town cut down that tree when they wanted to—never know what kind of vermin's going to climb up it."

Jack ignored the bane of his teenage existence and tested the branches that came closest to the window, looking for one strong enough to hold him.

"What are you talking about, Patrick? The boy's wooing his wife. Making up for lost time," Fred defended Jack.

Murray snorted. "A lot you know. He was messing around with another woman, and Gracie caught him at it." He looked up at Jack. "You broke Libby's heart, and I'll not be letting you do the same to Gracie. You get yourself down here now."

Before Jack could tell Murray to go to hell, Ted piped up, "You got it all wrong. Me and Fred were there. He wasn't messing around with the girl. He was looking out for her. Poor thing's having a hard time of it. Jack's honor bound to be there for her. She might be a civilian, but over there she was one of his."

Just what he needed to hear. Now Jack felt guilty for abandoning Maria at the hospital. She was in good hands, he reminded himself. And as much as he wanted to deny it, Murray was right. Grace was hurting, and that was on Jack. He should've told her about Maria instead of putting it off.

"Ted's right. You were never in the military, Patrick. You don't know what it's like. Me and Ted do. We look after our own."

"I look after my own, too," Murray said with a smirk in his voice as he whipped out his cell phone.

"Women like chocolate, Jack. Might help soften Grace up. I've got a box in my truck. They're from Valentine's Day, but they should still be good. How 'bout I go get them for you?" Fred called up.

"Appreciate the offer, Fred, but I'm good. Thanks," Jack said, testing the last branch with the bulk of his weight while he kept a wary eye on Murray. Jack didn't like the self-congratulatory expression on the old man's face.

"I'm going to text Nell and get you that book, Jack. Patrick, why don't you help him out and cut some of them lilacs Grace likes so much?"

"I've got a better idea. I'm gonna make sure Jackson here gets exactly what he deserves," Murray said.

"Good idea. Go get your ladder. That branch he's on doesn't look like it's going to hold out much longer," Fred said to Patrick Murray's retreating back.

On the off chance Fred was right, Jack quickly shim-mied along the branch. He grabbed the ledge, then pushed on the bottom of the window frame. Releasing a gratified breath when he got it open, he eased it higher. With both hands now gripping the ledge, he started to pull himself through the window. As he did, the branch cracked.

"Jack!" the two men yelled.

He turned his head to tell them to relax when the branch gave way. "Watch out," he shouted as it crashed through the tree and onto the pavement. Jack worked his elbows onto the ledge. The muscles in his arms quaked, belying his reassurances to Fred that he was okay. Anchoring his feet between the wooden slates, he got his head and shoulders through the window. He grabbed on to the edge of the change table and pushed off with his feet. The momentum sent the table crashing to the floor with him following after it.

Jack lay flat on his back on the Thomas the Tank Engine area rug. He wondered if he should yell, "Honey, I'm home." Taking in the broken table and jars scattered across the dark hardwood floor, he had a feeling his wife wouldn't be amused.

"Don't move or I'll shoot. The sheriff's on his way."

Oh, come on. He understood her being mad, but this was ridiculous. He decided she must be joking, but couldn't be sure since the crib and his position on the floor blocked her from view. All except her bare feet and hot-pink-painted toes.

"Drop your weapon," she ordered in a no-nonsense tone of voice, one that reminded him of her father and made him rethink his position.

"Grace, it's me." He shoved the basket of diapers and

bath toys from his legs and levered himself up. Through the rungs of the crib, he saw her. She looked like an avenging angel standing there in a white robe, her hair a golden cloud around her face as he stared down the barrel of the gun she pointed at him. *Jesus, she looks hot* was his first thought, followed quickly by *Shit, she looks like she knows what she's doing and she's not kidding around.*

*　　*　　*

"Ah, Grace," her rat bastard husband said as he slowly came to his feet, "a gun isn't something you want to fool around with. Why don't you give it to me?"

She rolled her eyes at his condescending tone. She didn't need instruction from him. Eyeing her warily, he slowly came around the crib. At the sight of the tear in the knee of his well-worn jeans and the scratches on his arms, she swallowed the biting retort she was about to make. She drew her gaze from his well-defined biceps and noticed the bruising and the cut at the corner of his mouth. "What happened?" she asked, fighting the urge to touch his mouth. "You're bleeding."

He rubbed his jaw. "Sawyer," he said, then looked down at himself with a rueful twist of his lips, "and the tree."

As she was getting into her bath, she'd received a text from Madison about the fight on Main Street and Sawyer and Jack's brief stay in jail. She hadn't mentioned they'd been hurt, though. Whatever sympathy Grace might have felt vanished with the memory of why they'd been fighting. "There's a first aid kit in the bathroom. You can clean up before you leave."

He moved closer and reached for the gun she'd yet to

lower. "I'm not leaving. I know you're mad, princess. But we have to talk about this."

"*This* as in you making out with another woman in front of half the town, is that what we have to talk about?" She jerked the gun away.

"Be careful with that thing."

"It's not loaded. I only had enough time to unlock the case after receiving Patrick's text and hearing the crash. I have a precocious—"

"What do you mean, *Patrick's text*?"

"He texted me that an armed intruder was climbing through little Jack's bedroom window and that he'd called the sheriff."

"What the hell was he thinking? He could've gotten me killed."

Jack was right. Patrick was protective of her, but this time he'd gone too far. Still, she felt the need to come to his defense. "He knows I don't keep the gun loaded."

"You don't need a gun."

"Yes, I do." She eyed him pointedly. "You never know when someone's going to climb a tree and break into your home."

"If you would've answered the door or your phone, I wouldn't have been forced to." He smoothed his rough hand down her arm. Her skin tingled at his touch, at the feel of him standing so close, and her mind sort of blanked out. He took advantage of her moment of inattention and removed the gun from her hand. His eyes lingered on her chest. She blew out an annoyed breath and closed her gaping neckline, meeting his heated gaze as it drifted back to her face.

"If I were an armed intruder, what good is an empty

gun?" he asked in a low, raspy voice. Twirling the gun on his finger, he looked at her as though she was a helpless female who didn't know how to take care of herself.

"He wouldn't know that. And if the gun didn't stop him, I'd push the crib at him to throw him off-balance, then run to the bedroom, lock the door, and load my gun," she said, repeating the scenario she'd gone over in her mind as she'd hurried to unlock the case in her closet.

The corner of his mouth twitched. "Good plan, but now that you've got your gun loaded, what do you do when he breaks down the door?"

"Shoot the gun out of his hand." She scowled as a smile spread across his too-gorgeous face and took back her gun. Striding from the room, she said, "Laugh all you want, Jackson Flaherty, but I'm an expert marksman."

He followed behind her. "Since when?"

"Since someone broke into the bakery and the apartment."

He took her arm and turned her to face him. "When?" His expression was fierce and pained. She knew what he was like and hadn't intended to tell him. He'd feel guilty for not being there to defend his family. "Tell me, Grace."

She sighed. He wouldn't let up until she did. "A couple of months before I moved in with Jill." Just as she suspected, guilt shadowed his eyes. It wasn't his fault. "After that, Jill took me to the shooting range every day for a month. So you better be careful, Flaherty. I'm a really good shot," she said, as a way to show him she hadn't been traumatized by the break-in, twirling her gun as he had.

"Don't make light of it. Were you or little Jack hurt?" His fingers tightened on her arms.

"No. We were coming home from dinner at Patrick's,

and I noticed a couple of chairs were out of place in the bakery. I was going to go in and straighten them when I saw that the display case had been smashed. I called Jill and waited for her at Patrick's."

"I should've been here." He tenderly stroked her cheek, and for a second, she forgot how angry she was.

Then she caught a whiff of a musky feminine fragrance. Earlier, he'd been touching that woman in exactly the same manner. Grace jerked away from him and turned to head into her room. "I'll get you the first aid kit."

She went into the bathroom and opened the cupboard below the sink. Kneeling, she reached past the cleaning supplies for the white plastic container. She stood up, catching sight of Jack in the mirror. Her jaw dropped. He'd stripped off his T-shirt and was unbuttoning his jeans.

He looked up and gave her a dangerously sexy smile. "I'll just grab a quick shower. Get rid of the dirt before you fix me up."

She stood staring at him like an idiot when he stepped out of his jeans, then his boxers. "I..." She couldn't tear her gaze from his incredible physique. "I'm not..." Her voice trailed off as he walked into the shower. The view from the backside was as mouthwateringly gorgeous as the front. Forget it. She'd tell him to see to his own injuries once he was dressed and she'd regained the ability to speak.

Closing the bathroom door, she hurried to her dresser. She placed the first aid kit on top, then pulled a pair of lacy beige panties and matching bra from the drawer, keeping her ears peeled for the sound of running water. If he thought her ogling him meant he could simply seduce her into forgiving him, he was wrong.

She strode to the closet and removed her robe, tossing it on the bed. She stuffed her legs into her panties, then put on her bra. As she pulled a sundress from the hanger the door to the bathroom creaked open.

She turned. Jack leaned against the doorjamb, water dripping from his hair and rolling down his powerful chest and his hard, flat stomach to disappear beneath the towel wrapped around his narrow hips. He was impossible, she thought, clutching the dress to her chest.

A desperate squeak escaped her parted lips when he started determinedly toward her. "You're wet. Go dry off before you track water across the floor."

Ignoring her, he smiled, revealing his strong white teeth, and kept coming.

"No, I'm serious, Jack." She scrambled to pull the dress over her head. His warm, damp hands clamped on either side of her waist. Jerking the fabric from her face, she said, "No, you can't come in here and think you—" Her helpless moan swallowed the rest of the words as he trailed the tip of his finger along the edge of her panties.

He leaned in—his damp chest brushing up against her—and whispered in her ear. "Think what?"

Overwhelmed by the heat from his warrior's body, she was tempted to give in. She wished she could, wished she hadn't seen what she did. She'd just gotten him back. It wasn't fair. None of it was fair. She pulled away and pushed him, angrily stuffing her arms in the capped sleeves of the floral sundress. "Don't."

He waited her out, then took her hand and brushed his lips across her burning cheek. "I'm sorry. Come here." He led her to the bed, sat on the end, and tugged her down with him.

Her gaze flickered to the parted towel, the muscled thigh that lightly touched her leg. She cleared her throat. "Can you put some clothes on, please?"

"Sure, but I thought you packed everything I owned."

He made it sound as though her request amused him, but there was another emotion in his voice besides humor. She wasn't sure what it was. And there was nothing amusing about the situation, at least not to her. She went to the open closet and tugged his robe from the hanger. He took it from her, dropped the towel, and shrugged into the white terry-cloth robe as he held her gaze.

Swallowing hard, she forced her eyes to remain on his face. "Would you like a cup of tea?" She cringed. She sounded like she was entertaining the Queen of England.

"No. I want to get this settled once and for all." The underlying tension in his voice made her nervous. She realized then that she'd been hoping he had a perfectly reasonable explanation. Like Maria was a very demonstrative woman and had thrown herself at him. And of course he cared for her, in the same way he cared about the other members of his crew.

He laced his fingers through hers and gently caressed the back of her hand with his thumb. "I love you, Grace, and the last thing I want to do is hurt you."

She heard the "but" and felt sick. "I know that." She forced the words from her dry throat. He smiled, a tender smile, just like the one he'd given...

"Don't blame Maria for today. It was my fault." He bowed his head, gave her hand a gentle squeeze, and blew out a breath. "Jesus, this is hard." He raised his gaze to hers. "Grace, I didn't tell you what happened between me and Maria right away because, as soon as I found out about you and little Jack, it didn't matter. And once I got my memory back, other than wishing it hadn't happened, it meant nothing to me. But it did to Maria."

She slowly withdrew her hand from his. "What happened?"

Another deep inhalation expanded his chest. "While we were held captive, we got close. We kissed a couple of times. When we escaped and were on the run…" He speared his fingers through his damp hair. "We didn't have sex, but we, ah, we came close."

She took small, shallow breaths to ease the tightness in her chest. When she was finally able to speak, she said, "I see."

"No, you don't. Look at me." He grasped her chin between his fingers, forcing her gaze to his. Whatever he saw in her eyes made him groan and take her in his arms. "I didn't remember you, princess. I didn't remember us. If I had, nothing would've happened. You gotta believe that."

She held herself stiff in his warm embrace. There was a question on her lips, a question she was afraid she knew the answer to, but had to ask. "If you didn't get your memory back, would you be with her now?"

He moved his hands to her shoulders and drew back to look at her. "I'm here. When I found out I was married and had a son, I came here."

"But you would, wouldn't you? You're an honorable man. You always do what's expected of you. But what if you hadn't gotten your memory back, what then? Were you going to stay with us?" She saw the answer in his eyes and nodded even as her heart crumpled in her chest. "I see."

He shook her as though desperate to make her understand. "I remember us. I remember you. You're the only woman I have ever loved. The only woman I want to be with."

"Have you ever wondered why you forgot me?"

"I had a fuc...I had a head injury, Grace. Don't read anything more into it than that."

"If it were you, wouldn't you wonder?"

"Okay, maybe it was because my wife told me if I walked out the door, we were done. She wanted a divorce. Maybe that's what I wanted to forget. And maybe I wanted to forget about losing Charlie when I was home instead of in the pilot's seat. Forget about you moving to Christmas when you knew I didn't want to. Forget about not being able to do anything right when I came back. Forget about Libby...Or have you thought about this: maybe I had to put the two people I loved more than anything in this world out of my head just to survive." Electric-blue eyes hot with temper speared her. "But in the end, none of it matters. I'm home now. What you saw today doesn't matter. Maria shouldn't have kissed me, but I should've gotten in touch with her and made it clear that whatever she thought we had was over. She knows that now."

"But what about you, are you sure you want it to be over?"

He put his face in his hands and shook his head before looking at her. "How many times do I have to tell you I love you before you believe me?"

"I know you do. But sometimes love's not enough. I need you to be sure. A few days ago you—"

He held up a hand. "No, I never once told Maria I loved her. And before you ask, no, dammit, I did not and do not love her." He hauled her onto his lap and buried his face in her neck. "I wish we could turn the clock back and ask for a do-over, but we can't."

She stroked his damp hair. "I wish we could, too."

He lifted his head. "Are we good?"

Were they? It was a lot to take in. To know how close he and Maria had been. Yet even knowing that didn't change how much Grace loved him, but...

A cell buzzed. It was Jack's. He averted his gaze from hers and gently eased her from his lap. "It's probably Maria. A truck backfired on the street. She had a flashback and went down. I'm worried about her, Grace. She's at the hospital and doesn't know anyone here. You understand why I have to take her call, right? I just need to make sure she's okay."

She understood how Jack would feel it was his duty to look out for the woman. But after what he'd revealed about their relationship, after what had happened today, did he really expect Grace to be *okay* with him taking her call?

He pulled his phone from his jeans pocket. "Hey, Maria, can you hang on a minute? Grace?" he said as she stiffly got up from the bed.

"It's fine, Jack," she said wearily and left the room.

A few minutes later, as she swept up the broken glass, he came into little Jack's bedroom.

He searched her face, then took the broom from her. "Let me do that."

She didn't have the energy to argue and went to sit on the narrow cot.

He frowned. "Are you okay?"

"Fine," she said, and the furrows in his brow deepened.

"Are you worried about little Jack? I can go get him now if you want. Gage offered—"

"No." She had to say what was on her mind before she lost her nerve. "Jack," she cleared her throat, "I think it might be best if you stayed with Jill for a while."

"What the hell are you talking about? Is this because I took the call from Maria? Because if—"

That was part of it. "No, of course not." She wrung her hands in her lap, trying to find the words to make him understand. "We've been separated for a long time. We've changed. I need to be sure you're not staying out of a misplaced sense of duty." *Like the way my father stays with my mother.* She held up her hand when he went to interrupt her. "We've had a lot to deal with in a few short days. You especially. Little Jack, too."

A muscle pulsed in his clenched jaw, his eyes a glacial, furious blue. "Are you having second thoughts about us?"

"No, my feelings for you haven't changed. I love you, and I want us to be together. I just thought..." She trailed off as he slammed the broom against the wall.

"That's what you want, Grace? Okay, you got it," he said and headed from the room.

She followed after him, trying to keep up with his long, angry strides. He flung open the front door and grabbed his duffel bag off the landing, then pivoted to face her. His mouth twisted in a grim smile. "This feels real familiar."

She gave an empathetic shake of her head and went to him. "No, it's not the same." Rising up on the tips of her toes, she wrapped her arms around his waist and kissed him deeply, passionately. For several terrifying beats of her heart, he held himself stiffly erect. Then she heard the thud of his bag hitting the floor, and he gathered her in his arms, kissing her back with as much desire and emotion as she kissed him.

When he drew away, his breathing was ragged. "I don't like leaving you alone."

"We'll be fine." She touched his cheek and forced a smile. "This will be good for us, Jack. It'll be like starting over with a clean slate. We can date."

His gaze narrowed. "You want us to date other people?"

"No, I meant each other. Did...did you want us to date other people?"

He picked up his bag. "If you have to ask, we're in bigger trouble than I thought. I'll call you later. We have the interview in the morning. Unless you've changed your mind about that, too."

"No, I haven't changed my mind about you, us, or the interview."

He held her gaze for a brief moment, then headed down the stairs. She watched him leave. He didn't look back. Her heart hurt. Jack was right; it felt all too familiar. Closing the apartment door, she leaned against it, praying she hadn't just made the biggest mistake of her life.

Chapter Fourteen

Jack waited impatiently for Grace to open the door. The least she could've done was give him a key yesterday when she kicked him out. It was his apartment as much as it was hers. What the hell had he been thinking giving in to her asinine suggestion? He never should've left. As soon as she'd voiced the idea, he should've shot it down. But he'd been in shock, feeling guilty after revealing the extent of his relationship with Maria.

He hadn't been the only one who'd been furious Grace had asked him to leave. Jill had been livid when he'd arrived at her door with his duffel bag in hand. He'd ended up on the defensive, protecting Grace from his sister's anger. He made Jill think he was on board with it. She didn't need another excuse to lay into his wife. It hadn't been easy playing it cool, acting as if he wasn't as pissed off with Grace as his sister was. The run he'd taken last night and again at dawn had helped deal with his anger.

The frustration and, as much as it pained him to admit, hurt, weren't so easy to get rid of.

Suck it up, Flaherty, and deal.

In the end, it was his fault it'd come down to this. He had to make it right. For now, he'd do as Grace asked. She wanted to start with a clean slate. All the better. She wanted to *date*. He could do that, too. How hard could it be to win back a woman who loved him, who'd never given up on him? Jack grinned as he thought of ways to "woo" his wife. Maybe he'd borrow that book from Nell after all.

He always felt better when he had a plan, a strategy to go into battle, even if this time the fight was to save his marriage. The heavy weight that had rested on his shoulders since yesterday lifted. He rapped on the door for the second time—just not as hard as a couple of minutes ago.

"Sorry," said a breathless Grace as she opened the door, carrying a naked little Jack under her arm. "Your son decided he's not wearing a diaper today and flushed it down the toilet before I could stop him."

"How come he's my son when he does something wrong?" Jack teased as he closed the door behind him. His humor faded when he took a closer look at Grace. There were shadows under her eyes, and her usual peaches-and-cream complexion was a pasty gray. She looked like she hadn't slept. Jack could commiserate. He hadn't slept much last night, either. "Here"—he held out his arms for his son—"we'll take care of it for you."

"Thanks, but I already did. I've gotten really good at fixing clogged toilets." She glanced at her wet robe and gave him a tired smile. Little Jack squirmed in her arms, and she put him on the floor.

It shouldn't bother Jack that she could handle things without him, but it did. And it bothered him that she hadn't handed over his son like he'd asked. He didn't say anything. Now wasn't the time to be making waves.

"Stay..." Little Jack took off, and Grace released a weary sigh as his naked white body disappeared from view. "There's coffee in the kitchen. Muffins, too, if you'd like some," she said and went to give chase.

"I'm not a guest, Grace. If I need something, I'll get it."

She turned, worrying the neckline of her robe between her fingers. "I'm sorry. I didn't mean..." A crash from the back of the apartment cut her off.

Jack jogged past her. "I've got it. Get dressed. Interview's in fifteen minutes."

"Fifteen minutes?"

He heard the squeak of panic in her voice and went to respond. Then he saw his son, sitting on the floor in his bedroom, shaking baby powder over himself. The kid must've climbed onto the table—the lamp was lying on the floor—to get the powder off the shelf. "Whoa, buddy, you're in trouble now."

"No, me..." His son started to choke. Jack opened his mouth to call for Grace, then shut it. *What are you, a wuss?* he asked himself. *You can handle this.* As soon as Jack took the container from him, the kid stopped choking and started screaming. Jack went to cover his son's mouth with his hand.

"What's wrong?" Grace called from their bedroom.

Jack handed him the baby powder. "Nothing."

His son beamed up at him. *Smart kid. Pretty damn cute, too,* he thought with a grin. Five minutes later, Jack was rethinking the cute part. His son was a terror. He eyed Jack's fingers as he fought with the tiny buttons on the short-sleeved plaid shirt he'd put him in. "Don't bite me again or I'll bite you back," he warned his son.

"Jack," Grace gasped as she entered the room.

"Thanks a lot, kid," he muttered.

She took in the mess and came to kneel beside Jack on the floor. Nudging his fingers aside, she took over. "You weren't really going to bite him, were you?"

"No, Grace, I wasn't." His irritation faded as he watched her with their son, as her warm body brushed against his, and he inhaled her floral scent. "But I might bite *you*. You smell good."

She shook her head, but a small, encouraging smile played on her lips. "No fooling around. We don't have time."

"I'll cancel the interview."

"Honestly, Jack, you're incorrigible."

"No, just a guy who wants to spend some time with his wife." He tucked her hair behind her ear. "I missed you last night."

She leaned in and kissed the corner of his mouth. "I missed you, too."

Scowling at them, little Jack put his hands on his hips. "No kiss my mama."

"Hey, she kissed me."

Grace tugged little Jack into her arms and kissed his mouth, his nose, and his eyes. "Four kisses for you." She turned to Jack and cupped his face between her soft hands. He was ready for her when she reached his mouth and gave her a kiss she wouldn't soon forget. "And four kisses for daddy," she said breathlessly.

Little Jack looked from his mother to his father, then picked up the empty powder container. "All gone."

Jack smiled, inordinately pleased over the small victory. "I think we should try that again, just to be sure it worked."

"I don't think so." Grace laughed. "Interview, remember?"

"It was worth a try." He came to his feet and helped her up.

Gathering little Jack into her arms, Grace brushed off some leftover powder from his hair, then did the same for Jack. "Do you want to come to dinner tonight?"

"Hmm, dinner with you and little Jack or dinner with my sister? It's a tough decision."

She winced.

"I'm kidding. I have to work on the house on Sugar Plum Lane after the interview." And wasn't that going to be fun times. "I'll be here around six, if that's okay."

"No, no, that's good. It's just when you mentioned Jill..." She shrugged, redoing the top button on little Jack's shirt. "I imagine she's pretty mad at me right now."

"She'll get over it." He glanced at the clock on the kitchen wall and placed his hand at the small of Grace's back. "We better get going. The reporter will be arriving at the bakery any time now."

She stopped in her tracks and looked up at him. "Bakery? I thought you said the interview was here. I..." Her gaze flitted around the room.

"Didn't Madison tell you?" She shook her head. "Sorry, I thought she did. She called last night to suggest we have the interview at the bakery. She thought it'd be good publicity."

Madison had assured him Grace would be happy with the change of venue, so he agreed. But now that he took in the spotless apartment, a hint of lemon oil in the air, he realized his wife had probably spent hours making sure everything was perfect.

"You cleaned all night, didn't you? And don't try and deny it, you look exhausted." The words were out of his mouth before he could take them back.

Her hand went to her cheek, and her gaze shot to his. "Do I look that bad?" Before he could respond, she passed him their son. "I'll just be a minute. I'll put on some blush, maybe some cover-up, too. I'll never hear the end of it from my mother if I don't," she muttered, more to herself than to him, as she speed-walked to the bedroom.

By the time she'd fixed herself up and changed into the yellow dress she'd worn to his homecoming, a strand of pearls at her neck, they were ten minutes late. Grace locked the door, and Jack ushered his family down the stairs. As they stepped onto the sidewalk, Grace turned to him.

"Jack?"

"Um-hmm," he said, distracted by the number of white news vans parked outside the bakery. What the hell was going on? He'd agreed to do the interview with one reporter only.

"Jack." She tugged on his arm to regain his attention and leaned into him. "No one knows we're not living together, do they?"

"No." And he planned to keep it that way. He made his sister promise to keep the news to herself. He didn't want Maria to find out. If she did, he had a feeling she wouldn't leave.

"Okay, that's good."

"Yeah, it is. Because, Mrs. Flaherty, I plan to be back

home with you before the week is out. And you know I'm very good at getting what I want."

He took comfort in the half smile she gave him. At least she didn't say no.

As they walked into the bakery, which was jam-packed with customers, cameramen, and reporters, Grace groaned. Madison McBride stood beside a woman with long, curly butterscotch hair, who wore a pair of denim shorts, a "Save the Planet" T-shirt, and hiker boots. "Set up your cameras over here. You'll get a great shot of the bakery that way," Madison said, catching sight of Jack and Grace. She waved them over. "Here they are now."

"I'm sorry, princess. I had no idea they were all going to be here."

"I know you didn't. I should have realized Madison wouldn't be able to resist the free publicity."

The woman in question overheard Grace and grinned. She walked toward them with her friend in tow. "Don't be mad. I did it for you." Madison gave Grace a one-armed hug, ignoring Jack, "Well, you and the bottom line. You remember my friend Skylar Davis, don't you, Grace?"

"Of course I do." She smiled and went to shake the woman's hand but was pulled in for a hug instead.

When they finished, Jack introduced himself. Obviously Madison had been bad-mouthing him to Ms. Davis, because the woman greeted him with a cool nod.

Whatever.

Three reporters came forward and introduced themselves. John Ryan, the guy Jack had agreed to do the interview with, would take the lead. They sat at one of the tables. When his son started to squirm in Grace's lap, Jack took out the small book he'd stuffed in his pocket and handed it to him. Grace rewarded him with a dimpled smile.

"Just a sec," Madison said as a photographer went to take their picture. She came over and pinched Grace's cheeks. "That's better. You looked a little pale."

Jack sighed, then whispered in his wife's ear, "Don't listen to her. You're beautiful."

The smile she gave him faltered as the bell tinkled over the door. Whatever color Madison had forced into Grace's cheeks drained away. He followed her gaze. Several more people entered the bakery, his sister and Maria bringing up the rear.

* * *

Jack shot Grace a worried look. She tried to force her lips to curve. But they felt frozen, just like the rest of her face. Madison cleared her throat. Grace glanced her way, and Madison touched her neck. *Oh.* Grace released the stranglehold she had on her pearls and tried to focus on the reporter instead of Maria DeMarco. It was hard not to look at the gorgeous brunette wearing the white, body-hugging halter dress that skimmed the tops of her well-toned bronzed legs. Grace self-consciously smoothed her dress, trying not to compare herself to the other woman. It was too depressing. Especially given the intimate relationship she'd had with Jack.

Instead, Grace tried to focus on the reporter's questions and her husband's responses. Jack was good at this. He was intelligent and charming, deflecting Mr. Ryan easily when the reporter asked a couple of pointed questions about how they'd escaped their captors.

Maria hadn't taken her eyes off Jack, not for a minute.

Grace wished she could say the same for Jill. Her sister-in-law's censorious stare was beginning to wear on Grace's nerves. Her son would choose today of all days to be well behaved, she thought. It wasn't like she could use him as an excuse to escape.

Jack laid his hand over hers. She glanced to where she'd unconsciously lined up the packets of sugar in the bowl. He laced his fingers through hers, then drew her hand to his thigh, giving it a comforting squeeze. When one of the other reporters asked Jack how it felt to be home with his family, the cameras zoomed in on Grace and her son. It was then that Grace realized she and little Jack were only along for the photo op. That was fine by her. Normally she didn't mind dealing with reporters. She'd handled the press for her father on many occasions. But with Jill and Maria looking on, she was just as happy to be ignored.

Grace glanced up at the sound of a derisive snort. Jill's blue eyes flashed with temper as she stared Grace down. Maria patted her arm and whispered something in her ear.

"Grace, John asked you a question," Jack said.

She drew her attention from the two women's silent exchange. "I'm sorry."

"No problem, Mrs. Flaherty. I asked how it felt to have your husband back."

"It's hard to describe how incredible it feels to have him home. It's a miracle, really. Our prayers were answered." She looked into Jack's eyes and smiled. "I guess you could say it feels like Christmas."

Jack squeezed her hand, then he tensed.

"Hello, Mr. Ryan." Maria sauntered toward the table.

"I'm Maria DeMarco, a reporter with the *Washington Daily News*. Would you mind if I asked the happy couple here a few questions?"

"We've had enough questions for today," Jack said and pushed his chair back.

"Your wife has only answered one, Jack. Surely she can handle a couple more, can't you, Mrs. Flaherty?"

Grace lifted her chin. "Certainly. Ask away."

"Hey," one of the other reporters said, "aren't you the woman who was held captive with Chief Flaherty?"

She kept her challenging gaze locked on Grace when she spoke. "Yes, I am. Jack and I've been through a lot together."

"If you're willing, Ms. DeMarco, we'd like to ask you a few questions. Maybe get a couple of pictures of you and Chief Flaherty?"

"By all means. But I have to tell you, I'm saving most of the juicy details for my book."

Grace pressed a hand to her stomach. Little Jack, as though sensing her distress, started to cry. Jack stood. "Come on. We're done here."

Out of the corner of her eye, Grace saw her sister-in-law reach for Maria. "No, Maria, don't—" Jill began, but the woman ignored her, holding up a chocolate sugar plum.

"Mrs. Flaherty, I've heard all about your cakes since I've come to Christmas and how the wishes in a sugar plum like this one come true. I was told you made one for your husband's birthday with your own wish in it, and moments later it was announced he'd been found. It's almost like they're magic."

The saliva in Grace's throat dried up. She couldn't speak. Madison gave her a concerned look before saying,

"That's exactly how it happened. Grace's cakes *are* magical. And very soon we'll be introducing everyone to the reason for the magic...the Sugar Plum Cake Fairy."

Maria arched a sardonic brow. "Really, how...interesting." Returning her attention to Grace, she said, "Perhaps you can tell me, Mrs. Flaherty, if you wished for your husband to come home, why his wedding ring was in the chocolate sugar plum along with this note saying good-bye to him and a wish for you and your son's future. One you planned to have without him." Cameras flashed as she went to Jack and handed him the contents of the sugar plum. "I'm sorry, Jack. But your wife lied to you. She wasn't waiting for you to come home. She'd given up on you a long time ago."

Chapter Fifteen

The reporters vied for Jack's attention at the same time as Grace, Jill, and Maria did. He couldn't tell which one of the women said what. He felt like he was in a wind tunnel with the air and sound sucked from the room. All he could do was stare at the evidence lying in the palm of his hand—the pieces of paper and his wedding band. Everything Grace had told him had been a lie.

She hadn't kicked him out of the apartment because of Maria. She'd already moved on with her life the night she'd asked him for a divorce. And he had a pretty damn good idea who she'd moved on with. He should've killed Anderson when he had the chance. Some of his sister's earlier innuendos began to make sense. She'd known all along that Grace had given up on him.

He raised his gaze to his wife. "Jack, it's not what you think. Let me explain," she pleaded in a hoarse whisper, tears welling in her eyes. He couldn't feel sorry for her. His sympathy was frozen inside him.

"I think this about covers it," he said, displaying the items in his open palm.

She shook her head, patting little Jack's back, gently bouncing him in her arms. "No, it doesn't. You have to... Shh, baby, it's okay," she murmured when their son cried harder.

Madison and her friend ushered the reporters from the bakery. Several customers also left. Shaking their heads as they passed Grace on their way out the door, they offered Jack sympathetic smiles.

He took his son from her. "You're upsetting him." Jostling little Jack in his arms, he patted his back. His son's crying subsided, and he released a shuddered sob, lifting tear-filled eyes to Jack. "Mama's sad," he whimpered.

Makes two of us, Jack thought.

Maria moved closer. "I didn't mean to upset your son." Her dark gaze softened as she rubbed little Jack's arm.

Grace stepped between them, pushing Maria's hand aside. "Do. Not. Touch my son." She pointed to the door. "Get the hell out of my bakery now."

Everyone froze. Jack's jaw dropped, as shocked as his sister and the remaining customers appeared to be. He'd never heard Grace swear or raise her voice in public.

"Jack, I—" Maria started to say, sidestepping Grace.

"If you are not out of my bakery in two seconds, I'm calling the sheriff," Grace threatened in a steel-edged voice.

Jack was too stunned to intervene. His sister wasn't.

"Grace, calm—"

His wife whipped her head around. She stalked to Jill and stabbed a finger in her chest.

Jack groaned. No one messed with Jill and walked away unscathed. Unless it was him. And while he was so mad at his wife he could spit, he wasn't about to let his sister hurt her. "Grace, let's—"

Without looking at him, she raised her hand, palm out, then, in a cutting voice, said to his sister, "If you think I'm letting you get away with this, you better think again. You've been a hurtful, vindictive bitch, and I'm not going to take it anymore. I'm done with you, Jillian Flaherty."

For the first time in a long time, his sister looked truly shaken. But it didn't take her long to recover. *Here we go*, Jack thought, and started toward them. Maria touched his arm. "Jack?"

He shook her hand off. "I think you better do as my wife asked and leave."

Madison came inside, took one look at what was going on, and said, "Give me little Jack. I'll take him to the kitchen." Her gaze went to Jill, who poked Grace in the chest. "Do you think I should call Gage?"

"No," he said, passing her his son, "I've got this."

The handful of customers who'd stuck around avidly watched his sister and Grace. Jack was about to send them on their way when Grace shoved Jill's hand away with such force, his sister took three startled steps back. Jack reached out to steady her. "Grace, that's enough."

"You don't want to mess with me, Jill," she said, ignoring Jack, her tone eerily similar to her father's. Jack flashed back to the image of her holding the gun on him. His wife was more her father's daughter than he'd realized. And that did not bode well for his sister.

Jill shot him a grateful glance. Then, as if Jack's presence bolstered her confidence, she turned on Grace. "You've got some nerve putting this on me, Grace Garrison." She didn't flinch when his sister turned the knife. Jack did. "The last time he was home you asked him for a divorce, and this time you kicked him out of *his* home."

He heard the low, censorious remarks the onlookers directed at Grace, but it was Maria's reaction that set his internal warning system on high alert. Her lips curved in a triumphant smile. He was going to strangle his sister. If his wife didn't beat him to it.

Grace arched a brow and lifted her chin. Jack and everyone else in the room held their breath. Giving his sister an intimidating look, she pivoted on her heel. "Take your friend and get out of my bakery. Neither of you are welcome here." Holding the door open, she glanced at the clock on the wall. "You have one minute to do as I ask."

Jill's lip curled. "Or what?"

Grace gave her a smile that set off the warning tingle in the back of Jack's neck. Taking his sister by the arm, he grabbed Maria's on the way by, ushering both women onto the sidewalk.

"Jack," Grace called after him.

"Not now." Once he got himself under control, they'd talk. He thought about taking a run, but heat already shimmered off the asphalt. In the distance, the mountains with their snowcapped peaks beckoned.

His sister reached for him as he went to walk by. "Don't be mad at me. I was just trying to protect you."

"Bullshit. What you pulled in there—"

"Your sister isn't the one you should be angry with. It's your wife who lied to you," Maria interrupted him, moving out of the way to let a furious Stu Thomas pass.

"You didn't deserve what she did to you," the kid said, jerking a thumb in Grace's direction. "You're a hero, and she asks for a divorce, kicks you out of your own goddamn home?" He shook his head. "I don't care how bad I need the money. I'm not going to work for her. They're all the same. Can't trust the bitches . . ."

"Okay, that's—" Jack tried to cut him off, but Stu was too caught up in his rant to hear him.

"You're better off without her. But take it from me, get yourself a good goddamn lawyer if you don't want to lose your kid." He threw a glare at Maria and Jill, then started down the sidewalk.

Jack stared after him. "You better keep an eye on that guy," he told Jill.

"Yeah, yeah, but, Jack, you don't think Grace would keep us from little Jack, do you?"

"No. Jesus, of course she wouldn't. I can't believe you'd even . . . What?" he said when Maria arched a brow.

She shrugged. "You've been gone a long time. And after what you found out today, she obviously isn't the same woman you married. Maybe you should consider—"

"Don't. Not another word. You've caused enough trouble as it is."

"Jack, wait, where are you going?" his sister asked as he headed off.

"I'm taking my bike out."

*   *   *

Jack hooked his helmet on the handlebars of his black Harley. Years ago, all he'd need was an hour on his bike, taking the mountain roads at breakneck speed, feeling the wind in his face, to alleviate the suffocating tightness in his chest. Didn't work today. There'd been no adrenaline rush when he'd taken the hairpin curves at full throttle. Just the knowledge he was getting too old to take stupid risks. He had a wife and son who depended on him.

Right.

His wife sure as hell didn't seem to need or want him to take care of her these days, he thought, kicking the stand into place. He pulled out his phone. Three messages from Grace, two from Gage, and one from the dickhead who leaned against the doorjamb of the run-down pink Victorian on Sugar Plum Lane with his arms crossed.

Sawyer nudged up the bill of his ball cap with his finger. "About time, flyboy. You were supposed to be here two hours ago."

Jack pushed open the gate attached to the peeling white picket fence. It came off in his hand. With a muttered curse, he tossed the gate on the ground and stalked up a stone path overrun with weeds. Pounding up the steps to the front porch, he got in Sawyer's face, and stabbed his finger into the other man's sweat-stained Colorado Flurries T-shirt. "Stay away from my wife. She may have given up on me, but I haven't given up on her." He yelled the last as a chainsaw started up inside.

"Get out of my face, Flaherty." Sawyer tried to push him back.

Jack didn't budge. He shoved the aviators on top of his head and drilled Anderson with a hard look. "No."

Sawyer frowned, his gaze searching. "What's this about?" he shouted when a couple of hammers joined in with the saw.

"As if you don't know." Jack waved his hand in front of his face. "You reek." He moved toward the swing on the end of the porch and went to sit down.

"Don't..."

The chain gave way, and Jack ended up on his ass.

"...sit on the swing." Sawyer fought back a grin.

Jack blew out an aggravated breath and shifted his position to lean against the house. Sawyer joined him, and Jack pulled a face.

"Get over it. I'm sure you've smelled worse."

Thinking back to his months in captivity, Jack agreed, "Yeah, I have."

Sawyer gave him a long look. "What is it I'm supposed to know?"

"Huh, I thought it'd be all over town by now."

"Been a little busy here, Jack. Not a lot of time for idle chitchat. You said something about Grace giving up on you. Where the hell did you get an idea like that?"

"From the ring and good-bye letter she left in the sugar plum the night you found out I was alive. You knew, didn't you? You knew that she gave up on me?" The muscles in his neck tensed as he steeled himself for Sawyer's answer.

"Yeah, I did."

Jack's hands balled into fists. "Are you in love with my wife?"

Sawyer cleared his throat. "Yeah." Ducking, he closed his hand over Jack's fist and pushed him back. "Nothing happened. She's in love with you, not me." He tipped his head, resting it against the house. "I didn't know you were coming back. Be honest, if any of your guys had been MIA for as long as you, how much hope would you have held out for their return?"

None, but that wasn't the point. "I sure as hell wouldn't have moved in on his wife."

"I didn't."

Jack narrowed his eyes at him.

"I wanted to, but she wasn't ready." Sawyer shoved him. "Stop snarling at me, I'm being honest here. If it makes you feel better, I feel bad about it. I never meant to fall in love with her." He shrugged, a smile playing at the corner of his mouth. "But you have to admit, she's pretty easy to fall in love with."

"Nice, dickhead, real nice," Jack muttered, then slanted him a look. "So if she didn't give up on me for you, why did she?"

"Because it was killing her. The guilt, the worry, it was eating her up inside. She blamed herself."

"So you knew she'd asked me for a divorce the night I left?"

"Yeah, and you know as well as I do that she asked out of desperation. I was there when she got the call from her father that you were MIA. I've never seen a woman in that much pain, and I don't ever want to see it again. But she pulled it together, did everything she could to lobby the military to take action. After months of coming up against a brick wall, she turned her focus to making everything perfect for when you came home. She used her savings to renovate the bakery and the apartment."

And he hadn't said a word to her about the changes, other than to slam her decision to keep the bakery and stay in Christmas. "So when did she decide to move on?"

"Well, I, ah, might've had something to do with that. Now, don't go getting your shorts in a twist. You would've told her the same thing. You heard Dr. McBride the other night. In the last few months, she'd lost a lot of weight. Her father's a general, she knows the score. I think she'd finally admitted to herself that you weren't coming home. Leave it to you, flyboy, to beat the odds." He lifted a shoulder. "I told her to let you go, and no, it wasn't about me. It was about her."

Sawyer was right. In his place, Jack would've told her the same. And while it wasn't easy to hear his best friend had feelings for his wife, who knew how much more difficult it would've been for Grace without Sawyer to lend his support. "Thank you for being there for her," he said gruffly and extended his hand.

Sawyer grinned. Instead of taking Jack's hand, he got him in a headlock and gave him a noogie.

"Okay, enough already. I'm going to puke." Jack reached up to break his hold and they ended up rolling around on the porch.

"Are they fighting again or playing?" Jack looked up to see Fred ask Ted, from where they watched in the doorway.

"Playing, I think," Ted answered, adding, "Boys, you better watch..."

Sawyer and Jack hit the porch railing and rolled right through the rotted posts. They fell off the porch, landing in the weeds.

They looked at each other and grinned. "Just like old times," Jack said.

"Yeah." Sawyer punched him in the shoulder. "Good to have you back, buddy."

"Good to be back, dickhead." Jack punched him in the arm.

Fred waved them in with a hammer. "Don't want to interrupt the reunion, boys, but there's work to be done."

"I guess we better get in there or they'll report us to Gage. I was late, and you were later. They're making us put in overtime," Sawyer said.

Jack looked up at the Pepto-Bismol-pink eyesore. "They should just tear the place down." He never understood why people would tie themselves to a house. As far as he was concerned, they were money pits. He dug his phone from his pocket. "I'll be in in a minute. I have to call Grace, let her know I'll be late for dinner. Although, after this morning, she may have withdrawn the invitation."

Sawyer frowned. "What happened?"

Jack figured he might as well tell him. He was going to hear about it anyway. So he did. He told him everything—about Maria, about Grace kicking him out of the apartment, and about the shitshow at the bakery earlier.

Sawyer whistled when he finished. "You've got a tough road ahead of you, buddy."

"What do you mean?"

"You and I both know how amazing Grace is, but someone did a number on your wife. Don't take this the wrong way, I know it's not like you had any control over it, but the fact you forgot her and little Jack didn't help. And after what you told her about you and Maria, you're going to have a hard time convincing her you weren't in love with the woman. The sooner you get Maria out of town, the better. Once she's gone, the odds of winning back your wife are good."

Good wasn't good enough for Jack. He had to figure out a way to strengthen the odds. "Since you know my wife so well, how about you give me some help winning her back?"

"You're killing me, man. Have some pity on a guy and give me time to fall out of love with her."

"You really are a dickhead, you know."

Sawyer grinned, then looked up at the house. "If you're serious about winning her back, you should buy this place for her."

"Did you hit your head when you fell off the porch? I don't want a house, and even if I did, it sure as hell wouldn't be this one."

"Too bad, because your wife wants one. She always has. And I hate to tell you, buddy, this is the one she wants."

"You can't be serious. How do you figure that?"

"Haven't seen a sugar plum cake yet, have you?"

"No." And after learning about Grace's sugar plum wish, he wasn't sure he wanted to. "But I couldn't get Nell and Madison to shut up about them yesterday."

"Well, we're here on Sugar Plum Lane, and your wife owns the Sugar Plum Bakery and puts a pink Victorian on all her sugar plum cakes. Sensing a pattern here?"

"Yeah," he muttered, like staying in Christmas, buying a house that looked like it belonged in a horror movie wasn't on his bucket list. But it sounded like it was on his wife's, and at that moment, Jack would do anything to win her back. "How much do you think it'll go for?"

"They're auctioning it off, but my guess would be around two fifty once the renovations are done."

"I doubt the bank would approve me for that much."

At the roar of an engine, Sawyer glanced over his shoulder as a red Mustang squealed in behind Jack's Harley. "Too bad, but at least you'll be able to take care of the Maria problem."

Jack shoved his hands in his jeans pockets. Sawyer was right. After what she'd pulled at the bakery, it was time for Maria to leave town.

"Looks like the lady's on a mission," Sawyer said.

"Jack," Maria called out, slamming her car door. "I'm glad I found you."

"What's up?" he asked as she picked her way along the stone path toward them.

She glanced from him to Sawyer and extended her hand. "Hi. Maria DeMarco."

"I know who you are," Sawyer said, giving her an unfriendly, assessing look. A couple of awkward seconds passed before he relented and took her proffered hand. "Sawyer Anderson. Grace's best friend."

Jack rubbed a hand over his mouth to hide his grin. Maria gave Sawyer a tight smile, then said, "Jack, I need to talk to you about something."

"Yeah, I need to talk to you, too."

She shot Sawyer a buzz-off look. It didn't work, which suited Jack just fine. "Maria?" he prompted.

"Oh, right," she said, obviously flustered. "I just got a call from my publisher. They want the completed manuscript by July fifteenth. I really need your help with this, Jack."

"I don't think that's a good idea. Not after what you pulled today. My wife—"

"Please don't say no." She gave him a desperate look. "I'm getting a seven-figure advance. I'll pay you fifteen percent to consult on the book."

Jack was about to say no, when Sawyer gestured toward the house. "You might want to think about her offer before you reject it out of hand, buddy."

Chapter Sixteen

Are you sure you don't mind?" Grace asked Skye as they loaded up the afternoon's deliveries in the van. Stu had stormed from the bakery after the press conference, accusing Grace of being just like his wife. He didn't give her a chance to explain. Instead, he roughly shoved the van's keys at her and quit.

Grace was grateful that Skye had stuck around when Madison left to drop off little Jack at the sitter on her way to a meeting at the town hall.

"For the last time, no, I don't mind," Skye said as she got in the white van. "Now go talk to your husband."

"Thanks, Skye. I will." Hopefully he was in the mood to listen.

She hadn't heard from him since she'd lost it in the bakery, and he hadn't responded to her phone calls and texts. Her cheeks heated at the memory of how she'd acted. Yes, her rat fink sister-in-law and Maria had pushed her beyond her limits, but Grace should've known better and kept her temper in check. She couldn't lose Jack, not over a misunderstanding. And that's why, after her last attempt to reach him, she decided to head to the house on Sugar Plum Lane and explain to him face-to-face.

It would've been hard enough for him to hear that she'd said good-bye to him that night, but to hear it in the way that he had, in the middle of a press conference with everyone looking on, must've been unbearable. There was nothing he valued more than honesty—honesty and trust. A small part of her rebelled at the thought he expected her to trust there was no longer anything between him and Maria. A woman who with every look, with every action, said she wanted Jack and she intended to have him.

Grace's pulse kicked up at the thought, and she opened the door to the bakery, calling out to the pretty brunette with the purple streaks in her hair. "Desiree, if you're okay, I'll leave now. I should be back in about an hour."

The twenty-four-year-old looked up from spraying the display case with glass cleaner and took in the two teenage girls sitting at the table by the window. "Shouldn't be a problem."

But it was. And five minutes after searching the apartment from top to bottom, Grace returned to the bakery.

Desiree lifted a pierced brow. "How come you're back so soon?"

"I couldn't find Jack's keys to the truck." She tried not to think of him tearing up the mountain roads on his bike. She'd been worried ever since she'd seen him take off on his Harley, looking big, bad, and very mad.

"You can borrow my bike if you want," Desiree offered.

"That's a great idea. Thanks."

*   *   *

Fifteen minutes later, Grace realized accepting Desiree's offer had been a bad idea. Her breath sawed painfully in and out as she pedaled up the hill, sweat dripping into her eyes. She swiped a hand across her brow, then pulled her pink ruffled, sleeveless blouse from where it stuck to her chest. She hadn't realized how out of shape she was until now.

A relieved breath pushed past her dry throat upon reaching the top of the hill. Then noting the steep descent, she groaned, "Oh no." So much for taking the shortcut to Sugar Plum Lane. With a light squeeze to her brakes, she stopped pedaling and prayed. She sailed down the hill like a four-year-old who'd had her training wheels removed for the first time. At Grace's squawk of panic, two older women toddling up the sidewalk stopped to look at her.

From behind came the roar of an engine, and Grace nervously edged closer to the curb, veering to the right to avoid getting hit when a red Mustang zoomed past her. The bicycle's tire bounced against the sidewalk at an awkward angle, causing an out-of-control wobble. Grace lost her balance, and both she and the bike toppled over.

"Are you all right, dear?" the older woman with blue-gray hair asked, shuffling to her side.

"Yes, thank you," Grace said, as she levered herself up on her hands and knees, wincing at the sharp sting in her palms.

The woman's friend righted the bike while Grace unsteadily came to her feet. "Hooligan. We should call the sheriff," the stern-faced woman muttered, scowling after the Mustang that turned onto Sugar Plum Lane.

The woman was right. They should call Gage, Grace thought as the car took the corner at a dangerous speed. She went back to brushing off her black pants and winced. The left knee was torn, and there were dark streaks where she'd wiped off the dirt. She turned over her hands to discover they were scraped and bleeding. Pulling tissues from their purses, the older women made sympathetic noises. With their help, Grace cleaned herself up. Five minutes later, she'd set herself to rights and thanked the two women, inviting them to stop by the bakery anytime for a complimentary coffee and cupcake.

Grace walked the bike to the bottom of the hill, then got back on, releasing a pained yelp when she tightened her grip on the handlebars. This, she decided, was one of the worst ideas she'd ever had. The feeling increased tenfold when she turned onto the tree-lined street and saw the red Mustang parked in front of the pink Victorian. Maria, who still had on the sexy white body-hugging halter dress, stood with Jack and Sawyer in the front yard.

Grace's gaze dropped self-consciously to the old-school blue metallic bike and her conservative clothes. Well, it wasn't as if she could wear a dress while riding a bike, now, was it? she thought peevishly, putting on the brakes. She got off the bike and started toward them. Jack said something to Maria, and the gorgeous brunette tossed her long hair like a model in a shampoo commercial. Grace pictured what her own sweat-dampened hair must look like beneath the pink Hello Kitty helmet, and lost her nerve. She went to wheel the bike around before they saw her. At least Jack was safe. She'd call him once she got back to the bakery.

Then she heard his low, raspy laugh, and a spurt of temper overcame her self-consciousness. She spun the bike around. He wouldn't be laughing when he found out that Maria had run her off the road. Dragging in a going-into-battle breath, she straightened her shoulders and strode down the sidewalk to the house. Sawyer saw her and nudged Jack.

Her husband glanced over his shoulder, his gaze moving from the bike to her head. His lips twitched. "Hey, I was just going to call you," he said as he started toward her.

Sure he was, she thought, with a hard kick to the stand. She went to meet him on the path, then remembered she had on the stupid helmet. She didn't know which was worse, leaving it on or taking it off. She took it off. "I've been trying to call you. I was worried about you."

He opened his mouth, then frowned. "What happened?" Crouching in front of her, he gently moved the torn fabric to check out her knee.

"Maria ran me off the road."

He blinked. "Come again?"

She told him what had happened, and he came to his feet. Aiming a censorious look at Maria while placing a protective hand on Grace's shoulder, he said, "You ran my wife off the road?"

Sawyer, who'd overheard the last part as he came to join them, lobbed an accusatory stare in the other woman's direction.

"I didn't run anyone off the road."

"Yes, you did, and I have witnesses. But at the speed you were going, I was probably just a blur, and you didn't notice me." Or maybe she thought it was a good way to get Grace out of the picture once and for all.

"I was going pretty fast," the woman admitted with a nervous glance at Jack, "so I guess it's possible, but I honestly didn't see you."

Grace snorted inwardly, because she'd never snort out loud.

Maria continued, "I'm sorry if I ran you off the road. I hope you weren't hurt." Grace had to admit, she appeared to be genuinely sorry.

"Not badly, no."

Rubbing his thumb over her collarbone, Jack angled his head. "You sure you're okay?"

"I'm fine. But I . . ." She glanced from Maria to Sawyer. "I really need to talk to you."

He turned Grace to face him and lifted his hand, smoothing back the hair plastered to her cheek. "I know why you did what you did. Sawyer told me everything," he said, his voice low and gentle.

Maybe not as low as she thought, because Sawyer gave Grace a conspiratorial wink, and Maria's eyes narrowed. Grace sent Sawyer a grateful smile before saying to Jack, "You're not mad at me anymore?"

"No." He kissed her forehead. "Not at you."

Maria moved closer, extending her hand. "We haven't been formally introduced. I'm Maria DeMarco."

Like I don't know who you are, lady. Grace snorted. Oops. She cleared her throat and took the woman's hand. "I have allergies." The corner of Jack's mouth quirked. "Grace Flaherty."

"I'm sorry we got off on the wrong foot. I'm sure you understand, given the circumstances, that I was just trying to protect Jack." Maria smiled up at him then returned her attention to Grace, giving her an expectant look.

Did she actually expect her to apologize? *Yeah right.* "Of course I do. Jack's the type of guy who brings out every woman's protective instincts. Goodness knows, a six-foot-three man carrying two hundred and ten pounds of lethal muscle needs all the protection he can get."

Jack's brows shot up. The sweet smile Grace gave him faltered when she caught Maria eyeing all those muscles before she twisted her gorgeous face in a hurt expression.

"Grace, I think…" Jack began, looking uncomfortable.

She frowned. He can't be serious? The woman sabotaged her at the press conference and ran her off the road.

"Don't get angry with your wife on my account," Maria intervened, rubbing his arm.

Grace fought back the urge to rip the woman's red talons from her husband's bicep. Instead, she searched Jack's face. What was Maria talking about? He wasn't angry. Embarrassed, maybe—which was ridiculous, he had no reason to be, not on her account.

She returned her attention to Maria, who continued speaking. "I totally understand where Grace is coming from. I just hope that you won't let our petty differences interfere with Jack working on the book, Grace. He doesn't deserve to lose out on a fabulous opportunity because you feel threatened."

Petty… threatened… Grace fumed, then focused on the important part. "What book are you talking about?" she asked at the same time Jack said, "Maria, I told you I wanted to talk to Grace before I gave you my answer."

"Your answer on what?"

"Maria asked me to consult on her book."

Sawyer, who'd remained quiet up until then, must've noticed the shocked expression on Grace's face, because he said, "Maria's offered Jack a lot of money to consult on the book. I think he should do it."

It wasn't a secret that they could use the money. But she'd bet her last dollar Maria DeMarco wanted more from Jack than help with her book. Honestly, Jack and Sawyer were clueless if they couldn't see through the woman. Then again, most men acted like idiots around a beautiful woman. And Maria DeMarco was beautiful.

Grace wasn't about to let the woman think she'd pulled the wool over her eyes. She'd have to be some kind of masochist to let her husband work with Maria. No, it was time to nip this in the bud. "I'm not sure what petty differences you're referring to, but Jack has a lot on his plate right now. He's very busy doing volunteer work for Gage, and I'm busy with the bakery. Taking on a project like this would interfere with our family time. And money isn't an issue. The bakery's doing very well."

"I'm sorry, are you saying Jack *can't* work on the book with me?"

"The timing isn't right, that's all." Too late, Grace caught the telltale tic in Jack's clenched jaw, and the subtle warning shake of Sawyer's head.

Sawyer took Maria's arm. "I think we should let Jack and Grace talk about this."

"Sure, I guess. I hope you can convince your wife to *let* you work on the book, Jack. It'd be a shame if our story didn't get told." Maria got in one last jab before allowing Sawyer to walk her to her car.

You idiot, Grace thought. *You walked right into that.* Now Jack really was angry at her. Couldn't he see that the woman was simply using the book as a way to spend time with him? "Why wouldn't the story get told, Maria?" Grace called after her. "You're a journalist. Surely you're able to write—"

Jack cut Grace off with a curt "That's enough."

"But it's true, Jack. Don't you see what... You can't seriously be thinking of working with her on this?"

"Yeah, I am. Sawyer's right. She's offered me a lot of money. I want to contribute to our family, too."

"You are. You still get paid, and the bakery's doing better every day." There was more she wanted to say, but hesitated. Speaking her mind had only gotten her into trouble in the past. Then again, Jack blamed Grace's unwillingness to share her feelings for some of their problems. She decided now was as good a time as any to start sharing. "I don't want you to work with her on the book." There, she'd said it. She felt better for telling him the truth, until she saw the hard set of his square jaw.

"It's not your decision to make. It's mine. There are two people in this relationship, Grace. You don't get to call all the shots."

"But you—" she began before being interrupted by Fred, who hollered at Jack and Sawyer from the front porch, "You two get in here or you'll be working till midnight."

"I gotta go. We'll talk about this later. I'll be over as soon as I finish up here. Probably around eight."

"Okay, I'll see you then. But, Jack," she said as he started up the path, "I won't change my mind."

He stopped midstride, turning to face her, his gaze roaming her face. "Then we have a problem."

"I guess we do," she said quietly and walked away.

Grace reached the sidewalk as Maria sped off in a cloud of dust. "Don't draw a line in the sand. He needs to do this," Sawyer said, coming to stand beside her.

She shoved the helmet on her head. "No, he doesn't. You didn't see her today. She's in love with him. She's using the book as an excuse to get close to him."

"Don't confuse love with hero worship. Jack protected her over there. It's because of him they got out alive. He's in love with you, not her." Sawyer adjusted the strap under her chin, struggling, she could tell, not to laugh.

She got on the bike. "Talk to him, Sawyer. For me. Make him understand why I can't back down on this. For goodness' sake, the woman destroyed my reputation this morning, and then she tried to run me over."

"Grace, she didn't—"

"Try, please."

"Okay, but I'm not making any promises. And I want you to think about it, too. Think about it from Jack's perspective."

*   *   *

Drenched in sweat and frustration as she pedaled toward the bakery, Grace spotted the delivery van. She didn't think she'd been gone that long. Although, considering the amount of time she'd spent on the ride back trying to come up with a rational, unemotional argument against Jack working with Maria, it was possible she had been.

She propped Desiree's bike against the wall and walked into the bakery. As she noted the empty tables, an anxious knot tightened in her chest. It was just as well, she decided. She'd take the rest of the day off. It would give her the opportunity to set the stage for a romantic dinner. She'd make Roberto's lasagna and her chocolate caramel cupcakes for Jack. Surely he'd be more receptive to her argument then. Now that she had the beginnings of a plan, she felt somewhat more hopeful until she saw the fretful expression on Desiree's face.

"What's wrong? Did the van break down?"

"Um, no. Five minutes after you left, three of the customers called in to cancel their orders. I got in touch with Skye before she made the trip for nothing."

"Why did they cancel?"

"Word's gotten out about the press conference and..." Desiree gave a pained grimace. "They all said they won't do business with a woman who lied to them."

A loud buzzing sound reverberated in Grace's head. She felt faint. Her legs were boneless, and she leaned against the counter for support. Then she realized the buzzing was from the phone. It was off the hook, and she went to replace it.

Desiree grabbed her hand. "No, don't."

"Why?" Grace asked, even though she had a feeling she didn't want to hear the answer.

"The three customers who canceled, they're not the only ones who are upset. Seems like the whole town is worked up about you lying about your sugar plum wish and, you know, asking Jack for a divorce..." Desiree's head bobbed back and forth. "...kicking him out of his house..."

"I think I get the picture. I'm sure it'll blow over in a couple of days." It had to. She'd be unable to pay her bills if it continued much longer. "If you don't mind, I'm going to take—" She stopped at the look on Desiree's face. "There can't be more."

"You know the two sugar plum cakes that you made for the Pines tasting tomorrow morning?"

"Yes," she said warily. The resort wanted to sample the cakes before signing on the dotted line.

"They're destroyed. I didn't notice until I had to go in the cooler to get Mrs. Tate's order. I think Stu must've done it. I'm so sorry, Grace, if I would've known—"

Grace sagged against the counter and bowed her head. Swallowing past the hard lump in her throat, she said, "It's not your fault."

It was Maria DeMarco's. In less than two days, she'd destroyed Grace's reputation, put her business at risk, and did a number on Grace's marriage and confidence. And today, she'd almost killed her. So if Jack thought Grace was going to change her mind about him working with the woman, he had another thing coming.

Grace glanced at the clock; it was two. She'd be lucky to finish the cakes by eight. Maybe she could push Jack off by an hour. Pulling out her phone to text him, she winced. She'd forgotten about her injured hands. They were going to slow her down. Her fingers froze over the keys. What was she supposed to tell Jack? He'd made it clear how he felt about her long hours. In his eyes, this would be one more strike against the bakery, another nail in its coffin. But the contract with the Pines was too important for Grace to jeopardize, especially now.

She squinched her eyes closed, took a deep breath, and tapped out the text. *Jack, I don't think it's a good idea for you to come over tonight. I don't want to fight with you, and we will. I need more time. We'll talk tomorrow.* As soon as she sent the text, she turned off her phone.

Skye rushed into the bakery with an earthenware bowl

in her hands. "Don't you worry, Grace. I've got it covered." She lit a match, putting the tip to the end of a small stick. Sage-scented smoke filled the bakery as she walked around the tables. "I'm going to get rid of all the negative energy for you."

Chapter Seventeen

Jack took a seat at the end of the bar. Sawyer, wearing a Colorado Flurries ball cap, cut Jack a sidelong glance as he fixed a girly drink for a tall, leggy redhead. Sawyer shook his head with a laugh when the woman asked for his phone number. She walked away with a pout and her drink.

Sawyer lifted his chin. "Wanna beer?"

"Sure." He could use a cold one after the day he had. Maybe a couple of them.

Sawyer popped the cap off a Twisted Pine Stout and slid the bottle across the bar. "Didn't think you'd show. Figured you'd be busy making up with your wife."

"Little hard to be making up with her when she won't take my calls, don't you think?" He took a long pull of the beer, letting the ice-cold brew assuage his thirst and his temper. He'd been tempted to stop by the apartment on his way to the Penalty Box from Jill's, but it was late, and he was tired and on the far side of testy. Not the best combination for a heart-to-heart.

"Didn't stop you the other day."

"Yeah, and look how that turned out. She wants time. I'm giving it to her."

"In my experience, giving a woman more time to think never works out how you hoped."

"Just what I wanted to hear. Thanks, pal," Jack muttered, his eyes going to the flat screen behind Sawyer when the eleven o'clock news came on. They were leading with this morning's press conference. A photo of Jack staring at his open palm and Grace looking at him with a devastated expression on her face flashed across the screen. Jack cursed under his breath and took another pull on his beer.

A thirtysomething bald guy two barstools over shook an old-fashioned tumbler, ice cubes tinkling, at the TV. "Heard what went down at the bakery today, man. Gotta hurt when a wife pulls shit like that. You got my sympathies."

Sawyer shot the customer a censorious look and aimed the channel changer at the TV, tuning in to the last minutes of play-off hockey.

The guy glanced to his left and grinned. "I bet she could help ease your pain."

Maria flashed the man a smile and sidled up to Jack. "I'm surprised your wife let you out to play," she said, tangling her fingers in the hair at his nape.

He moved her hand to the bar. "She's not my keeper."

Sawyer's eyebrows disappeared under his ball cap before he turned to grab a bottle of scotch off the well-stocked glass shelf. Okay, so maybe that was harsh.

"Huh." Maria reached for his beer. "Sure sounded that way to me. Never thought of you as the type of guy who lets his wife wear the pants in the family." She lifted the bottle to her lips, holding his gaze as she took a deep swallow.

Sawyer uttered a low "Ouch" as he handed the bald guy another scotch and soda. Jack removed the bottle from Maria's hands. "She doesn't."

"So you're accepting my offer, then?" Maria asked, a challenge in her voice.

"Yeah, I am." The words were out of his mouth before he could take them back. But if he was honest, he didn't want to. His wife had used her savings to renovate the bakery and the apartment, and that didn't sit well with Jack. Nor did Grace telling him what he could and couldn't do.

Maria's face lit up with a smile. "That's the best news I've had all day. You don't know how happy you've made me." Her smile dimmed, a hint of pain in her dark eyes. "I don't think I could've handled it by myself. It's hard, you know, remembering…" She leaned in, his stomach roiling at the smell of wine and beer on her breath. She brushed her lips across his cheek. "Thank you."

"Don't make me regret my decision, Maria."

"Of course not. Come on, let's celebrate. A bottle of your best champagne, Sawyer. You do serve champagne, don't you?" she asked when Sawyer crossed his arms, his gaze narrowed at Jack.

Taking note of her over-the-top happiness, the slight slurring of her words, the way her body swayed into his, Jack said, "I think you've had enough to drink, Maria."

Her gaze softened, and she stroked his arm. "You

always took such good care of me. If it weren't for you ..."
She blinked back tears, reminding him how vulnerable
she still was. Less than a month ago they'd been running
for their lives.

"Amazed," his and Grace's song, came through the
speakers. Maria tugged on his fingers. "Dance with me."

Sawyer looked like he was about to say something, but
a couple of women approached the bar, presenting their
glasses for a refill.

"No." Jack removed her hand. "This is what I'm talking about, Maria. I'm married. You have to remember that
or I can't work with you. You can't pull shit like you did
the other day."

"What harm is there in a dance between friends?"

"Small town, remember?"

"Yeah, Jack, I remember everything," she said softly
and held his gaze. He wondered if he'd bitten off more
than he could chew. Would she be able to put their past
behind them? And how the hell was he supposed to make
Grace understand why he needed to do this without coming off as a sexist jerk? He thought of the house on Sugar
Plum Lane. Maybe if she knew he was thinking of buying
it ... No, he still wasn't sure he could go through with it.

He returned his attention to Maria. "I remember how
you felt about this town and the bakery," she said, caressing his bicep. "You can't be happy here. And life's too
short to waste a single minute of it being unhappy, Jack.
You and I know that better than anyone in this place." She
gestured to the people in the bar. "Get rid of the bakery,
and get out of this town before it sucks the life out of you."

It felt like a steel band wrapped around his chest as
her words hit too close for comfort. "You're forgetting

my wife and son. It doesn't matter where I am—as long as I'm with them, I'll be happy." He said the words for Maria's benefit. He wasn't exactly in a happy place right now. Maybe because, thanks to Grace, he wasn't living with her and little Jack.

The lyrics from "Amazed" drifted above the hum of conversation and laughter. They were as true now, Jack realized, as on his wedding day. He wanted Grace in his life forever. Somehow he had to make her remember what they'd once had. What they could have again.

Maria tilted her head to search his face, then nodded with a sad smile. "You deserve to be happy."

A guy with dark, slicked-back hair called to Maria and waved her to his table. She patted Jack's shoulder. "Let me know when you can start on the book. The sooner the better."

"Sure, I'll call you tomorrow to set up a time."

As she turned to walk away, he saw her force a come-hither smile onto her lips.

"She sure knows how to push your buttons, doesn't she?" Sawyer observed dryly, his eyes on the table where she took a seat.

"Okay, just for one minute, imagine yourself in my place. How would you react if your wife told you you couldn't take a job that's going to pay you a shitload of cash?"

"Is Grace my wife?" He grinned when Jack gave him the finger. "Kidding aside, I get where you're coming from. But I understand why Grace reacted the way she did. It's pretty obvious Maria has the hots for you. And, intentional or not, she ran your wife off the road a few minutes before she mentioned the book deal."

An image of Grace in the pink helmet came to him, and Jack found himself smiling. She'd looked pretty damn cute.

"You're thinking about Grace, aren't you?"

"Yeah, how did you know?"

"You get a moony look on your face. Go home and work things out with your wife."

Jack set his empty beer bottle on the bar. "I think I'll do—"

"If she keeps that up, I'm going to have to put her in the box."

"What are you..." Jack began, following the direction of Sawyer's gaze. Maria was getting down and dirty on the dance floor with the guy who'd called her to his table.

"I have a feeling that show's all for you, buddy. She's trying to make you jealous."

"She's going to a lot of trouble for nothing, then." He went to turn away when he saw the change come over Maria. Her dance partner had come up behind her and grabbed her by the hips, grinding against her. She froze, her mouth opening on a silent scream. The guy kept grinding, oblivious to her reaction.

Jack shot off the barstool and across the dance floor. Shoving the man back, he grabbed Maria, who swayed on her heels.

"What the fuck?" her dance partner said, reaching for Jack.

Sawyer stepped between them. "You don't want to do that," he advised the guy and took him by the arm. "Party's over. Time to leave."

"Maria?" Jack gave her a small shake, trying to snap her out of it. He ignored the curious stares of their attentive audience and wrapped an arm around her waist. She leaned heavily against him as he guided her off the dance floor. "Jesus, Maria, what—"

"I'm okay. Too much to drink, that's all," she whispered. "I need to leave."

"Sit for a minute," he said, settling her on a stool.

Sawyer came around the bar, took one look at Maria, and grabbed a mug off the counter.

She wouldn't look at Jack. "Thanks," she said, accepting the cup of coffee from Sawyer.

Jack shrugged at the question in Sawyer's eyes. He didn't know if she was okay or not. The color had returned to her face, and her hand no longer shook. Whatever happened out there, she was pulling it together. "Did you talk to Dr. Trainer?" he asked, keeping his voice low.

"I'm okay."

"What just happened to you out there doesn't qualify as *okay*, Maria. Make an appointment with him tomorrow or I'm not working with you on the book."

"I . . . All right, I'll call him. Happy?" she said, her dark eyes flashing.

The knots in his shoulders relaxed at her reaction. Better anger than that vacant stare.

"I'll give you a ride to the lodge," Sawyer offered when she slid off the barstool.

"Thanks, but I'd rather walk. I need the fresh air." She patted Jack's chest. "I'll talk to you tomorrow."

"Maria, I'm serious. I want—"

She waved him off as she walked away. "Don't worry about me, Jack. I've got it covered."

But she didn't, and that's what bothered him.

"What happened to her over there?" Sawyer asked.

Jack told him what he knew. But she'd been there a couple of months before he and his crew were taken captive, so he didn't know the whole story.

Sawyer poured himself and Jack shots. Tossing his back, Sawyer wiped his mouth with his hand. "I get it now," he said. "I get why you need to help her through this."

"Yeah." Jack rubbed his jaw. "I shouldn't have let her go off on her own." He could tell by the look on Sawyer's face that he thought the same thing. Jack got off the stool. "I'll try to catch up with her, walk her to the lodge, then head over to see Grace. I'll pick up my bike on my way back."

"Try the River Walk. Saw her down by the water when I went for a run this morning," Sawyer said, waving him behind the bar. "It'll be faster to go through the back."

Ten minutes later, Jack reached the end of the planked walkway. From where he leaned against the rail, he took in the empty bench under the lamppost and the gazebo to the right of the weeping willow. No sign of Maria. And in her white dress, she'd be easy to spot. Jack figured it was a lost cause and headed for the shortcut to the park. As he dug his cell from his jeans pocket to call her, it rang.

He checked caller ID. Sawyer. "Hey, I can't—"

"Jack, there's a fire at the bakery."

*   *   *

Pushing down the panic and fear before it closed off his airway, Jack raced toward the park. When he reached Main Street, he smelled the smoke and shoved past the small groups of people huddled in their pajamas on the sidewalk.

He thanked God when he caught sight of old man

Murray standing in front of the lane with little Jack. Sirens blared in the distance as Jack jogged the last few yards toward them. His relief at seeing his son safe in the old man's arms faded at the panic on Murray's face.

"Grace, she's in there. I tried to stop her. She hasn't..." The old man began in a strangled voice.

Jack ran down the smoke-filled lane before Murray finished what he was about to say: *She hasn't come out.* He blocked out the words, same as he did his son crying for his mother.

"Grace," Jack yelled, as he rounded the side of the building. The heat of the fire and smoke burned his eyes even before he flung open the back door. "What the hell do you think you're doing?" he said at the sight of his wife, standing in one of his T-shirts and a pair of pink slippers, with a fire extinguisher in her hand.

"I'm trying to save the bakery. Help me, I can't get this to work." She pushed her matted hair from her soot-covered face, shoving the extinguisher at him. With a quick visual sweep, he took in the flames that engulfed the stove and licked across the ceiling, spreading to the counter. "We're getting out of here. Now," he said as he grabbed her hand. "The fire department's on the way."

"It'll be too late. I..." She let out a small shriek and ducked at the sound of several loud pops. Flames shot up from the garbage can on the opposite wall.

Sawyer came through the door. "Holy hell."

Jack tossed the extinguisher to him and grabbed Grace around the waist. "No, let me go," she said, pushing his hands away.

"Stop it, Grace," he said, dragging her toward the door. She fought him every inch of the way, and damned if she wasn't a lot stronger than he'd given her credit for. He turned, bent down, and threw her over his shoulder.

"Put me down." She pounded his back as he jogged up the lane after Sawyer. "You don't care if it burns to the ground, do you?"

"No, I don't. The only thing I care about is you," he said, setting her in front of him once they were a safe distance from the building. He closed his hands over her shoulders and gave her a small shake. "What the hell were you thinking?"

"That I could put the fire out before it destroys everything." She flung her arm at the extinguisher Sawyer carried. "And I would have if I could've made that thing work."

"I'll get Grace a blanket," Sawyer said.

Jack nodded and returned his attention to his wife. "The fire's out of control." And he was about to lose his. "There's nothing you could've done."

"The lad's right," Patrick Murray said as he limped toward them. "That was a damn fool thing you did running in there like that."

"You don't understand. None of you understand." She swiped at her eyes and reached for little Jack.

"Mama owie," he whimpered, touching her cheek.

"I'm all right, baby," she responded with a forced smile.

She was, and some of the fear that had been fueling Jack's frustration and anger diminished. Siren screaming, the fire truck turned onto Main Street. He put his arm around Grace, drawing her close. "Look, they're here now. Everything's going to be all right," he said, as the truck pulled up to the curb, the flashing lights illuminating the lane and Grace's tear-streaked face.

"No, it won't," she said, but the fight went out of her. She sagged against him, turning her head to watch the black smoke billowing from the bakery, the static pop and hiss of the flames audible from where they stood.

The firefighters jumped out of the truck and began attaching the hose to the hydrant. Gage, who'd been handling crowd control across the street, signaled for his deputy to take over and jogged toward them. "Let's move down the sidewalk a ways," he suggested, giving Grace's shoulder a comforting squeeze. "You okay?"

"No." She gave a brittle laugh. "I'm not okay, Gage. Everything I worked for, everything I own, is going up in flames."

Before Gage could respond, Jack intervened. "We were in there a couple of minutes ago, princess, and the fire was contained in the kitchen." He hoped it still was because it'd been moving terrifyingly fast. But he had to say something positive before she lost it. "The apartment will be fine."

Sawyer caught the last of the conversation as he rejoined them, draping a blanket over Grace's shoulders. "Jack's right. The building's up to code. Fire walls will do their job."

"Do you have any idea how it started, Grace?" Gage asked.

She stroked their son's head while staring at the bakery. "Little Jack got out of his crib. When I went to put him back to bed, I smelled smoke. The window was open."

Gage frowned. "Smoke detector didn't go off?"

"No. I don't think so. I didn't remember hearing it when I opened the door. But maybe I was so panicked—"

"I didn't hear it, either," Jack said, taking his son from

Grace. "We okay on Murray's porch? Grace needs to sit down."

Gage glanced at two firefighters who rounded the side of the building and nodded. "Should be safe enough." He narrowed his eyes at Madison, Nell, and Mrs. Tate, who hurried down the sidewalk toward them as Jack settled Grace on the porch steps. "I thought I told the three of you to stay put," Gage said.

The women ignored him and moved in to fuss over Grace. "You come with Auntie Nell," Nell said, taking his son from Jack. "We'll see if Patrick has a treat for you and make some tea for your mommy."

"Me want cake."

"Don't have cake, but I've got those cookies he likes. And forget about the tea, what Gracie needs is a good stiff drink. So do I," Patrick said as he followed Nell and Mrs. Tate into the house.

"Sheriff." A tall man in uniform waved Gage over.

Assuming he had news about the fire, Jack, along with Sawyer, followed Gage to the edge of the lane. Once they'd been introduced to the deputy chief, Jack asked how the fire had started.

"It looks like a burner on the stove hadn't been shut off and an apron or something had been left too close on the counter. Couple of aerosol cans were left out, too. With the heat..." The man shrugged. "It doesn't take much."

Intent on the man's answer, Jack didn't realize Grace had joined them until he heard her say, "No, that's not right. I didn't leave the stove on, and I'd never leave anything out on the counters."

"Grace, you were tired. Accidents happen. It wasn't your..."

"It doesn't matter how tired I am, Jack. I didn't leave the stove on, and there was nothing on the counters."

"Well, ma'am, it looks like you did. But a fire inspector will be doing an investigation. He'll be able to tell you more." When Jack asked the reason behind an investigation, the man said, "There's been an uptick in the number of kitchen fires purposely set by their owners. Over the last year, it's become standard procedure."

"I wouldn't do that. I'd never..." she began, then looked at Jack.

"Oh, come on. You can't seriously believe I'd do something like this." He struggled to keep his voice low in case she wasn't implying what he thought she was. Not to mention Gage and the deputy fire chief were standing there when his wife accused him of arson.

"Someone left the stove on, and it wasn't me. You haven't exactly kept your opinion of the bakery to yourself, Jack."

She did think he'd done it. At least from the expressions on the men's faces, they didn't. Jack struggled to not lose his cool. Seeing the desperation and defeat in Grace's red-rimmed eyes made it easier. "You're upset, so I'm going to pretend you didn't say that." He took her by the shoulders. "You're human, Grace. You make mistakes just like the rest of us. You were tired and forgot to turn off the damn stove. It'll be ruled the accident that it was, and we'll rebuild."

"Jack's right, Grace. We'll all help out. You'll be up and running in no time," Sawyer said. Madison assured her that Gage would do all that he could to fast-track the insurance claim, despite her husband giving her a zip-it look.

Maria ran across the road. "Jack"—she touched his shoulder—"are you all right? What happened?"

"You," Grace said, pointing a trembling finger at Maria. "It was you. You did this."

You've got to be kidding me, Jack thought, dragging a hand down his face.

"What . . . what did I do?" Maria looked from Grace to Jack.

"Nothing, Maria. Grace is upset and—"

"Don't patronize me, Jackson Flaherty. I know what I saw, and I saw her standing across the street staring at the bakery when I ran to Patrick's with little Jack."

Murray, who'd been sitting on his porch with a beer, came down the steps. "It's true. I saw her, too. Seemed odd the way she stood there staring at the place."

Jack shared a look with Sawyer. He could think of a couple of reasons Maria might've been staring at the bakery, most of which he wouldn't want Grace to hear. But would Maria go as far as setting the place on fire? No way.

"You see, it's not just me. And she tried to run over me today, too. Arrest her, Gage."

"Hold it, why am I only hearing about this now?" Madison said, narrowing her gaze at Maria before turning back to Grace.

"I did not try to run you over. I didn't see you."

Grace snorted. "Tell that to someone who believes you." She looked at Jack. "Oh, right, you did."

"You believed her, too. You accepted her apology."

"Not anymore, I don't. Not after this." She flung her hand at the bakery.

Gage rubbed the back of his neck. "Grace, honey, this wasn't arson. It was an accident."

"Why won't any of you listen to me? Someone did this on purpose—"

With her gaze fixated on the smoldering building, Maria rubbed her ring finger with her thumb. "You think someone set fire to the bakery?"

"I *know* someone did. Why were you here? What were you doing?"

"I-I was walking back to the lodge. I wasn't doing anything." Her gaze flickered across the street, then back to the building.

"Did you see anything out of the ordinary?" Gage asked.

"No." Maria averted her gaze. "If there's nothing else, I have to get going."

"That's fine. You can go," Gage said.

"I'm glad no one was hurt. I'll talk to you tomorrow, Jack," she said and headed off in the opposite direction.

"That's it? You're just going to let her go?" Grace's temper flared as she aimed an infuriated look at Gage. "It's because of her that this happened. I've had threats phoned in against me, orders canceled, and my cakes destroyed. And if you won't do anything about it, Gage, I will. I am going to find out who did this."

"Look at me." Jack cupped Grace's face with his hands. "You're exhausted, and you've had more than your share of crap to deal with today. But you need to calm down, princess, and think this through." She was breathing like she'd run a hundred-yard dash in two seconds flat. Drawing her into his arms, he stroked her back while directing his question to the deputy fire chief, whose gaze had bounced from one accused to the next with his mouth agape. "Can we stay in the apartment tonight?"

"No, but you should be good to go back in tomorrow. I'd better get over there."

"I'll join you. And you," Gage said, taking his wife by the arm, "are going home. Say good night."

"Good night," Madison said and hugged Grace. "We'll talk in the morning. And don't worry about the Pines. I'll call them."

"No, we can't afford to lose that contract, especially now. I..." Her gaze flitted nervously from Jack then back to Madison. "I made two more cakes. They're in our refrigerator upstairs."

Once Madison and Gage left, Jack nudged Grace's chin up. "You'll stay with me at Jill's tonight, and we'll—"

"After what she pulled today? I don't think so. I'll stay with Patrick, if that's all right?" she said to the old man.

Murray patted her arm. "I'll get your bed made up." He looked like she'd just made his day. Now Jack was going to ruin it. Because after what had just happened, he had no intention of spending another night apart from his family.

"You got room for me?" Jack asked.

The old man looked at Grace. She gave him a small nod. "I suppose," Murray said, then headed for the house.

"Go with him. Grab a hot shower, and I'll be in in a minute." When she looked set to refuse, Jack said, "There's nothing more you can do. We'll deal with it tomorrow. And if you still believe that it wasn't an accident in the morning, I'll help you look into it."

She blinked. "You will?"

"Yeah, I will."

Giving him a grateful smile, she went up on her tiptoes and kissed his cheek. "Thank you."

She touched Sawyer's arm as she went to walk away. "Night, Sawyer."

"Night, Grace." Together they watched her head to the house, then turned as the firefighters regained their attention. "So," Sawyer said, "was it just me, or was there something off about Maria's reaction?"

"There was, but I think it had more to do with what happened at the bar."

"I don't know. What if she—"

"What? Had a mental break and burned down the bakery without knowing what she was doing?"

"Well, yeah. It's possible, isn't it? After what she said at the bar, maybe she'd think she was doing you a favor."

"Keep those kind of theories to yourself, will you? My wife doesn't need any encouragement."

"So you were just humoring her?"

"Yeah. There's nothing to look into. It was an accident. You heard her. She had to deal with the fallout from the press conference and then spent half the night making those damn sugar plum cakes. No wonder she forgot to turn off the stove. She's wearing herself out trying to make a go of the bakery. Libby couldn't do it. I don't know why Grace thinks she can." Staring at the building, he absently rubbed the back of his neck. He didn't need his internal warning system to tell him the place was dangerous. "Maybe we shouldn't rebuild. Maybe we should just—"

From behind them came a soft, feminine gasp. Sawyer gave him a you're-screwed look before Jack turned to face his wife.

Chapter Eighteen

The next morning, Grace walked into the bank with as much confidence as her sleep-deprived body could muster. Through no fault of her own, she'd given Jack the perfect excuse to get rid of the bakery. Grace wasn't about to let that happen. No matter what her husband thought, the fire was not a result of her being too tired to think straight. Last night, she'd mentally retraced each and every step she'd taken before locking up. There was no doubt in her mind that she'd turned off the stove, hung her apron on the hook by the door, and cleaned off the counters.

But until the fire inspector came back with his report, no one would believe her. For now, she had to focus on getting the bakery up and running as soon as possible. Which is why she'd called the bank first thing this morning to set up an appointment with Mr. Powell, the branch manager. She needed her line of credit increased. Because if what the deputy fire chief had said was true, it would take more time than she could afford to settle the insurance claim.

Opening her purse, Grace checked for Madison's list of talking points in case she forgot one of them. With a surreptitious tug on the hem of the black pencil skirt she'd paired with a white blouse, she smiled at the frizzy-haired teller. "Hi, Wanda, I have an appointment with Mr. Powell."

Wanda pressed a hand to the side of her face. "Girl, that was just a darn shame about the fire. Don't you let anyone make you feel bad for leaving the stove on like you did. I've done it a hundred times myself. All that matters is that you and your adorable little boy are—"

Grace hoped the fire inspector hurried up with his report, because she was getting tired of everyone thinking this was her fault. "Thanks, Wanda. Is Mr. Powell ready to see me?" She felt bad for interrupting Wanda, but the woman liked to talk and Grace had to be at the Pines for the tasting in three hours.

"Your husband's with him now." Wanda obviously didn't register Grace's jaw dropping at the news because she leaned on the counter, cupped her chin in her hand, and released a dreamy sigh. "I heard he rescued you from the fire last night. That's so romantic."

"Jack? Jack's with Mr. Powell?" Grace repeated, her voice raising on a panicked note. There was only one reason for him to be here.

"Well, yes, isn't that what I just said?" Wanda's brow furrowed, then she shot a glance to the frosted window of Mr. Powell's office and lowered her voice to a conspiratorial whisper, "What is wrong with you, girl? How could you ask that man for a divorce? He is hot, like smoking hot." She made a sizzling sound and touched her finger to her arm. "Yowza."

Grace would've rolled her eyes if she weren't battling her nerves and temper. How was she supposed to convince Mr. Powell to advance her more funds with Jack looking on? *Ask him to leave*, she thought. But since, from Mr. Powell's perspective, Jack had as much right to be there as Grace, that wouldn't work. Then the answer came to her. She'd channel Madison. Grace stiffened her spine. "I'll go in now," she said and walked with fake confidence toward the office, ignoring the way the black high heels pinched her toes.

"Girl, did you hurt yourself in that fire?"

Hand raised to knock on the bank manager's door, Grace turned. "No, why?"

"Well, honey, you're walking like you have a poker up your derriere."

Grace sighed. "Good to know. Thanks." Forcing herself to relax, she pasted a smile on her face and opened the door. "Mr. Powell, Jack, I hope I'm not interrupting. Wanda said I should come on in." The sight of the bald and bearded Mr. Powell with what looked to be a balance sheet open on the computer screen threw her for a loop. Or maybe it was the sight of her husband exuding all that testosterone-laden confidence. It was as if his commanding presence ate up all the air in the small space, and the lack of oxygen short-circuited her brain.

"No, of course you're not. Please." Mr. Powell waved her into the office.

Jack stood, his intent blue gaze focused on her face. "You okay?" he asked, an edginess in his deep voice. He was probably still ticked at her for making him sleep on the couch last night. Well, too bad. She hadn't exactly been feeling the warm fuzzies after hearing his comments to Sawyer. And she was afraid this meeting wasn't going to help matters.

"I'm fine. It's just my shoes," she said, sitting in the chair he held out for her.

He rubbed a hand along his stubbled jaw, looking dangerously hot and slightly confused. "Come again?"

"I thought you were talking about the way I was walking. It's because of…Never mind," she said in a perturbed tone of voice as his eyes drifted from her feet to the skirt riding up her thighs.

A slow smile curved his lips as he took the seat beside her and leaned in to whisper, "Wasn't what I meant, but I really like those shoes."

Mr. Powell cleared his throat. "I hope you don't mind that I asked Jack to join us, Grace. I have some papers he needs to sign."

"No, not at all." She waved her fingers at the papers and files scattered across his desk. "Go ahead, I can wait. I know Jack has to get to work." The nervous flutter in her stomach calmed at the thought he'd be leaving before she made her pitch to Mr. Powell.

"I'm good." Jack folded his tanned arms over his black T-shirt, his long, muscular legs encased in well-worn jeans stretched out before him as he casually crossed his steel-toed boots at the ankles.

"Really, Jack, I can wait."

The teasing light in his eyes disappeared. "Grace, I'm not leaving."

"All right, suit yourself, but don't blame me if you're bored."

"I won't be bored."

"I have another appointment after yours. So if you don't mind getting to the point of the meeting..." Mr. Powell said.

At the hint of impatience in the bank manager's voice and Jack's hardheaded attitude, Grace's palms began to sweat. "I need you to extend my line of credit. Thirty thousand dollars should about cover it," she blurted out.

Mr. Powell's bushy brows slammed together, while beside her, Jack speared his fingers through his hair. Since indirectly Grace was responsible for the situation she was now in, she'd wanted to be the one who solved the problem. Considering the men's reactions, she should've let Madison handle it. But it was too late for Grace to second-guess her decision, so she forged ahead.

"Think of it as a short-term loan," she suggested. "I'm sure it won't take more than a month for the insurance claim to be settled."

"You're being overly optimistic, Grace. I've seen it take up to a few months. As it is, you'll have a hard time meeting your existing loan payments. I don't think—"

"I realize that, but"—she leaned forward in her chair and tapped the papers on his desk—"sales in the last quarter surpassed our forecast. We accelerated the payments on our business improvement loan. Surely that counts for something. And I have business interruption insurance. I can clear off the line of credit as soon as the settlement comes in." From Mr. Powell's expression and the frustration emanating from Jack, Grace knew it was time to hit them with some hard facts. By rote, she listed Madison's talking points. After a somewhat halting start, Grace thought she'd done a pretty good job of it until she saw Mr. Powell staring openmouthed from his desk to Grace's hand.

She followed the direction of his gaze to the pens she'd unconsciously been organizing according to height and color. She put them back in the holder. It looked like she'd also straightened the papers and folders on his desk. Embarrassed, she sat back in her chair, gripping her purse in her hands. Jack's cough sounded suspiciously like a laugh. She shot him a glare. "It's not funny."

Laugh lines crinkled the corner of his eyes. "I know it's not," he said once he got his amusement under control. "Dave, Grace made some good points. You—"

"I did?" she asked, unable to contain her surprise.

"Yeah, you did." He patted her leg, then returned his attention to the bank manager. "You floated Libby, and her profit margins weren't anywhere near as good as Grace's. Besides, there's no risk here. It's a bridging loan until the claim is settled. You do them all the time."

Grace couldn't believe it. She was in total shock at Jack's one-eighty. And so happy about it that she wanted to jump in his arms and shower that too-gorgeous face of his with grateful kisses.

Jack must have sensed her surprise because he winked and smiled before saying to Mr. Powell, "And, as I mentioned to you, I'll be bringing in extra income from consulting on the book. So you—"

Grace's mouth fell open. "Wait. What do you mean you're..." Her voice trailed off as she caught the change in Mr. Powell's expression. Seconds ago, he'd looked like Jack had won him over, and now in the face of Grace's objection...If she wanted the money, she had no choice but to agree to Jack working with Maria. "Go ahead," she said, leaving little doubt by her tone of voice that she wasn't pleased at how Jack had outmaneuvered her.

He cocked his head and gave her a long look.

Mr. Powell clicked away on his keyboard, adjusting numbers on the computer screen. "All right, you've convinced me, Jack. I'll approve the increase on your line of credit. Good luck with the tasting at the Pines, Grace. That contract should keep you afloat until the claim is settled." Grace was going to use her kitchen, and Patrick's if need be, to fulfill the Pines' orders as well as her regular customers'.

If she still had regular customers, she thought, remembering yesterday. After the damage Maria had wrought, the idea of Jack working with the woman rankled. And she couldn't get past the feeling that Maria had had something to do with the fire. But Grace had accomplished, with Jack's help, what she'd set out to. And for now, she'd be satisfied with that.

Jack stood and shook Mr. Powell's hand. "Thanks, Dave."

"We can discuss that other matter at another time, Jack," the bank manager said.

Before Grace could ask about "the other matter," Mr. Powell shook her hand. "Good luck."

She'd barely gotten out her "Thank you" when Jack ushered her from the office with a firm hand at the small of her back.

Wanda, who had a long line of customers, gave Grace an exaggerated wink and a thumbs-up. "What's that about?" Jack asked, holding the door open for her.

"Nothing," she said, stepping into the morning sunlight, "but maybe you'd like to explain to me why I had to hear that you'd accepted Maria's offer from Mr. Powell. How could you do that to me, Jack?"

He took her by the hand and drew her to the side of the building. "I'm not going to argue with you about this, Grace. I have my reasons for working on the book. And because I am, you got what you wanted, didn't you?"

"Well, yes, but—"

"Thanks for helping me out in there, Jack," he said with a flash of strong, white teeth.

She sighed. She wasn't going to win on this, and she did appreciate what he'd done. Besides that, she was thrilled he'd come around about the bakery. "I do appreciate you going to bat for me. Thank you. Why didn't you tell me you'd changed your mind about keeping the bakery? It would've saved..." The words stalled on her lips when he averted his eyes. "But I thought—"

"Yeah, I know what you thought." He rubbed his chin. "Whether we sell or keep the bakery, it doesn't change the fact it needs to be rebuilt. And after last night, you already know which way I'm leaning."

Grace had a new appreciation for how her son felt when he didn't get his way. She'd like to throw a temper tantrum, too. Since nothing she'd done or said so far had changed Jack's mind, she decided to change tactics. Stuffing down her true feelings had worked in the past. Sort of. "Yes, and I understand why." She did. He'd been worried about them, and he was worried about her. She reached up and brushed her lips over his. "Let's not talk about the bakery anymore."

His eyes narrowed. "What are you up to?"

"Nothing." She smiled, looping her arm through his as she walked him to where he'd parked his truck. "Are you coming over after work?"

"Yeah, I planned... You know, princess, you're making

me kind of nervous here," he said, pressing the button on his keys.

"I'm smiling. How can that make you nervous?"

"It's just . . . You're right. How about I pick up little Jack from the sitter and grab a pizza on the way home?"

"Great. That sounds great. We can celebrate . . ." Not talking about the bakery was going to be more difficult than she thought.

"Good luck with the Pines. I mean it," he said at her doubtful look.

"Thanks." She smiled as he got in the truck.

"If we're going to be celebrating tonight, make sure you wear that outfit and keep on the shoes."

*　　*　　*

Grace still had on her outfit and shoes, but they wouldn't be celebrating tonight.

The manager at the Pines had withdrawn their offer before the taste test had even begun. Due to the negative publicity generated from the press conference, they didn't feel Grace's sugar plum cakes were a good fit with their clientele.

"Don't worry about it," Madison said as they stood by the stove in Grace's apartment waiting for the water to boil. "We're going to fix this."

"Whoa, you two are putting out some wicked negative energy," Skye said as she joined them in the kitchen. "Do you have any sage, Grace? I can . . . What's with the face?"

"Um, well . . ." Grace trailed off.

"You did your energy-clearing thingy yesterday and look how that turned out. Grace's bakery went up in flames," Madison said.

"I didn't do the kitchen. I did the eating area. And FYI, Miss Doubting Thomas, that escaped unscathed."

The kettle's piercing whistle ended further discussion. Grace removed it from the stove and automatically turned off the burner. Madison met her gaze. "I know what you're going to say. And I spent half the night trying to convince Gage of the same thing. But we just have to wait until the fire inspector renders his decision. Right now, let's focus on how we're going to repair your reputation," Madison said.

"Here, let me." Skye took the kettle from Grace's hand. "You go take a load off. Well, Maddie needs to take a load off, anyway."

"Thanks a lot," Madison said as she led Grace to the living room.

Grace flopped onto the couch, numb with disappointment. Madison and Skye had accompanied her to Aspen. She didn't know what she would've done without their support. She'd probably still be crying at the side of the road if not for them.

"Grace, where do you keep your herbal tea?" Skye called from the kitchen.

"First shelf in the cupboard to the left of the sink."

"Got it."

"Please tell me your tea's organic and from a fair-trade company. If it isn't, we're going to have to endure a twenty-minute lecture from her, and I don't think I can take another one."

As someone who'd had to endure Madison's lectures on finances more often than she cared to think about, Grace had a hard time working up any sympathy for her.

"I can hear you, you know." Skye popped her head

out of the kitchen, waving a bag of jasmine tea. "You see, I'm not the only one. And Grace"—she held up a cupcake—"these are amazing."

"I don't know why I'm friends with the two of you," Madison grumbled. "I've got Miss Thing there, who can eat like a horse and never gain an ounce. And then there's you, Mrs. Perfect, who doesn't have to scour two counties for organic, fair-trade tea bags. You have them in your frigging cupboard. I'm starting to get a complex. I need some normal friends."

Grace snorted. "After yesterday, I seriously doubt anyone thinks of me as Mrs. Perfect."

"You're right. Thanks. I feel better now." Madison grinned, then grew serious. "But honestly, with all you're dealing with, you're handling it a lot better than I would."

"That's true. Our little mama bear has been a tad cranky these days," Skye said, placing the tray with the Dresden-blue teapot and teacups on the coffee table.

"What are you talking about? I'm not cranky."

Skye sat cross-legged on the floor and poured the tea. "It's all right, sweetie. You're pregnant. It's all those nasty hormones overloading your body. But if you'd listen to me and get rid of the sugar and dairy products, you'd be back to your old sweet... Well, you'd feel much better."

"Name one instance where I've been cranky."

Skye named ten, ticking off her fingers as she did.

Grace decided to throw herself under the bus in the name of friendship. "So," she said as Madison opened her mouth to refute Skye's list, "how am I going to turn this mess around?"

Skye stared at something above Grace's head. "Maybe I should've made chamomile instead," she murmured, then said, "Breathe in the jasmine." Grace lifted the cup to her nose and inhaled the exotic, floral scent. "That's it, nice deep breaths. All right, now I want you sit back and get comfy." Skye was beginning to make her nervous, but Grace did as she directed. "See how she listens, Maddie? You could take a lesson from her. Okay, now find your happy place. Got it?"

"Yes." Grace was making a sugar plum cake in the bakery with her husband and little Jack at her side. Jack loved the bakery, and her son adored his father as much as Grace did. And Maria, well, she was doing time for arson.

"Maybe you should sprinkle some fairy dust on her, too."

Grace blinked her eyes open. "Madison, that's it. Skye's the Sugar Plum Cake Fairy."

"I'm a what?" Skye asked as Grace got up and went to the bookshelf along the far wall. Withdrawing her sketch pad, she flipped to the page where she'd been doodling ideas and handed it to Madison.

"There is a resemblance with all that curly, long hair, but..." Madison began.

"Hang on." Grace opened the drawer of the coffee table and took out a pencil. Looking at Skye, she started to sketch. A few minutes later, she showed Madison.

"Okay, that's incredible and depressing at the same time. Grace, I didn't know you could draw like this. Is there anything you can't do?"

Grace gave a self-conscious shrug. "I'm not bad, but it's not like they're good enough to sell."

"Let me see." Skye reached for the pad. "Wow, that actually looks like me. Stop underselling yourself, Grace. You're really talented. But what's with the wand and the skimpy costume I'm wearing? Hey, is that a cake on my head?"

"Thanks. Umm, it's actually a crown. But we can work on the costume. It's just what I envisioned a cake fairy would wear. But once Vivi finishes the story, we can play around with it. And Mrs. O'Connor is really good with this sort of thing. I'm sure she—" Grace stopped to frown at Madison, who shook her head, drawing a finger across her lips.

"I really wish you'd stop acting as if I'm not here. I can see you. And Grace, Mrs. O'Connor is more likely to design a body bag for me than a fairy costume. Honestly, talk about an overprotective mama bear. The woman got bent out of shape because I had a difference of opinion with he who will not be named."

Madison sighed. "You dumped the bowl of champagne punch on his head."

"How would you feel if he said Fred and Ted shouldn't marry? Love is love, that's what I say, and gay couples have as much right to marry as you and me."

"I didn't know Fred and Ted were gay. When did that happen?" Grace asked, wondering how come she was the last to know.

"They're not. I've explained this to you before, Skye. They were both married. They live together to share expenses."

"Just because they were married doesn't mean they're not gay. As a society, we certainly don't make it easy for them to come out." Skye wound a long, spiral curl around her finger. "I think I'll offer them my services. I can marry them, you know. I'm a licensed minister."

"No, I, ah, didn't know that," Grace said.

"You got your license off the computer."

Skye waved Madison off and started flipping through the pages of the sketchbook before Grace thought to stop her. "Oh my, if your husband looks like this naked, I don't know why you kicked him out." Skye grimaced. "Sorry, I didn't mean that. His hotness fried my brain for a minute."

"Let me see," Madison gestured for the sketch pad.

"No. Those are not for public viewing," Grace protested.

"You're pregnant. You're not supposed to be looking at naked men. It's not good for your blood pressure," Skye informed Madison.

"He's not naked. He has his pants on," Grace said as her face heated.

"I know." Skye turned the sketch pad toward them, doing a Vanna White impersonation. "But look at that back, those shoulders, and those arms—they're enough to raise anyone's blood pressure." The sketch was of Jack from the back, wearing a pair of low-riding jeans, throwing a laughing little Jack in the air. Grace had filled the sketch pad with moments she wished would happen while he was missing.

"Oh, that's beautiful," Skye said, as she turned to a drawing of Grace and Jack kissing, her hand on his face.

Skye flipped to another page. "This is the house on your cakes." It was a sketch of Jack walking up the path through the wildflower garden with their son on his shoulders. *Foolish dream*, she thought. Jack didn't want to live in Christmas, and he'd never wanted to be tied down to a house. She'd known that from the beginning, but once she'd had little Jack, she'd hoped he'd change his mind.

"We've gotten off track, ladies," Grace said as she got up to take the pad from Skye. "I need to come up with a plan to counter the bad press." At least if she was doing something, she'd feel as if she had some control over the situation.

Skye stood up and retrieved the sketch pad from Grace. She opened to the drawing of herself as the Sugar Plum Cake Fairy. "Here's your answer, ladies. Grace will give an interview to that nice reporter and explain that she never stopped loving her husband, but she had to move on because it was making her sick and she had her son to think about. That's why you wrote the note, isn't it, sweetie?" she asked Grace.

"Yes," Grace said, her throat painfully tight as she remembered how she felt the day she wrote her good-bye letter to Jack.

"All right, be prepared to be awed by my brilliance. Grace made her wish, and as soon as the sugar plum was opened, they learned Jack was alive. And that's because, my sweets, the Sugar Plum Cake Fairy granted the wish Grace really wanted but was too afraid to ask for." Skye grinned. "Don't hold back your applause."

Madison slowly nodded. "It might just work." Then she started to laugh. "You're right—it's not only brilliant, I have a feeling we won't be able to keep up with orders after we go to the press with this."

"When you're given lemons, make lemonade, that's what I always say," Skye said.

"It's a great idea," Grace said, but there was one problem with the plan. The press would want to know why she'd kicked Jack out of the apartment. And even though Grace loved him and knew he loved her, too, she had to be sure he was *in* love with her and wasn't just doing the honorable thing before he moved back in.

"So, how much does this gig pay?" Skye asked.

Madison frowned. "What gig?"

"Umm, me playing the Sugar Plum Cake Fairy."

"You're joking, right?" Madison asked.

"Are you kidding me? Of course I am," Skye said on a half laugh.

Grace didn't think Skye was joking, which didn't make sense, because trust-fund baby Skylar Davis had more money than God, according to Madison. But Madison had also said Skye was too generous and would one day end up broke. Grace had a feeling that's exactly what had happened. Because now that she thought about it, the Skylar Davis Madison talked about would have offered to keep the bakery afloat until they received the check from the insurance company.

"We'll take pictures of you in costume for the book and publicity material, but don't worry, we'll get on it ASAP. I'm sure you don't want to be stuck in Christmas for long," Madison said.

"Uh, no, I'm good. Footloose and fancy-free, that's *moi*. I thought I'd, you know, stay for a while. Help you with the baby and the girls."

Madison's eyes widened. "But...but I'm only four months pregnant."

"I know. Won't it be great?" Skye asked, her face stuck in a frozen smile.

No doubt about it, Grace thought. Trust-fund baby Skylar Davis was broke.

Before Madison could respond, there was a knock on the door. Grace went to answer it. "Uh, hi, what are you all doing here?" she asked, as Holly, Hailey, Brandi, Nell, Mrs. Tate, and Mrs. Wright trooped into the apartment.

"We thought you could use some cheering up," Holly said with a sympathetic smile.

Brandi held up a box filled with mix and liquor. "To help drown your sorrows. Sawyer created a new drink, Christmas in July. We're going to try it out."

"Ignore them," Nell said. "We're here to help figure out who set fire to the bakery and how to catch them. I'm real good at solving mysteries, you know."

Mrs. Tate nodded enthusiastically. "She is. She always figures out who the murderer is before the cops do on *Law & Order*."

"Yeah, it's damn annoying," Mrs. Wright muttered as she trailed behind the other women into the living room.

Grace stared after them, tears welling in her eyes, and closed the door. This was why she loved Christmas. From the first day she'd moved to the small town, the women had made her feel like part of an extended family. They were always there for her. They had her back. She wished she could find a way to make Jack see that.

"Okay," Madison said, holding up her cell phone as Grace entered the living room. "One thing taken care of. I talked to John Ryan. They had a cancellation on *Good Afternoon Denver*. They're fitting you in the day after tomorrow. He felt responsible for how the press conference went and wants to help turn this around for you. He wondered if Jack would be joining you, but I told him he was busy." At Grace's raised brow, she said, "We need the focus to be on you and your sugar plum cakes, not your husband the hero."

Grace supposed she was right, but didn't get a chance to question Madison further because Nell was already off and running.

"Now," Nell said, sitting on the couch with a pad of paper and a pen in hand, "let's figure out who set fire to the bakery."

"I'll make the drinks," Brandi said and headed for the kitchen.

An hour later, they had a list of suspects. Grace didn't know how half of them ended up on there, but she was afraid to argue with Nell. "Well," Nell said, clicking her pen, "that Maria gal, Jack, and Stu are our primary targets."

"Nell, you're making me nervous," Madison drawled. "What do you mean, our primary targets?"

"You're married to an officer of the law. You should know what that means."

"That's why I'm nervous. And I know you, which makes me more nervous."

"We're going to do a little digging, nothing illegal."

The way the three older women were carrying on, Grace didn't blame Madison for being nervous. So was Grace. Then again, maybe the drinks were making the older women a little loopy.

"I think we can eliminate Jack from the suspect list, Nell," Grace said.

"You're the one who put him on there."

She'd forgotten about that. A sure sign that Grace was a little loopy, too. But no matter what she'd said last night, she knew Jack had nothing to do with the fire. Her accusation had been made in the heat of the moment. Her anger and fear had gotten the better of her. Today it had been three drinks on an empty stomach.

"So did we," Mrs. Wright said, nodding at Mrs. Tate. "He fits the profile. Remember, when he was twelve, he nearly burnt down the church hall."

"And he did set the garbage can on fire in the boys' changing room when he was fifteen," Hailey added.

"Not on purpose, Hailey. He was smoking, and the janitor walked in. He'd already been suspended twice that year. He didn't want to get kicked out, remember?" Holly said.

"More like he didn't want his grandmother to tan his behind," Nell said.

Poor Jack, Grace thought, feeling the need to come to his defense. "I'm sure all of us have done things when we were young that we're not proud of." She certainly had. "But you guys know the man he's become. And he'd never do anything that would put little Jack and me at risk."

Several of the women agreed with her, and Nell crossed Jack's name from the list. Grace didn't think Stu would put little Jack in danger, either. His MO was more to beat up things than set fire to them, but she was vetoed. He remained at the top of the suspect list along with Maria. Nell expected a surveillance report from all of them in three days' time. She followed up her directive with detailed instructions on interrogation and investigative techniques. "All right, meeting's adjourned," Nell announced at the end of her display of self-defense moves. In case, as she put it, "the unsub had to be taken down."

"Okay, y'all, I think a cup of tea is in order before you leave," Madison said, then whispered to Grace, "Hopefully clearer minds prevail or we could have a real problem on our hands. Gage is going to kill me if he gets wind of this."

Jack wouldn't be too happy, either.

Skye, along with a not-so-sober Holly, headed to the kitchen.

Thirty minutes later, Grace ushered the women from the apartment. "Remember, Grace, keep your friends close, and your enemies closer." Nell did a two-finger point to her eyes, then to Grace. "Don't let that Maria gal out of your sight."

"I won't," Grace promised as she closed the door. Suddenly exhausted, she leaned against it. What she needed was a nap. She walked into the living room and lay down on the couch. She closed her eyes, waiting for the room to stop spinning. Once it did, sleep dragged her under, and she got lost in a dream.

And it was a very nice dream, until she heard a deep voice say, "Jesus, Grace, you left the stove on again."

Chapter Nineteen

If you ask me, this is a colossal waste of time." Jack gave his head a frustrated shake when the wind whistled through the cracked windows. "They should just tear the place down."

An ungodly moan greeted his statement. Sawyer chuckled. "I don't think the house agrees with you, and neither would your wife."

"Maybe she just likes the name of the street and pink Victorians. She hasn't mentioned anything about the house to me." He hoped she wouldn't. Because the more Jack thought about it, the more convinced he became that buying the house was a bad idea. And not just because the Victorian sounded like it was going to fall down around them; he didn't like the idea of being locked in to Christmas.

"Why don't you ask her?"

"On the off chance she does, I don't want to get her hopes up."

"In case you can't commit to staying in Christmas?" Sawyer asked as they headed through the freshly painted grand foyer.

Yeah. "No, in case the house goes for more than we can afford." *Or more than I'm willing to pay.*

Sawyer nodded as he opened the dark-paneled door with its tempered glass inserts. "You might be right. When the bank foreclosed on the place, Madison bought it for a song with town funds. She figures once the renovations are done, she can make a tidy profit. And she's not the type of woman who'd settle for anything less. She's been advertising the hell out of the auction."

Knowing Gage's wife as he'd come to, if Jack actually wanted the house, he'd be concerned. "She'll make a profit. She's got free labor."

While he waited for Sawyer to lock the door behind them, water poured through the cracked boards onto their heads. Drenched, Jack scowled up at the porch ceiling. "I'm really starting to hate this place," he muttered as he headed down the steps. He tripped on a loose board and grabbed the banister. The rotted wood broke off in his hand.

"I don't think the house likes you much, either." Sawyer laughed as they started down the stone path on the way to their vehicles. "But, hey, look at the bright side, you get to spend time with me." He clapped Jack on the back. "You coming to the bar for a beer?"

"I'll take a rain check. I want to spend some time with little Jack before he goes to bed, and Maria's coming over later to work on the book."

"I'm surprised Grace agreed to have her work at the apartment."

"She's the one who suggested it." Although she looked like she was sucking on a lemon when she did.

"That's a pretty dramatic turnaround, don't you think? I wonder..."

"Wonder what?"

"If Grace's about-face is connected to how Brandi acted with Maria last night in the bar. She was pretty chummy with her. Which is strange given how protective Brandi is of Grace. Then, and this is where it gets weird, Maria went to the ladies' room, and Brandi took her empty glass, wrapped it in a napkin, and passed it off to Mrs. Tate. Nell happen to be at that little get-together at your place yesterday?"

"I think so. My wife wasn't exactly forthcoming when I asked her about it."

"Before or after you gave her hell about leaving the stove on?"

He'd come home with little Jack, pizza, and flowers to find his wife passed out on the couch and the stove on. Grace had woken up long enough to place the blame for the stove on Skye and Holly. It was when he tucked her into bed that she'd suggested he work with Maria at their place before falling back to sleep. After what Sawyer had just told him, the invitation now made sense.

"Both—she was pretty much comatose. What was in that drink Brandi made them?"

"Kahlua and vodka. I think Brandi might've gone a little heavy on the vodka. They polished off a twenty-sixer."

"Jesus. No wonder Grace was still asleep when I left this morning." A circumstance that played out in Jack's favor. He'd been able to stay the night, sleep with his wife in his arms, and have some one-on-one time with his son. Tonight, he planned to talk to Grace about moving back in.

"She had a rough day. She was probably exhausted. Tough break about the Pines."

"Yeah. Might be for the best, though."

Sawyer grinned. "Give it up, buddy. You don't have a chance in hell of changing her mind about the bakery. What you should be focusing on is pulling the plug on whatever plan Nell put in motion."

Jack ignored the first part of his comment, and said, "Why? It's not as if Maria has anything to hide. Besides, how much trouble can a seventysomething-year-old woman cause?"

Sawyer laughed all the way to his truck.

*   *   *

Jack's cell rang as he started up the stairs. "Hey, I'm on my way up."

"Maria's here," Grace's whispered over the line, then the apartment door opened.

"Sorry, I thought she was coming around eight," he said as he joined his wife on the landing. Taking in the pink jogging suit that hugged Grace in all the right places, he decided he'd much rather be working on getting his wife out of her clothes than working on the book with Maria.

Grace leaned heavily against the closed door. "It would've been nice to have a heads-up. I didn't get a chance to clean the apartment."

"Is there a pillow out of place, a smudge on the coffee table?" he teased, tugging on her ponytail.

Unamused, she pressed her lips together. He lowered his

head and gave her a long, lingering kiss. It took a couple of seconds for him to kiss her tension away, then she leaned into him, molding that sweet body to his. As he stroked the strip of warm, bare skin between her midriff-baring top and her jogging pants with his fingers, she shivered and deepened the kiss on a breathy moan. Reluctantly, Jack eased away from her. "I'm going to get you wet."

"I'm already wet," she murmured.

"Sorry about…Jesus, Grace," he said when he realized she wasn't talking about her clothes. He lowered his forehead to hers. "You're killing me, princess. But I promise, as soon as Maria leaves, I'll take care of that for you."

"If the pile of papers she set out on the table are any indication, you'll be working all night."

"Trust me, she's not going to be here for more than a couple of hours." Not if Jack could help it. With Grace's words playing over in his head, he probably wouldn't be much use to Maria anyway.

* * *

Jack gritted his teeth as Grace banged another pot in the kitchen. She'd been going at it for the last twenty minutes. "Excuse me for a sec," he said, getting up from the couch. "You want something to drink: coffee, tea, pop?"

"Wine?" Maria asked, looking up from the computer screen. "All right," she responded to his pointed look. "Tea, then."

On her hands and knees, Grace rooted around in the kitchen cupboard. He crouched beside her, waiting for her to pull her head out. When she did, she dragged out another pot and thumped it on the floor beside the others. Her gaze collided with his, and she gave a startled yelp.

"You got something you want to get off your chest, princess?" He kept his voice low to avoid Maria overhearing him.

"No, why?" She reached for the damp cloth hanging on the edge of the sink and went to scrub the cupboard's shelf.

He closed his hand over hers. "Because you're making enough noise to wake the dead, not to mention little Jack, and we're having a hard time hearing ourselves think in there. You were the one who suggested we work here, remember?"

Admittedly, he wasn't only frustrated with her banging the pots and pans. He hadn't been happy to discover she'd put his son to bed before he'd had a chance to see him. She'd made it clear she wouldn't change little Jack's routine, even for him. If Maria hadn't been in the living room, avidly hanging on every word, he would've had more to say about that.

"I know I did, but I didn't think I'd have to watch her practically crawl onto your lap and touch you every five seconds."

"You can't be serious." The look she skewered him with said she was. He gave a disbelieving shake of his head and stood up. Grumbling under her breath, she took out her temper on the cupboard, scrubbing viciously.

Jack stepped over her and the pots to grab the kettle off the stove.

"If she takes off any more of her clothes, she'll be naked. Give her a cold drink instead of tea and open the window," Grace muttered.

He turned off the tap, slammed the kettle onto a burner, and with an impatient flick of his wrist, turned it on. Grace's gaze jerked to his and widened when he fit his hands under her arms and lifted her off the floor. "What..."

Taking her by the hand, he hauled her into the hall and backed her against the wall, then proceeded to kiss her senseless. Since it'd worked earlier, he hoped it would work again, because she was pissing him off. When Grace wrapped herself around him, making those sexy little noises in the back of her throat, the sound of the kettle's whistle was the only thing that stopped him from taking her right there, right then. Slowly he pulled away, more frustrated than before he'd put his brilliant plan into action. Grace sagged against the wall with a dazed expression on her face. Jack planted his palms on either side of her head and brought his mouth to her ear. "As soon as Maria's out of here, I'm in you."

She blinked, then opened her mouth. Whatever she planned to say was interrupted by a loud knocking on the front door.

He gave her a fast, hard kiss. "You better get that." He dropped his gaze to the front of his jeans when she started to protest, silently pointing out the obvious.

"Okay." She nodded, a dimpled smile curving her lips as she turned to walk away.

Satisfied that he'd at least put his wife in a better mood, he walked into the kitchen. As he removed the whistling kettle from the burner, he sensed Maria's intent gaze upon him. Unlike his wife, she wasn't in a good mood. Self-consciously, he angled his body toward the stove. A couple of seconds later, he heard Grace introduce Skylar Davis to Maria.

His wife came into the kitchen while the two women

talked in the living room. "I'll get that," Grace said, taking the kettle from him.

He lifted his chin to the two women. "They know each other?"

"No, Maria recognized Skye. Her father was the governor of Texas. Maria interviewed him several years ago." As she poured the hot water in the teapot, Grace glanced at him from under her lashes. "Maybe Maria and Skye would like to talk for a bit. You haven't eaten. I'll fix up a tray, and we'll join you."

Remembering his conversation with Sawyer, Jack held back a grin. "Sure, that'd be great."

Twenty minutes later, Jack wished he'd shot down Grace's suggestion. And from the tight expression on his wife's face, she did, too. If the two women had hoped to discover something to use against Maria, they'd be disappointed. Maria had turned the tables on them. Jack was about to suggest they get back to work when Maria said, "Sorry, Grace, you must be bored to tears."

"Not at all," his wife responded. "It's incredible how much the three of you have in common, especially you and Jack."

He grimaced at Grace's snotty tone. He understood how she might feel as though Maria was trying to one-up her, but he didn't think it was intentional. The problem was that he and Maria did have a lot in common, at least when it came to their interest in extreme sports and travel. And, admittedly, they'd spent a lot of time together.

"Yes, we do, don't we, Jack?" Maria smiled, smoothing her palm along his thigh.

He didn't have to look at Grace to know how she'd react to Maria touching him. She wouldn't understand that Maria meant nothing by it. She was a touchy-feely kind of person and not only with him. "Um-hmm," he said, shifting away from her. Plucking another cupcake from the tray, he smiled at his wife. "These are amazing, princess."

She held his gaze. "Thanks."

So much for getting lucky tonight, he thought as he bit into the moist chocolate cupcake with the caramel center.

"They look so good, I wish I could have one. Sadly, I have to watch what I eat. Unlike you," Maria said with a laugh, looking at Skye, who was on her third. "And you, Grace—I don't know how you stay so *skinny* working in a bakery."

Okay, that was a backhanded compliment if he'd ever heard one. He opened his mouth to say something, but Skye intervened. "Don't kid yourself. A body as fantastic as Grace's doesn't come without work. She runs every morning before she opens the bakery. She swims and bikes, too."

With each activity Skye said she participated in, Grace's eyes widened farther. Jack grinned into the cupcake. His wife didn't run, she was afraid of the water, and if the sweat pouring off her the other day was anything to go by, she didn't bike much, either. But Skye had succeeded in putting Maria in her place, which was all Jack cared about.

"Really? I didn't know you were such an athlete, Grace. I guess I'll have competition in the triathlon after all," Maria said with a tight smile.

Jack choked on his cupcake.

"Triathlon?" Grace croaked.

"Yes, the one on July Fourth. Surely you've heard

about it. I signed up yesterday. The proceeds go to The Home Front Cares. I don't recall seeing your name on the list, Grace."

"No, I..."

"She was waiting for me to sign up..We're going to do that first thing tomorrow morning, aren't we, Grace?" Skye said.

Grace gave the other woman a deer-caught-in-the-headlights look. "We are?"

"You both should know, I plan on winning that race. It'd be the perfect photo to end the book with." She shifted to face him. "Jack, you should sign up. We'll cross the finish line together."

"I, ah..."

"Come on, you have to do this. It's a great cause."

"We'll see." He wiped his mouth with a napkin. "We probably should be getting back to work."

"We should, too. Grace and I are working on a book, you know."

Maria arched a brow. "Is that right? What's it about?"

"Me," Skye said. "I mean, it's about the Sugar Plum Cake Fairy. Grace is doing the illustrations, and my best friend Vivi's writing the story. But we're going to have to do some serious edits. That girl sucks at writing happily-ever-afters."

"I didn't know you're an artist, Grace," Maria said in a skeptical tone of voice.

"I'm not an artist. I..."

"Are you kidding me?" Skye got up from the floor and headed for the bookcase.

"No, Skye, don't..." Grace said, half rising from the chair.

The woman ignored her and retrieved a sketch pad from the shelf, holding it out of Grace's reach. "Don't be so modest," Skye scolded her, flipping it open. "Now do you believe me?" she asked Maria.

Jack lifted his stunned gaze from the sketch of him holding his laughing son. If he'd ever doubted Grace loved him, all he'd have to do is look at that image. Her love for him and his son imbued every line of the drawing.

"Do you like it?" she asked, fiddling with the zipper on her top.

"No. I love it. It's incredible."

She gave him a shy smile.

Maria's narrowed gaze moved from him to Grace before she tilted her head, reaching out to trace the sketch of his back with her fingers. "It's fantastic. You captured him exactly, right down to that small scar at the base of his spine."

Maria's eyes widened at the are-you-fucking-kidding-me look he shot her. "I'm sorry, I-I didn't mean to say that."

He stood up. "You know what, I think we should call it a night."

"No, please let me explain." She reached for his hand. "Grace, I know how that sounded, but I meant it as a compliment. Truly, I did."

"Thank you," Grace said in an excruciatingly polite tone of voice, her whitened fingers gripping the arms of the chair.

Skye's gaze rocketed between the three of them, and she started babbling about the book and the Sugar Plum Cake Fairy, showing Grace's sketch to Maria's over-the-top praise. Skye skipped a couple pages, then held up another sketch. "Grace, maybe you should give Jack this one so they get the house exactly right."

He was screwed. Because as much as he could tell she loved him from her sketch, it was obvious she felt the same about the damn house on Sugar Plum Lane.

Chapter Twenty

You sure you don't mind dropping me off?" Skye asked as Grace drove Jack's truck along I-70.

"Of course not. It's the least I can do," Grace said, casting a grateful glance at the butterscotch blonde wearing white capri pants and a white T-shirt. "I really appreciated you coming along for moral support."

"Like you needed it. You were fan-freaking-tastic. And bringing a sugar plum cake was a stroke of genius. Did you see John's face when he opened the sugar plum?" Skye asked, referring to John Ryan, who'd done the interview with Grace on *Good Afternoon Denver.*

Grace smiled. "It was the perfect wish, wasn't it? I wouldn't have known he'd just gotten engaged if it weren't for Madison."

Skye was right: bringing the cake had been an inspired idea. Jack would probably disagree. He hadn't been pleased when Grace started baking as soon as Skye and

Maria left last night. But after enduring three hours in the company of Maria the Magnificent, Grace had needed to relieve her stress and, she supposed, to boast her own self-esteem by doing something *she* was good at. After listening to how much Jack and Maria had in common, she couldn't shake the feeling that the other woman was his perfect match. It didn't help that Grace and Jack weren't in the best of places right now. Every time they took a step forward, something knocked them two steps back. Last night had been no exception. Frustrated with Grace's inability to let Maria's comments go, Jack had left for Jill's.

Skye made a face. "I think Nell's rubbing off on Madison. And speaking of Nell, we better complete our surveillance report on Maria. It's due tomorrow."

"We don't have much to report." Grace glanced at the other woman. "Did you get the feeling Maria knew what we were up to last night?"

"Yeah. I think Jack did, too. I saw him trying not to laugh a couple of times." Skye slipped off her sandals and put her feet on the dashboard. "And I have to tell you, your husband's smokin' hot on a bad day, but when he smiles, he's off the charts." She fanned herself.

"I get that a lot," Grace said, thinking of Wanda, and waited for Skye to continue in the same vein.

"I bet you do. And I'm sure you had your reasons, but honestly, I don't think I could've kicked him out. It's like cutting off your nose to spite your face. I'm just glad you guys worked it out, and he's back home now."

"Um, he's not," she admitted, focusing on the road as it wound its way through the valley, the snowcapped Rocky Mountains looming in the distance.

"But you told John...Okay, gotcha. Smart move. Probably wouldn't have gone over well with the viewers if you'd told the truth."

Grace's fingers tightened convulsively around the steering wheel as she thought about how Jack would react to her lie. She'd wanted to take the words back as soon as they'd popped out of her mouth. But the interview had been going so well up until then that she couldn't do it. She was desperate to turn the publicity nightmare around, and it felt like she had.

"Don't stress about it. I'm sure Jack will understand."

Grace made a noncommittal sound in her throat. She knew better. And when her cell rang, she mentally prepared herself to deal with her ticked-off husband. Skye picked up Grace's cell phone from where it lay on the console between them. "It's your mom. I'll put her on speakerphone," Skye said at the same time Grace said, "Don't pick...Hello, Mother." She'd rather talk to a ticked-off Jack than Helena any day.

"Sorry," Skye whispered.

Grace forced a smile and mouthed, *It's okay*.

"Grace Garrison Flaherty, I have never been more humiliated in my life. I had to hear from Major Talley's wife about that...that press conference. How could you do that to your father and me? And Jackson! I can't imagine how humiliated he was. For a hero to be treated like that, and by a general's daughter..."

Out of the corner of her eye, she saw Skye staring, openmouthed, at the phone. Her face awash with heat, Grace said, "I was as unhappy about what happened as you are, Mother. But Jack understands why—"

Helena cut her off with a haughty sniff. "I highly

doubt it. Your disgraceful behavior has brought shame to both the Garrison and Flaherty names. I expect you to—"

Hands cupped to her mouth, Skye made loud whooshing and crackling sounds, then picked up the phone and pressed End.

Stunned, Grace looked from the phone to Skye. Most of her mother's calls ended with Grace wishing she'd hung up on her, but she'd never had the nerve.

Skye shrugged. "I'm sorry, but no one deserves to be spoken to like that. I don't care if she is your mother. She didn't even ask about the fire."

"I'm used to it. And I doubt my dad told her." Grace had talked to her father yesterday morning. With the possibility the fire had been her fault, he wouldn't breathe a word to Helena. He'd wanted to come to Christmas, but afraid her mother would join him, Grace had convinced him not to.

"You know, you should come zip-lining with me. It's a great way to relieve stress. And, ah"—she glanced at the top of Grace's head—"you really need to relieve yours before it makes you sick."

"I'm not very adventurous, so zipping across a cable a hundred feet above a gorge isn't my idea of stress relief. If anything, I'd have a heart attack. And why do you keep looking at me like that?" Grace asked, touching the top of her head.

"You have a black cloud hanging over you . . . literally."

"Over my head?"

Skye nodded. "I know you've been dealing with a lot lately, but for an aura to be as black as yours, it's more than that. Something happened to you in the past, and whatever it was, you're hanging on to a lot of guilt and grief. You gotta let it go." She tilted her head and grinned. "And I know exactly how to do it."

"How?" Grace asked, unable to keep the hope from her voice. Because Skye was right; that particular cloud had been hanging over her since she was twelve.

"Primal therapy," Skye said, opening her window and directing Grace to do the same. "It'd be better if we had a convertible. We could have a Thelma-and-Louise moment. But this'll work."

"Didn't they die in the movie?"

"Oh, right, but I love that scene with them driving, wind blowing in their hair, female bonding and all that." She waved her fingers at Grace's open window. "Stick your head out and scream all the pain you've repressed to the universe, sweetie."

"I don't think I can."

"Sure you can." Skye stuck her head out the passenger-side window, her long, curly hair flapping in the wind as she screamed her lungs out. Pulling her head back in, she said, "Don't think, just do it."

Taking a deep breath, Grace did as Skye instructed. The wind swallowed her first attempt, a pitifully weak warble. And then, with Skye's encouragement, Grace released a scream from deep inside her, a noise so loud and pain-filled it was embarrassing. But it was also one of the most incredibly freeing moments she'd ever experienced. And once she started, Grace couldn't stop.

Until she heard the siren.

She glanced in her rearview mirror and groaned at the sight of the dark-haired woman behind the patrol car's wheel. Grace pulled the truck to the side of the road and braced herself. She hadn't seen Jill since the morning of the press conference.

"Well, that sucks. You were doing so good."

Grace didn't have a chance to respond because her sister-in-law stared at her through the open window with a look Grace was becoming familiar with. She'd seen the same have-you-lost-your-fricking-mind expression in her husband's eyes a lot lately.

"It's all right, Grace. Everything's going to be okay. I'm just going to help you out of the van," her sister-in-law said in a soft, concerned voice as she opened the driver-side door.

Something terrible must have happened. It was the only explanation for Jill's uncharacteristic behavior. Jill was being sweet, and she was never sweet. "What's wrong? Did something happen to little Jack...to Jack?"

"No, they're good. Everything's good." Grace tugged down the hem of her pink eyelet sundress as Jill gently helped her from the van. As soon as Grace's feet touched the pavement, Jill released a choked sob and pulled Grace into her arms. "I'm so sorry. I didn't mean for any of this to happen. I love you. You're going to be okay. We're going to get you help."

From behind Grace came a snort and a gasping sound. She looked over her shoulder to see Skye, a hand pressed to her mouth, an arm around her waist, trying to contain her laughter.

Realization dawned at Skye's reaction. Jill actually thought Grace had lost it. She patted her sister-in-law's back. "I'm okay, Jill. Honest. And I love you, too. Even though you have to admit you've been a... Well, you know."

Jill drew back, looking from Grace to Skye, who'd

broken into loud guffaws of laughter. Jill scowled, her cheeks stained pink, and fisted her hands on her hips. "So if you're not having a breakdown, what in the hell were you doing?"

She's back, Grace thought with a sigh. "I—" she started to explain.

"You're drunk."

"Of course, I'm not drunk. I'd never drink and drive." At Jill's skeptical look, she said, "Okay, if you don't believe me, watch this." Grace proceeded to walk a straight line down the side of the road. She wobbled a little in the white high heels, but otherwise she thought she'd proven her point. And to ensure that she did, she stuck out her arms and balanced on one foot, and that's when she saw the black Harley coming toward them, its driver looking all big and badass.

While Grace looked like a flamingo.

She lowered her leg and arms and turned on her sister-in-law. "I don't believe you. You called Jack."

Jill threw up her hands. "What was I supposed to do? I thought you were having a nervous breakdown."

Jack pulled onto the opposite shoulder and turned off the engine. Kicking the stand into place, he held Grace's gaze as he took off his helmet and leather jacket. He didn't look happy. What he did look like was dangerously sexy and hot in a black T-shirt and jeans. He crossed the road, that intent blue gaze of his taking everything in. When he reached them, he gently grasped Grace's chin between his fingers and searched her eyes. "You okay?"

"Yes, Jill—"

"Sorry I called you, Jack, but she didn't look okay ten minutes ago," Jill muttered, her arms crossed. "She looked like she'd lost her fricking mind. She was hanging out the window, screaming her head off, and driving erratically."

"I wasn't driving erratically, was I?" she said to Skye, who'd climbed into the driver's seat.

Brows raised, Jack lowered his hand. "But you were screaming?"

"Well, yes, but I can explain. I—"

"This I gotta hear," Jill muttered.

"It's not Grace's fault," Skye said. "She's totally stressed-out, and I recommended she try primal therapy. And it was working."

"Primal therapy?" Jack and Jill said in unison, giving Skye an odd look.

Considering their reaction, Grace figured it was a good thing Skye hadn't mentioned the black cloud.

"Yes, it's a trauma-based psychotherapy. You release repressed pain by screaming it out."

Okay, Grace had to intervene before they wondered where her repressed pain came from. "Yes, and I found it a very helpful way to relieve my stress. And, as you both know, I've had a lot of stress to deal with lately. Like a huge amount."

A hint of amusement in his eyes, Jack opened his mouth to speak at the same time Jill said, "Yeah, you have. But don't worry, now that I'm back in town, my first priority is to find out who set fire to the bakery. I'll—"

Grace hadn't known Jill was out of town. She guessed, given their strained relationship, it shouldn't come as a surprise. Still, it made her a little sad. But Jill's belief that the fire was set on purpose... "You don't believe it was an accident, either?"

Jill gave her an as-if look. "I lived with you for over a year, remember? I don't care how upset or exhausted you were, you'd never leave the stove on or anything out of place."

"Aw, come on, Jill. They don't need any encouragement. They're already trying to pin the fire on Maria. I was at the diner today and Holly pulled a strand of Maria's hair. Last night at the Penalty Box, Brandi and Mrs. Tate stole the glass she'd been drinking from."

"Really?" Skye said. "Grace, we've got to up our game. They're making us look bad. We have to get some evidence—"

"No, what the both of you are going to do is shut this down right now before it gets out of hand. Grace, I mean it."

"But, Jack—"

"No buts."

"Jack's right," Jill said. "Leave the investigating to us. You're going after the wrong person, anyway. You should be looking at Stu."

"Real helpful, Jill." Jack interlaced his fingers with Grace's. "Come on."

"Where are we going?"

"To get rid of your stress. Maybe then you'll see how crazy this all is." He started leading her across the road.

She tugged her hand free. "I'm not acting crazy, and even if I were, I can't get on the bike with you." She gestured to her sundress and shoes.

"Yes, you can," Skye said, leaning over the seat. She reappeared with a white "Animals Have Feelings Too" T-shirt and a pair of denim Daisy Duke shorts in her hand. "And you can borrow my sandals."

"But those are your zip-lining clothes."

"It's too late to go now. And riding on the back of the motorcycle is perfect for primal therapy."

"Not exactly what I had in mind," Jack muttered. "Jill, do me a favor and pick up little Jack from the sitter."

"I canceled the sitter. Madison has him today."

"I'll pick him up there," Jill said cautiously, as if expecting Grace to refuse her offer.

"He'd love that," Grace said, accepting the clothes from Skye.

"Do me a favor, Jill. Pack up my stuff and bring it over to the apartment with you." Grace glanced over her shoulder as she climbed into the truck to change her clothes. Jack held her gaze. "I just found out that I've been invited back home. Nice interview, princess."

*   *   *

"I wouldn't have come if I'd known that was the stress relief you had in mind," Grace said, her voice hoarse from trying to talk to Jack over the roar of the engine and screaming at the top of her lungs. She swung her leg over the motorcycle to stand on the side of the old mine road.

Jack took off his helmet and grinned. "It's not." Lifting the bottom of his T-shirt, he checked out his washboard abs. "The way you were digging your nails in me, I'm surprised there's no marks." He dropped his T-shirt, reaching out to unsnap the strap under her chin. "You're a big baby. I wasn't even going that fast."

"You were so." Not really. An expert driver, he handled the motorcycle like he did everything else. It was the narrow, windy mountain roads and the other not-so-expert drivers that scared her. She brushed her fingers over his abs. "I'm sorry if I hurt you. I can kiss your boo-boos better if you want."

"Oh, I want." He gave her a slow, breath-stealing kiss before sliding his leather jacket down her arms. "Let's get up there before we miss the sunset." He took a blanket, flashlight, and to-go bag from his saddlebag. "Bring my jacket, you might want it later."

"How long are we going to be up here?"

"As long as it takes to get rid of your stress, princess." He winked and took her hand. "And since you seem to be really, really stressed, we could be here all night."

"Probably a better idea than taking those roads in the dark."

He chuckled. "I forgot what a wimp you are."

"I am not."

"Yeah, you are, but I like when you get all girly on me." He released her hand when they reached the rocky path through the Aspen grove. "Go ahead of me."

As she started up the steep incline, she asked, "Why do you like when I get girly on you?"

Several moments passed before Jack finally said, "Because it makes me feel like you need me. I like taking care of you. Lately, it's felt like you haven't needed me to."

As she reached the top of the boulder, she turned, about to tell him it wasn't true, but maybe it was. "I guess without you here, I got used to doing everything for myself. But it doesn't mean I don't need you."

He closed the distance between them, standing below her on the path. He reached up to stroke her cheek. "I probably shouldn't complain. I knew how strong you were when I married you. It's one of the reasons that I did. But it would be kind of nice, if every now and then, you let me take care of you."

"I promise, from now on..." Something slithered across her toes. "Jack," she shrieked, shaking her foot at the same time she flung herself at him.

He grunted and stumbled backward, grabbing hold of a branch to regain his balance. His arm tightened around her. "Princess, I really appreciate you trying to prove that you need me, but next time, a little warning would be nice."

"I wasn't faking, Jack. A snake...There was a snake." She shuddered, pointing to where she'd been standing.

"Really?" He looked to where she pointed and grinned. "It's a ground snake. They're harmless."

"It didn't feel harmless when it slid hissing across my toes." She shivered, unconsciously shaking her foot. "So gross."

Jack watched her with an amused glint in his eyes. "You want me to carry you or are you okay to walk?"

"I'll walk behind you."

"No, you take the lead, that way I can catch you if you slip on the rocks. Don't worry, I'll keep an eye out for snakes. Spiders, too." He turned her, giving her a light swat on the butt. "And the view's too good to pass up. You should keep those shorts."

"Ha. Next time it's long pants and tennies," she said as she scrabbled the rest of the way up the steep incline. Several feet ahead, a golden light shimmered through the trees, signaling that they'd reached their destination. Grace stopped and held out her hand. This was their special place, and she wanted them to see it together.

Jack didn't say anything, just took her hand. But from

the emotion in his eyes, she knew sharing this moment meant as much to him as it did to her. They climbed the last rock together. And stood hand in hand at the top of the Alpine meadow with the Indian paintbrush glowing red, and the white columbine glowing pink in the setting sun. As it had always done, the sheer majesty of the view stole her breath and her eyes filled. Far below them the last rays of the fading sun turned the lake to gold and cast the rolling hills and rock in shadows.

Jack let go of her hand and gathered her in his arms. "Have you been here since we came the last time?" he asked, his voice gruff.

She shook her head, her voice muffled against his chest. "No, I couldn't. I couldn't come here without you."

His chin resting on her head, he nodded. "I would've felt the same."

They stayed that way, wrapped in each other's arms, and watched as inch by inch the orange ball of flame descended behind the snowcapped mountain peaks. The sky above was bathed in a red-gold light.

Jack draped his jacket over her shoulders. "It'll cool down now," he said as he led her deeper into the meadow. He handed her the to-go bag and spread the blanket.

Grace sat beside him and pulled the containers from the bag.

Jack grimaced. "Probably cold and soggy now. Thought we'd be eating a lot earlier than this."

"They look okay," she said, handing him a chicken quesadilla. "You were bringing dinner for us?"

"Yeah," he said around a mouthful, then swallowed. "Figured we had some stuff to hash out after your interview."

"I'm sorry. I shouldn't have lied. But the interview was going so well, I didn't want to ruin it."

"It's not a lie now. I am moving back in." He raised a brow, a challenge in his eyes.

"I know."

"Don't sound so enthused," he said dryly.

"I didn't mean it the way it sounded. I'm glad you're moving back home. It didn't exactly turn out the way I hoped anyway. The dating thing, I mean. We're both so busy." She frowned at her half-eaten quesadilla. "At least I *was*."

Nudging her with his shoulder, he said, "You will be again. You rocked the interview."

"Thanks," she murmured, unsure how he felt about that.

He offered her some nachos. "No, thank you. Jack," she said at the same time as he said, "Grace." He smiled. "I'll go first since I have a pretty good idea what you're going to ask." He brushed his hands on his jeans, then looked at her. "Today was the first time I saw the infamous sugar plum cake. And the first time I listened to you, really listened to you, talk about the bakery. I get it now, Grace. You're not like Libby. You love what you do. You couldn't make a cake like that if you didn't. I'm not going to stand in the way of you doing something that makes you happy. We'll keep the bakery."

"Oh, Jack, I—"

"I'm not finished. The twenty-four-seven thing still stands. You gotta hire some help, princess. I don't want you overworked and stressed-out. You, me, and little Jack, we have to be able to do stuff like this." He gestured to the meadow.

"Yes, absolutely." She nodded, then, mentally crossing her fingers, asked, "Does that mean we're going to live—"

He cut her off with a kiss. "One thing at a time, baby. One thing at a time. Let's celebrate with dessert, and then I'm going to help you with that screaming therapy of yours."

The promise in his eyes sent a heated shiver up Grace's spine, ending any thought of pursuing her line of questioning. He was right. They had a lot to celebrate tonight. They were here, together, and only a few weeks ago she never would've believed that was possible. But with Jack, she realized, anything was possible.

He withdrew another container from the bag. "Hailey says you'll know what to do with this."

Grace opened the Styrofoam lid, a smile tipping up the corner of her lips at the sight of the plump strawberries and containers of whipped cream and chocolate sauce. She told Jack what Hailey had suggested *she'd* do with them at the last meeting.

"Great idea, but this has to go"—he tossed the container of cream back in the bag, then reached for the bottom of her T-shirt— "and so does this." He removed the top slowly, stroking her bared skin as he did. "And these," he said, nudging her onto her back. Head bent, he unzipped the denim shorts, his clever fingers making her squirm as he took his time stripping them off her. Tossing the shorts on the blanket, he lay down beside her and raised himself on his elbow. Dipping a strawberry in the chocolate sauce, he brought it to her lips.

Grace held his gaze as she licked off the chocolate before biting the strawberry in half. He made a tortured sound in his throat, his heavy-lidded gaze fixated on her mouth.

"Tease," he rasped. His slow, dangerous smile promised payback. She didn't have long to wait. Kissing the chocolate from her lips, he unhooked her bra. "You're not the only one in this family who's an artist, you know. I was real good at finger painting. And don't worry," he said, drawing his chocolate-coated finger between her breasts and down her quivering stomach, "I clean up my messes, too."

*   *   *

"You know," Jack said, as they packed up to leave beneath a full moon, stars twinkling like diamonds in the clear night sky, "if we weren't already married, I'd propose to you right now."

She briefly closed her eyes. He had no idea how much those words meant to her. Overcome with emotion, she wrapped her arms around his waist. "Even with all the craziness?"

"Oh yeah, even with the craziness, baby."

"I'd say yes a thousand times over, Jack."

He dipped his head and gave her a long, breath-stealing kiss before draping the blanket around her shoulders. "We better get going. Hop on," he said, crouching down.

"I don't think that's a good idea. I'll—"

"Get on, Grace." He handed her the flashlight. She decided not to argue. After three sessions of Jack's version of stress-relieving therapy, Grace's body was boneless. She wasn't sure she'd be able to walk. "Keep the light on the path," he said.

A quarter of the way down, something whooshed past Grace's head. She let out a girly scream, batting the flashlight at whatever had dive-bombed her. "Jesus, Grace, I can't see where I'm going."

"What was that? I didn't think birds came out at night," she said, searching the trees while aiming the light at the ground.

"Sure they do," he said, laughter in his voice.

"You are such a liar," she said, pulling the blanket over her head. "That was a bat, wasn't it?"

"All that work I did getting rid of your stress blown by one itty-bitty bat." He patted her leg. "Don't worry, princess, I'll take care of that when we get home."

Her cell phone pinged before she could respond. She stuck her fingers in the front pocket of her shorts. Unable to reach her phone because of her position, she shifted.

"Stop wiggling around, you're throwing me off-balance. You can answer it when we get to the road," he said, then his cell pinged.

"Maybe something happened to little Jack." Panicked, she raised herself up to dig deeper in her pocket.

"Grace, stay still. If it was something important, Jill would call, not text."

As soon as they reached the road, Grace scrambled off his back. She whipped her cell phone from her pocket and shone the light on the screen. Jack raised a brow, shook his head, and pulled out his own phone.

Grace read Madison's text and let out a whoop of joy. "We got it. We got the Pines contract. They saw *Good Afternoon Denver* and..." She trailed off at the stunned look on Jack's face. "What's wrong?"

"The fire investigator's report came in. It was arson."

Chapter Twenty-One

All eyes were upon Grace as she took a seat beside Skye in the conference room at the town hall. "Um"—she self-consciously touched her hair, wondering if Jack had messed her up when he'd sent her off to the meeting with a toe-curling kiss—"is something wrong?"

Nell, who sat beside Mrs. Wright and Mrs. Tate, waved a fistful of papers at her. "Investigation's at a standstill. We've got nothing. And now that the fire's been ruled arson, we need something fast or they'll send Jack up the river."

Grace's stomach did a slow, nausea-inducing roll. Only this morning, she'd had the exact same thought. She'd told herself she was overreacting. Knowing Jack would say the same thing, she hadn't mentioned her worries to him. But the thought had to have crossed his mind. And it would be her fault if they investigated him. In a fit of panic and temper, she'd leveled the accusation against him in front of Gage and the deputy fire chief. How could she have been so stupid? Like Nell and her friends had initially done, they'd use his youthful indiscretions against him.

At the sound of someone hurrying down the hall, Nell said, "As of now, Maddie's out of the loop. I don't trust her not to tell Gage. So zip it." She nodded toward the door. "Same goes for Jill. She might put the blame on you, Grace, to take the heat off her brother."

Grace had been about to say they should at least keep Jill in the loop, but couldn't help wondering if Nell had a point.

Madison rushed into the room. "Sorry I'm late. Hey," she said to Grace, taking a seat at the head of the table. "That's great you and Skye entered the triathlon. Not enough women have."

"Oh, right, slipped my mind." Skye gingerly passed Grace a sheet of paper, as if afraid she'd slap her hand. "Everyone sponsored you for the triathlon. All you have to do is complete the race, and you raise three thousand dollars for The Home Front Cares."

Grace gave a panicked shake of her head. "I didn't enter the race. I mean, that's very sweet of all of you to sponsor me, but I can't..."

"Sure you can," Nell said. "Skye already signed you up. Better get training. Course isn't an easy one and you don't want that Maria gal to beat you. Saw her out running the other morning, and she looked to be in pretty good shape."

Grace ignored Nell's comment about Maria and shot Skye an exasperated look. "You entered me in the race?"

"Yeah, both of us." She slid another piece of paper in front of Grace and fluttered her long lashes. "Sponsor me?"

"I'll sponsor you, but I can't enter the race. I'm not in good shape and"—she lowered her voice—"I can't swim."

"Holly, Hailey, and Sophia, you guys should sign up, too," Madison said as she sorted through her papers.

"What about me, Stella, and Evelyn? How come you're not telling us to enter? Do you think we're too old?"

"Uh, no, but don't you think..." Madison trailed off when the three older women put their heads together to talk among themselves.

"That's settled. We're signing up," Nell said after their brief powwow.

"Remind me to see if we can get an extra EMT in for the day," Madison murmured to Grace.

She held back a smile and nodded. If not for the swimming part of the race, now that Nell, Mrs. Tate, and Mrs. Wright were entering, Grace might have considered taking part. At least she wouldn't come in last. She felt bad that her inability to push past her fears would result in The Home Front Cares losing out on the funds. Although she probably could convince everyone to sponsor Jack instead. If he wasn't in jail by then. She squashed the thought. He was innocent. And if she couldn't prove it, surely Gage and Jill would.

Skye glanced at the top of her head and leaned closer. "You've gotta do it. The exercise will help get rid of your tension. You need to loosen up."

"You think I'm uptight?"

Skye's eyes danced with amusement. "Sweetie, you're beyond uptight."

Of course she was. She didn't need Skye to tell her that. Last night Jack had vanquished the majority of

Grace's worries, but her fear he might be charged with arson brought a new level of crazy to her life. And despite his reassurances, she couldn't help but think if she kept it up, she'd drive him crazy, too. Maria wasn't uptight. Possibly a pyromaniac, but she was also fun, adventurous, and exciting. And Maria was entering the race.

"Okay, I'll do it," Grace said in a competitive fit, instantly regretting doing so at the thought she'd have to get in the water.

"So will the three of us," Holly announced. "And we'll sign up Brandi and Autumn."

"Okay, ladies, now that that's settled, let's get on with tonight's agenda," Madison said.

"Hey, sorry," Jill said, hurrying into the room. "Ray just called to ask me to take his place." She cast Grace an apologetic smile.

Maria and Jack were working on the book again tonight. He'd invited Jill to join them. Most likely for Grace's benefit, even though he didn't say so. Despite Grace doing her best to keep the green-eyed monster at bay, every so often it reared its ugly head. Grace no longer voiced her concerns to Jack, but obviously, he knew she still had an issue with Maria.

So while Jill's smile was welcome, her news that Jack and Maria were without a chaperone wasn't. A toddler didn't count. Grace ignored the nervous flutter in her stomach. She trusted Jack.

Her cell pinged, and she surreptitiously checked her message as Madison called the meeting to order. Jack had sent her a photo of his masculine hand. He was wearing his wedding ring.

The image blurred, and she sniffed, wondering how

she'd gotten so lucky. It made her more determined than ever to be the woman he deserved.

"What's wrong?" Skye asked, tugging Grace's hand from under the table, smiling when she saw the picture. "Aw."

Of course Skye's reaction drew everyone's attention, and they wanted to see the reason for it. Before Grace could stop her, Skye stole her phone, and her cell made its way around the table.

"You're such a sap," Jill said, but like everyone else, she had a smile on her face.

* * *

By the time the meeting adjourned two hours later, Grace was anxious to get home. Despite her best intentions, she was once again battling her insecurities. It had started about an hour ago when talk turned to the triathlon, and Hailey and Nell debated the likelihood of any of the women beating Maria in the race, or at anything else.

As Grace rose from her chair to collect her belongings, Jill came over. "That's great that your dad was able to get permission for Jack to be presented with the medal on the Fourth," she said, handing Grace her notes.

"Thanks." She smiled, tucking the notepad into her purse. "You know my dad. He's good at pulling strings."

Jill shifted from one foot to the other, then cleared her throat. "I probably should've told you this yesterday, but, uh, I'm sorry for being such a bitch. I should've had your back when Maria came to town." She looked away, then returned her gaze to Grace. "I wasn't sure you loved him anymore. I should've known better."

"Yes, you should have. But honestly, your brother deserves a medal for putting up with me this last while."

"How so?"

"He's had to deal with my raging insecurity over Maria. I overreact to everything where she's involved." As she said the words, Grace wondered if her insecurities were behind her suspicions about the fire. But she couldn't get the look on Maria's face the night of the fire out of her mind.

"Don't beat yourself up. Maria…" She shrugged. "She's using Jack as a crutch. She needs help. And now that Jack's back home with you, where he belongs, maybe she'll realize it's time to move on and open up to Dr. Trainer."

Madison motioned for Jill. "I need to talk to you about extra EMTs for the triathlon."

Jill nodded, then grinned at Grace. "If you need any help with your training, let me know. I'll whip you…"

"Didn't know you were into the kink, Jill. That Christian Grey fella, he uses one, too," Nell said as she walked by.

Grace and Jill stared after the older woman. With a slight shake of her head as if to clear it, Jill finished what she'd been about to say. "…into shape in no time."

"Thanks, but no thanks. I don't know why I agreed to enter." Of course she did. It all went back to her issues with Maria. And after what Jill just said, Grace wondered how deeply affected Maria had been by her experiences in Afghanistan. And how far she would go to keep the man who'd saved her in her life.

"Don't chicken out now. The training would be a good way to help you alleviate the crazies, keep you calm until we can get Maria out of town."

Getting rid of both the crazies and Maria sounded like a good plan. "I'll think about it."

"I'll get you on a program starting tomorrow." Jill put an arm around her. "It'll be good to hang out again. I've missed you."

"I've missed you, too, but I can think of better ways to hang out together," Grace said. It was hard to sound grumpy about it when she'd gotten her best friend back.

Madison's gaze went from Jill to Grace, and she smiled. "Nice to see you two are friends again." She tugged a folder from her briefcase. "Before I forget, here's Vivi's revised manuscript."

Taking the folder and putting it in her purse, Grace asked Madison, "How is it?"

"Prince Charming's death wasn't quite as gruesome as in the last one, but he still meets an unhappy ending courtesy of the Sugar Plum Cake Fairy."

"I killed my Prince Charming?" Skye said.

"Umm, you know you're not really the Cake Fairy, don't you?" Madison asked, a hint of the South creeping into her voice.

"I sort of am."

"Right." Madison rubbed her brow. "And we need someone else to work on the costume. Mrs. O'Connor won't be back in time."

Madison rolled her eyes when Skye did a happy dance, then looked at Nell. "Do you think you could make the costume?"

"Oh no," Mrs. Tate said. "Nell's much too busy working on her book."

"Good Lord, is everyone writing a book?" Madison said, then her eyes widened. "Please tell me you're not writing a *Fifty Shades* for the geriatric population."

"FYI, girlie, we're not geriatrics, and…"

"No," Mrs. Wright interrupted. "She's writing a book about you and Gage. She's got a title and everything. It's called *The Trouble with Christmas*. Don't you just love it?"

"What?" Madison exploded.

Skye, struggling not to laugh, motioned to Grace. *Let's go*, she mouthed. They quickly said their good-byes and left.

"Do you think we should call Gage? Madison looked like she might have a coronary," Grace said as they exited the building.

Skye held up her phone. "Already texted him. I would've stuck around for the fun, but you looked like you were antsy to get out of there."

Grace sighed. "I didn't think it was obvious."

"Maria working with Jack on the book again?" Skye asked as they stepped into the warm night air.

"Yes, and I'm trying not to come off as the insanely jealous wife who runs home to check on them."

"So don't. It's the perfect opportunity to get the goods on her. We'll go to her room at the lodge and see if we can find anything incriminating."

"You mean like break into her room?"

"Sort of, I guess. It's not like it's a house or anything. Maids go in and out of hotel rooms all the time. If it makes you feel better, we'll tidy up while we're there."

"I don't know, Skye. If Jack found out, he'd kill me." And honestly, the idea of breaking the law terrified Grace. She was a good girl. Always had been. At times she wished she wasn't. The bad girls seemed to have all the fun. But this wasn't one of those times.

"No one's going to find out. And you heard Nell. We

have to find something pronto or they'll be coming after Jack."

Skye's remark reinforced Grace's own fears, and she said, "Okay, but we have to hurry."

"You have wheels?" When Grace said she didn't, Skye gave her a once-over, taking in her lavender ballet slippers, black capri pants, and purple sleeveless blouse. "Good a time as any to start your training, I guess. Come on." Skye waved her arm and took off down the sidewalk in her sandals and a tie-dyed pink tunic and Daisy Duke shorts.

When she finally caught up with Skye in the lodge's parking lot, Grace doubled over, hands on her thighs. "I think I'm going to pass out," she wheezed.

"Look on the bright side—if you train every day, you should be able to beat Mrs. Tate." Skye grinned, then her expression grew serious as she contemplated the rustic wooden motel. "Someone might recognize you, so hide behind that tree," Skye said, pointing to the twenty-foot blue spruce in the center court.

"What are you going to do?"

"Find out which room is Maria's."

"You can't just walk in and ask someone at the front desk. They'll—"

"I might be blonde, but I'm not stupid. Leave this to me," Skye said and darted across the parking lot. Grace bowed her head when Skye started peeking in windows. Skye was wrong. Grace was blonde, too, and this *was* really, really stupid. She was about to call out to Skye when the other woman knocked on a door. A big man in his undershirt and striped boxers answered with a bottle of Jack Daniel's in his hand. He gave Skye a lopsided grin, nodded, and pointed to a room down from his. Once he closed the door, Skye discreetly waved Grace over.

"You're the lookout," Skye said, pulling a pink Swiss army knife from the back pocket of her shorts. Grace slumped against the building, her knees weak with nerves. After working on the lock for several excruciatingly slow minutes, Skye said, "I can't do it." She rose from her crouched position and peeked in the window.

Relief swamped Grace. "We tried. We'll just—"

"No, come on. I've got an idea," she said, latching on to Grace's hand.

"Where are we going?"

"To the back of the building. There's a patio door," she said, running along the walkway, dragging Grace after her. "I'm sure I can get it open."

"Skye, I've got a bad feeling about this. I don't—"

"Jack in an orange jumpsuit. That's all I'm going to say."

"Okay, okay. Let's do this."

A spotlight over the inground pool illuminated the back of the lodge. Skye flattened herself against the building and gestured for Grace to do the same.

"This is the one," Skye whispered when they reached the only obviously empty room in the row. Putting the knife between her teeth, Skye tried the patio door. She gave Grace a triumphant thumbs-up when the door slid open. Grace didn't know whether she was happy or disappointed at their easy access. They crept into the darkened room. Grace knew it was the right one. She could smell Maria's vanilla perfume.

"You start going through her garbage and desk. I'll take the dresser and closet," Skye said, turning on a lamp.

Ten minutes later, Grace said, "I can't find anything other than papers and files related to her book. How about—" Her eyes widened at the sound of a key in the door. The lamp clicked off. "Skye," Grace called out in a panicked whisper. "Where are you? We have to get—" As her eyes adjusted to the dim light, she made out Skye flattened against the wall beside the door, a bottle raised over her head and a finger pressed to her lips.

The door opened. Three figures dressed from head to toe in black crept into the room. "Skye, no!" Grace shouted, but it was too late.

Chapter Twenty-Two

Her white jean–clad hip resting against the table, Maria surveyed the kitchen. "I can't believe your wife actually left us on our own and hasn't called to check on us."

"Why would she?" Jack asked as he poured her a coffee.

"Oh, come on, it's pretty obvious she doesn't trust you alone with me. My God, Jack, the woman is so desperate to get me out of town, she and her friends are trying to frame me for arson."

"She was upset the night of the fire, and her friends are protective of her. They won't be bothering you anymore." He thumbed his wedding band. "And if she didn't trust me, she'd be here now." Since Grace hadn't come home early, he figured the photo had done the trick, and he better get used to wearing the ring. Fine by him if it helped her feel more secure.

"Thanks," Maria said when he handed her the cup. The

smile she'd given him faltered, and her face fell. "You're wearing your wedding ring." Her dark eyes searched his. "Why?"

"Because I'm married," he said, pouring himself a cup of coffee.

"But you're separated. You don't even live together."

"I moved back in last night. And no matter how it might've looked, we were never separated."

She followed him into the living room. "Come on, Jack, open your eyes. I'm the reason she took you back. Even if she doesn't want you, she can't stand the thought of you with someone else."

"Look, I get that with what happened between us, this isn't easy for you," he said as he took a seat on the couch. "But I don't know how to make it any clearer. I love my wife, and she loves me. And I never doubted that for one second. Have we had some problems? Sure. But that's not surprising since I've been gone for almost two years."

"I don't know the man you used to be, but the man I know could never be happy with her." Her lip curled and she flung out her hand. "This isn't you, all perfect and...beige. How can you live like this? She's a Stepford wife. What are you going to do, Jack, stay in this shitty little town where you can't make a move without everyone talking about it? It was bad enough they were trying to frame me for the fire—now I hear they're looking at you."

He let her comments about Grace slide. It was useless to argue with the woman. As to suspicions being cast in his direction, he'd heard the same thing. Conversations ended abruptly when he walked into the diner or Penalty Box, but not soon enough that he didn't catch references to his misspent youth. But he wasn't about to share his frustration with Maria. "Being held prisoner for seventeen months kind of changes your perspective on things. You should know that as well as I do."

She ran the tip of her tongue over her teeth, then nodded. "Time will tell," she murmured, setting her cup of coffee on the table to pick up the hard copy of the manuscript.

Her reaction, or lack thereof, surprised him. Maria wasn't the type of woman who gave up easily.

Twenty minutes later, as they discussed the best way to lay out the last chapters, he realized she hadn't. She'd regrouped and come at the problem from another angle. Good strategy, if he didn't see through her.

She moved closer, her breasts pressed to his arm as she pointed to the end of the page. "I don't know if you want me to keep this part in. It might be hard for your wife to read."

"I have nothing to hide, but this"—he tapped the printed page with his finger—"doesn't add anything to the story."

"I disagree. All of our relationships, Josh, Quinn, and Holden's included, are what readers care about."

"All right. Whatever. Keep it in."

She turned to another page. "This would probably be more difficult for her to read."

He scanned the page, then lifted his eyes to hers. "You're not writing a romance. This is totally over-the-top, not to mention untrue."

"That's how I remember it."

"Bullshit." He tossed the chapter on the coffee table and stood up. "If you leave that in the book, I'm done." She'd included the night when they'd almost made love.

Only she'd written it as if they had, and she'd written it in graphic detail. She'd also had him telling her he loved her, which he hadn't, and them making plans for their future. Again, a blatant lie.

She held up her hands. "I'll take it out. But I'm not changing the book just so it's easier for your wife to read."

"Grace won't be reading the book."

"Wow, really? I knew she was insecure, but color me shocked."

He dragged his hand down his face. If she weren't paying him a shitload of money and he didn't need the cash to buy the house, he'd be done. From his son's bedroom came a muffled cry. "I'll be back in a minute."

"Take your time. I'll read over the next chapter." If the uneasy look in her eyes was anything to go by, she'd been putting her imagination to good use again.

Little Jack took a while to get settled. He wasn't impressed that it was his father, and not his mother, who'd come in to check on him. "Sorry, I..." His jaw dropped when he walked into the living room. "What the hell do you think you're doing?" he growled at a topless Maria bent over scrubbing the couch.

"I spilled my coffee, okay? What's your problem? It's not like you haven't seen me in less than this."

"Not once I knew I was married and not when my wife could come home at any minute. Get your top on." He snagged her T-shirt from the area rug and went to give it to her.

She straightened, dropped the coffee-stained cloth on the table, and moved into him, putting a hand on his arm. "Are you sure your reaction isn't because you remember what we had? I know how much you loved touching and kissing me, how much you loved my body." He removed her hand from his arm and stepped back. She ran a finger down his chest. "Funny how you professed to love my curves and you're married to a woman without any, how much you loved my passion, how uninhibited I was, yet you're married to..."

He clenched his jaw, fighting to keep his temper under control and shoved the T-shirt into her hands. "Get dressed and get out. We're done."

She shot him a frantic look. "No, you can't send me away, not because of this. I...I just thought if you remembered what we had..." Her voice trailed off as she took in his unyielding stance. "You never loved me, did you?"

The anger that had been building inside him deflated. He'd forgotten how vulnerable she was. Bowing his head, he dragged in a harsh breath before raising his gaze to hers and giving her the answer she didn't want to hear. "No." Her face crumpled, and he drew her into his arms, holding her for a minute before saying, "I'm sorry, Maria. You're a beautiful woman, and I was attracted to you, but no, I never loved you."

She took a step back. "I loved you," she said in a broken whisper.

"I'm sorry."

She swiped at her eyes, then jerkily pulled on her top. "I'll pay to have the couch cleaned. I didn't do it on purpose."

The apartment door opened. "Jack...what the hell is going on here?" his sister snapped upon entering the living room.

He moved in front of Maria. "I spilled coffee on Maria and the couch. We were cleaning it up."

"That's not how it looks to me," Jill retorted, leaning back to look down the hall. "Where's Grace?"

"She's not home from the meeting yet." Thank Christ.

Frowning, Jill said, "She left over forty-five minutes ago with Skye."

"I'll, um, just get going," Maria said, sidestepping Jack as she bent to gather the papers.

"They probably went out for coffee," he said, at the same time digging his cell from his jeans pocket. He found it hard to believe, ring or no ring, that Grace hadn't come home as soon as the meeting let out. "Did she—"

Jill held up a finger when her cell rang. "Hey, Ray." She listened to the deputy on the other end. Her eyes widened. Nodding, she bit her bottom lip. "Yeah, we're on our way."

Jack's fingers tightened on his phone. "What's going on?"

"Calm down, Grace is all right." Jill's nervous gaze darted from him to Maria. "I'm sure it's a misunderstanding. We'll straighten it out at the station."

"Are you telling me my wife's in jail?"

"Um, yeah, kind of. They're charging her with breaking and entering. But like I said, I'm sure there's been a mistake."

*   *   *

Grace wasn't all right. She'd lost her fucking mind.

Jack dragged his hand down his face, splaying his fingers over his mouth as he stared at the five women in the cell. Nell, Mrs. Tate, and Mrs. Wright, dressed in black pants and tops, camouflage stripes painted on their cheeks and black knit hats on their heads, sat together on the cot, talking on their cell phones. Skye sat cross-legged on the floor. She looked like she was meditating or something. And Grace, head bowed, fiddled with the buttons on her blouse.

"They broke into my room, Jill. My room," Maria ranted at Jack's sister, who tried to calm her down.

"Om," Skye chanted.

Gage came into the holding area with a what-the-hell look in his eyes. "Get off your damn phones," he barked at the older women.

"Hold on, there, sonny. Don't forget who you're talking to," Nell said. Then, to whomever she was on the phone with, "I've gotta go. I'll call you when I get out of the slammer."

"It'll be a good long while before that happens, lady. You broke into my room!"

Jack could hear Gage, who stood beside him, grind his teeth. "Ms. DeMarco, not another word or I'll have to ask you to leave. Now, before we go any further, do any of you require medical attention?"

Skye opened one eye, her "Om" rising a couple of decibels as Nell leaned forward to check out Mrs. Wright, who remained on the phone. "Skye there hit Stella over the head with a wine bottle, but Stella's got a hard noggin. She's not slurring. So she's good." Mrs. Wright nodded, then proceeded to tell whomever she spoke to a colorful version of the event.

"Don't think Grace needs a doctor, but she's got a shiner. Sorry about that, Grace," Nell said with a wince.

"It's okay, Nell," she mumbled.

Jack had hung back, afraid he'd lay into his wife if he didn't. But upon hearing she'd been hurt, he strode to the cell. "Grace, come here."

Her shoulders rose and fell on a sigh, then she did as
he asked. He put his hand through the bars and nudged
her chin with his knuckle. "Look at me." She did. He grimaced as he took in her bloodshot right eye and the angry
red and vibrant purple surrounding it. "That's gotta hurt,
princess. Can you see okay?"

She nodded. Jill elbowed him out of the way and
handed Grace a bag of ice, talking quietly to her as she
did. Before Jack could ask his wife what the hell she'd
been thinking, Gage said, "All right, which one of you
wants to tell me what you were doing in Ms. DeMarco's
room?"

"I'll tell you what they were doing. They're trying to
frame me for arson," Maria said, arms crossed, white
high-heeled sandal tapping on the floor.

Skye stopped Om-ing and said, "No, we weren't. Grace
and I dropped by to say hi. The patio door was open, so
we went in to wait for you. We thought Nell, Mrs. Wright,
and Mrs. Tate were burglars."

Grace's mouth dropped open. As though sensing Jack's
attention, she quickly closed it.

Maria snorted. "Seriously? Grace knew I was with
Jack."

"And maybe that's why she wanted to talk to you,"
Skye said, giving Maria a take-that look.

Gage rubbed the back of his neck. "Okay, Nell, what's
your story?"

"Me and the girls are offering our services to local
businesses. We're showing them how easy it is to break
into their establishments. We didn't know it was Maria's
room. And we didn't break in." She held up a hotel pass-
key. "The lodge has some serious security issues. We're

going to write up our report as soon as you let us out of here." Her cell rang, and she answered, despite her nephew telling her not to. "Hey, Ethan, thanks for getting back to me. Yep. Sure thing." She got up from the cot, gave her nephew a smug smile, and handed him the phone through the bars. "My lawyer would like a word."

Gage scowled at his aunt and took the phone. Maria came to stand beside Jack. "I won't press charges. But if I don't, I want something in return," she said for his ears alone.

He raised a brow. "Looks like they're going to get off anyway."

"I have a lot of connections, Jack. And I have no problem pulling in a few favors. All I want is for you to continue working on the book with me."

He knew better than to underestimate Maria, but he didn't take kindly to blackmail. He'd tell her to go to hell if it weren't for Grace. His wife didn't need to take another hit in the press. Besides, he needed the pay from the book now more than ever. The insurance company wouldn't settle their claim until Grace and Jack were eliminated as suspects. "All right, but the deal's off if there's a repeat performance of tonight."

"It won't happen again. I promise."

Maria talked to Gage after he got off the phone with Ethan, and the women were released. But not before Gage laid down the law. While Grace said good-bye to her partners in crime, Jill came to his side. "Don't be too hard on her. She did it to protect you," she said, confiding his wife's fears to him.

"Of all the..." he began, and his sister elbowed him none too gently in the gut. "All right already, I'll go easy on her."

"You'd better," his sister said in a warning tone. Grace approached with an apprehensive look in her eyes. "Come on, princess. It's past old man Murray's bedtime," he said, taking her by the hand. He'd called Murray to come stay with little Jack.

"I know you're upset with me, Jack. I'm kind of upset with me, too. But I had to do something," Grace said, holding the ice pack to her eye. She glanced over her shoulder when Maria gave a flirty laugh while speaking to Gage. Grace's good eye narrowed. "What is she up to now? Did you hear her, Jack? Did you hear Maria accuse us of trying to frame her?" Grace made a frustrated sound in her throat. "Now when we, um, they, find evidence against her, she'll say we planted it. Oh, she thinks she's pretty smart lying for us like she did, but I've got her number. When they find out she's behind the arson, she's going to blackmail us. But it won't work. I—"

"Grace, seriously, baby. Be quiet before I turn you over my knee and spank you."

"Jack!"

"Hey, don't knock it till you try it, Grace," Nell said as she headed for the door. "I just read a scene in my book where Christian Grey paddles that Anastasia gal's behind. She seemed to like it just fine, let me tell you."

Jack stared after her. "What the hell kind of book is she reading?"

Chapter Twenty-Three

Two weeks later, all was well in the Flaherty household. And Jack couldn't be happier. Surprisingly, it was thanks to the bakery that his wife no longer had time to run around with the geriatric crime solvers. But Jack had done some investigating of his own.

Whoever had set the bakery on fire had put his family in danger, and he wouldn't rest until they were behind bars. As soon as the official report came in, Jack went to Gage with his suspicions about Stu. The kid had gone to ground, but last night they caught a break.

They knew Stu's motivation; opportunity had been tougher to nail down. Whoever had set the fire had a key. And now they knew where he'd gotten it...Desiree. The two it seemed were more than friends. Gage had Desiree's home under surveillance. It was only a matter of time before they had Stu in custody. But for today, Jack was going to kick back and enjoy his first Father's Day with his son.

"You wanna watch *The Smurfs*?" he asked little Jack, who lay beside him in bed eating toast.

His son nodded, stuffed the rest of the bread in his mouth, and reached for the channel changer. "Me do," he said, crumbs spraying over Jack and the breakfast tray.

Jack brushed the soggy bits of bread from his bare chest, eyeing his wife as she came into the bedroom loaded down with presents. "You didn't have to do that, princess. The show you put on last night covered you for a couple years' worth." He grinned when her cheeks pinked. That was just one of the things he loved about Grace. No one other than him knew that his classy, demure wife was a wildly passionate, uninhibited woman in the bedroom.

"Come here." He patted the bed. "We're going to watch *The Smurfs*."

Grace set the wrapped boxes on the end of the bed. "You've already watched it twice. Why don't we watch *The Little Mermaid* instead?"

"We're guys. That's a chick flick," he said, holding back the covers for her.

She gave an amused shake of her head. His son glanced from his father to his mother, then patted his side of the bed. "No sleep Da. Sleep me."

"Oh, Jack," Grace said as she crawled in beside their son. "He called you Da."

He'd almost given up hope his son would call him anything other than Jack. "Yeah, best present ever," he said, his voice gruff as he struggled to keep his emotions in check. He ruffled his son's hair. "Thanks, buddy."

Her golden eyes misty, Grace leaned across their son to kiss him. "Happy Father's Day."

"Thanks." He went to meet her halfway, but little Jack shoved his head between them and wrapped a small arm around each of their necks. "Kiss me."

Laughing, they did as he asked. Then Grace said to their son, "Do you want to give Daddy his presents?"

For the next ten minutes, Jack opened his presents with his son's enthusiastic help. By the time they were finished, the bed was littered with wrapping paper, Jack wore his "#1 Dad" T-shirt, and his son had on Jack's "#1 Dad" ball cap. Jack ducked when his "#1 Dad" coffee mug whizzed past him, knocking the clock off the bedside table.

Jack chuckled. "Gotta admit he has a good arm."

Grace sighed. "Good thing it's plastic. Here, we'll put on your movie," she said, deftly removing the controller from little Jack's hand before it went the way of the mug.

Jack leaned over and picked the digital clock off the floor. "I didn't realize it was that late. We better get going or Gage and the girls will leave without us." Jack caught the apprehensive look in Grace's eyes. "He'll be fine. I won't let him out of my sight."

"But…Okay, just promise you'll use his harness and put him in a life jacket."

"Gonna be tough to fit his harness over the life jacket, don't you think?" And a little overkill, if you asked him. They wouldn't be on the water. They were fishing from the shore.

"Maybe he should stay home. He's going to miss his nap, and he'll be cranky when we go to Gage and Madison's—"

"I'm taking him fishing," Jack said, unable to keep the frustration from his voice as he climbed out of bed. He'd thought they'd moved past this. "Come on, buddy."

He held his arms out to his son. Jack's frustration faded when he saw the look of fear in his wife's eyes. This had nothing to do with her need for control. She was terrified.

"Hey." He crouched in front of her with little Jack in his arms. "You okay?"

"Fine." She took their son's hand in hers and kissed it. "I know I'm being overprotective. It's just..." She shook her head and gave him a weak smile. "Sorry."

"Come with us."

"No, this is your special day with him. Besides, I promised to bring a sugar plum cake to Madison's. Which reminds me, I have to get it out of the oven." She got off the bed and headed for the door.

"Princess, I'll put him in a life jacket, harness, and water wings."

She turned at the door and smiled. "Thank you."

Well, shit, he'd been joking about the water wings.

*   *   *

Finger poised over the Send button, Grace chided herself for being ridiculous and put the phone in her pocket instead of texting Jack. Like the last couple of weeks, this morning had been perfect, and she'd nearly let her irrational fears ruin it.

She picked up the cake and walked to the door, awkwardly balancing the board against the wall as she locked the apartment. Her decorating supplies had arrived last week, and she'd restocked the bakery's kitchen. All that was left was for the new stove to arrive and the painting to be done before she reopened for business. And hire staff, she reminded herself.

Unlike Jack, Grace had a hard time believing Desiree had quit because she felt guilty. Although, she had to admit, Desiree's remorse about the fire had seemed over-the-top. Maybe Grace didn't want to believe Stu had set the fire because it meant she'd been wrong about Maria. She still got embarrassed thinking of the night they'd broken into the woman's room. Grace had been so worried about Jack ending up in an orange jumpsuit, she'd nearly ended up in one herself.

Well, that was the last time she was going to let her bad girl out to play, Grace thought as she unlocked the bakery door. She looked around the room. It would be nice to see the tables filled with happy customers again. And if the number of people popping by to ask when she'd reopen were any indication, they would be.

Smiling at the thought, Grace pushed through the swinging doors and swallowed a panicked yelp. A man stood with his back to her, cell phone in hand. It was Stu, and he had a gun tucked in the waistband of his jeans. Grace took a careful step back, attempting to ease her way out of the kitchen without alerting him to her presence. He whipped around.

She smoothed the fear from her face and forced herself to walk to the prep table. "Hi, Stu," she said, setting the cake down.

"Grace, what are you doing here?" He slammed the cell phone on the counter, jerking his fingers through his unkempt hair.

"Decorating a cake. What are you doing here, Stu?" she asked, holding his gaze as she edged her fingers to her pocket. His eyes were bloodshot behind his wire-framed glasses, his movements jerky. She had to get him to calm down. Distract him so she could let Jack know he was here.

"It's your husband's first Father's Day with his boy, isn't it? You made him a cake. That's nice, real nice." He nodded, kept nodding.

"I'm sorry. I know how difficult this day must be for you."

"Don't...don't be nice to me. I did this." He gesticulated wildly to the kitchen. "You know I did. I thought you were like my wife, but you're not. I saw your interview. Wish I'd have known. Wouldn't have done this."

"So why are you here, Stu?" Her hand closed around her cell phone. She needed to keep him talking so he wouldn't notice her texting. "Did you come to apologize?"

He reached into his pocket, set down a key and a pack of matches. "I was going to frame that Maria broad. I've seen her with your husband. She's the same as that lowlife who went after my wife. Stealing what doesn't belong to them."

Grace ignored his accusations and pressed another key. So far she'd typed in *Stu*.

"But now it's too late," he continued, nodding at his phone. "Desiree says the cops are at her place. Won't have her lying for me."

As he continued to talk about Desiree, about how his wife would find out what he'd done and how he'd never see his kids again, Grace typed *is here. Has gun.*

"Turn yourself in, Stu," Grace said, raising her voice as she sent the text. "I'll make a statement on your behalf. We'll get you help. I'll talk to my dad and Ethan. They'll know what you need to do." She felt a glimmer of hope when he didn't shut her down and continued, "If you run, you'll never see your kids. This way, you might have a chance. There are organizations that can help you. And one day, it'll be up to your kids if they want to see you, not your wife. You can have a relationship with them, Stu, but only if you make the right choice now.

"I'm not making excuses for you. What you did was wrong, but what Lisa did to you was also wrong. Everyone deserves a second chance." She thought about how much Stu loved his kids and realized something. "You made sure little Jack woke up that night, didn't you?"

"Yeah, I threw stones at his window. I wouldn't have let him get hurt— you, either. I just wanted you to suffer like you'd made your husband suffer. Like I *thought* you'd made him suffer."

"Will you do it, Stu? Will you turn yourself in?"

Before he had a chance to answer, Jill pushed through the swinging doors. "Grace—" She broke off when she saw Stu and went for her gun at the same time he did.

"No." Grace put her hands up and, without thinking, stepped between them. "No, don't shoot. Put your guns down. No one has to get hurt."

"Grace, goddammit, get the hell out of my way."

"Put your gun down, Flaherty, or I'll shoot Grace," Stu threatened in a menacing tone of voice.

"Oh, stop it, Stu. You're not going to shoot me, and you darn well know it," Grace said. "You've got your safety on. So stop bluffing before you get yourself killed. Jill, put your gun down."

"Seriously, Grace, you're starting to tick me off. Get out of my way."

"No. He won't shoot me, but he might shoot you."

Stu and Jill started trading insults. "Stop right now,

the two of you," Grace yelled. "Now lower your damn guns."

They stopped fighting, shared a look, and slowly did as she asked. "All right, that's better. Now we're going to figure out the best way to do this." Recalling the text she sent Jack, Grace pulled out her phone. The last thing they needed was for him to arrive on the scene. She typed *All good. Happy fishing.*

Arms crossed over her chest, Jill said, "Why do you think I'd do anything to help him?"

"You remember how you felt when you thought I'd asked your brother for a divorce and kicked him out of the house?" Jill looked at the ceiling, then gave her an almost-imperceptible nod. "Well, just think how'd you feel if I did to him what Lisa did to Stu."

"All right, you made your point," Jill grumbled and took out her cell.

"Good, now let's see what Ethan thinks we should do," she said once Jill hung up from the station.

As Grace disconnected from Ethan, Jill prepared to take Stu in. "Thanks," Grace said, giving her a hug. She knew backing down hadn't been easy for her sister-in-law.

Eyes narrowed, Jill pointed a finger at Grace. "Don't think I won't tell my brother how you put yourself between two loaded guns."

"We can discuss what we'll tell your brother later. Right now I have to—"

"Explain to your husband what the hell you were thinking," Jack said from where he stood at the back door with Gage.

Chapter Twenty-Four

Sawyer turned off the sander as Jack joined him on the front porch. "Last day on the job, buddy. What's your wife up to today? Disarming bad guys? Breaking and entering?"

Sawyer had been ribbing Jack about Grace for the last ten days. He hadn't teased him immediately after because he had been as upset with Grace as Jack had been. "You need to get some new material," Jack said, tossing his helmet on the now-repaired swing. He grabbed a can of paint, frowning as he poured it into the tray. "I thought the house was supposed to be pink, not purple."

Sawyer snorted. "As if you want to live in a pink house."

"Uh, first off, we don't know that I'll get the house—bank only approved me for two hundred and fifty thousand." Oddly enough, over the last couple of days, Jack started to see the benefits of buying the old Victorian.

Not only would it make his wife happy, but they could use the extra space. He'd gone so far as mapping out the backyard—where the swing set would go and the barbeque and fire pit. And there was an old oak that would be perfect for a tree house. He hadn't had any of those things growing up and liked the idea of providing them for his son.

As word got out, thanks to Sawyer, that Jack was interested in buying the house on Sugar Plum Lane, they'd had an uptick in volunteers. Volunteers who knew what they were doing. "Second, purple's not much better than pink. You run the color change by the historical society?"

"Damn, forgot about that, but I'm sure they'll be fine with it. Like you say, purple's not much different from pink. Besides, the house is on Sugar *Plum* Lane. It should be purple."

"You're starting to worry me. Next you'll be telling me you watch HGTV."

"What's wrong with that?"

Before Jack could respond, Fred, Ted, and old man Murray walked up the stone walkway carrying paint guns. "Jack," Fred said, "think your wife might've gone a little crazy again."

He rested the roller on the edge of the paint tray. "What do you mean?"

"Saw her driving down I-70 and that Skye gal had her head stuck out the window screaming."

"Shut up," Jack said to Sawyer, who started to laugh.

"That gal's a bad influence, if you ask me. Gracie never got in trouble before she came to town. She's always been a good girl," Patrick Murray said. "You better sit your wife down and have a talk with her, Jackson."

"I don't know, Patrick. Jack always had a thing for bad girls. Maybe he's the problem and not Skye," Sawyer said.

"Thanks, dickhead," Jack muttered.

"Patrick's right, it's that Davis gal's fault. She's a bit of an odd one," Ted said.

Fred agreed with him, and the two men started listing everything that was odd about Skylar Davis. Her being a tree-hugging liberal topped their list.

"All right, quit your jawing. If we want to have this old lady painted in time for the auction tomorrow, we'd best be getting to it," Murray said, heading for the side of the house.

Murray'd started showing up the day after the fire. Knowing how the old man felt about Grace, Jack figured he'd heard he planned to buy the house for her and wanted to lend a hand. Patrick Murray was a master carpenter. The dark wood cabinets in the kitchen were incredible.

Jack pulled out his phone to call Grace at the same time a text came in. "You've got to be kidding me," he muttered upon reading his wife's text. No sense in calling her now.

Sawyer stopped sanding. "What's up?"

He turned his phone, showing his best friend the picture of Grace standing on a platform with a helmet on her head. "She's zip-lining."

"Huh, guess you cutting off little Jack's hair sent her to the dark side again."

"How was I supposed to know when I told him not to swallow his gum he'd stick it on his head? And I didn't cut his hair, Dan did." It'd happened two days ago, and Jack wasn't sure Grace had completely forgiven him. Good thing Dan had thought to send him home with a couple of little Jack's curly, long locks for his baby book or there'd be no doubt she wouldn't have. "Maybe the thing with Stu scared her more than she let on."

"Not from what I heard. Jill said it was like she'd channeled her father," Sawyer said.

His sister had told Jack and Gage the same thing. Gage had even suggested she'd make a great hostage negotiator.

"Do you think she has any idea you're going to bid on the house?"

"Surprisingly, since everyone in town seems to know I am, no." He'd even dropped subtle hints, feeling her out.

Five hours later, they'd finished painting the front of the house. Ted, Fred, and Murray had finished up the rest. Jack, along with the three older men, accepted a beer from Sawyer's cooler. Doors slammed as they toasted one another on a job well done. They turned to see Nell, Mrs. Tate, and Mrs. Wright getting out of the red pickup. "Get over here and give us a hand," Nell called, unloading plants from the flatbed.

The older men groused, and Sawyer grinned. "Looks like Grace is going to get her wildflower garden."

As Jack opened the gate on the freshly painted white picket fence, he looked back at the house. If he could give her her dream, maybe it would make up for all that she'd gone through without him.

Gage pulled up behind the red pickup. He got out of the SUV and looked up at the house. "You guys did a great job. Better keep your noses clean. Madison has her sights set on a Victorian on Taffy Lane." Gage's radio went off, his smile fading as he listened to whoever was on the other end. He glanced at Jack. "Yeah, thanks, Roy. I'll take care of it."

Gage rubbed the back of his neck and eyed Jack. "Roy just responded to a call at the lodge. People reported a woman screaming. It was Maria. He thinks she's been drinking and fell. She has a bruise on her cheek. He tried to take her to the hospital, but she refused. Wasn't much else he could do."

Jack frowned. He thought she'd left town. After she'd pulled a repeat performance of the night of the break and enter, Jack had told her he would no longer consult on the book. He'd done his best to avoid her since then. She didn't make it easy, turning up here, showing up there. Three days ago, frustrated when she'd once again filled his voice mail, he'd finally had it and called her to suggest she leave town.

Jack glanced at Nell ordering Ted and Fred around. "I'll head over as soon as we finish up here."

"I'd feel better if you checked on her now. I'd go myself, but I doubt she'd open up to me. You're the only one she'll talk to, Jack. I'll help out here."

"You're probably right," he admitted and went to retrieve his helmet off the porch swing.

"Come over to my place when you're done. Skye and Grace are picking up Jill and little Jack and heading over now. Thought we'd celebrate the house being done, and the girls have work to do on Skye's costume."

"Sounds good. If you don't mind, keep it on the down-low where I am. Grace doesn't need to hear about it." Obviously, since she was zip-lining, he didn't want to add to whatever had set her off this time.

*   *   *

As soon as Maria opened the door to her room at the lodge, the memory of the morning Jack's mother died assaulted him. It was the smell—puke and booze. He swallowed hard, forcing himself to put one foot in front of the other and go inside.

"Jack, what is it?" Maria asked, standing before him in a short, stained white robe, her long hair matted around her pale face.

He closed the door, then gently clasped her chin between his fingers, turning her face to study the bruise. "You look like hell. What did you do to yourself?" he asked, lowering his hand.

She touched her cheek. "I heard something and got up to check it out. The room was dark, and I tripped on the chair."

"Bullshit," he said, taking in the four empty wine bottles on the table. The heavy brown drapes were drawn, the bed unmade, the desk cluttered with papers and her computer. He walked across the room, pulled the drapes aside, and opened the patio door. Sunlight sparkled off the kidney-shaped pool, where two young boys were splashing their parents, the family's laughter filling the room with light and life. Digging his phone from his pocket, he turned to her. "Have a shower. I'm taking you to Dr. Trainer."

She sat on the edge of the bed. "No. I had a bad night, that's all." She gestured to the computer. "I've been working a lot. It's been hard. It's been hard going through it by myself."

Jack pulled out the chair at the desk and sat down. "I'm

sorry." And he was; the last thing he wanted to do was hurt her, to see her suffer. But he couldn't be what she wanted or needed. "You have to get help, Maria. Gage told me they got a complaint about you screaming."

Wrapping her arms around her waist, she averted her gaze from his and stared out the patio doors. "I didn't get much sleep last night. I, ah, fell asleep a couple of hours ago. I had a bad dream, that's all."

"The nightmares are getting worse, aren't they?"

She went to shake her head, then choked back a sob and nodded.

"Is there anyone I can call . . . friends, family?"

"I burned those bridges a long time ago, Jack." She got up from the bed and headed for the bathroom. "I'll be okay. Thanks for checking on me."

Jack rubbed his jaw, glancing at the open document on the screen. He started reading and couldn't stop. Even though he wanted to, he couldn't.

"Jack?" Maria said, coming out of the steam-filled bathroom ten minutes later, a white towel wrapped turban-style around her hair, another around her body.

"Why didn't you tell me?"

Her eyes flicked from him to the screen, then she shrugged. "I thought you would've guessed."

"No. Jesus"—he held her gaze—"I'm sorry, Maria. I shouldn't have touched you like I did. You didn't need someone coming on to you, not after what you'd been through. I wish you would've told me. I wouldn't have . . ."

"You have nothing to apologize for. I needed you to kiss me, to hold me, to touch me. After what he did to me, I didn't think I'd ever be able to bear the feel of a man's hands on me again. You changed that."

"Let me call Dr. Trainer. I'll go with you."

"I finally forced myself to write the chapter last night. That's why I had the nightmare. I've got it out of me now. It's over."

He went to the table beside the chair and scooped up the bottles, tossing them in the wastebasket. "No more drinking," he said as he walked to the door. "Get dressed. I'll wait for you outside."

"God, you're stubborn. I'm not going to see Dr. Trainer."

"You're not staying alone, either. You need to be around people. I'm taking you with me to the McBrides'."

*   *   *

"I guess I won't be able to participate in the triathlon," Grace said, doing her best to sound disappointed as Dr. McBride gently removed her tennis shoe. She made sure to wince when he carefully bent her foot. Skye winced along with her, Madison arched a brow, and Jill crossed her arms. Sawyer snorted a laugh, turning at the sound of Jack's voice. Gage led her husband into the living room. When she saw who accompanied him, Grace sighed.

It appeared the honeymoon was over. The last seven Maria-free days had been blissfully perfect. Well, aside from the day that Jack had cut their son's hair. Grace wasn't sure she believed the gum story.

Jack frowned and came to her side. "What happened?"

"They didn't adjust the tension for Grace's weight, and she kind of used her foot as a brake," Skye explained.

Dr. McBride patted Grace's knee. "There's no bruising or swelling. You should be fine to continue your training, honey."

Grace gaped at him. For goodness' sake, if you had the sniffles, he confined you to your bed for a week. "Are you sure . . ." She no longer held his attention. "But you, young lady, are not fine," he said, giving Maria a concerned frown. He stood up and went to her. The others did so as well.

Everyone except Jack. Grace felt his gaze upon her as she picked up her tennis shoe. "How did Maria hurt herself?" she asked.

Jack shared a silent exchange with Sawyer, then came to sit beside Grace on the couch. "We'll talk about that in a minute. Right—"

Nell popped her head through the French doors off the dining room. "We're ready for the burgers."

"Too nice out to waste it standing around in here," Sawyer said, ushering everyone from the living room onto the deck.

Lifting Grace's legs, Jack draped them over his lap. "Right now, I want to talk about you," he said, taking her foot in his hand. "I thought we'd agreed how to handle your stress." His strong fingers gently kneaded her instep. "You promised no more crazy stuff."

"Zip-lining isn't crazy." He raised a brow. "Okay, maybe for me it is. But it wasn't my stress we were dealing with today, it was Skye's."

"Come on, princess. You expect me to believe that a woman with more money than God is stressed?"

Grace glanced over her shoulder to make sure no one was in the room. "I'm going to tell you something, but you have to promise not to tell anyone else." She waited until he agreed. "She's broke. She told me today."

"Are you kidding me?"

She explained how Skye managed to lose all her money due to her overly generous nature and bad investments. "She's going to work for us at the bakery."

"Madison doesn't know?"

"No one does but me, and now you."

"I won't say anything, but she might feel better if she got it out in the open."

"It's not like I can force her. She'll open up to Madison when she's ready. Now, are you going to tell me what happened with Maria?"

"Yeah, in a minute," he said, drawing her onto his lap. And then, after giving her a long, sweetly tender kiss, he told her how he'd found Maria and what had happened to her.

"I feel terrible, Jack. If it weren't for me, she wouldn't have had to deal with the memories on her own."

"I feel bad, too. But I'm not equipped to help her deal with this and, let's be honest here, she wanted more than my help on the book. I shouldn't have cut her off like I did, though."

"She needs to talk to someone." Who was she to make that call? It wasn't like Grace had opened up about her sister's death. She hadn't even told Jack about Faith. Then again, it wasn't the same. Maria wasn't to blame for what happened to her. Unlike Grace, she was the victim.

"I know that," Jack said. "But it's like Skye. Until she's ready to, I can't force her."

No woman should have to deal with being raped, especially on her own. Grace didn't fool herself into thinking that Maria would accept her sympathy or help. But that didn't mean she couldn't support her indirectly. "What if

Dr. Trainer happened to show up tonight? He's a friend of Gage, and he works with Dr. McBride."

"Good idea if he's free and they don't mind giving him a call."

"I'm sure they won't. I'll go talk to Madison," she said, moving off his lap.

"Hey, princess," he said as she walked away. She turned, and he held up his hands. "I must have the magic touch. You're not limping. Guess we can go for a run tomorrow after all."

Chapter Twenty-Five

Panicked, Jack searched the crowd attending the auction in the backyard of the house on Sugar Plum Lane for his son.

"There he is. He's headed your way." Sawyer gestured over the heads of the people gathered in the side yard.

Jack crouched and caught sight of his son crawling through a woman's legs. She let out a shriek. Jack jumped to his feet. "Grab him," he ordered the woman.

"Got him," an older man called out.

Great, it was Murray. Patrick was a fan of the leash. He'd probably tell Grace. Sure enough, Patrick shook his head as he handed off little Jack. "When are you going to listen to your wife, boy-o? Put the lad on the leash. Where is Gracie?"

"We're taking little Jack up to the meadow later. She's getting the picnic ready."

"You proposed to her there." The old man gave an

approving nod. "Good place to give her the key to the house."

Jack thought so. Murray smiled, and Jack's jaw dropped.

Ever since the night of the fire, the old man didn't lecture or curse Jack out as much as he used to. But smiling... It took a couple of seconds for Jack to recover. "I've got a limited budget. Hopefully no one pushes the price too high."

Patrick scrutinized the crowd. "Know most of them... You should be good. Stop by my place before you bring her the key and get some flowers. Gracie likes her flowers."

It wasn't long into the auction when Jack knew he'd have no need for the flowers. He didn't realize until now that he'd actually thought he had a chance. How much he had wanted to see Grace's face when he handed her the key.

"Shit," Sawyer said. "I'm sorry, buddy."

"Shit," little Jack echoed.

Jack scrubbed his face. "All I had to do was figure out a way to keep working with Maria. If I had the extra money, I could've gone higher."

"Don't beat yourself up. You did what you had to. There'll be another house."

"It's not the same. She wanted this one. And I...I wanted to be the one to make her dream come true." He shrugged, embarrassed for coming off a sentimental sap.

"You did. You came home."

"Thanks." Jack appreciated him saying so, but at the moment, it didn't help.

Fred, Ted, Patrick, and Nell came over to commiserate.

Then Madison, who'd been shaking hands with the new owners, walked over. "I'm so sorry, Jack. I wish there were something I could do."

"Don't worry about it. At least Grace didn't get her hopes up."

"That's true," she said. "Well, you guys have a nice picnic. We'll talk later."

"Yeah, thanks." As Madison walked away, Jack noticed Maria standing with the well-dressed couple who had the winning bid. His eyes narrowed as they shook her hand. Sensing his attention, she looked up, then excused herself and walked across the lawn to where he stood.

"I'm sorry you lost the house, Jack. But in the end, you know you'd never be happy here."

She ran her hand over little Jack's buzz cut. "Hey, cutie."

"You made sure I didn't get the house, didn't you?"

"What I did is save you from making the biggest mistake of your life. You don't belong here."

"Who are they?"

"A former colleague and his wife who moved to Colorado a couple of years ago. He'd always talked about how they wanted to open a bed-and-breakfast. He's close to retiring, so I let them know. I . . ."

He turned and walked away. If he didn't, he'd say something not fit for his son's ears. "You don't want to do that," he warned her when she followed after him.

"Hey, Jack," Sawyer called out, jogging in his direction.

Jack waited for him on the sidewalk, forcing himself not to look back at the house. "What's up?"

"Five-acre wildfire on Blue Mountain. We've got a

scout troop locked in up there. One of our pilots is down sick. You okay to take a chopper up?" Sawyer had been volunteering with search and rescue since he'd retired.

"Yeah." Jack ignored the uptick in his pulse and started for his truck. "I'll take little Jack home and meet you at the field." With his son buckled in his car seat, he called Grace before getting behind the wheel.

As soon as he pulled up to the bakery, Grace ran to the SUV. "Jill called. Dr. Trainer's going up with you, too," she said, opening the door to get little Jack out of his car seat. "Are you going to be okay?"

"Sure, why wouldn't I be?"

With their son on her hip, she reached through the open window to caress Jack's cheek. "Because you haven't taken up a chopper since the day you were shot down."

*   *   *

Grace sat on the landing outside their apartment door, anxiously waiting for Jack to come home. Gage and Jill had been giving her updates on the hour. As of thirty minutes ago, all the boys and their troop leaders had been rescued.

The door opened. Jack saw her and cocked his head, a slow smile curving his lips as he started up the stairs. "Hey, princess."

"Hey, flyboy. I hear you were playing hero again."

He laughed, hauling her off the steps and into his arms. He kissed her, walking her backward into the apartment as he did. She was breathless and weak-kneed by the time he drew his mouth away to rest his forehead against hers. "Hold that thought. We'll take up where we left off once I grab a shower."

All Grace could manage was a nod. He grinned then headed for the bedroom, stopping in his tracks as he went to walk by the living room. He swung his gaze to hers. "You're amazing, you know that?"

She shrugged. "I thought if we couldn't go to the meadow for our picnic, I'd bring it home to you." She'd pushed the furniture back, spread a blanket on the floor, and filled the room with flowers. "Patrick let me raid his garden. I don't know what happened today, but he seems to have a crush on *you* now."

"Jesus, don't tell me that." He reached for her hand, tugged her closer, and kissed the top of her head. "I won't be long."

She was arranging the food on the blanket when he returned to the living room.

"Looks great," he said, stretching out on the blanket beside her. He snagged a piece of fried chicken. "I checked on little Jack. He's down for the count."

She scooped a big helping of potato salad and one of macaroni salad onto his plate. "I kept him up as long as I could."

"You let him stay up past his bedtime?"

She caught the amusement in his voice and sighed. "Just because I think a structured environment is important doesn't mean I won't deviate from his schedule every now and then, you know."

"I know, princess." The corner of his mouth twitched, and he patted her leg.

She watched as he dug into his potato salad, noticing a change, a lightness in his manner that had been missing earlier. "You loved flying again, didn't you? It makes you happy."

"Yeah, I did. I didn't realize how much until I got up there."

"I was worried you might have a flashback." She'd had them for a long time after her sister's death. After what Jack had been through, she imagined he did, too.

He wiped his hands on a napkin. "I did."

"How bad was it?"

"Bad. Would've been worse if Sawyer and Dr. Trainer hadn't been with me. They knew what was happening. They talked me through it."

"Did you have the flashback when you were in the air?"

"No, thank God, on the ground. I wasn't going to take her up, but they convinced me it was something I needed to do."

They talked about the rescue, Afghanistan, and how much Jack had missed flying. "Have you thought about what you're going to do? Are you going to retire?"

"Your dad asked me the same thing the other day. I'll tell you what I told him—I'm not sure."

"Oh, I see," she said, trying to hide her disappointment. She started to pick up the dishes.

"I know that's not the answer you want to hear, but it's a big decision. I'm not ready to make it yet, but when I am, we'll talk about it."

"Okay." She forced herself to smile.

He took the dishes from her hands, placing them on the floor. "Come here." Drawing her between his legs, her back to his chest, he wrapped his arms around her. "Let's talk about something else."

"I heard from Madison. She sounded happy with what the house brought in." Grace had done her best to act pleased. It wasn't that she thought there was a chance she'd ever live in the house on Sugar Plum Lane, but before it was sold, at least she could dream.

"Yeah, I'm sure they made a hefty profit. Free labor and all. She say anything else?" he asked in a wary tone of voice.

"No, why?"

"Nothing, just Nell was giving me a hard time about little Jack losing his long hair. Thought she might have mentioned it. I don't know what the big deal is. If you ask me, he looks pretty darn cute."

"Of course he's cute. But I miss his curls. He doesn't look like a baby anymore."

He wrapped her hair around his hand and gently tipped her face back. "You ever think about having another one?"

"I'd like to. What about you?"

"Yeah. I missed out on a lot. I didn't hear his first word, didn't see him learn to crawl or walk." His hand caressed her stomach. "Didn't get to feel him kick."

"But, Jack, if you're not going to retire, you could end up missing out on—"

"There's always a possibility an instructor's position might come up," he murmured against her lips, silencing her response with a hot and demanding kiss.

"You want to start trying now . . . tonight?" she asked breathlessly when he finally let her up for air.

He rolled her beneath him. "Yeah, right now, right here."

Chapter Twenty-Six

A week later, Jack decided he needed to have his head read for thinking adding a baby to their family was a good idea. With the bakery back up and running, Grace had been inundated with orders for her sugar plum cake. Despite the promise she'd made to him, she worked from morning to night and had an excuse at the ready every time he approached her about bringing in more help. Add her parents' impending arrival to the mix, and her stress levels were through the roof. She was driving him crazy.

"Stop." He took the cloth from her hand. "You wiped down the counter twenty minutes ago."

"Maybe if you'd cleaned up after you made little Jack's lunch, I wouldn't have to." When he didn't release the cloth, she tried to tug it from his hand. When that didn't work, she got another one from the drawer, slamming it shut.

At the end of his patience, Jack threw the cloth in the sink. "I did. And I loaded the dishwasher, only you had to reload it. I also threw in a load of wash, and you redid that, too."

"You put little Jack's clothes in with the sheets. I told you—"

He gritted his teeth, put his hands on her shoulders, and turned her to face him. "Look, I get that you're tired and stressed, but I'm tired of you giving me hell when all I'm doing is trying to help out."

"I appreciate your help. It's just that…" She trailed off, looking at him from under her lashes.

"Just what… that I'm not doing it to your standards? Well, let me tell you something, princess, no one can live up to *your* standards."

Her shoulders sagged under his hands. "I just want everything to be perfect."

Some of his anger faded at the sight of her blinking back tears. "Baby, they're your parents. They don't care if the house is spotless. Little Jack and I sure as hell don't. We'd rather have you happy and relaxed than stressing out over a few crumbs on the counter and tie-dyed sheets."

"My dad doesn't care, but my mother does. I'll never hear the end of it if everything doesn't meet her expectations. I wish she weren't coming," she murmured into his chest, wrapping her arms around his waist. She looked up at him. "I'm sorry. I know I haven't been easy to live with the last couple of days."

Try a week. "Why don't we go for a walk once little Jack's up from his nap? It's just drizzling out. The fresh air would do you good."

"I wish I could, but with the tourists starting to arrive

for the Fourth of July celebration, it's really busy today, and the Pines doubled their order for this week." When he gave her an exasperated look, she wrinkled her nose, something he used to think was cute. "I promise, as soon as we slow down, I'm going to advertise for another baker. Skye and the girls are great with the customers, but I need help with the sugar plum cakes. And now we can afford someone with experience." She gave him a hopeful smile. "That's good, isn't it? We're making money now."

And that was another thing that was starting to get to him. His wife was providing for the family, not him. He decided to talk to the general about his options tonight. Because as much as Jack enjoyed spending time with his son and Grace, when she wasn't acting like a Stepford wife, which admittedly had been much of the time lately, he needed to be doing something productive. He needed a job. At least when he'd been working on the house or the book, he'd felt like he was contributing something.

Grace looked at him expectantly, waiting, he imagined, for an enthusiastic response. "If you're able to hire someone to take the load off you, then yeah, it's good." But he wasn't holding his breath. He doubted his wife would be able to give up control to anyone, no matter how experienced they were.

A crash came from little Jack's bedroom. Grace sighed, her arms dropping to her sides. "I've got it," he said, heading to his son's room. He opened the door. "Okay, Houdini, what did you do now?"

Little Jack, who'd escaped from his crib, tossed a basket from his change table onto the floor and pulled off his diaper. "Me go pee."

Jack didn't need to look at Grace to know what her reaction would be. He steered her from the room. "I'll take care of it."

"Thanks," she said wearily. Halfway out the door, she turned. "Um, Jack, do you think you could take him to the park or visit with Jill until my parents get here? They're supposed to be here around two."

Right, because God forbid there was a pillow out of place when they arrived.

*   *   *

"Hey, Jack," Matt Trainer called out as Jack buckled his son into his car seat. He'd decided to take little Jack to Jill's instead of taking him to the park to play. With the rain they'd had, the playground would be a giant mud puddle. All he'd need was to bring little Jack home dirty for his visit with his grandparents.

Jack straightened. "Hey, Matt. How's it going?" The thirtysomething-year-old doctor reminded Jack of Sawyer. He liked the guy. So did most of the women in town. They'd nicknamed him Doctor McSexy.

"Not bad." Matt looked like he had more to say, but was weighing whether to tell him or not. Jack had an uneasy feeling it had to do with Maria.

She'd waited a couple of days after the auction to get in touch with him. By that point, Jack figured she'd done him a favor by screwing up his bid on the house, so he didn't walk away when she caught up with him on Main Street. Besides that, no matter what she'd done, he couldn't help worrying about her.

They'd met for coffee a couple of times—she'd completed the first draft of the book and wanted his opinion—and everything was good...until yesterday. Madison had come over to their table at the diner and teased him about working on baby number two. And that'd been it: Maria had had a meltdown.

Little Jack fired a ball at Matt through the open window. "Good arm." Matt smiled, tossing it back before he glanced at Jack. "You hear from Maria today?"

"No, why?" Oh yeah, something was definitely up, Jack thought, feeling the electrical buzz at the back of his neck.

"She didn't show up for her appointment this morning."

"You're worried about her?"

"You more than anybody knows what she's dealing with. So yeah, I am. And up until today, she's kept her appointments."

Remembering the shape she'd been in only a few weeks ago, Jack took out his cell. "I'll give her a call." An uneasy feeling came over him when she didn't pick up. If she answered for anyone, it would be him. "I'll head over and check on her."

"Thanks, Jack. I'd go myself, but I'm due back at the hospital."

"No problem. I'll give you a shout once I talk to her."

"Appreciate it."

"Okay, buddy, change of plans. Got an errand to run and then we'll go see Auntie Jill," Jack said as he pulled onto Main Street. Once he made sure Maria was all right, he'd have Jill do some checking for him. The best thing he could do for Maria was to find her friends and family. She needed ongoing support, and he knew it couldn't be him who gave it to her.

As he pulled into the parking lot of the lodge, Jack

spotted the candy-apple-red Mustang in front of her unit. He tried her cell again. When she didn't respond, he got little Jack out of his car seat and walked to the door, turning the knob. Locked. "Maria, open up."

"'Ria open," little Jack echoed, banging his small fist on the door.

"You're pretty damn cute, you know that?" he said to his son.

Little Jack nodded, pulling on his orange T-shirt. "Me cute."

When another round of loud knocking didn't draw a response, Jack set his son down beside a planter. "Okay, buddy, you pick some flowers for Mommy while Daddy opens the door."

The short hairs on the back of his neck had been standing on end since his conversation with Matt, and Jack knew he didn't have time to hunt down the manager for a key. He put his shoulder to the door and, when it didn't budge, kicked it in. Scooping up little Jack, he entered the dark room, once again overwhelmed by the smell of stale wine and vomit. Maria was in bed, wine bottles cluttering the nightstand, one lying empty on the floor.

"Maria," he called out.

Closing the door behind him, he set little Jack on the floor and approached the bed. Images from the day he discovered his mother assaulted him. He froze. Fighting back the memories, he forced himself to put a hand on Maria's chest and his cheek to her mouth. A faint, shallow breath whispered across his face. He shook her, shouting her name. Like a rag doll's, her head fell back. He got on the bed, moving in behind her to prop her against his chest. Her head lolled onto his shoulder. With an arm around her, he continued calling to her as he dialed 9-1-1. Her eyes opened to slits.

"What did you take, Maria? Open your eyes. Come on, that's a girl. The ambulance is on the way. Hang in there." He wouldn't let her die like his mother. If she did, it was on him.

At the thought, he scanned the nightstand for a pill bottle. When he didn't find one, he swept his hand over the comforter, his fingers closing around a plastic container. He shoved the prescription bottle in his pocket to give to the paramedics. At least they'd have a better idea what they were dealing with. In the distance, he heard the scream of the siren, and his body sagged in relief.

And that's when he remembered his son.

"Jack." His gaze shot to where he left him. He wasn't there. Lowering Maria to the bed, he did a quick, panicked scan of the room. "Jack," he called out again, about to race to the front door when he saw the drapes by the patio door flutter. His heart pounded so hard it felt like it was going to explode from his chest. He whipped open the drapes, the curtain rod falling off the wall. Through the misty rain, he made out something orange in the pool.

*   *   *

Grace cast a critical eye on the wildflower garden she'd just finished up on the sugar plum cake. The sunflowers weren't as perfect as she'd wanted.

Skye, who'd been watching her as part of her training, grabbed her hand. "No, not again. There is not a single thing wrong with the sunflowers."

"But..."

"No buts." Skye put her hands on Grace's shoulders and brought her face close to hers. "We're friends, right?"

"Yes, of course we are."

"Okay, so I'm saying this to you as a friend, as someone who cares about you . . . sweetie, you've got a problem, and you've gotta deal with it before you drive yourself and everyone around you crazy."

Grace closed her eyes and bowed her head. After how Grace had acted with Jack, Skye wasn't telling her anything she didn't know. She was overwhelmed and out of control. Nothing she did seemed to help. "I know," she said on a choked whisper.

"Maybe if you talk to me, it'll help. I know how busy you've been, but it's more than that, isn't it?"

She sniffed and nodded. "My mother's coming. No matter how hard I try, I can't please her."

"Heard your phone call, remember? You're thirty, Grace. It's time to cut the apron strings. If she makes you feel this bad, she doesn't deserve to be a part of your life." Skye's eyes narrowed at her. "You're holding something back. What is it?"

Grace's fingers unconsciously latched on to the gum paste and cutter. She couldn't tell Skye what had happened to Faith. How, even after all these years, being around her mother brought everything back.

Skye covered her hand with hers. "Okay, your problems with your mother aside, is there anything else?"

"Jack and I are trying to have another baby."

"I know, but that's a good thing, isn't it?"

"It would be if I knew Jack's plans. Every time I ask him, he tells me we've got lots of time to figure it out. I'm afraid if I push him for an answer, he'll feel pressured and shut me out like last time. But I need to know if he's going back to active duty, if he'll be deployed again, if he's willing to live here or he wants to move back to Fort Carson. It was hard enough raising one child on my own. How would I raise two?"

"What do you want, Grace?"

"I don't want him to return to active duty." As the daughter of a general, she felt guilty and selfish for even thinking that, let alone voicing it out loud. But she knew Skye wouldn't judge her, and she felt a little better being able to confide her fears to someone. "I don't know if I can do it again, Skye. The last seventeen months..." She twisted her wedding band, her heart racing as all the emotions she'd battled while Jack was missing came back to haunt her. "I don't know how I'd cope if he was deployed again." She gave a brittle laugh and held out her trembling hand. "Just thinking about it makes me feel faint. How do I pretend everything's okay, that I'm okay, if he leaves again? But I want him to be happy, I wouldn't be if he wasn't, and I'm afraid the only thing that will make him feel truly fulfilled is remaining in the military and flying a Black Hawk."

"I'm not sure it's my place, since it's obvious Jack hasn't told you, but given how you're feeling, I think you need to know. He bid on the house for you, Grace."

"My...I mean, the house on Sugar Plum Lane?"

"Yeah. Everyone in town knew he was going to. That's why they planted the wildflower garden. It's why Sawyer thought the house should be purple instead of pink."

Grace covered her mouth, holding back a sob. She couldn't believe it. She couldn't believe Jack would do that for her. She'd already been feeling guilty for how she'd been acting, and this just made her feel worse. She didn't deserve him. "Thank you," she said around the thick lump in her throat. "Thank you so much for telling me. I wish Jack had."

"He was probably afraid of getting your hopes up. And then when he lost the bid, he knew you'd be disappointed."

"No." She shook her head emphatically. "It doesn't matter. Just knowing he did that for me…" She shrugged helplessly, unable to continue, afraid she'd start crying and wouldn't be able to stop.

Skye smiled and rubbed her shoulder. "Take it from me, everything's going to work out for you and Jack. But honestly, Grace, whatever issues you have with your mother, deal with them when she's here. And if you can't work it out with her, let both your mother and whatever hurt you in the past go."

Skye was right. Her mother had punished her long enough. It was time for Grace to let go of her past before it ruined her future. "Do you think you guys would be okay without me for an hour? Jack asked me to join them for a walk earlier."

"Definitely. And while you're gone, I'll try my hand at making a sugar plum cake."

"Oh, I-I don't think…"

"Just checking." Skye grinned. "Progress, but you still have some work to do on your control issues."

"Thanks for pointing that out. I…" Smiling, Grace turned as Madison and Gage came through the doors. Her smile faltered at the grim expression on Gage's face and Madison's red-rimmed eyes. "What's wrong?"

"Grace." Gage came and took her hand. "There's been

an accident. Little Jack's in the hospital. He fell in the pool at..."

Gage's face went out of focus, his words garbled as the room spun around her. From a distance, she heard someone say, "...in shock." Something warm enveloped her body at the same time everything went black.

Chapter Twenty-Seven

Jack ran toward the hospital elevator. Gage had called to let him know Grace had gone into shock when he'd broken the news about little Jack. They'd started an IV in the ambulance. As the elevator doors opened, Jack pushed past the nurse. "Grace." Her beautiful eyes haunted in her pale face, she looked at him, and he reached for her hand. She turned her head.

"Sir," the orderly said, "we have to get her to her room."

Jack let his hand drop to his side. She'd never forgive him. He stepped back as they wheeled her past him and down the hall. He didn't think he'd be able to forgive himself.

Jack followed behind and leaned against the wall outside the room where they'd taken Grace. "Come with me. We'll check out your knee," Dr. McBride said, appearing at his side.

"No, I..." He scrubbed his face. "I've gotta talk to Grace. Just for a minute. All I need is a minute." To tell her how fucking sorry he was and to try to explain what had happened.

"Son, look at me." Dr. McBride put a hand on his shoulder and waited until Jack dragged his gaze from the floor. "Let them examine Grace and let me look after you. They'll have completed the tests on little Jack by then, and you'll have some news for her."

"Be straight with me, what are..." He swallowed painfully before continuing, "What are his chances?"

"Good. You gave him CPR, and the EMTs were able to start treatment almost immediately." The EMTs had told him the same thing.

Jack tipped his head back against the wall, struggling to contain his emotions. He'd shut them down seconds after realizing little Jack was in the pool. The gate had been locked. Jack had to climb an eight-foot wrought-iron fence to reach him. No one but his son would've spotted the opening at the bottom. He started CPR on little Jack before he had him out of the pool, yelling for the EMTs when he heard them enter Maria's room.

Dr. McBride nodded at whoever approached and said, "I'll be right back." As he moved away, Jack found himself pulled into a hard hug. "I'm so fucking sorry, buddy," Sawyer said, drawing in a ragged breath, as if he, too, was having a hard time keeping it together. "What can I do for you?" he asked once he released Jack.

"Pray."

"Got it covered. Nell activated the town's prayer line. How's Grace doing?"

"I haven't had a chance to talk to her yet." He didn't tell his best friend that he didn't think she'd ever speak to him again.

Sawyer must've read the fear on his face and put a hand on his shoulder. "It was an accident. It could've happened to anyone. You saved both little Jack and Maria. Don't beat yourself up over this."

Jill, her complexion stark white, her eyes tormented but dry, strode down the hall toward them with the change of clothes he'd asked for. She was holding it together for him.

She gave Sawyer a brisk nod and handed Jack his clothes. "Any word yet on little Jack?"

"They're running tests. They took him for a CT scan a few minutes ago."

"That's good. He's stable, then," Sawyer said, keeping an eye on Jill as he did.

"Yeah, that's what they said."

"Jack." Dr. McBride motioned for him from the other end of the hall. "Let's get an x-ray of that knee."

Sawyer frowned, taking in Jack's torn jeans and his bruised and swollen knee. "Doc's right, you better get that looked at. We'll stay here in case Grace needs us."

Jack was about to protest until Jill said, "Please, I don't want to worry about you, too."

He knew neither of them would let up and started to walk toward Dr. McBride. As he did, Sawyer tucked Jill's hair behind her ear. "How you holding up?"

"Good. I'm good."

"Yeah, I know you're tough, shortstop," Sawyer said, tugging her into his arms.

Halfway down the hall, Jack heard her sobbing.

* * *

Sitting in the pew in the small hospital chapel, Jack buried his face in his hands as he relived the moment he saw his son facedown in the pool. The moment Grace, lying pale on the stretcher, looked right through him. The door behind him creaked open, and he straightened, knuckling his eyes with his fists.

Patrick Murray sat down heavily beside him. "Done beatin' yourself up, boy-o?"

"Nope. Go ahead, get your licks in."

The old man leaned back, crossing his arms over his chest. "That girl and the wee devil mean a lot to me. I'd be first in line to give you those licks if I thought you deserved them, but you don't." He looked around the chapel. "Libby spent a lot of time in here praying for you, you know."

"Yeah, I can imagine."

"I can see you don't believe me. She wasn't easy on you kids, I know that better than most. But she did the best she knew how. It wasn't easy on her, either. Your lad's a handful, and you were the same. Only you were an angry ten-year-old. Your mother taking her life like she did hit Libby hard. She blamed herself and was going to make damn sure nothing happened to either of you kids. She'd be proud of the man you turned into, Jackson Flaherty."

Until that moment, Jack had never thought of what it must've been like for his grandmother raising him and his sister on her own. He had a tough time keeping up with his son, and he was only thirty-five. Libby'd been close to sixty when she'd taken them in. And old man Murray was right: Jack had been an angry and scared kid and acted out because of it. "Appreciate you saying so, sir."

"Now let's go check on that wife of yours." Murray heaved himself from the pew.

"She doesn't want to see me." After Dr. McBride had x-rayed him and taped his knee, Jackson had gone to her room, only to be turned away by the nurse. Sawyer and Jill had seen her, though.

"We'll check on the wee devil, then. He'll be waking up in no time and wantin' to see his da." As Murray limped beside Jack to the door, the old man cast him a sidelong glance. "Don't you worry about Gracie. Give her time. I'll put a good word in for you. Give her a talkin' to, if need be."

It surprised him that the bane of his teenage existence had turned into his champion. And oddly enough, Jack was able to let go of the anger and resentment he'd nursed against his grandmother for all these years, thanks to the old man. As for him helping to change Grace's mind, that was debatable, but Jack would take all the help he could get.

When they reached little Jack's floor, they learned he was still undergoing tests.

"There's been no change. The doctor should be finished in about fifteen minutes. Why don't you get yourself something to eat, Mr. Flaherty, and come back then? And, sir," the nurse on duty said to Patrick, "only family allowed."

The old man's face fell, and Jack heard himself say, "He is family."

Murray nodded with a smile. "Yeah, I am family."

"Thank you," the old man said as they once again got on the elevator.

Jack shrugged. "You mean a lot to my wife and son. I appreciate you being there for them when I couldn't be."

When the doors opened on Grace's floor, Murray stayed behind. "I'm going to get some flowers for Gracie. Help you win her over. I'll be back in a bit."

It would take a lot more than flowers to win his wife over, but he thanked the old man. As Jack rounded the corner, he heard General Garrison's booming voice. Sawyer and Jill were with him and so was Grace's mother.

"Sir, Mrs. Garrison," Jack said as he reached them, bracing for the general's harsh rebuke.

"Jack." Garrison surprised him by ignoring Jack's proffered hand and pulling him into a hug. "Sad business, son. Damn shame what happened. How's my baby girl?"

They must've just arrived. "The doctors—"

"Oh, stop it, Frank. She's fine. And if you hadn't coddled her growing up, she wouldn't have reacted as badly as she did," Mrs. Garrison said in an icy tone of voice, offering her cheek for Jack to kiss. "I'm sorry, Jackson. You must be as ashamed as I am by her behavior, especially after how badly she treated you."

Was she for real? Jack looked from Sawyer, to Jill, to his father-in-law, to see if he'd heard her right. From his sister and Sawyer's shocked expressions and the general's angry, flushed face, he had. "Mrs. Garrison, my wife suffered one of the worst shocks a parent can have. She didn't react badly. She reacted like any parent would who is worried they might lose their child. I don't know if you're aware of this or not, but my son is upstairs fighting for his life." Jack's voice broke, and he struggled to regain his composure. Sawyer squeezed his shoulder.

Grace's mother sniffed, lifting her nose in the air. "You're as bad as her father. I know very well what she's going through, Jackson. I lost my child because of your wife."

"What? What did you just say?"

"Helena"—the general took his wife's arm, looking like he wanted to shake the woman—"that's enough. Jack, we'll..." His voice trailed off. "Grace, baby," he said on a pained whisper.

Jack turned to see his wife leaning against the door frame, holding on to her IV.

*   *   *

Grace held up a hand as Jack came to her side, shaking her head when he suggested she get back into bed. She'd heard everything her mother had said. Skye was right. It was time for Grace to deal with her mother once and for all. What had happened to their son was as much Grace's fault as Jack's. If she hadn't been trying so hard to make everything perfect for her mother, she wouldn't have told him to take little Jack out for the day. She would've gone for that walk with them like Jack had wanted her to, been with him when he went to help Maria.

She smiled at him to temper her rejection. She imagined her refusal to see him earlier had hurt him. He was suffering as much as, probably more than, she was. It wasn't until her visit with Sawyer and Jill that she'd learned what had happened at the lodge.

Facing her mother, Grace said, "You've never been able to forgive me, have you?"

"This is not the time or place, Grace. We do not air our private affairs in public."

"Moot point, mother. You already did." She cleared her throat, her gaze moving from Jill to Sawyer to Jack. "When I was twelve, my sister, Faith, drowned. My mother blamed me. Until today, I thought it was my fault.

Because of what happened to little Jack, I know now it was an accident." She took Jack's hand. "I'm sorry I turned you away earlier. I just needed a little time to get myself together. It wasn't your fault, Jack. You saved our son. You saved Maria."

He kissed her temple. "Baby, you don't have to listen to her. Let me—"

She caressed his clenched jaw. "Yes, I do. I have to do this for me, for us."

"Faith's death was not an accident. You were the best swimmer on the swim team. You could've saved her if you'd wanted to- "

"My God, Helena, how can—"

"No, Daddy, please let her finish."

"How, Frank...How can I blame her? I'll tell you how. I heard her that day. I heard her tell her seven-year-old sister, who followed her around like an adoring puppy, that she was sick to death of her. That she hated her and wished she'd never been born."

Tears welled in Grace's eyes and spilled down her cheeks. It was true. She'd yelled the words in the heat of anger and frustration. Words she'd regret to her dying day. "Children say cruel and hateful things. I loved my sister, but I didn't want to spend every waking minute with her. I was twelve, and it was the summer holidays. I wanted to spend time with my friends, and I wasn't allowed to because I had to look after Faith."

The edges of her mother's mouth whitened. "Are you blaming me?"

"No, it was an accident. I didn't know she'd followed me when I snuck out of the house. And I didn't know you were..." *too drunk to pay any attention*, she silently finished. There was only so much dirty laundry she'd air in public. "And I didn't know she'd gone in the river until I heard her screaming for help. And I did help her, Mother. I almost died getting her out of that undertow. We'd just started our CPR course, but I did my best. It took the ambulance thirty minutes to get there, and I never stopped trying to save her." She was crying now—so were her father and Jill—and the last words came out garbled. Jack had left her side a few moments ago and returned now with a wheelchair. "Sit down, princess," he said, helping her into the chair.

Her father came and crouched in front of her, taking her hands in his. "Never, not once, did I blame you."

"You sent me away."

He bowed his head and briefly closed his eyes before raising his gaze to hers. "I did what I thought was best for you. Your mother…" He gave a weary shake of his head. "We should've talked about this before now." With a squeeze of her hands, he stood up. "I have to do something, something I should've done a long time ago. I'll be back. You take care of my baby girl, Jack."

He went to Grace's mother, who stood clutching her purse in a grip as tight as her face, and took her by the arm.

"I hope your son is all right," Helena said stiffly.

"Thank you," she said quietly as her father led her mother away. Grace didn't know if her mother would ever forgive her, but she thought she'd finally be able to forgive herself.

*　　　*　　　*

Grace woke up in the middle of the night to the steady beep of the monitors. Since she'd refused to leave her son's side, Dr. McBride had had a bed brought in for her. She reached through the bars and touched little Jack's small hand, startling at the sound of Jack's voice. The room was dark enough that it made it difficult to see him sitting in the chair across from their son's hospital bed.

"Matt checked him an hour ago. He's happy with his progress. He's going to be fine, Grace."

They'd spent the day and most of the evening talking about little Jack and her sister, and why Grace had never confided in him. Jack seemed to understand that the topic had been forbidden in her home, her guilt so difficult to deal with that she'd followed the course her mother'd mapped out all those years ago.

"I thought you were going home to get some sleep."

He smiled as he came to her side. "I tried. Got to the front doors of the hospital and couldn't leave. I grabbed a coffee, talked with Nell, Ted, Fred, and old man Murray for a bit."

She patted the bed, and he lay down beside her. Curving his arm around her waist, he tucked her against him, resting his chin on top of her head.

"He looks so small," she said, stroking little Jack's arm through the bars.

"Yeah, but he's a fighter."

"Just like his dad."

"Just like his mom."

She turned her head to look at him, and he kissed her nose. "Are you okay?" After going through a similar experience, she knew how those images remained burned in your brain.

"Getting there. How about you?"

"Same. Did Sawyer tell you about the time I lost little Jack?" He shook his head. "It was the night we found out you were alive. I was making a sugar plum cake in honor of your birthday and little Jack was helping. He smushed a flag into the wildflower garden, and I couldn't let it go. I couldn't stand that the last cake I made for you wouldn't be perfect. While I was fixing the flowers, he escaped through the back door. If it weren't for Sawyer finding him in the alley, who knows what would've happened."

"It's good to know I'm not the only one he takes off on."

"I'm going to work really hard to relax, Jack, to not worry so much if everything isn't perfect. Now that I've come to terms with my guilt, it should be easier, but…" She shrugged. "I'm going to try."

"So am I."

She frowned. "You're not controlling or a perfectionist."

He laughed, low and deep. "Yeah, you've pointed that out to me occasionally. The perfectionist part. But in talking with Skye tonight, I realized I've got some control issues of my own. I've made things harder for you by not deciding what to do with my life."

"You don't have to—"

He gently pressed a finger to her lips. "Let me finish."

"No." She kissed his finger before removing it from her lips. "Since you've come home, you've bent over backward to make me happy. Even though you hated the bakery, you kept it. Same goes for the house on Sugar Plum Lane. The only reason you bid on it was to make me happy. It's my turn, Jack. You're going to take your time and figure out what *you* want to do. To figure out what will make *you* happy. And if that means you want to move back to the base, we'll move. If you… What?" she said as he looked down at her, an unreadable emotion in his eyes.

"Grace Flaherty, I adore you," he said, brushing his lips over her hair. "And I appreciate what you're trying to do. But part of my problem with Christmas and the bakery, even buying a house, was tied up in the past. To be honest, the idea of having our own home was starting to grow on me. And the bakery's doing well, better than well. Our future is the only thing that matters, baby—yours, mine, and little Jack's. So what do you think about living in Christmas?"

"Are you sure, Jack? I need this to be as much about you as it is about me."

"Yeah." He smiled. "Half the town showed up today to check on you and little Jack. We've got a good support system here, lots of friends and family."

"We do. We're very lucky."

"Yeah, we are. And, princess, I have a job if I want it. Sawyer talked to the head of search and rescue. They're looking to hire."

"That would be perfect..." she began, then decided to banish that word from her vocabulary. Life wasn't perfect. It wasn't meant to be. If you didn't go through the bad times, the sad times, you wouldn't appreciate how incredible the good times were. "I mean, it sounds like something you'd enjoy. What do you think?"

"I get to come home to you and little Jack every night and keep flying—can't get much better than that."

She was about to agree with him when little Jack's fingers moved in her hand. "He's waking up."

Jack was off the bed and to their son's side before Grace had pushed herself upright.

"Hey, buddy," he said gruffly as he lowered the rail and took little Jack's other hand.

"Da, me want cake."

"Okay, we'll see what we can do about that." Jack looked at Grace, his eyes glassy. "I think we're all going to be just fine."

"I think so, too," she said and kissed her son's head. "Hi, baby."

Chapter Twenty-Eight

With his son in his arms, Jack stood among the spectators crowded near the starting line and anxiously scanned the triathlon participants for his wife. Dr. McBride wouldn't let him take part because of his sprained knee. Grace had been hoping he'd tell her she couldn't participate, either, and wasn't too happy when he declared her good to go. "There's Mommy," Jack said when he spotted her honey-blonde head. He smiled at the sight of her in the purple bathing suit that showed off her incredible long legs and toned body.

A hand clapped him on the shoulder, distracting him from thoughts of what he planned on doing to her gorgeous body later that night. "Hey, Jack," Grace's father said, taking little Jack from him. He frowned. "Why's he wearing a leash?"

Jack ignored the general's question. He'd argued with one Garrison about the harness already today. Grace now worried they might be harming their son psychologically by using the leash and thought a good compromise would be using a stroller. Jack heartily disagreed.

"Grace'll be glad you made it. She was worried you weren't going to be back in time." His father-in-law had put Helena on the plane and stayed in Christmas until he was sure his grandson and daughter were going to be all right. He'd returned home four days ago to start divorce proceedings, something he and Grace had talked about before he did.

"Wouldn't miss it. Now, where's my baby girl?"

Jack pointed Grace out just as the starting pistol went off. Everyone surged into the water, everyone except his wife. After what she'd been through, Jack knew this was the part of the race that worried her most. But this morning she'd seemed determined to conquer her fears, excited even to get back in the water. It was as if she needed to do this one last thing to be able to move forward. Jack went to duck under the barrier. He didn't want her to face this alone. His father-in-law's hand on his arm stopped him.

"No, son, she's gotta do this on her own."

Jack's hands balled into fists at his sides as he watched her stand on the water's edge with her arms wrapped around her waist. "What's wrong with her?" a few people behind him asked. Jack was about to ignore Frank's directive when Maria glanced in Grace's direction.

He'd seen Maria a couple days ago in the hospital. She'd been teary-eyed and apologetic. She'd asked his permission to speak to Grace and see little Jack. It hadn't been an easy meeting for either of the women.

Maria ran back to Grace and tugged on her hand. He

held his breath, releasing it when his wife entered the water.

Ten minutes later, he watched in awe as Grace's powerful strokes cut through the white-capped waves, and she took the lead.

His father-in-law chuckled. "Guess I should've mentioned that Grace had Olympic times the last swim meet she participated in." Frank sobered. "If she weren't as strong a swimmer, I would've lost them both that day."

"Mamma," Jack shrieked, pointing at his mother, who ran onto shore.

Jack and his father-in-law, along with the crowd, cheered. Grace waved, then gave Jack that dimpled smile he adored and a thumbs-up. He returned both, his chest tight with pride. His wife was one amazing woman.

Since the bike trails they'd be taking next weren't easily accessible, they decided to head for the finish line instead. Gage and Madison were there with Annie and Lily. "How's she doing?" Madison asked.

"She's in the lead after the swimming event," Jack said, unable to keep the proud smile from his face.

Madison threw up her arms. "Is there anything she's not good at? Please tell me there is, because I'm seriously thinking about not being friends with her anymore. It's too hard on my self-esteem."

Two hours later, his wife crossed the finish line just ahead of Nell, Mrs. Tate, and Mrs. Wright.

Grace fell into his arms. "Please tell me I beat them. I'll never live it down if I didn't."

"You beat them by a nose."

Madison came over and pinned a ribbon on her. "I love

you, and I'd miss being your friend, so I'm glad you suck at biking and running."

"You wait until next year," Frank said, handing a sleepy little Jack to Grace. "I'm going to take over her training, and you'll be pinning a first-place ribbon on her."

Grace glanced down at her purple ribbon. "One hundred and fiftieth. How many participants were there?"

"You don't want to know." Madison grinned.

"How did Maria do?" Grace asked, bouncing their now-wide-awake son on her hip.

"Twentieth overall, first in the women."

Grace smiled. "That's great. I hope someone took her picture for her book."

Madison waggled her brows. "Dr. McSexy did."

Jack rolled his eyes and Gage did the same.

"I'm thinking of having him deliver my baby." Madison patted her stomach. Gage shot her a not-going-to-happen look.

"Me, too. No, I'm not pregnant yet," Grace said when they all looked at her. "At least I don't think I am. Come on." She took Jack's hand. "Ceremony's in two hours."

Jack slanted her a look as they headed to the truck. Caught up in his conversation with Nell and her friends, her father trailed behind. "Just so you know, Dr. McSexy is not delivering our baby. Dr. McBride is."

"We'll see. I have to get pregnant first."

"How about we work on that tonight?"

*   *   *

Maybe they should've held off on the baby making until tonight after all, Jack thought with a grin. They had ten minutes to spare before the ceremony.

"Grace, are you guys ready?" Jack asked as he walked into the living room, tucking his uniform shirt into his pants. Grace knelt on the floor wearing a white sundress, looking from the framed picture of her sister that she'd set on the bookshelf yesterday to little Jack, an odd expression on her face. "What is it?" he asked.

"Did you tell him who this is?"

"No, why?"

She turned the picture to their son, pointing at the cute little blonde with the gap-toothed smile. "Tell Mommy who this is again?"

"Fafe."

"You're right, baby. It's your auntie Faith."

"Fafe kiss Jack."

"Oh." Grace covered her mouth, blinking back tears.

Jack crouched beside her, sliding a supportive arm around her shoulders. "Where did you see your auntie Faith, buddy?"

"Pool. Fafe love you." He threw himself at his mother, wrapping his arms around her neck. "Fafe say..." His brow furrowed. "Jack kiss Mama for..."

"Your auntie Faith told you to kiss your mommy for her?" Jack asked him.

His face brightened, and he nodded, then frowned when his mother started to sob, burying her face in his neck. "Mama sad."

"No, baby." She lifted her head and sniffed. "Mommy's happy." She looked up at Jack. "Do you think it's really possible?"

He wiped her tears away. "Yeah, I do."

"The hardest part of losing her was not being able to tell her that I loved her, that I didn't mean what I said."

"She knew that, princess. She saw you coming to save her that day, didn't she? Saw you risking your life to save hers."

"Just before she went under that last time, I told her to hang on and not panic. I told her I'd get her out, but..."

Little Jack framed his mother's face with his small hands. "Fafe loves Mama."

Smiling through her tears, Grace nodded, then whispered, "I love you, Faith."

*   *   *

Beneath a cloudless blue sky, Grace stood toward the front of the crowd gathered in the park. Her husband, looking so handsome he could've stepped off the big screen, released a surprised laugh when his three crew members, Josh, Quinn, and Holden walked up the two steps to the stage. Grace met Jack's gaze and smiled. He gave his head a bemused shake and mouthed, *Thank you*.

"What is it about a man in uniform?" Skye, who came to stand beside Grace in her Sugar Plum Cake Fairy costume, mused. "I mean, Jack's hot, but today, wow, just holy fricking wow."

"He's mine, get your own." Grace laughed. "And where were you today? I didn't see you at the race. In fact..." She looked at each one of her friends standing in the row. "Where were *all* of you? I didn't see any of you at the triathlon. I know there were lots of people, but I should've seen at least one of you." And she would've heard Sophia.

"Flu, sprained ankle, was that today?" Grace lost track of which one of them made which excuse. Sophia opened her mouth to make hers, then stopped when something behind them caught her eye. "You girls can take the men in uniform. Me, I will take the one in the suit."

Ethan O'Connor, the sun glinting off his blond head, walked through the smiling crowd wearing a light-gray suit paired with a red tie. Shaking people's hands, he stopped when he reached them and flashed a movie-star smile. With his chiseled jaw, his eyes hidden behind a pair of aviators, the man was totally swoon-worthy.

"Ladies, you're all looking as gorgeous as ever," he said in an equally swoon-worthy voice. Because his eyes were hidden, it was hard to tell, but, Grace thought, although his comment was directed at all of them, his entire focus was on Skye, who ignored him.

"So are you, Senator," Sophia said in her singsong voice. The other women agreed.

He laughed. "Hey, don't jinx me. Lots can happen between now and November." Skye snorted while keeping her gaze on the stage. "Miss Davis, I didn't recognize you in your costume. What are you supposed to be… a cupcake?" His firm lips twitched as he fought back a grin.

Skye rolled her eyes. "The Sugar Plum Cake Fairy, and if you really want to win the election"—she raised her wand—"I'll turn you into a Democrat. Better yet, an Independent."

"Haven't changed, have you, cupcake?"

When Skye went to lift her wand again, Grace grabbed her hand and said, "Ethan, thanks so much for coming today. I know how busy you are."

He nudged Skye out of the way to kiss Grace's cheek. "Wouldn't miss it. Look forward to catching up with Jack. And you"—he crouched beside little Jack's stroller—"I heard you gave everyone quite the scare. Glad you're okay, buddy." He rubbed little Jack's head and stood up.

A statuesque brunette wearing a conservative red sundress came toward them.

Skye turned to face Grace, her eyes wide. "Do not let her see me," she said in a panicked whisper.

The woman touched Ethan's arm and gave them a practiced smile. "We need to get you onstage."

"Right. See you ladies after the ceremony. Grace, you might want to take Ms. Davis's wand from her."

The woman frowned, leaning past Ethan to get a look at Skye. "Kendall Davis, is that you?"

"I'm going to kill him," Skye muttered before taking a deep breath and plastering a smile on her face. "Claudia, as I live and breathe, what are you doing here?"

Ethan, with a what-the-hell expression on his face, watched the two women air-kiss.

The brunette patted Ethan's arm. "What I do best, making sure our boy here wins the election. But a better question would be, Kendall, what are you doing here and dressed like *that*? Oh my God." She tittered. "The girls back home are going to die when they see this. You have to let me take your picture."

Ethan, who hadn't taken his eyes off Skye, took the other woman by the arm. "Claudia, you can catch up with...Kendall later."

"Yes, of course." Claudia mimed clicking a camera and said, "Later."

"What's she supposed to be?" they heard Claudia ask Ethan.

"A cupcake, I think."

"She always was a fruitcake," the other woman said, laughing as they walked toward the stage.

"Who is that woman and why did she call you Kendall?" Sophia asked the questions they all wanted the answers to.

Skye crossed her arms over her chest. "Claudia Stevens. Old money with deep connections to the Republican Party. If they're behind Ethan, it means they're looking at him going all the way to the top."

The speeches began, ending further conversation. Madison gave the opening address, then introduced Ethan. Grace thought he gave a great speech. Skye didn't. Grace's father spoke next. He looked the most relaxed she'd ever seen him. Her parents hadn't been happy for years, and it was about time that one of them did something about it.

When her dad presented Jack with his medal, Grace blinked back tears. Blinking didn't help when Jack gave his short and poignant speech. He talked about what the country and the freedom they enjoyed as Americans meant to him and what he'd missed the most when he'd been a POW. At the end, he thanked his sister, Patrick, and Sawyer, and the people of Christmas for being there for his family when he couldn't be.

Grace frowned when he unpinned the Purple Heart from his chest and held it up. "It means a lot to me that you think I deserve this medal, but there's someone here who I think deserves it more. It's not easy being the one who's left behind, the one who has to keep on keeping on, to stay strong and brave. My wife did that and more." Grace covered her mouth to hold back a sob, tears welling in her eyes. "As much as you call me a hero, she's mine. Grace, will you come up here, please?"

Grace turned when someone touched her arm. It was her mother. "Go to your husband. I'll look after my grandson."

She was speechless. She didn't know what to say, didn't know what to feel.

"Your husband's right. You deserve that medal," her mother said, adjusting the neckline of Grace's sundress.

"Thank you. That means a lot coming from you." It did. More than her mother probably knew. She hesitated, then kissed her mother's cheek before making her way through the cheering crowd. Jack held out his hand, helping her onto the stage. "It's true, you know," he said as he carefully pinned the medal to the front of her dress. "You *are* my hero. I love you, Grace Flaherty."

Fingering the medal, she sniffed back her tears. "And I love you, Jack Flaherty." She rose up on her toes and wrapped her arms around his neck. "You've always been my hero, and you always will be."

He gave her a breath-stealing smile then lowered his head and kissed her to the delight of their audience. "We'll finish this later in private," he murmured when Madison tapped them on their shoulders.

"Sorry to break it up, guys, but we have one more item on the agenda," Madison laughingly said as she drew them with her to the podium. "We have a little something for the two of you."

Sawyer and Jill walked toward the stage carrying a cake between them. "Sawyer, slow down. I'm going to drop it," Jill huffed, and the two of them started arguing as they awkwardly made their way up the steps. Since little Jack's accident, Jill and Sawyer had actually been getting along, to the point Grace had begun to think something was going on between the two of them. Now it looked like they were back to normal.

Grace gaped at the lopsided black cake they set down on a small table. There was a purple fondant house, at least she thought it was supposed to be a house, surrounded by store-bought candy roses.

Her mother handed little Jack to Grace. "That was a lovely speech, Jackson," she said, then went to stand beside Grace's stunned father. Skye crowded onto the stage along with all their friends. "So, what do you think?" Skye asked, gesturing to the cake. "Everyone helped out."

Grace looked at the faces of her friends and smiled. "It's beautiful. You guys did an amazing job."

Jack, who stood behind her with his arms around both her and little Jack, whispered in her ear, "I'm impressed, princess. You actually sound like you mean it."

"I do," she whispered back.

"Wonder what the bakery looks like."

"That's not funny," she murmured, nudging him with her elbow.

Skye chewed her nail, eyeing the cake. "We had a little trouble getting the icing the right color and making the roses, but I think it works." She shrugged, then smiled. "But don't worry, even if it doesn't look like a sugar plum cake, the Sugar Plum Cake Fairy is on the job. Make a wish."

Grace tipped her head back. "What do you want to wish for?"

"I don't know. I've got everything I want right here," he said, tightening his arms around them.

"Me, too."

Skye rolled her eyes. "I'll make the wish for you. Okay, it's done. Open the sugar plum."

When Jack and Grace looked at her blankly, she sighed. "Under the house."

Jack lowered his arms, nudged Grace out of the way, and lifted the house to reveal a chocolate sugar plum twice its normal side. He opened it and took out a key and a scroll tied with a yellow ribbon. "What's this?" he asked, holding up the key.

"Just unroll the scroll, flyboy," Sawyer said with a grin. Jack's crew laughed, and Holden said, "Yeah, flyboy, open the deed. What?" he said when everyone shushed him.

Jack frowned and unraveled the scroll. He scanned the paper and lifted a disbelieving gaze to Grace. "It's the deed to the house on Sugar Plum Lane." He showed her the paper.

"How? I don't understand," Grace said, looking at the smiling faces of their friends and family.

Everyone started to talk at once. Ethan whistled loudly. "Quiet."

"Thanks, Ethan," Madison said. "All your friends"— she shot a look at Skye, who shuffled closer to Grace—"well, most of us, pitched in to buy the house. You can make monthly payments just like you would to the bank. And with the way the bakery's going, you'll pay us back in no time."

"But I thought that couple bought the house," Jack said.

"They did. Maria convinced them to sell it back to us."

Maria, who'd joined Jack's crew onstage, smiled and said, "It's the least I could do."

The smiling faces blurred in front of Grace's misty vision, and Jack slid his arm around her shoulders. "Thank you, all of you. We're deeply touched, but it's—"

"You can't refuse, Jack. It's a done deal," Madison said

firmly. "And don't worry, we're charging you the same interest the bank would have."

Jack looked down at Grace and grinned. "Sounds like we have a house, princess."

All Grace could do was nod as the tears slid down her cheeks. "I love you, all of you," she managed to choke out.

"It's Santa," Gage's daughter Lily cried, pointing to a wagon rolling down Main Street.

"Come on, your carriage awaits. Let's go check out your new home." Madison ushered them off the stage. People hugged and congratulated them as they made their way to the wagon. A big sign announcing Christmas in July, from the twenty-fourth to the thirtieth, was attached to the back rails.

Jack lifted Annie and Lily into the wagon then helped Grace up, handing her little Jack.

Her friends looked at the wagon, and Sophia said, "We will meet you at the house."

Pretty much everyone said the same thing. Skye was walking toward them when Ethan climbed in. She turned and headed off after Sophia and the girls. Sawyer jumped on and went to offer Jill a hand. She rolled her eyes and heaved herself onto a bale of hay.

"Okay, giddyup, Santa," Madison said, sliding in beside her husband.

"You owe me big-time for this, honey," Gage muttered.

"Hey, it's great advertising for Christmas in July. We had to find some way to take advantage of all the media here to cover the ceremony."

Sitting behind them, Grace looked at Jack and laughed. "I can't believe it. We own the house on Sugar Plum Lane."

Ethan smiled. "I guess it's safe to say you guys are happy about the house. Have you decided what you're going to do next, Jack?" Jack told him about the job with search and rescue, and before long, the four men were reminiscing about old times. Lily and Annie were amusing little Jack, and Grace, Jill, and Madison were talking about the plans for Christmas in July when Nell, Mrs. Tate, and Mrs. Wright flagged them down.

"Keep going," Madison told her husband.

"Honey, it's hot out. I can't let them walk."

"I'm warning you, if she says one thing about that book, I can't be held accountable for my actions," Madison said, as Jack, Sawyer, and Ethan went to help the older women into the wagon.

Nell must've heard Madison because she grinned when Lily said, "Auntie Nell, am I going to be in your book?"

"Sure you are, sweetpea."

Grace pursed her lips to keep from laughing. Jack leaned into her. "What book are they talking about?"

"The one she's writing about Madison and Gage."

"It sounded like it would make a pretty good story."

"Aunt Nell, I don't want to be in the book."

"Don't worry, Annie, if I have anything to say about it, there won't be a book," Madison said, giving Nell her don't-mess-with-me face.

"Hate to disappoint you, girlie. Stella's granddaughter is working with me. She's a real author, you know, and her publisher is interested in taking a look."

Madison appeared ready to explode. Grace reached back to pat her arm. "Don't worry about it. Even if she sells the book, no one will know it's about you and Gage," Grace said, trying to make her friend feel better.

"Me in book," little Jack said.

Mrs. Tate smiled. "You're in the next one."

"What?" Grace said, her voice raising an octave.

Nell grinned. "Yep, I'm writing yours and Jack's story next. Even got the title—*Christmas in July.*"

Madison patted her arm. "Don't worry about it, no one will know it's about you and Jack."

Grace's reply flew out of her head as they turned onto Sugar Plum Lane. "Oh, Jack," she said instead, taking his hand. People lined the street waving American flags, and in the middle of a wildflower garden in full bloom sat their house wrapped in a yellow ribbon. As Grace took it all in, she thought back to that day in May when she'd given up on her husband ever coming home, on ever having a home like the one that was now their own. Maybe, she thought, there was something magical about her sugar plum cake after all.

Skylar Davis has a secret she must
protect at all costs.
No such luck, due to all the
local gossips in little Christmas,
Colorado…

Please turn this page for a

preview of

It Happened at Christmas.

Chapter One

Skylar Davis stood in the middle of Main Street wearing a sparkly purple dress with a wand in her hand and a cupcake tiara on her head, wondering where the magic had gone. For the last ten years she'd flitted through life like a butterfly wearing rose-colored glasses.

Seven months ago she'd had those glasses ripped right off her face, and her life had become stomach-churningly horrible. Six weeks ago, it had gone from horrible to downright scary. Which was why she was hiding out in the small town of Christmas, Colorado. Well, that and she only had a couple hundred pennies to her name.

Another reason for choosing Christmas, she had free room and board courtesy of her best friend, Madison McBride—although she had a feeling that wasn't going to last much longer. The fact her best friend was married to a big, hot sheriff didn't hurt, either. At least Skye had protection if Scary Guy discovered where she was. But right now, the person she needed to avoid was her best friend.

Skye cast a nervous glance behind her, releasing a relieved breath when she didn't spot a familiar face among the crowd. In the middle of a wave of people heading down Main Street, she bent her knees and bowed her head in an effort to make herself less visible. Granted, it was a little hard to be inconspicuous wearing a Sugar Plum Cake Fairy costume. And somehow she'd wound up in the middle of a group of tourists from Japan. Up ahead, she spotted a couple of men taller than she was and started toward them.

One of the tourists snagged her arm. "Picture." He smiled, holding up his camera.

Two more men held up their cameras. "You. Picture."

"At the park. Okay?" Skye smiled, pointing to where the Fourth of July festivities were being held. They'd draw less attention there, and if she spotted Madison, Skye could duck behind a tree. She went to walk away and caught a glimpse of a tall, broad-shouldered man in a light-gray suit, the sun glinting off his tawny blond hair as he held court on the sidewalk with a statuesque brunette at his side.

Skye's smile froze on her face, a drawn-out "no" echoing in her head. She'd overheard someone say that senatorial candidate Ethan O'Connor had another speaking engagement and was heading out of town. If she'd known he was sticking around, she would've hidden out at the bakery. She'd been humiliated enough for one day, thank you very much.

Her gaze shot to the pastel-painted shops across the street to her left. *Seriously?* she thought, at the sight of her best friend Madison standing beneath the purple-and-white-striped awning of the Sugar Plum Bakery. How could anyone's luck change so dramatically?

Since bemoaning the situation wasn't going to save her further humiliation and neither was standing there, Skye did the only thing she could think of and dropped to her knees. Forcing a smile for the worried faces looking down at her, she said, "I lost my wand," surreptitiously tucking the aforementioned item beneath her dress.

"Excuse me. Pardon me. Lost wand," she explained, duckwalking through the crowd as fast as the position allowed.

"I'll help you find it, Sugar Plum Cake Fairy," a little girl, her dark curly hair caught up in red, white, and blue ribbons, offered.

"Me, too," volunteered a little boy, a miniature American flag clutched in his small hand.

Before long, Skye had a line of children waddling after her. She was like a mother duck with her ducklings following behind. They looked so darn cute that she would've had an "aw" moment if she didn't feel like throwing up.

She'd been feeling that way a lot lately. And it wasn't because the jig was up and Madison had found out that her best friend, who'd once had more money than God, was now as poor as Jesus. Or that Ethan O'Connor, the man Skye'd had a one-night stand with—and Skylar Davis did not do one-night stands—was in town and looking even more breath-stealingly gorgeous than she remembered. Or that the first time she saw Claudia Stevens, the bane of her teenage existence, she'd be in Christmas on Ethan's arm instead of Texas, where she belonged.

An old family friend, Claudia's name came up in every single it's-time-to-grow-up conversation Skye had with her father, William Davis. "Why can't you be more like Claudia?" was his constant refrain as he compared the other woman's many accomplishments to Skye's non-existent ones.

Nope, none of them were responsible for her upset stomach. It was the stress. However, they were responsible for her humiliation, which, she supposed, could indirectly lead to stress. So, yeah, maybe they were responsible for her upset stomach after all.

As she made her way to the front of the crowd, beads of perspiration rolled into her eyes, blurring her vision. She went to rub the drops away with the hand that held the wand. *Oops.* "Look at that," she said, turning to the children. "It's my magic wand. Silly me. I should've wished for it sooner."

She winced at the crestfallen expressions on their cute little faces because she'd found her wand without their help. In an effort to counter their disappointment, Skye raised it, nodding at the sparkly sugar plum on the end. "You know what, my wand just told me it didn't find me because of *my* wishes—it was because of all of yours. Yay, you guys." She clapped her hands, relieved when they joined in.

"That makes us your fairy helpers, doesn't it?" said the first of her volunteers.

"Yes, it does." Skye smiled, looking through a sea of legs to get her bearings. A few more yards, and she'd be on the path to the park. She felt like clapping her hands again. "I have to go now. Thanks for all your help."

"Can we have tiaras like yours?" asked a little girl, her blue eyes hopeful behind her pink-framed glasses.

Skye fingered the jeweled crown with the tiny cupcakes glued to each point. She'd frigging love to give the tiara away. When Grace, her friend and boss, had first broached the idea of Skye being the Sugar Plum Cake Fairy, she'd jumped at the chance. But that's when she thought it was a paid position. When she found out it wasn't, she kind of thought it was cool that she'd be the face of the Sugar Plum Cake Fairy in the book. It wasn't until they fitted her with the costume, and she realized they meant for her to wear it in public, that she wanted to say "no way, no how." But she couldn't. Even though Grace didn't have the money in her budget to hire Skye, she'd given her a job at the bakery. So Skye had no choice but to accept the role as the bakery's mascot to repay Grace for her kindness.

Today was Skye's debut as the Sugar Plum Cake Fairy. And as her newfound bad luck would have it, she'd been in costume when she saw Ethan for the first time in three months, and Claudia for the first time in ten years. Ethan had restrained his laughter. Claudia, not so much. And the woman was bound and determined to get a picture of Skye, looking like an idiot, to post on social media.

"I wish I could, sweetie, but there's only one tiara like this in the whole, wide world." At the little girl's disappointed look, Skye did a quick head count. She got paid next week, so she should be good. "But because you're all my special helpers, you get a free cupcake from the bakery this week. You just tell them the Sugar Plum Cake Fairy sent you."

"Yay." The little girl bounced up and down and her friends joined in.

Oh, gosh, they were getting kind of loud. Afraid they were going to draw unwanted attention, Skye put a finger to her lips. "Shush, we don't want anyone else to know. It's our secret. Okay?"

They nodded and Skye went to stand up. Several of the children threw their arms around her. "We love you, Sugar Plum Cake Fairy."

"Aw, I love you guys, too." Maybe this job wasn't so bad after all, Skye thought. She'd always enjoyed spending time with kids. Some people told her it was because she still thought she was one. She didn't know what the big deal was. In her opinion, the world would be a better place if more adults kept their inner child alive, holding on to that natural curiosity, the ability to appreciate the simple things in life and have fun. She supposed that was easy for her to say. She'd never had to work for a living or worry about paying bills or putting a roof over her head or clothes on her back.

She sighed. Not until now she hadn't.

Skye waved good-bye and speed-walked to the path.

"Auntie Skye, I've been looking all over for you. Mommy wants to talk to you." Madison's stepdaughter Lily ran toward Skye, her chestnut-colored ponytail bouncing, and caught her by the hand.

Skye couldn't help but smile. She loved that Madison's stepdaughters called her Auntie. In a way, it was true. Since she was an only child, Skye thought of her best friends Madison and Vivi as her sisters. But she wasn't quite ready to face her *sister* just yet. Skye needed time to put a positive spin on her situation.

Her gaze darted to the park, and she spotted the bright-blue Porta-Potty in the distance. "Tell Mommy I'll catch up with her in a bit. I have to go." She nodded in the direction of the outdoor toilet.

Lily frowned. "Mommy's at the bakery. It's closer."

Too bad Lily was as smart as she was adorable. Skye shot a look at the crowd working its way up the street and caught sight of the tourists. "Right, but I promised some people I'd take a picture with them. I won't be long."

Skye waved and headed down the path. To her left, a man shouted out for Ethan. *Please, let it be another Ethan.* She glanced in the direction he'd called from. Sure enough, there was the man himself entering the park with Claudia on his arm. Skye took off at a run. By the time she reached the Porta-Potty, she was out of breath.

This hiding-out crap is exhausting.

A big, burly man with a full beard stepped out of the Porta-Potty and gave her an apologetic shrug.

How bad could it be? Skye thought, stepping inside. She slapped a hand to her mouth and nose. It smelled like someone had died in there. Several someones, and a long time ago. She whipped around, about to get out, when she heard, "Is that Kendall?"

Skye ducked inside, slammed the door, and locked it. There was only one person who called her by her legal name and that was Claudia. Skye had started using her middle name when she left Texas. The one her mother had chosen. It suited her better. It was Skye's way of thumbing her nose at her father's attempt to change her into the daughter he wanted her to be. Someone William Davis, the former governor of Texas and right-wing Republican, could be proud of.

Someone like Claudia.

Breathe, Skye told herself in hopes of calming her jack-rabbiting pulse. *For goodness' sake, you idiot, don't breathe!* She lifted the hem of her dress and pressed it to

her face, gagging into the silky fabric. The claustrophobi-
cally small space was closing in around her, the temperature about twenty degrees hotter than outside. Holding
her breath, she fanned herself with her dress. When the
lack of oxygen began to make her dizzy, she once again
buried her nose in the purple fabric and released it.

*Okay, relax, think of walking through the forest in winter,
the snow crunching underfoot, your breath a crystallized
cloud.* Yes, she almost cheered, it was working. The room
felt cooler, the space less confining. But the smell…she
retched, automatically leaning toward the black hole. She
jerked back when she realized what she was doing. *Hurry
up, think of…think of something that smells amazing, something you want to…Do not think of that!*

She couldn't help it. Once the images started, she
couldn't make them stop. The memory of that night with
Ethan played out in her mind. *Oh, but he had smelled
amazing, and all that lean, sculpted muscle, his large…
arms, his arms!* Voices coming in her direction snapped
her back to the here and now.

Good, that was good.

"Claudia said she saw her going in there, Madison."

Bad. Very bad.

That was Ethan's voice. Ethan's incredible, swoon-
worthy voice. She scowled as the thought popped into
her head. The sewage must be poisoning her brain, she
decided, pinching her nose and breathing through her
mouth. The man was a right-wing, judgmental conservative who was as critical of Skye's lifestyle as her father.

Oh no, now she could taste it. She made small retching
sounds as the cupcakes she'd eaten earlier curdled in her
stomach.

"Skye, are you in there?" Madison asked, tapping on the door. "Skye?" She tapped again.

If Skye stayed quiet, maybe they'd leave. She moved away from the door, which put her closer... She started gagging, loudly, and stumbled backward, bouncing off the wall.

"Skye, Lily said she saw you running over here. Are you okay? Do you need help?"

"Fine, I'm fine. I'll be out in a minute. You can go..." She started gagging again before she got "back to the bakery" out.

"You don't sound *fine*, and we're not going anywhere until we know you're all right," Ethan said, his voice whiskey smooth and deep.

"I am. It's the door." She rattled it for effect. "It's stuck, and I can't get out. So if you could go and get someone... if *all* of you could go and get someone, that'd be great. Thanks." And when they did, she'd escape to the woods. The sweat trickling down her chest and back had turned the sparkly purple fabric to shrink-wrap, while the humidity had rolled her long, wavy hair into a frizz ball. There was no way she was going to face Mr. and Ms. Perfect looking like something the dog had dragged in and shaken a couple of times before he did.

"Okay, I'll try and get it to open," she heard Ethan say.

"No, no, that's not a good idea." The door handle moved, a metallic scraping sound coming from the other side. "What... what are you doing?"

"Picking the lock."

"You can't pick locks," she blurted in desperation, swiping her arm across her damp forehead. "You're a lawyer, and you're running for political office."

"Appreciate the concern for my reputation, cupcake. But it's a Porta-Potty, and I'm rescuing a damsel in distress." She heard the amusement in his voice.

"Don't call me cupcake, and I don't need rescuing. Go away." She stupidly took a deep breath to calm herself and started retching again. She sounded like she was horking up a hair ball. Covering her mouth and nose with both hands, she turned away, hoping to muffle the noise.

"Hang in there, sweetheart. Just a little bit... There, got it."

Her eyes widened, and she whipped her head around, reaching for the handle just as it turned. She dug her heels into the damp floorboard and held on with both hands.

"Huh, the lock released, how come..." He pulled on the door, a sliver of light entering the space.

They played a silent game of tug-of-war; she leaned back, he inched her forward, she leaned back, he inched her forward. Then, with one last yank from his side, she went flying out the door. Landing hard on her hands and knees at his feet, her tiara askew, Skye threw up on Ethan's Italian leather shoes.

THE DISH

Where Authors Give You the Inside Scoop

♥ ♥ ♥ ♥ ♥ ♥ ♥ ♥ ♥ ♥ ♥ ♥ ♥ ♥ ♥ ♥ ♥

From the desk of Debbie Mason

Dear Reader,

While reading CHRISTMAS IN JULY one last time before sending it off to my editor, I had an "oops, I did it again" moment. In the first book in the series, *The Trouble with Christmas*, there's a scene where Madison, the heroine, senses her late mother's presence. In this book, our heroine, Grace, receives a message from her sister through her son. Grace has spent years blaming herself for her sister's death, and while there's an incident in the book that alleviates her guilt, I felt she needed the opportunity to tell her sister she loved her. Maybe if I didn't believe our departed loved ones could communicate with us in some way, I would have done this another way. But I do, and here's why.

My dad was movie-star handsome and had this amazing dimple in his chin. He was everything a little girl could wish for in a father. But he wasn't my biological father; he was the father of my heart. He came into my life when I was nine years old. That first year, I dreamed about him a lot. The dreams were very real, and all the same. I'd be outside and see a man from behind and call out to him. He'd turn around, and it would be my dad.

I always said the same thing: "You're here. I knew you weren't gone." Almost a year to the day of his passing, my dad appeared in my dream surrounded by shadowy figures who he introduced to me by name. He told me that he was okay, that he was happy. It was his way, I think, of helping me let him go.

I didn't dream of him again until sixteen months ago when we were awaiting the birth of our first grandchild. I "woke up" to see him sitting at the end of my bed. I told him how happy I was that he'd be there for the arrival of his great grandchild. He said of course he would be. He wouldn't be anywhere else.

A week later, my daughter gave birth to a beautiful baby girl. When I saw my granddaughter for the first time, I started to cry. She had my dad's dimple. No one on my son-in-law's side, or ours, has a dimple in their chin. He used to tell us the angels gave it to him, and we like to think he gave our granddaughter hers as proof that he's still with us.

So now you know why including that scene was important not only to Grace, but to me. Life really is full of small miracles and magic. And I hope you experience some of that magic as you follow Grace and Jack on their journey to happy-ever-after.

Debbie Mason

♥ ♥ ♥ ♥ ♥ ♥ ♥ ♥ ♥ ♥ ♥ ♥ ♥ ♥

From the desk of Kristen Ashley

Dear Reader,

Usually, inspiration for books comes to me in a variety of ways. It could be a man I see (anywhere), a movie, a song, the unusual workers in a bookstore.

With SWEET DREAMS, it was an idea.

And that idea was, I wanted to take a hero who is, on the whole, totally unlikable, and make him lovable.

Enter Tatum Jackson, and when I say that, I mean *enter Tatum Jackson*. He came to me completely with a *kapow!* I could conjure him in my head, hear him talk, see the way he moved and how his clothes hung on him, feel his frustration with his life. I also knew his messed-up history.

And I could *not* wait to get stuck into this man.

I mean, here's a guy who is gorgeous, but he's got a foul temper, says nasty things when he's angry, and he's not exactly father of the year.

He had something terrible happen to him to derail his life and he didn't handle that very well, making mistake after mistake in a vicious cycle he pretty much had no intention of ending. He had a woman in his life he knew was a liar, a cheat, and no good for anyone and he was so stuck in the muck of his life that he didn't get shot of her.

Enter Lauren Grahame, who also came to me like a shot. As with Tate, everything about Lauren slammed into my head, perhaps most especially her feelings, the disillusionment she has with life, how she feels lost and really has no intention of getting found.

In fact, I don't think with any of my books I've ever had two characters who I knew so thoroughly before I started to tell their story.

And thus, I got lost in it.

I tend to be obsessive about my storytelling but this was an extreme. Once Lauren and Tate came to me, everything about Carnal, Colorado, filled my head just like the hero and heroine did. I can see Main Street, Bubba's Bar, Tate's house. I know the secondary characters as absolutely as I know the main characters. The entirety of the town, the people, and the story became a strange kind of real in my head, even if I didn't know how the story was going to play out. Indeed, I had no idea if I could pull it off, making an unlikable man lovable.

But I fell in love with Tate very quickly. The attraction he has for Lauren growing into devotion. The actions that speak much louder than words. I so enjoyed watching Lauren pull Tate out of the muck of his life, even if nothing changes except the fact that he has a woman in it that he loves, who is good to him, who feeds the muscle, the bone, the soul. Just as I enjoyed watching Tate guide Lauren out of her disillusionment and offer her something special.

I hope it happens to me again someday that characters like this inhabit my head so completely, and I hope it happens time and again.

But Tate and Lauren being the first, they'll always hold a special place in my heart, and live on in my head.

Happily,

Kristen Ashley

♥ ♥ ♥ ♥ ♥ ♥ ♥ ♥ ♥ ♥ ♥ ♥ ♥ ♥ ♥

From the desk of Rebecca Zanetti

Dear Reader,

I'm the oldest of three girls, and my husband is the oldest of three boys, so we grew up watching out for our siblings. Now that we're all adults, they look out for us, too. While my sisters and I may have argued with one another as kids, we instantly banded together if anybody tried to mess with one of us. My youngest sister topped out at an even five feet tall, yet she's the fiercest of us all, and she loses her impressive temper quite quickly if someone isn't nice to me.

I think one of the reasons I enjoyed writing Matt's story in SWEET REVENGE is because he's the eldest of the Dean brothers, and as such, he feels responsible for them. Add in a dangerous military organization trying to harm them, and his duties go far beyond that of a normal sibling. It was fun to watch Matt try to order his brothers around and keep them safe, while all they want to do is provide backup for him and ensure his safety.

There's something about being the oldest kid that forces us to push ourselves when we shouldn't. When our siblings would step back and relax, we often push forward just out of sheer stubbornness. I don't know why, and it's sometimes a mistake. Trust me.

SWEET REVENGE was written in several locations, most notably in the hospital and on airplanes. Sometimes

I take on a bit too much, so when I discovered I needed a couple of surgeries (nothing major), I figured I'd just do them on the same day. Why not? So I had two surgeries in one day and had to spend a few days in the hospital recuperating.

With my laptop, of course.

There's not a lot to do in the hospital but drink milkshakes and write, so it was quite effective. Then, instead of going home and taking it easy, I flew across the country to a conference and big book signing. Of course, I was still in pain, but I ignored it.

Bad idea.

Two weeks after that, I once again flew across the country for a book signing and conference. Yes, I was still tired, but I kept on going.

Yet another bad idea.

Then I returned home and immediately headed back to work as a college professor at the beginning of the semester.

Not a great idea.

Are you seeing a trend here? I pushed myself too hard, and all of a sudden, my body said…*you're done*. Completely done. I became sick, and after a bunch of tests, it appeared I'd just taken on too much. So at the end of the semester, I resigned as a professor and took up writing full time. And yoga. And eating healthy and relaxing.

Life is great, and it's meant to be savored and not rushed through—even for us oldest siblings. I learned a very valuable life lesson while writing SWEET REVENGE, and I'll always have fond memories of this book.

I truly hope you enjoy Matt and Laney's story, and

don't forget to take a deep breath and enjoy the moment. It's definitely worth it!

Happy reading!

Rebecca Zanetti

RebeccaZanetti.com
Twitter @RebeccaZanetti
Facebook.com

♥ ♥ ♥ ♥ ♥ ♥ ♥ ♥ ♥ ♥ ♥ ♥ ♥ ♥

From the desk of Shannon Richard

Dear Reader,

When it comes to the little town of Mirabelle, Florida, Grace King was actually the first character who revealed herself to me, which I find odd as she's the heroine in the second book. I knew from the beginning she was going to be a tiny little thing with blond hair and blue eyes; I knew she'd lost her mother at a young age and that she was never going to have known her father; and I knew she was going to be feisty and strong.

Jaxson Anderson was a different story. He didn't reveal himself to me until he literally walked onto the page in *Undone*. I also didn't know about Jax and Grace's future relationship until they got into an argument at the beach. As soon as I figured out they were going to end up together, my mind took off and I started plotting everything out, which was a little inconvenient as I wasn't even a third of the way through writing the first book.

Jax is a complicated fella. He's had to deal with a lot in his life, and because of his past he doesn't think he's good enough for Grace. Jax has most definitely put her on a pedestal, which is made pretty evident by his nickname for her. He calls her Princess, but not in a derogatory way. He doesn't find her to be spoiled or bratty. Far from it. He thinks that she should be cherished and that she's worth *everything*, especially to him. I try to capture this in the prologue, which takes place a good eighteen years before UNDENIABLE starts. Grace is this little six-year-old who is being bullied on the playground, and Jax is her white knight in scuffed-up sneakers.

Jax has been in Grace's life from the day she was brought home from the hospital over twenty-four years ago. He's watched her grow up into the beautiful and brave woman that she is, and though he's always loved her (even if he's chosen not to accept it), it's hard for him think that he can be with her. Jax's struggles were heartbreaking for me to write, and it was especially heartbreaking to put Grace through it, but this was their story and I had to stay true to them. Readers shouldn't fear with UNDENIABLE, though, because I like my happily-ever-after endings and Grace and Jax definitely get theirs. I hope readers enjoy the journey.

Cheers,

♥ ♥ ♥ ♥ ♥ ♥ ♥ ♥ ♥ ♥ ♥ ♥ ♥ ♥ ♥

From the desk of Stacy Henrie

Dear Reader,

I remember the moment HOPE AT DAWN, Book 1 in my Of Love and War series (on sale now), was born into existence. I was sitting in a quiet, empty hallway at a writers' conference contemplating how to turn my single World War I story idea, about Livy Campbell's brother, into more than one book. Then, in typical fashion, Livy marched forward in my mind, eager to have her story told first.

As I pondered Livy and the backdrop of the story—America's involvement in WWI—I knew having her fall in love with a German-American would provide inherent conflict. What I didn't know then was the intense prejudice and persecution she and Friedrick Wagner would face to be together, in a country ripe with suspicion toward anyone with German ties. The more I researched the German-American experience during WWI, the more I discovered their private war here on American soil—not against soldiers, but neighbors against neighbors, citizens against citizens.

A young woman with aspirations of being a teacher, Livy Campbell knows little of the persecution being heaped upon the German-Americans across the country, let alone in the county north of hers. More than anything, she feels the effects of the war overseas through the absence of her older brothers in France, the alcohol troubles of her wounded soldier boyfriend, and the disruption of her studies at college. When she applies for a teaching job in hopes of escaping the war, Livy doesn't realize she's simply traded one set of troubles for another, especially when she finds herself attracted to the school's handsome handyman, German-American Friedrick Wagner.

Born in America to German immigrant parents, Friedrick Wagner believes himself to be as American as anyone else in his small town of Hilden, Iowa. But the war with Germany changes all that. Suddenly viewed as a potential enemy, Friedrick seeks to protect his family from the rising tide of injustice aimed at his fellow German-Americans. Protecting the beautiful new teacher, Livy Campbell, comes as second nature to Friedrick. But when he finds himself falling in love with her, he fears the war, both at home and abroad, will never allow them to be together.

I thoroughly enjoyed writing Livy and Friedrick's love story and the odds they must overcome for each other. This is truly a tale of "love conquers all" and the power of hope and courage during a dark time in history. My hope is you will fall in love with the Campbell family through this series, as I have, as you experience their triumphs and struggles during the Great War.

Happy reading!

Stacy Henrie

♥ ♥ ♥ ♥ ♥ ♥ ♥ ♥ ♥ ♥ ♥ ♥ ♥ ♥ ♥

From the desk of Adrianne Lee

Dear Reader,

Conflict, conflict, conflict. Every good story needs it. It heightens sexual tension and keeps you guessing whether a couple will actually be able to work through those serious—and even not so serious—issues and obstacles to find that happily-ever-after ending.

I admit to a little vanity when one of my daughters once said, "Mom, in other romances I always know the couple will get together early in the book, but I'm never sure in yours until the very end." High praise and higher expectations for any writer to live up to. It is, at least, what I strive for with every love story I write.

Story plotting starts with conflict. I already knew that Jane Wilson, Big Sky Pie's new pastry chef, was going to fall in love with Nick Taziano, the sexy guy doing the promotion for the pie shop, but when I first conceived the idea that these two would be lovers in DELICIOUS, I didn't realize they were a reunion couple.

A reunion couple is a pair who was involved in the past and broke up due to unresolved conflicts. This is what I call a "built-in" conflict. It's one of my favorites to write. When the story opens, something has happened that involves this couple on a personal level, causing them to come face-to-face to deal with it. This is when they finally admit to themselves that they still have feelings for each other, feelings neither wants to feel or act on, no matter how compelling. The more they try to suppress the attraction, the stronger it becomes.

In DELICIOUS, Jane and Nick haven't seen each other since they were kids, since his father and her mother married. Jane blames Nick's dad for breaking up her parents' marriage. Nick resents Jane's mom for coming between his father and him. Jane called Nick the Tazmanian Devil. Nick called her Jane the Pain. They were thrilled when the marriage fell apart after a year.

Now many years later, their parents are reuniting, something Jane and Nick view as a bigger mistake than the first marriage. Their decision to try and stop the wedding, however, leads to one accidental, delicious kiss, and a sizzling attraction that is as irresistible as Jane's blueberry pies.

I hope you'll enjoy DELICIOUS, the second book in my Big Sky Pie series. All of the stories are set in northwest Montana near Glacier Park, an area where I vacationed every summer for over thirty years. Each of the books is about someone connected with the pie shop in one way or another and contains a different delicious pie recipe. So come join the folks of Kalispell at the little pie shop on Center Street, right across from the mall, for some of the best pie you'll ever taste, and a healthy helping of romance.

Adrianne Lee

♥ ♥ ♥ ♥ ♥ ♥ ♥ ♥ ♥ ♥ ♥ ♥ ♥ ♥ ♥

From the desk of Jessica Lemmon

Dear Reader,

A *quiz*: What do you get when you put a millionaire who avoids romantic relationships in the same house with a determined-to-stay-single woman who crushed on him sixteen years ago?

If you answered *unstoppable attraction*, you'd be right.

In THE MILLIONAIRE AFFAIR, I paired a hero who cages and controls his emotions with a heroine who feels way too much, way too soon. Kimber Reynolds is determined to have a fling—to love and leave Landon Downey, if for only two reasons: (1) She's wanted to kiss the eldest Downey brother since she was a teen, and (2) to prove to herself that she can have a shallow relationship that ends amicably instead of one that's long, drawn-out, and destined to end badly.

When Landon's six-year-old nephew, Lyon, and a huge account for his advertising agency come crashing into his life, Landon needs help. Lucky for him (and us!) his sister offers the perfect solution: her friend, Kimber, can be his live-in nanny for the week.

The most difficult part about writing Landon was letting him deal with his past on *his terms* and watching him falter. Here is a guy who makes rules, follows them, and remains stoic...to his own detriment. Despite those qualities, Landon, from a loving, close family, can't help caring for Kimber. Even when they're working down a list of "extracurricular activities" in the bedroom, Landon puts Kimber's needs before his own.

These two may have stumbled into an arrangement, but when Fate tosses them a wild card, they both step up—and step closer—to the one thing they were sure they didn't want...*forever*.

I *love* this book. Maybe because of how much I wrestled with Landon and Kimber's story before getting it right. The three of us had growing pains, but I finally found their truth, and I'm *so* excited to share their story with you. If Landon and Kimber win your heart like they won mine, be sure to let me know. You can email me at jessica@jessicalemmon.com, tweet me @lemmony, and "like" my Facebook page at www.facebook.com/authorjessicalemmon.

Happy reading!

Jessica Lemmon

www.jessicalemmon.com

Find out more about Forever Romance!

Visit us at
www.hachettebookgroup.com/publishing_forever.aspx

Find us on Facebook
http://www.facebook.com/ForeverRomance

Follow us on Twitter
http://twitter.com/ForeverRomance

NEW AND UPCOMING TITLES

Each month we feature our new titles
and reader favorites.

CONTESTS AND GIVEAWAYS

We give away galleys, autographed copies,
and all kinds of exclusive items.

AUTHOR INFO

You'll find bios, articles, and links to personal websites
for all your favorite authors—and so much more.

GET SOCIAL

Connect with your favorite authors, editors, and
other Forever fans, and share what's important to you.

THE BUZZ

Sign up for our monthly romance newsletter,
and be the first to read all about it.

VISIT US ONLINE AT

WWW.HACHETTEBOOKGROUP.COM

FEATURES:

OPENBOOK BROWSE AND SEARCH EXCERPTS

•

AUDIOBOOK EXCERPTS AND PODCASTS

•

AUTHOR ARTICLES AND INTERVIEWS

•

BESTSELLER AND PUBLISHING GROUP NEWS

•

SIGN UP FOR E-NEWSLETTERS

•

AUTHOR APPEARANCES AND TOUR INFORMATION

•

SOCIAL MEDIA FEEDS AND WIDGETS

•

DOWNLOAD FREE APPS

BOOKMARK HACHETTE BOOK GROUP
@ WWW.HACHETTEBOOKGROUP.COM